D0252452

Counterfeit Lies

Oliver North

and Bob Hamer

Threshold Editions
New York London Toronto Sydney New Delhi

Threshold Editions
A Division of Simon & Schuster, Inc.
1230 Avenue of the Americas
New York, NY 10020

First Threshold Editions hardcover edition June 2014

Interior design by Aline Pace
Jacket design by Jae Song

Manufactured in the United States of America

10 9 8 7 6 5 4 3 2 1

ISBN 978-1-4767-1435-6
ISBN 978-1-4767-1438-7 (ebook)

For Betsy, “The wife of my youth . . .”

[Proverbs 5:18–19]

ACKNOWLEDGMENTS

JERUSALEM, ISRAEL, 2014

This is a story about those of us who have had to confront the ultimate moral quandary: doing what's right when everything around us seems wrong. For some that's a once-in-a-lifetime event. For others it's an everyday occurrence.

In this ancient capital the prospect of Iran acquiring nuclear weapons is a very real existential threat. Here the phrase "Never again!" isn't a political slogan. It's a way of life. That's why the scenario at the heart of this story is so frightening—and why those who shared it with me must remain nameless. For their trust, I am grateful.

There are others who helped make this book possible who can be thanked *and named.* Foremost among them, my mate and muse—to whom this work is dedicated. Thank you, Betsy, for being my most fervent advocate and best friend.

My gratitude to FOX News chairman Roger Ailes, senior vice president Bill Shine, and general counsel Dianne Brandi for making it possible for me to travel the globe in the company of *real* heroes akin to those in this work of fiction.

Bob Hamer—true friend, fellow Marine, and real "UC"—has "been there, done that." He and his lovely wife, Debbie, are the reason this story resonates with authenticity. Thankfully, Gary and Kim Terashita reminded us that *they* are Peter Newman's best friends.

Robert Barnett and Michael O'Connor—the Williams & Connolly QRF (quick reaction force)—somehow managed to elicit the agreement of "all concerned parties" so we could tell this story without endangering other relationships or ourselves any more than usual. But it really took the help of Marsha Fishbaugh—my loyal assistant for more than a quarter of a century—and her husband, Dave, a fellow Vietnam War vet—to help us meet our deadline for this work.

Thankfully, Louise Burke, Mitchell Ivers, and their team at Simon & Schuster were ready, willing, and able to ensure we could "get it done." Natasha Simons, Mary McCue, Kevin Smith, Al Madocs, George Turianski, and Aline Pace became "secret agents" to help get this book into your hands.

Duane Ward and his team at Premiere Centre and Sheena Tahilramani have once again stepped into the breach to introduce this story to the widest possible audience at just the right time—without interfering with Josh & Emily's wedding plans.

And perhaps best of all, every person who buys this book helps support the work of Freedom Alliance, an organization devoted to serving real American Heroes and their family members. A brief description of how Freedom Alliance helps and honors those who have sacrificed so much for all of us is on pages 325–26.

Oliver North
Jerusalem, Israel
4 February 2014

PROLOGUE

INTERNAL USE ONLY

THIS IS CERTIFIED AS THE TRANSCRIBED ORAL PSYCHOLOGICAL INTERVIEW WITH FBI SPECIAL AGENT JAMES JACOB "JAKE" KRUSE AND IS HEREBY SUBMITTED UNDER SEAL IN ACCORD WITH FBI DIR. 32014.12 AND HIPAA REG. 7319.

PREPARED BY MICHAEL R. TWILLIGER, PHD, UNDERCOVER EMPLOYEE SAFEGUARD UNIT, NATIONAL COVERT OPERATIONS SECTION, CRIMINAL INVESTIGATIVE DIVISION, FBI

Q. Special Agent Kruse, I understand you do not want to be here.
A. That's right.

Q. And that you've objected to this evaluation.
A. It doesn't really do me any good to object. Look, I'm tired and was looking forward to a few days off before I picked up another assignment. I spent all day yesterday with OPR and I was ordered back here today. I took a red-eye and I'm here. Let's get this over with so I can catch an afternoon flight back to L.A.

Q. I see by your file you were benched from undercover work seven years ago for a three-month period because of an adverse psychological evaluation.

A. That's correct. I was fairly new to the undercover program, and the psychologist and I didn't hit it off. She decided I needed a few months of desk duty. I objected and she won. I've learned since then. I know your evaluation will determine whether I can go back on the street, so all I'm asking you to do is check off the "approved" box and send me on my way.

Q. But you understand given what happened in Los Angeles, this is mandatory?

A. It's mandatory every six months or when ordered by an administrator due to special circumstances. This one's necessary because lots of bad people got killed.

Q. Would you please give me a brief description about how all this got started?

A. Sure. Every undercover case is different, but this one started out as a straightforward UC operation. Our target was an Asian organized-crime ring—of which there are dozens in L.A. Every ethnic group on the West Coast has one or two; different players, same sheet music. To the extent any undercover operation—the kind of thing the press calls a "sting"—is routine, this one should have been. It wasn't quite the simple example you find in an FBI Academy textbook—"a one-off"—you know, nab a criminal violating a single federal law. But we didn't expect it to take us in the directions it did. Typically, the UC meets a target dealing contraband, negotiates for the product, and when the delivery is made, the cuffs come out. Connect the dots—A to B to jail for the bad guy. In this one, the UC was targeting an organization rather than an individual.

Q. When you say "the UC" you mean . . .

A. The undercover agent. How long have you been at this?

Q. I'm new to the unit. You're only my second evaluation.

A. That's not very comforting.

Q. So you were the "UC" in this operation. Do you often refer to yourself in the third person?

A. Yeah. I was the UC. I really hadn't thought about this "third person" stuff. Does it bother you?

Q. Not really. Just wondering. People who refer to themselves in the third person—using terms like "he" or "they"—sometimes have disconnected from reality. Tell me what you think went right and what went wrong on this operation.

A. Every operation is a crapshoot. There are no guarantees of success. An experienced undercover agent can often negotiate the crooked trail and take the investigation in directions never dreamed of in the initial planning stages. But those journeys aren't always easy to navigate and are seldom welcomed by management. Each detour requires a new level in the approval process.

Q. Do you feel frustrated by what you call the "detours" in the "approval process"?

A. Look, I'm a big boy. I've been doing UC work for the past eight years and before I joined the Bureau I was a Marine. I understand the chain of command. And I know in Washington, Congress demands that whenever an operation diverts from its original approved path more administrators are going to get involved. That's what happened here.

Q. Why did you leave the Marine Corps and join the FBI?

A. I had the privilege of serving under a really great leader during the invasion of Iraq in 2003. After I was wounded he came to see me in the field hospital. . . .

Q. What was your job in Iraq?

A. I was a rifle company commander in the Third Marine Regiment. My regimental commander, a guy everybody admired, visited me in the hospital. He wanted me to stay in the Marines but he understood. I had lost a lot of men over there and the Bureau seemed like a better fit.

Q. Why?

A. Because in the Bureau I wouldn't be responsible for the lives and safety of hundreds of other people like I had been in Iraq. That takes a toll, watching the men you command die, makes you question whether you could have done something differently . . . then, writing letters home to their loved ones . . . Death is never easy when you know the people doing the dying.

Q. How about when you don't know the people doing the dying? How do you feel when you kill others . . . criminals . . . enemies?

A. To be quite honest, it doesn't bother me a whole lot. Maybe that's not healthy, I don't know, but in every case where I've killed people, it was either me or them. I don't spend a lot of time thinking about who they were before they tried to kill me or what they might have been if they had chosen a different line of work. The Marines never asked me "touchy-feely" questions about killing enemy combatants, but the Bureau gets all sensitive about it.

Q. So what's easier for you to deal with: the FBI structure or the Marines?

A. It's not a matter of easier or even better but as an undercover agent it's usually just me. I answer to myself unless the operation changes. Then I deal with the bureaucracy. A UC gets approval to buy illegal drugs but guns show up . . . a new approval's needed ASAP. You're authorized to buy stolen cars and your targets now want to launder money . . . new approvals. If the investigation implicates a judge, a politician, a member of the incumbent administration—expect FBI HQ and DOJ to go ballistic and demand lots of new approvals, which can take weeks, even months—while the UC's butt is on the line.

Q. Did you ever talk about these frustrations with your wife, Katie?

A. Let's come to an understanding real quickly. We're not going to talk about my wife.

Q. Okay. So what happened on this investigation? Did the FBI "approval process," as you call it, cause so many people to get killed?

A. We knew going in it would take more than L.A. Field Office approval to authorize the operation. Because it involved smuggling goods across the Mexican border, we had a "sensitive" circumstance from Jump Street. But we were trying to contain the violations to the L.A. Division just to avoid more Headquarters or DOJ involvement. Nobody in Washington gave a damn about counterfeit jeans and cigarettes. It seemed pretty simple at the time.

Q. So what changed? Why do you think HQ and DOJ got involved? Do you think it was personal?

A. Personal? Only so far as what they did could have gotten me—and some *real* innocents—killed. Look, this isn't my first rodeo. In an operation a few years ago, we were targeting a Chinese national we knew to be the biggest importer of counterfeit cigarettes on the West Coast. I took possession of a forty-foot container of counterfeit Marlboros, about ten million cigarettes. Our guy wanted them delivered to a Russian Mafia crew operating out of Allentown, Pennsylvania. I personally delivered the container to their warehouse, which the FBI didn't even know existed, and I watched Russian thugs affix counterfeit New York tax stamps to packs of fake cigarettes destined for New York City. It all went smoothly and I returned to L.A.

The Chinese kingpin now knew I could deliver the goods—and he ordered five more containers from his pals in Beijing. But then some genius at Headquarters, concerned this whole thing could disrupt our "relationship" with the Chinese communists, suddenly declared the operation to be "sensitive"—requiring Headquarters and DOJ authorization.

I was ordered to "cease and desist" all undercover operations until

DOJ approval paperwork arrived . . . a process that usually takes weeks. I sent an email to the L.A. SAC reminding him that I was "dealing with Chinese and Russian crime bosses who routinely 'off' people in L.A. but had, to date, never killed any Bureau humps in Washington." It took a month for the approval to come down. Meanwhile, I had to tap-dance because these guys would have killed me if they had figured out what was going on.

The SAC never offered a solution to my problem of blowing off meetings with the Chinese, but he did call me in for counseling and placed a notation in my personnel file that I had been admonished to use more professional language when communicating with Headquarters.

Q. I notice you're gripping both arms of the chair. Does it distress you to discuss Bureau hierarchy?

A. It's a coping mechanism. I'm okay. Next question.

Q. So have you always questioned authority?

A. No. Remember, I told you I was a Marine. I know how to follow orders. I also know the difference between a real leader and a politically motivated, butt-kissing, flagpole-hugging bureaucrat.

Q. And can you give me an example of a good leader?

A. Sure, Peter Newman. He was my regimental commander when we liberated Iraq from Saddam in 2003. He was the one who came to see me in the hospital after I was wounded. He's the kind of leader who knows how to accomplish the mission *and* take care of his men. Everyone who served with him knew he always cared more about us than he did about himself. Whether he was commanding a regular Marine unit or conducting special operations, as he did later on, we all loved him for it.

Q. Interesting term, "loved." Would you describe one of those special operations so I have a context?

A. Sure, but then I'll have to kill you. You're not cleared for it. . . . Just joking, Doc.

Q. I'll take your word for it, Agent Kruse. But tell me, is this the same Peter Newman you called in the midst of this operation?

A. Yep.

Q. And did the two of you talk about Gabe Chong?

A. Yeah.

Q. Did you have authorization to talk to someone outside the government about this operation?

A. No.

Q. So how did you contact each other? As you undoubtedly know, none of the cell phones provided to you by the FBI for this operation have any record of the calls between you and this Peter Newman. . . .

A. I have already answered that question for the slugs from OPR. . . . But if it makes any difference to you, I still have a personal cell phone. . . .

Q. And according to NSA, that phone is registered in the name of your wife. . . .

A. I've already told you, we're not going to talk about Katie and I've told OPR all they need to know about how General Newman and I communicated during this operation.

Q. Let me rephrase the question. Do you think it was wise to call this General Newman?

A. Look, Gabe and I were both Marines. We both served with Peter Newman, just not at the same time. After the Marines, I went to the FBI and Gabe joined the Agency. General Newman retired from the Marines in 2011, but we've stayed in touch. Last December he became the CEO of a company called Centurion Solutions Group. CSG has contracts with all kinds of government agencies—including the Bureau and the CIA. I'm pretty sure his security clearances are far above yours and mine. So, yeah, I think it was wise to talk to him, don't you?

Q. Do you feel that Peter Newman or you are responsible in any way for what happened to Gabe?

A. Responsible? Sure, I'm responsible because I was inside the operation. Gabe had my back. I should have had his. General Newman may be a civilian now but he's very aware how the Iranians and North Koreans are working on nuclear weapons and ICBMs. He knows how counterfeit U.S. currency is being used to pay for R&D, the research and development, and the nuclear enrichment Pyongyang is doing for the ayatollahs in Tehran. The general tried to get the power brokers in D.C. to pay attention but the potentates on the Potomac wanted their "deal" with Iran to work—and nothing else mattered. Gabe's blood is on the hands of the clowns here in Washington—they betrayed us all.

Q. And how does that make you feel?

A. How does it make me feel? Like I want to puke. I really think we're done here. Do me a favor, put this in the report: "The agent conducted himself in a professional manner. He has not overadapted nor is he attached to his undercover persona. Neither is he detached from reality nor displaying an exaggerated sense of importance. He is adequately coping and not in need of withdrawal support." I've been through enough of these to know the verbiage. Check off the box clearing me to go back to UC work. Let me catch my plane and you and I can get together for my next session on the couch.

INTERVIEW TERMINATED WHEN SUBJECT SPECIAL AGENT ABRUPTLY DEPARTED.
PSYCHOLOGICAL EVALUATION: SEALED
SIGNED ________________
MICHAEL R. TWILLIGER, PHD, UNDERCOVER EMPLOYEE SAFEGUARD UNIT, NATIONAL COVERT OPERATIONS SECTION, CRIMINAL INVESTIGATIVE DIVISION, FBI

CHAPTER ONE

DAY 1

MONDAY, APRIL 28

"TEN DAYS PRIOR TO SPECIAL AGENT JAKE KRUSE'S MOST RECENT PSYCHOLOGICAL EVALUATION"

The sounds of mariachi music blasting from the run-down bar just north of the Otay Mesa border crossing were met by the rumblings of the Cummins diesel engine. The two men in the cab of the 2009 International 9200i weren't going to surprise anyone if stealth were important. Only the darkness provided a modicum of cover for the evening's criminal endeavor. Pulling off the pockmarked blacktop road, the driver slowly made his way past a half-dozen trailers parked in the dirt lot.

"There it is," said Jake Kruse with a late-night attitude as he pulled in front of the burnt-orange twenty-footer. The indefinable graffiti spray-painted on most of the side panels matched the description his border contact had provided. He threw the big rig in reverse and backed toward the trailer, stopping a few feet from the tongue hitch. Shutting down the engine, he and Tommy Hwan jumped out of the cab and headed to the back of the cargo container.

The two men had performed this ritual several times over the past two months, but this was the first time they would dance in the dark. A reluctant trust had been built but cautious doubt lingered.

Jake pulled a mini SureFire from a side pocket of his worn khaki cargo pants. Illuminating the thin metal surety wires intertwined between the latches on the steel doors of the shipping box, he said, "It hasn't been tampered with since it left China. You can check the serial number on the seal with what's on the bill of lading, if you want."

"I believe you. Let's just get out of here. Too many wets hanging out across the street," said Tommy, pointing to a half-dozen noisy men sharing beers in front of the bar.

"An Asian racist. I love it," said Jake as he handed the flashlight to Tommy. "I can't do this blindfolded, so light up the back as I hook up the trailer."

Jake climbed back into the cab and began to slowly ease the tractor in reverse, seeking to couple the tractor and trailer. He'd been to the CDL short course and could do this in daylight, but darkness added a degree of difficulty the six-week commercial truck driver's school failed to include in its curriculum. Apparently, the instructor for Trucking 101 didn't anticipate his graduates engaging in nocturnal crimes. Jake took a couple of stabs at lining up the kingpin and the strike plate before he heard the distinctive sound of the lockjaws engaging.

He jumped down from the cab, worked some late-night magic, and within minutes completed the final hookup, attaching the service, supply, and electrical lines. "It looks good. I think we're ready to get out of here."

Tommy was only too happy to return to the security of the semi and get as far north of Mexico as he could. Not only Customs, but border bandits would love to seize a rig of counterfeit Rolex watches smuggled into the United States.

As Jake started to climb into the cab, two men, both "stupid brave" on oxy washed down with a six-pack of cerveza, jumped out from behind one of the parked trailers. In the darkness it was impossible to identify the exact make and model of the semi-automatics they were carrying, but both men were waving their weapons like B-list actors in a cheap Hollywood movie.

"Manos arriba!" shouted one of the men as Jake and Tommy threw up their hands.

"Give me the keys, *jefe*," said the taller of the two in slurred, heavily accented English. The attacker was only about five foot seven but the gun he was holding made him seem bigger and his Corona-induced courage made him a bit more unpredictable.

Jake was slow in responding to the command as he assessed the situation. The only exit was to his left, retreating to an open field, leaving Tommy to fend for himself. As with most confrontations, and Jake had been in his share, this was more than flight-or-fight. Two other variables entered the calculus: posturing and submission. Without their guns, Jake would have beaten both men like cheap piñatas, but it was one thing to be cocky and another to be sloppy.

"Don't be stupid, *weddo*. Give me the keys!" screamed the leader.

"Give him the keys, Jake," said Tommy, fear evaporating what little mettle remained.

Jake slowly reached into his pocket with his right hand, keeping his left hand high in the air. He held up the keys, jiggling them at about eye level.

"Toss 'em, *jefe*!"

Jake did as instructed, the border thug snatching the keys in midair.

"You guys had to wait until I got my hands dirty hooking up the trailer. At least let me grab a towel out of the cab to wipe off the grease," said Jake with the bravado reserved for the truly brave or the really stupid.

"Quieto!" shouted the boss as he handed the keys to his partner.

The smaller of the two slipped his semi-auto in the front of his pants and fumbled with the keys as he prepared to climb into the cab.

"No need for any violence. It's just a tractor and a trailer. You can have it. You keep the truck and we keep our lives. Seems like a fair exchange," said Jake.

The predator seemed pleased his prey wasn't going to put up a fight.

"You guys are going to need a bill of lading in case you get stopped," said Jake.

Tommy threw him a confused look.

"Huh?" asked the spokesman for the two-man Latino criminal conspiracy.

"I'm just going to reach in my back pocket and pull out the shipping paperwork. This way if you get stopped they'll know what you're carrying. It makes you look legit to the cops."

Keeping his left hand high in the air Jake slowly reached toward his back pocket; no sudden moves, no quick jerks, just slipping his free hand behind him. He had a quiet confidence the late-night hijackers failed to grasp. . . . *Control the adrenaline and manage the chaos.*

In an instant everything changed!

With lightning speed and a practiced precision, Jake pulled a Glock 19 from the small of his back and fired two quick shots at the taller of the two, who dropped immediately; one round hit just below the right eye and the second through the throat. There was a slight gurgle and gasp but death was maximized; suffering minimal.

Jake pivoted as the smaller man, whose senses were dulled by alcohol and drugs, was reaching into his waistband for his weapon. The semi-auto never cleared the belt and Jake fired three times from only a few feet, all three center mass. The tight grouping of hollow-point rounds, expanding upon impact, ensured massive destruction of the internal organs. The thief was dead before his body folded to the dusty ground.

The two Mexican felons never had a chance; their criminal careers ended in a matter of seconds. It was quick, dirty, and ugly, but it was done.

"Are they dead?" asked a shaken Tommy.

Jake didn't answer as he did a quick search of the smaller gangster, grabbing the keys to the rig, a worn leather wallet, and the weapon, which he stuffed in the front of his pants. "Might need a throw-down someday," said Jake with a slight smile. From the other thief he took the wallet and semi-automatic.

Before jumping into the cab Jake kicked at both bloodied bodies, moving them from the path of the big rig.

The sideshow was complete.

With the music still blasting from the squalid tavern across the street, the five gunshots had failed to arouse the attention of those partying on the porch. Within seconds, Jake and Tommy were out of the lot and on the road, heading north toward Los Angeles.

CHAPTER TWO

Jake maintained a safe speed keeping in the far right lane. The traffic was minimal on the I-15, so he could have opened it up without arousing any suspicion, but he had no intention of alerting some chippie trying to make his monthly quota. He checked his mirrors often but saw nothing unusual. Their escape had gone unnoticed.

Tommy Hwan, a third-generation Korean-American with a criminal record dating back to his juvenile days, was in the passenger seat. Just twenty-four, the small-time street thug, what the Koreans called a *kkangpae*, had no idea Jake was anything but another member of L.A.'s criminal underworld.

Forty minutes of silence was interrupted by Tommy's plea, "You need to pull over. I gotta take a leak."

Jake smirked. "I thought you peed your pants back there."

"I wasn't expecting you to pull a gun. I thought you were giving him the bill of lading and couldn't figure out why."

"We've got too much unfinished business to let a couple of jackers get in the way."

"They didn't get in our way for long," said Tommy.

"What did you want me to do, give them your twenty-foot container of fake watches?" said Jake.

Tommy laughed. "They aren't mine till you get 'em to the warehouse. The deal includes safe delivery to L.A."

"Yeah, I guess it does say something like that in the fine print," said Jake with a brief grin.

"You showed me something back there."

"Yeah, so did you," sneered Jake.

"No, seriously. A gun ups the ante on any jail time, so I don't carry. I'm a lover, not a fighter. But you're not afraid to pull the trigger."

Jake merely nodded, questioning whether he'd become too comfortable with the violence that had become a part of his life.

"Killing comes easy to you," said Tommy.

With a slight shrug, Jake said, "I wouldn't say easy but it kept us aboveground tonight."

"Something came up the other day and you just might have the stones to pull it off."

"You want to give me a clue."

"After I pee."

Jake pulled off the freeway at State Highway 76, stopping in front of the Circle K–Mobil station. "You can run in there. Grab me a Coke on your way out. I'll turn this puppy around, then we'll head back north."

As soon as Tommy exited the cab, Jake was on his cell phone. He punched in a number and after three rings a sleepy voice answered, "Yeah."

"It's me. We need a cleanup on aisle four," said Jake with a slight smile in his voice.

"Jake, don't tell me that. I don't need any more paperwork."

"Hey, I removed two more idiots from the gene pool."

"What happened?" asked Trey Bennett, his case agent.

"At our usual off-loading spot in Otay Mesa, Tommy and I got hit by a couple of thieves. They're both dead. I've got their wallets and weapons. You better get somebody from the San Diego office involved. I don't think there were any wits. I didn't have much of a choice but it was righteous. I'm not sure if the video from the cab picked it up but the audio should have grabbed it."

"Is Tommy okay?"

"Yeah," and then with sarcasm, Jake added, "So am I. Thanks for asking."

Science-fiction author Robert Heinlein claimed fulfillment in life came from loving a good woman and killing a bad man. Veteran FBI undercover agent Jake Kruse had done both, but lately the killing came easier than the loving.

Jake wasn't the only person spilling blood in Southern California this evening. An honor graduate of the state's prison system was about to pull a trigger as well. Within days the lives of the assassin and the undercover FBI agent would intersect violently.

CHAPTER THREE

As the assassin threaded his way through the Wilshire Boulevard traffic, the female in the passenger seat rolled up her window and motioned for him to do the same. He gave her a sideways glance, sulking at the directive, but reluctantly complied. She offered an unassuming smile, then lowered the volume on B. B. King, who was soulfully singing through the sound system of the 2008 Honda Pilot LX. He playfully slapped her hand for touching his radio but knew the real business of the evening was about to begin.

In a matter of minutes sweat rained down the assassin's face, more heat than nerves. The evening was unusually humid and even though the sound system worked, the air-conditioning didn't.

They couldn't afford to roll with the windows down; the dark tint obscured faces and features. He would have preferred the accompanying breeze of opened windows, but the sealed-up Honda was the safe move for the short term.

To placate the driver, the female passenger unwrapped two

pieces of Korean ginseng candy, popped one in her mouth, and placed the second to his lips as they both savored the momentary pleasure.

He turned left off Wilshire, heading south. A few cars were parked on the street but traffic was minimal in the quiet upscale community. He slowed as he entered the block where the target lived. In the darkness it was hard to discern the house numbers and they both strained to find the residence. With her hands, the female motioned for him to slow down and then she pointed to a home on the right in the middle of the block.

As he edged the vehicle to the curb, stopping two houses past the target's location, he wiped his thick dark brow with his right hand before turning off the ignition and pocketing the keys. Rubbing his hand dry on his pants leg, he popped the center console and removed the German-made Heckler & Koch Mk 23 SOCOM. With his left hand he attached a sound suppressor, then racked a .45-caliber round into the chamber. The weapon was bulky but its stopping power made it a favorite of special forces worldwide. Second place in a gunfight meant death and the assassin was taking no chances with tonight's mission.

Though he never served in the military, he knew what it was like to take a life. He had done so on the streets of Los Angeles with a gun and in prison with his hands. It wasn't as hard as most people believed. He was nervous the first time he pulled the trigger in a drive-by shooting, but after watching his victim fall and receiving accolades from his "homies," the nerves quickly dissipated and he welcomed the attention.

In prison it was a matter of survival. Death to others meant life for him, and he wasn't about to forfeit his life to some convicted felon seeking to establish his bona fides on the yard. More than one prisoner felt the assassin's powerful hands around the throat, crushing the windpipe and snapping the neck. Few were willing to challenge his strength and no one was willing to discuss with prison authorities the killer's propensity for resolving conflicts through violence.

Each time he killed it became easier. Now it was a part of him. The prison psychiatrist was wrong. He really wasn't a sociopath, but another man's death meant nothing to him. He didn't necessarily kill for thrills but he admitted to enjoying the rush. He loved the adrenaline racing through his veins as he gripped the weapon and anticipated pulling the trigger. When he held his breath and squeezed the index finger, it was as pleasurable as anything he experienced, especially when he watched his intended victim collapse. He found a cause that welcomed his skills and now he justified his work because killing had purpose . . . tonight he would kill for preemptive protection.

He had been recruited in prison, where he had spent most of his adult life. At thirty-three, Kareem Abdul, the name he chose to honor his grandmother's favorite basketball player, was converted through the efforts of a prison imam. He found a different kind of fellowship with "followers of the Prophet." Kareem learned the ways of the faith but also learned the game many in prison played. Following his conversion, the strict discipline he evidenced while incarcerated served him well when the parole board met. They observed the changed man, his unblemished prison record since his conversion, and his willingness to admit to previous wrongs. Though still morally elastic, he sold the board on his sincerity and was given an early release on the armed-robbery conviction. With his demonstrated continued devotion to the faith after his prison stint and as part of a state cost-cutting move, he was also released early from parole. Islam served him well and as in prison, he was willing to exploit the religion to his advantage.

They paused briefly as he and his passenger assessed the situation, scanned their surroundings, and listened for the unusual. They nodded in agreement and quietly opened the doors to the Honda. In addition to switching license plates, Kareem had already removed the dome light, preventing a quick flash of the interior light, which would have alerted a neighbor when the car doors opened.

As she exited the car, the passenger tossed the candy wrappers on the ground as if in defiance of the community's wealth. Each carefully shut their door and padded down the sidewalk.

A large, powerful man, Kareem Abdul moved with commando-like stealth up the short driveway. She followed in trace. Dressed in black, he was easily concealed in the shadows on the darkest night of the month. She too was dressed in black and her slight build served as sufficient camouflage for the evening.

Though the streetlights illuminated the road, the mature thick trees in the front yard shaded the house. It was nearing eleven o'clock but they knew bedtime for the middle-aged Asian was immediately following the news. *Tomorrow he will make the news but miss the broadcast.* As they suspected, a flickering light from the living room creeping through the bamboo curtains signaled the target was watching television.

By Beverly Hills standards the residence was small, but as any real estate agent will tell you, "location, location, location." The diminutive home commanded a multimillion-dollar price tag merely because it had a coveted zip code.

While cautious, the intruders weren't really worried about nosy neighbors making a 9-1-1 call. The assassin would follow the motto of the military sniper: one shot, one kill. A single suppressed gunshot might draw someone's attention, but like most people, the listener would wait to hear a second sound. Failing that, he would dismiss the noise and go on about his business. Since few residents in this elite community exercised their Second Amendment rights, most knew the sounds of gunfire only from those provided by Hollywood. A quick subdued pop was hardly what any resident would expect. Stealth and speed would accomplish this evening's task.

The woman slipped behind a large crepe myrtle bush and spied into the living room through a small divide between the window and the curtain. The target was alone, resting comfortably, his feet propped up on a brown leather footstool as he watched TV in an exquisitely furnished home, antiques complementing the utilitarian furniture.

The man was guilty of betrayal, an offense worthy of death. His offhand comments at the bar and his inquisitive nature seemed more than just trying to impress a beautiful woman. When he bragged to her in private of his association with law enforcement authorities, his treachery was confirmed. But he was no government-sanctioned spy . . . he was a snitch, a rat. The law of the street prevailed. *Cheese-eaters must die!*

Some at the mosque objected to tonight's mission but the complaint was never about murder. Their concern was drawing undue attention to the "cause." Kareem assured everyone that what needed to be done would never be linked to them. When the cell leader concurred and the followers realized they wouldn't be participating, the men easily acceded to their leader's decision.

Kareem rang the doorbell, then flattened his body against the darkened wall, concealing himself should the quarry decide to peer out the living-room window.

The target was fighting to stay awake, his eyes growing heavy. He wasn't expecting company at this hour and was startled by the sound of the doorbell playing the first few notes of a traditional Korean ballad. Rising slowly from his wingback chair, the man shouted, "Who is it?" as he approached the door.

There was no response.

"Who is it?" he asked again, perhaps thinking it was a delivery of some kind. From surveilling the block over the past few days Kareem knew FedEx or UPS sometimes dropped off a package and rang the doorbell without waiting for a reply, but never this late.

With still no answer to his third inquiry, the target peered out the window, scanning in all directions, and saw nothing.

The assassin moved directly in front of the door, his focus straight ahead, his weapon just below the eyepiece. He rang the doorbell a second time. When the porch light came on, the assassin didn't flinch, remaining steady, prepared to strike.

The target hollered, "Yes!" then made the final mistake of his life. He put his eye to the security peephole.

When Kareem spotted the resident peering through the tiny opening, he raised the semi-automatic two inches and fired a single round. The suppressor minimized the muzzle flash, but the sound of the .45-caliber echoed against the heavy wooden door. It was louder than the assassin expected and he hoped he hadn't attracted a neighbor's curiosity. The gunman casually picked up the spent shell casing and put it in his pocket.

A wicked smile covered the woman's face as she watched a pink spatter flood the living room and the man crumble to the floor, his life extinguished in an instant, his account closed.

Kareem and his companion retreated down the driveway toward the Honda. They entered the vehicle, holding the doors closed, but waited until they were down the block before slamming the front doors shut.

The woman gave the assassin a congratulatory stroke of his thigh, and when he glanced over at her, she provided an approving smile. Turning right at Olympic Boulevard, the murderers disappeared into a steady late-evening stream of Los Angeles traffic.

CHAPTER FOUR

DAY 2

TUESDAY, APRIL 29

The mosque on Olympic Boulevard was in a run-down strip mall tucked away in the far corner of the complex between a bakery and a dry cleaners. It was no mega-mosque or Islamic cultural center like those being funded by Saudi oil money. In fact, most, including nonpracticing Muslims, didn't know the facility existed. The call to prayer didn't echo throughout the business district signaling believers of the hour. Most worshippers came and went without much fanfare.

The space had been a used clothing store, which should have benefited by the economic downturn, but like many businesses in the area it too failed. Even the secondhand-clothing market was impacted by the double-dip recession, and the Korean property owner was only too happy to find a new tenant.

Now the building answered the religious needs of those practicing Islam and living in the immediate neighborhood. The tiny facility consisted of three rooms and a single restroom: the larger area was used for prayers; the smaller area, meetings; the third room, a tiny office, doubled as a storage facility.

Though there was an authentic air of legitimacy to the mosque, it served a greater purpose for those members wishing to impose their own brand of sharia law upon America. Not every one of the several dozen in regular attendance sought self-segregation nor desired to participate in violent jihad. They evidenced no pent-up hostility toward the United States and had assimilated into Los Angeles's multicultural society. Many loved America and the freedoms and opportunities this country provided, but among those worshipping at the religious institution was a group of men who supported the pro-jihad, anti-America, anti-Jewish rhetoric flooding the terrorist websites. They believed in an ideology of hatred, demeaning all religions while extolling Islam.

These men viewed jihad as a violent, offensive confrontation against the enemies of a global *ummah*, a unified Islamic state. The Koran imposed such an obligation: "And fight them until there is no more dissent and the religion will be for Allah alone." It was their duty to pursue the infidels throughout the world, killing those who refused to submit to the will of Allah. "Fight and slay the pagans wherever you find them. Seize them and beleaguer them, and lie in wait for them in every stratagem."

The men were sleeper activists who would not be seduced by the infidel's culture.

The mosque provided a safe haven, serving as a staging area for terrorist activities. It birthed plans to destroy the *kafirs,* nonbelievers who were not worthy of an earthly life and were destined for hell.

Thanks to political correctness and the First Amendment, it was almost impossible for the FBI to monitor the happenings at any mosque. Since 9/11, government officials at all levels had gone out of their way to appear tolerant, inclusive, and accommodating. Politicians obscured the origins of violence, twisting uncomfortably in public hearings, and refusing to attribute terrorist acts to any one belief system. Whenever possible they blamed a lone wolf acting outside the religious norm or misguided social

outcasts seeking a perverted meaning to life. America's tolerance and self-imposed social engineering fueled the cause of those at the mosque. Presidents called Islam a religion of peace, with Muslim outreach a top priority for successive administrations. Christians opened dialogue while educators and politicians sought to answer the question "Why do they hate us?" and came up essentially empty, offering feckless concessions and indefensible appeasements.

More than a decade after 9/11, the efforts of law enforcement were mostly ignored or criticized. Several dozen terrorist attacks had been disrupted. Yet when a plot was discovered and a terrorist act prevented, the media quickly found fault, dismissing the investigation as government-inspired entrapment, blaming informants or paid operatives. "Experts" described the "root causes" of "extremism" to be inadequate education or limited economic opportunities and unemployment. Rarely would an academic or journalist acknowledge that radical Islamic terrorists frequently used children, the mentally challenged, and the infirm to do much of their bidding.

When Army major Nidal Hasan murdered thirteen at Fort Hood while shouting "Allahu Akhbar!" it was called "workplace violence"—not terrorism. When two young "students" from Chechnya killed three and wounded more than two hundred at the Boston Marathon, it was a "failure" for law enforcement. After alert civilians stopped Richard Reid and Umar Farouk Abdulmutallab from setting off bombs aboard aircraft headed for U.S. cities from overseas, the media described the events as intelligence failures. Those in the stands love to hurl epithets at those on the field.

The six men arrived at the tiny mosque for sunrise prayers and stood around outside before entering. They were convinced their terror cell, operating in plain sight in one of America's largest

cities, remained off the government's radar. . . . And they were right.

As the sun began to creep above the horizon, the heavy traffic on one of Los Angeles's busiest streets provided the cover they needed for a dangerously open conversation.

"Where is he?" asked one.

"Have you heard from him?" asked the smallest of the six men, looking around for Kareem.

"He called me last night. The deed is done," said Mohammed, the leader of the cell, who wore his leathery and scarred face as a badge of honor.

"That is good."

Mohammed smiled. "It is better to be the hunter than the hunted. Before peace there must always be war . . . or surrender. Although I wish to one day destroy this godless nation in its entirety, we must never forget that our ability to cripple the Great Satan can also rest in the small victories that go unnoticed and are not linked to the cause. We shall discuss this further after sunrise prayers. Let us go in and give thanks to Allah for last night's victory."

The words of Mohammed bound the men to the terror pact; they collectively basked in this most recent, yet seemingly inconsequential, success as they followed their leader into the mosque.

CHAPTER FIVE

Jake Kruse and Trey Bennett were sitting in Trey's Ford Fusion just down the street from the entrance to the CBS Studio City lot. Those walking past, more concerned with midmorning auditions, paid no attention to the two men.

Jake smiled at the question and answered with bureaucratic perfection, "I used a force-multiplying instrument to successfully stop the lethal threat."

"You shot them," said Trey.

"Okay, I shot them."

"You've been in so many shootings, you're beginning to sound like OPR," said Trey, referring to the FBI's dreaded Office of Professional Responsibility.

"It's all how you write up the paperwork," said Jake, offering a lopsided grin before passing a worn pillowcase to Trey. "This has the wallets and weapons from the two hijackers last night. I cleared both weapons and there isn't much in the wallets, but maybe you can come up with something."

Trey set his coffee in the cup holder before peering into the bag. "San Diego got an agent down there right after you called. The locals didn't seem too concerned and welcomed the Bureau's help. The agent called me this morning and said it didn't even make the paper."

"Those guys weren't virgins. I'm sure once they do some digging a few open investigations get closed. The video and audio tapes from the cab are also in the pillowcase. After you listen to it you'll see it was righteous."

"I didn't doubt that it was."

"I dropped the container off at their warehouse about two this morning."

As Trey was poking through the pillowcase, he said, "We should be able to pick up the delivery schedule from the phone traffic. We'll let a couple of small loads get through but then intercept the bigger deliveries with a traffic stop en route to the ultimate destination. It's worked so far and they haven't linked it back to you."

"I'm still golden with Tommy. How do you want to handle this latest issue?"

"We have to play it out."

Jake smiled. "I was hoping you'd say that. I always enjoy the chance to take down a lawyer. I'll set up a meet for tomorrow."

CHAPTER SIX

Through the window Kareem spied Mohammed sitting near the back and strained to look at ease as he entered the tiny diner across the street from the mosque. The prison convert suspected by the look on Mohammed's face he was in for another subdued tongue-lashing. Kareem had missed sunrise prayers . . . again. He had been admonished before about his lack of submission, which some saw as a lack of faith, but self-discipline and punctuality were never his strongest characteristics, even prior to his conversion.

He debated lying to Mohammed, telling him he had gone to another mosque or performed the ritual at home. The fifth-century Chinese author Sun Tzu, in *The Art of War*, stated, "All warfare is based on deception." Kareem was at war on an urban battlefield, and this morning might be a time to hone his skills, exercise deceit, and practice the art. Besides, Muslims believed in *taqiyya*, lying to safeguard oneself or to protect Islam. Kareem anticipated his pride was about to be attacked and might demand protection.

For months Kareem questioned whether he should move to another mosque, maybe one where more African-Americans attended. If not for Mohammed, he would have left shortly after he first began worshipping at the strip mall facility, which had been recommended by a visiting imam at the prison. Kareem was the only homegrown convert. The others, born in the faith, emigrated from Iran, West Beirut in Lebanon, or Syria's Shiite community.

He heard the rumors and backstabbing. Many recent failed terrorist plots were the actions of converts; men and women radicalized through the Internet, who brought too much attention to the jihadist agenda. Kareem had been lumped into this pot of offenders and for all his bravado, his ego was fragile. He sought acceptance and never felt welcomed, except by Mohammed, who nurtured him, praising his skills and devotion.

Mohammed clearly articulated the cell's mission: impose Allah's word on America so Islam would reign supreme. The means of accomplishing that goal seemed clear to a man of Kareem's limited religious background, yet for some, even those in the cell, it was not as defined as Kareem would have liked. The ex-con had an all-or-nothing vision of jihad.

Kareem had studied enough in prison to know Israel was not the problem, as many who were ignorant of the cause's true mission espoused. The Koran demanded *all* nations submit to Allah. The nation of Israel served as a fashionable excuse, a convenient scapegoat, for the current call to arms, but Israel wasn't even a recognized state when Muslims conquered the Middle East, North Africa, and most of southern Europe centuries earlier. As Kareem recognized from his readings, a homeland for the Palestinians wouldn't halt the efforts to implement sharia in America or worldwide.

Since he was taking risks others in the cell were unwilling or unable to take, maybe this morning was the time to be assertive. Kareem prided himself on never backing down from anyone in prison or on the street, so why was he fearful of the cell's leader?

Kareem towered over Mohammed and outweighed him by at least fifty pounds. Even larger OGs, or Original Gangsters, as the gang members in the hood referred to them, never instilled this much apprehension in the convicted felon. Though Kareem was still questioning his own religious foundations, he believed Mohammed had been ordained by Allah.

The ex-con had heard whispers of Mohammed's heroics in Lebanon during the most recent battle with the Israelis in 2006. It was rumored Mohammed was a member of Hezbollah, the Party of God, and trained by Iran's Islamic Revolutionary Guard Corps—the IRGC. Each time Kareem broached the subject, Mohammed dismissed the inquiry, reminding the novice jihadi that only through Allah could the cause succeed, and no one should seek individual glory.

In many ways the cell was autonomous, with Mohammed making the tactical decisions without much overseas input or oversight. It had been that way since he arrived in Los Angeles in 2009. Taking the "long route" from Beirut to California wasn't easy. It had taken him three months to travel by sea from Lebanon to Caracas, then by ferry to Panama and a dozen bus trips through Costa Rica, Nicaragua, Honduras, El Salvador, Guatemala, and north up Mexico's west coast to the cross-border tunnel in Tijuana.

But in the end, it was worth it. Since being smuggled into the United States there had been thousands of telephone calls, text messages, and emails between Mohammed and his Quds Force masters. Buried in trillions of NSA metadata files there were records of these communications. Yet for more than five years his true role as the leader of an Islamic terror cell had gone undetected.

Though government surveillance had failed to detect the cell's existence, the aggressive financial investigations by the FBI and Treasury agents in recent years made it difficult for the cell to receive funds. Mohammed was often forced to seek his own funding to recruit new jihadis for the cause or to move Hezbollah "sleeper agents" across the border into the States.

Kareem not only sought Mohammed's approval but was constantly looking for ways to benefit the cause. He hoped for a more prominent role for himself in the cell, and knew his aggressive ideas were not embraced by those who feared going beyond the safe confines of the mosque.

Kareem offered his hand and cautiously took his seat. The waitress approached with a second pot of tea and dropped a menu on the table.

"We missed you this morning," said Mohammed.

Kareem only nodded.

Maybe it was Mohammed's leadership skills but he chose not to admonish the newest member of the cell. "Well done last night. Allah be praised."

Kareem breathed a protracted sigh, a smile now growing on his face. "Allah be praised."

"Do you still believe we made the right decision?" asked Mohammed.

Kareem nodded.

"The fact you were successful only reinforces the belief Allah chose to honor our decision."

Kareem blew on the steaming tea before taking a sip, then said, "We couldn't let Sonny live. He told Candy he was working for the cops. We couldn't take a chance."

"What about the other one?" asked Mohammed.

"They both need to go but setting him up might be tougher. He's part of Yeong's security team."

"You are wiser in those ways because of your street experience in this country," noted Mohammed.

Kareem's smile grew. "Even if we're wrong, it's two less infidels."

Mohammed wanted to smile but didn't. "We can't resolve every question with a bullet."

Kareem shrugged as the waitress returned. Kareem quickly glanced at the menu, then said, "I'll take two eggs scrambled and pancakes."

"Would you like bacon or sausage with that?"

Kareem shook his head as she turned toward Mohammed.

"I'm fine. Just the tea," said Mohammed.

When she left the table, Mohammed smiled and said, "I guess your cover is still intact if she offered someone devoted to the cause pig for breakfast."

"Do you think she's an undercover fed who doesn't understand our beliefs? I hear they can be pretty stupid," whispered a smiling Kareem.

Suddenly serious, Mohammed said, "Americans are not stupid, but they are easily distracted. Look how excited they got about Russia and Ukraine. They also believe in diversity and believe we are a minority in need of protection." Mohammed laughed with contempt. "But they are ignorant of our ways and our calls for jihad. Though our fatwas have been most public they attribute these holy proclamations to religious 'fundamentalists.' The American media even refers to the imams who issue these fatwas as 'conservatives.' "

Kareem was no longer smiling, focused now on his spiritual mentor.

"The Americans are fools. The 'true believers' number in the millions. Allah's army actually outnumbers the American military. We have infiltrated their entire society. We live on their college campuses. We have supporters in their media, in their courts, even in their big businesses, who want to proclaim they are 'inclusive.' Like you, Kareem, we have sought out brothers in their prisons. Americans who remain neutral are on our side. Theirs is a nation of apathy, too consumed with depravity, self-indulgence, and decadence. They allow us not only to exist but to thrive."

Without even raising his voice, Mohammed instilled fire and passion in Kareem, calling for his service to the Islamist cause and its enemies. For Kareem, the enemy was an American society that had held him in chains for a lifetime.

Shaking his head, Mohammed said, "Our allegiance is not to

any flag, not to a political party, certainly not to the democracy they have deified. Our allegiance is to Allah alone and his will calls for a worldwide Islamic caliphate with a mandate of any means necessary. Not just one nation under God but an entire world in submission to Allah."

Uncharacteristic warmth overcame Kareem as he flushed with pride, knowing he was playing a part in a movement designed to destroy the corporate and personal demons in his own life.

CHAPTER SEVEN

DAY 3

WEDNESDAY, APRIL 30

For Jake Kruse, it was another restless night. In the past, only the undercover assignments brought such restlessness, his mind never quieting from the potential clashes racing through his "overactive imagination," as Katie used to joke. But for the past year, thoughts and images of her battled nightly with the issues of his job.

He always justified the job-related insomnia because it prepared him for the harsh reality of the street. The danger never really dies. But death didn't scare him, it never had; embarrassment did. He could take a bullet. In some ways he might even welcome it. He just didn't want a stupid mistake caught on a surveillance camera becoming a YouTube video in perpetuity. He knew the difference between humility and humiliation.

Jake was convinced he was a better undercover agent because he didn't sleep. He lived many of the confrontations, at least in his mind, and rehearsed his answers and reactions. His manufactured lies were grounded in the truth, but a near decade of undercover work had taught him the more convincing the lies, the more deadly the consequences. He needed to be prepared; he needed to be ready. Katie constantly reminded him each undercover encounter was a gift, a learning experience not to be ignored. So this morning was one more gift, one more adventure. With Katie gone, he lived for little else.

Jake parked just below the pier on Appian Way, a surface street paralleling the Pacific Ocean. As he exited the vehicle he slipped the Glock into his waistband. The 9mm was more for show than protection. When a person is too weak to pull the trigger, he usually doesn't pose an immediate threat to a professional killer.

Though the faded blue jeans and untucked denim shirt failed to make a Beverly Hills fashion statement, the Tony Lama ostrich-skin boots set him apart from the ordinary. Pretty didn't necessarily sell on the street but image was everything when you lived on the edge, and that's where Jake Kruse thrived.

Even his choice of weapons had purpose. Many federal law enforcement agencies issue .40-caliber pistols. Jake was comfortable with most handguns but his Glock 19 served him well. It was easily concealable and the 9mm might throw off a sophisticated criminal knowledgeable about a federal agent's arsenal.

It's impossible to categorize successful undercover agents. They come in all shapes and sizes, all types of personalities. Some UCs prefer working as part of a team. Others, like Jake, enjoy being on the high wire alone, without a net. Some are people persons, others loners. Jake liked playing lonely and independent. As Katie used to say, "It's not just humanity. Jake is also lactose intolerant." He was a team player only when the rules required. But he loved the adrenaline rush of each encounter and welcomed the unknown each assignment brought.

Today the biggest unknown was the subject's overall knowledge of L.A.'s law enforcement community. In spite of its size, Los Angeles is a small town, especially its criminal underbelly. This morning wasn't a "Kevin Bacon six degrees of separation" situation. In L.A.'s criminal underworld it was more like two or three degrees. Jake knew he had not personally encountered today's target but assumed those he previously met while undercover had. The risks, however, were balanced by the adventure.

CHAPTER EIGHT

Jake looked at his reflection in the car window, ran his fingers through his hair, pronounced himself fit for the role, and proceeded to the pier. With a few well-chosen admissions by H. Daniel Reid, Jake would be ridding the legal establishment of one more bottom-feeder.

The bright orange midmorning Los Angeles sun was beating on his back as he headed west on the Santa Monica Pier. His focus was on the moment. Reid might only be a lawyer but he could still be dangerous. He could panic and do something really stupid. Even one night in jail is more than most can take, and the thought of a perp walk on the six o'clock news can send the most genteel over the edge.

The waves were blasting ashore, breaking in rapid succession. The morning surfers rushed to the water, seeking the perfect ride. Joggers ran up and down the beach as the tides washed away any evidence of their physical efforts. Those not wealthy enough to run or surf for sheer enjoyment hugged the railing of the pier, fishing poles in hand, hoping to catch a meal for their hungry families. The Pacific Ocean offered something for everyone.

There was no way to lighten the footfalls as his boots clomped along the wooden planks of the pier. Jake fought hard to conceal a confident grin. The Duke and Gary Cooper would love the image: the lone lawman taking on society's evils one at a time. The heavy pounding of each step added to his essence. Successfully fighting off a smile, he was in character and devouring this persona: the contract killer . . . maybe his favorite role.

About halfway down the pier he sidled over to the railing at the prearranged meeting spot, a concrete bench on the north side of the pier. Jake took in the smells and sounds: fresh air, gulls crying out, and the sea splashing against the concrete pilings.

It was a little past ten and he was preparing to meet an obnoxious criminal defense attorney, a frequent guest of the TV talk shows. Reid represented most of the bad boys of Hollywood and served as their PR mouthpiece every time the stars and starlets decided the criminal statutes were meant only for the unwashed masses. Reid didn't need TV ads or billboards; his face was plastered across the screen often. If you didn't know better you might think he co-hosted *TMZ on TV* or *Access Hollywood*. The height-deprived, Harvard-trained lawyer gave Napoleon complex a bad name. He was short, lumpy, and sported a spray-on tan, but his money and power trumped any physical inadequacies. With his slicked-back dark hair and baritone voice, he wooed juries and the media.

Reid suggested the pier and Jake didn't balk. The experienced undercover agent knew he could get a better recording outside than in some crowded coffee shop.

Jake spotted his quarry out of the corner of his eye but maintained his attention on the water below as the pompous litigator with a cigarette dangling from his lips marched with purpose toward the designated meeting site.

An Asian homeless man followed Reid down the pier. When

Reid stopped to assess the people around him, the homeless man, reeking of alcohol and urine, approached the attorney dressed in his tailored Armani suit and Dolce & Gabbana shoes.

In a heavy accent the beggar pleaded, "Can you spare change?"

Reid removed the cigarette from his lips. Responding with the dismissive arrogance of the landed gentry, he grunted, "I gave at the office."

"Please," said the homeless man in a hope-filled voice as he reached for the suit and grabbed at the sleeve.

With his free hand Reid brushed the man's right arm aside, more disgusted than afraid. "Don't touch me," said Reid defiantly.

"You have very nice suit, you spare few dollars."

Reid picked up his pace and scooted past the beggar as a few fishermen who watched the exchange turned their attention back to their multiple fishing lines.

Reid hustled toward Jake, who was still looking out over the water.

"Do those guys just bathe in their own piss?" said Reid, flicking the cigarette into the ocean. "The smell, how do they stand living like that?"

Jake didn't turn to acknowledge the comment, his apparent focus on the surfers. There was an awkward silence as Reid reached inside his jacket and pulled a tricolor gold cigarette case from his pocket. As if stalling for time, he removed a cigarette and tapped it against the case.

The homeless man meandered over to a bench a few feet from where Jake and Reid were standing.

"You must be Jake," said Reid, squarely facing the undercover FBI agent.

Jake continued the long moment of awkward silence before turning slightly and sneered, "And why must I be Jake? I don't have to be anybody." He looked the lawyer up and down as if sizing him up. "Who are you?"

Reid was caught short. The encounter with the homeless man took the lawyer out of his game and now he was being ridiculed by some guy in cowboy boots who towered over him. "Maybe I got the wrong guy. Sorry." The words almost choked as the apology stumbled out of his mouth. Mea culpa didn't come easily to someone used to commanding those beneath his perceived place in society. He dropped the unlit cigarette and returned the case to inside his jacket. Reid turned to look at the others on the pier but Latino fishermen or the homeless didn't fit the description he'd been given. Confusion reigned and he stammered with a weak "Tommy sent me. I was looking for . . ."

"Yeah, maybe I'm the guy you want," interrupted Jake.

"I'm Daniel Reid," he said, offering his hand.

Jake forcefully grabbed the extended arm just above the wrist and pulled the lawyer forward, giving Reid a Mafia hug and obligatory pat-down, running his hands up and down Reid's back searching for a wire or a weapon.

Reid tried to push himself away but was no match for the undercover agent's strength. "What are you doing? Do you think I brought a gun?"

Jake released Reid, who stepped back, brushing off his suit and straightening his tie.

"No, I think you may be wearing a wire. This could all be a setup. You might be some slick attorney trying to work off a tax beef. I don't know you. Tommy said you needed help. But I don't know that I trust Tommy any more than I trust you."

"So are you satisfied?"

"Yeah."

"Do I get to check you out?"

Jake took a step back, held out his hands, palms up, and gestured with a perceptible wiggle. "Yeah. Come on."

Reid took a step forward and Jake said, "But if you don't find anything I'm going to throw your ass over the railing. And for a few bucks everyone on this pier will tell the same story . . . the guy in the suit jumped. He must have gotten scared by the homeless man."

Reid stopped in his tracks and screwed up his courage. "We aren't getting off to a very good start."

"Sure we are. You're not wired and you know I'm all about business. Now let's talk about your problem."

Reid had his head down, afraid to look Jake in the eye. Trying to defuse the volatility of the situation and make a little nice-nice, the lawyer said, "Good-looking boots."

"Ostrich skin. I can afford it and I'm worth it."

Reid reached inside his suit coat and again removed the gold cigarette case.

"Nice case," said Jake.

"It's a Cartier."

"You can afford nice toys, too."

"It was a gift but yes, I can afford nice toys."

Reid opened the case and began to remove a cigarette.

Determined to keep Reid off balance and uncomfortable, Jake said, "Leave the smokes in your jacket. Your cigarettes smell worse than your friend over there," referring to the homeless man.

Reid slowly replaced the case inside his suit coat. "Tommy told me you had a way of making problems disappear."

"Yeah, I'm a regular Criss Angel when it comes to problems, assuming the price is right. Why would a rich man like you need my services?"

"I need someone out of my life and I need it done quickly and quietly."

"Timing shouldn't be an issue as long as you're straight up with the facts. Who is the someone?"

"It's a girl."

"I don't do kids," snapped Jake.

"No, I mean a girlfriend."

Jake looked down and saw a diamond-studded gold wedding band on the lawyer's left ring finger. "Thou shalt not commit adultery. But I guess if you don't have a problem with murder, adultery shouldn't be an issue. Why don't you just break it off and walk away?"

Reid put his head down and in a near whisper said, "It's complicated."

"It always is; otherwise you wouldn't need me. What's the complication? Is it a celebrity? Some politician or a judge? Notoriety costs more."

"No, it's nothing like that. She's the daughter of what you might call a business associate and she's pregnant. I offered to pay for an abortion but she wants to keep the baby. That isn't going to happen. I won't be blackmailed with support payments for the next eighteen years."

"Does this business associate know you've been dipping your pen in the company inkwell?"

"She says she hasn't said a word but how can I believe her? She kept telling me she couldn't get pregnant."

"How do you know the baby is yours?" Jake offered with a hint of skepticism. "You said you can't believe her."

Reid reflected briefly on Jake's question. His ego wanted to believe she had been faithful and the child was his. "Look, under the circumstances a paternity test is out of the question."

"Why?" asked Jake. "Are you sure there aren't any other boyfriends?"

"Most of our dates have been at clubs catering to young Asians. Maybe she met someone there. I don't know, but waiting for the kid to be born and finding out he has round eyes is a chance I can't take. Her father would have me killed if I bet wrong."

Jake looked back out over the water and leaned against the railing. He paused for a long moment as if gathering his thoughts and knew he was making the attorney anxious. "I love the ocean. Each wave seems to bring new hope as it washes away the disturbances in the sand created by men and their problems." Jake paused again, this time for dramatic effect. "I understand your complication."

"So you can handle it?" There was a hint of excited anticipation in his voice.

"I can handle it. You want to send a message or just make the problem go away?"

"No, I want it to go away. If it looks like an accident, all the better."

"I can do accidents. How about a random act of violence?"

"Yeah, that would work. Maybe you could make it look like a robbery or a carjacking."

Jake turned to face the attorney. "I can do it. Fifty thousand. Half up front. Half when it's done."

There was a subdued look of shock on Reid's face. "Fifty thousand! Tommy didn't say it would be that much."

"If you're looking for a bargain, try Walmart, but two murders are more costly."

"Two?"

"Yeah, two. You said the girl was pregnant."

Reid hesitated a little too long. Jake thought the lawyer would bite but questioned whether he'd set the price too high. Jake hated to look desperate and from a legal standpoint didn't want to lower the fee as if enticing Reid to commit a crime. The moments ticked by but so were Reid's options if he wanted the job done professionally. The attorney might be a tiger in the courtroom but he was out of his league in these negotiations. Jake wanted to add one more ingredient to this recipe for murder. He'd give Reid an opportunity to call it off; Jake started to walk away.

"Wait!" cried the attorney, despair in his voice.

With a confident grin Jake turned and almost in a whisper said, "Listen, if you want a bargain-basement killing, hire some gangbanger down in the hood. Those hip-hop artists you represent must know plenty who would do it on the cheap, but if you want it done right and done professionally by someone who won't give up your pale white ass when he gets picked up on his next dope beef, you've come to the right man."

"I'll pay what you're asking. Just keep me out of it," said Reid, pleading for Jake's assistance.

"I know how to do my job and since you aren't interested in pulling the trigger, I'll do your job, too . . . if you bring the green. Meet me at three tomorrow afternoon. Bring the money, a picture of the girl, and all the descriptive information, like cars, addresses, phone numbers. I want the four-one-one. Everything you got. You understand?"

Reid nodded. "She's Asian—is that a problem?"

"Why would that be a problem? I'm not real fond of their driving but they bleed the same as Caucasians."

"Please don't say anything to Tommy about this. He doesn't know who I want killed, just that I need it done. It's between you and me," again almost pleading with the request.

"If that's the way you want to play, I don't have a problem. Your money buys my services and my silence."

Relief washed over the lawyer's face as he offered his hand. When Jake took it, Reid clutched Jake's with both hands, shaking with too much enthusiasm. "Thanks so much."

"Just be here tomorrow at three with the down payment."

"Oh, I will. I promise."

As Reid turned and retreated down the pier, the homeless man approached again. He grabbed Reid by the arm and spun him around, pushing him toward the railing, saying, "Can you spare something? I not eat in days."

Reid attempted to pull away, this time in fear rather than disgust. "I said leave me alone." His plea was loud enough to catch the attention of all the fishermen, who turned to watch the assault.

The man continued to push, shoving the attorney against the wooden railing. "I just need meal. Anything. You can spare buck or two."

Jake rushed to the encounter. He grabbed the homeless man from behind and pulled him off Reid. Jake spun the man around and grabbed the tattered shirt with a powerful grip. "My friend isn't interested in donating to the cause."

Jake noted the man's balance was a little too perfect for his apparent station in life; his motions too fluid, and his eyes too clear for a street dweller.

The homeless man muttered something, collapsed onto a concrete bench, and began to cry. Jake released his grip, confused by the performance. He looked to Reid, who was shaking as he straightened his suit coat. Jake took two steps, grabbed Reid by the tie, and with his free hand reached deep into the attorney's pocket, pulling out a money clip loaded with hundreds. Jake sorted through the bills until he came to twenties. He pulled a twenty from the wad of bills and turned to the homeless man who sought sanctuary on the Santa Monica Pier. Jake stuffed the money in the man's hand.

When Jake turned back to Reid he said, "Just my way of redistributing the wealth. Next time pay the toll or stay out of the man's neighborhood."

CHAPTER NINE

The morning commute was far from subsiding. The Pacific Coast Highway was still creeping along and even the majors like Wilshire and Santa Monica Boulevards were heavy with solo drivers hoping to get somewhere on time. With all their clamoring for liberal causes L.A. residents never quite caught the concept of carpooling. Even the carpool lanes on the freeways required only two people. Traffic jams in L.A. began decades ago and would dissipate when the oil ran out. It was usually a nightmare regardless of the hour and this morning was no exception.

Actually the traffic made Jake's objective a little easier. He checked his mirrors as he took a circuitous route through the residential streets of Santa Monica. A left, two quick rights, even turning left well after the light was red. He was looking for a tail but saw none. Surveillance wasn't as easy as they made it look on TV. Trying to follow someone, either on foot or in a car, was seldom a one-man show, especially in a city as congested as Los Angeles. If Reid hired a PI or had a gangbanger or two following, Jake was confident he would spot it.

He doubted the attorney or his stooges were shadowing him, but since Jake was wasting Bureau gas and not his own he didn't mind taking the long way to the Brentwood coffee shop.

The meet at the pier had gone a little too easy. This wasn't Jake's first dance recital, so maybe it was an undercover agent's paranoia. Reid seemed too eager to employ a man he just met while standing at the edge of the Pacific Ocean. You play to emotions but you live by logic. Cautious optimism would prevail.

Jake's vehicle, a 2013 Range Rover HSE, was his most recent reward for a short-term undercover assignment in San Diego. Jake did a quick hit on a cartel meth dealer who delivered ten kilos of the powder in his brand-new, paid-for-in-cash, luxury off-road SUV . . . *Oh, the joy of dealing with really stupid criminals who get to forfeit any property used to "facilitate" a narcotics transaction!*

He remained married to his rearview mirrors, making sure he wasn't being followed. A tail might even be another law enforcement agency. Jake couldn't be certain Reid wasn't setting up the entire scenario to avoid a prison vacation. The odds of that seemed remote, but when dealing with sleaze even the unlikely can become real. So far, the trip from the pier to the coffee shop appeared surveillance-free.

Jake pulled into the Chevron station at the corner of Santa Monica Boulevard and Bundy. He really didn't need to fill up but decided to top off. It provided one more opportunity to scour the landscape and see if anyone was on the high ground preparing an attack.

CHAPTER TEN

When Jake was satisfied he was clean, he headed east on San Vicente Boulevard and took a left at Barrington. He found an open parking spot on the street and threw a couple of quarters in the meter. As he was exiting the car, he glanced over at the outdoor tables of the coffee shop. The only two occupants practically screamed FBI: discount suits, white, button-down collar shirts, and ties that were stylish during the Bush administration—forty-one, not forty-three. He shook his head and walked onto the patio. As he passed the waitress, he ordered the no-frills coffee . . . black and hot.

Before Jake even sat down he took a shot. "Did the Salvation Army have a two-for-one sale on suits?"

Trey Bennett looked at the younger agent. "I told you he was a jerk."

Jake pulled up a chair and said, "You know this is L.A. You don't have to wear a suit and tie to every meeting, and I am trying to maintain some type of cover. Why don't you both get newspapers and cut out eyeholes?"

"Cover? You've got to be kidding me. Is your next gig the Grand Ole Opry? In those boots you look like an extra in some low-budget country-western music video. And don't even talk to me about ties. I'm guessing the only one you own is a bolo."

Jake laughed. "Bolo, that's pretty good. Too bad you don't apply that innovative imagination to your investigations."

The younger agent wasn't quite sure how to respond. He wanted to laugh but thought maybe the two were about to go to fist city.

"So why the suits? Was this picture day at the FBI?" asked Jake.

"It was a mandatory all-agents conference with some deputy director from D.C. Apparently you didn't get the memo," said Trey, a broad-shouldered former Division I linebacker.

"So what was the meeting about?" asked Jake.

Trey shrugged. "I don't know. I was finishing up a crossword puzzle and didn't pay attention."

"Who's your date?"

"This is Brian Carter. He graduated from the Academy about six weeks ago and he's been doing the new agent's rotation. You know, applicants, fugitives, banks, anything to get his feet wet. He's now assigned to our squad and I picked him up about an hour ago. As part of his training, he needs to check off a box 'interacting with a problem child' and yours was the first name that came to mind."

Jake reached across the table and the two shook hands. "Welcome to Hollywood. You from around here?"

Brian shook his head. "Upper Michigan, the peninsula."

"Did you want L.A.?"

"I was hoping for Detroit," said Brian.

Jake laughed. "Good to know the FBI hasn't changed the division assignment policy. Name your top choice and they'll send you to an office within five hundred miles of an airport that can fly you to your preference." Jake paused briefly. "Where'd you go to school?"

"The Naval Academy."

"The Boat School," said Jake. "Did you go blue side?"

"No, I went into the Marines."

Jake offered a welcoming smile.

Just then the waitress arrived with Jake's coffee, steam rising. Jake blew on the drink but it was still a minute or two from being consumed. "And your MOS?"

Trey interrupted. "Speak English."

"I forgot. We are in the presence of a civilian who was a cop in Bumrush, Iowa, before joining the Bureau," said Jake.

"It was Indianapolis," said Trey, feigning irritation.

"Special Agent Carter, please tell the Boilermaker from Purdue what your military occupational specialty was," said Jake.

"I was an 0302."

"English," said Trey.

Both Jake and Brian said simultaneously, "Infantry."

Trey wanted to hurry the conversation. "Enough with the pleasantries; how'd the meeting go?"

"But I need to brag about my illustrious Marine Corps career," protested Jake mockingly.

"Share your oorahs over another cup of coffee on someone else's watch," said Trey.

After signing the chain of custody, Jake turned over the FD-504 ELSUR envelope containing the micro-memory chip. The recording of the meeting with Reid was the first piece of electronic surveillance evidence in this phase of the investigation and the manila envelope held evidentiary gold. Jake then detailed the meeting with the notorious L.A. lawyer. "I'm not one to worry about administrative protocol, but this murder-for-hire case might bring down the rest of our investigation before we're ready."

Trey shrugged and threw up his palms in a muted surrender. "I'm not sure there is any way around it. Once Tommy brought up the fact Reid was looking to get somebody clipped, we had to act."

"Have you explained to Brian what's happening?" asked Jake.

"You do the honors," said Trey, gesturing with one hand as if offering the probationary agent entry into a fiery FBI netherworld of unknown dimensions.

The waitress approached and the three men quieted as she refilled the empty cups.

When she left Jake began: "We're taking a hard look at a Korean crime syndicate that's been operating in L.A. for years. They're into drugs and counterfeit goods, mainly cigarettes and name-brand clothing, but they brought in a container of counterfeit watches the other night. We just got started and I'm trying to work my way up the ladder. We began with a guy named Tommy Hwan. He's a member of the junior varsity but seems to be gaining credibility by bragging about his association with a 'round-eye who can get things done,' as he likes to call me. The night before last, he told me an attorney he deals with, a real slime bucket in L.A.'s legal cesspool, H. Daniel Reid, is in need of someone who does contract killings. I sold myself to Tommy in the early run-up as a person willing to do anything for a buck. So today Reid and I had our first kiss."

Brian sat there without saying a word but smiled with a slight nod.

"We were lucky Tommy solicited Jake and didn't shop this around," said Trey.

Jake looked to Brian. "When Tommy approached me I told him I'd give him a third as a finder's fee so I knew he wasn't going anywhere else."

Trey added, "Several agencies have taken a run at these Asian gangs doing cross-border counterfeit imports and haven't had much success. This seems like our best shot at making a real dent in Koreatown."

Jake nodded. "We're just getting started. We've got Tommy on importing counterfeit goods. I might be able to get his immediate boss and of course, assuming all goes well, we should nail Reid, but I had high hopes of this thing lasting awhile and taking us all over the map."

Trey was educating the new agent but also thinking out loud, trying to make the most of the situation. "We take it down when we have to take it down. You never know who is going to roll. Maybe one of these guys can take us even further or in directions we never anticipated."

Jake turned to Brian as he pointed to Trey. "His beer mug is always half full. I just wanted to stretch it out for months, even years, to avoid going into the office and dealing with the bean counters and feather merchants."

Trey looked at Brian. "Jake has issues with Bureau administrators. Once you understand that, it's easy to predict almost any move he makes." Then looking back at Jake, Trey said, "Getting back to the issue at hand, do you think Reid bought your act?"

"I think so," said Jake, giving Brian a cherub-like grin. "Most people do."

"So who does he want hit?"

"His Asian girlfriend, who happens to be carrying his love child. I'll get as much as I can when I meet him tomorrow afternoon."

"Are you still meeting with Tommy this afternoon?" asked Trey.

"Yeah, but Reid didn't want me to say anything to Tommy."

"Will you?"

"I'll see how it plays out. It's more important we keep Tommy in the loop than Reid, so I'll probably tell him about the meet and explain how his Johnnie Cochran wanted me to keep it a secret."

"It's your call," said Trey.

Jake grabbed the check and threw a couple of dollars on the table. Turning to the new agent, he said, "This isn't the Marines, Brian. Here's how it works in the Bureau."

Trey, now standing, just shook his head as Jake added, "I'll cover it this time. Now your training agent owes us both a free lunch."

CHAPTER ELEVEN

The thirtysomething athletic Korean bounded across the street during a break in the traffic. Dressed neatly in a solid dark green shirt and designer jeans, he contrasted greatly with H. Daniel Reid's homeless man. Even though the two men differed in appearance, their meeting didn't draw the attention of others. L.A. was a forgiving town when it came to fashion. Blue jeans were routine business attire and nothing the men did attracted the interest of those passing by.

After purchasing coffee from a beachfront vendor, the two men grabbed a seat at a concrete table near the entrance to the pier. The noise from the traffic on Ocean Boulevard to their east and the waves splashing ashore to the west provided all the "noise cover" they needed to openly discuss their business.

"Mr. Park was right. He is a problem," said the homeless man.

The other man nodded, his expression displaying frustration. "I knew that long before you got here and told Mr. Park even before this latest wrinkle surfaced." He paused to take a sip of coffee.

"It's clear Reid is weak and brings little to the table. Mr. Park was wrong to go outside the community. He could have laundered the funds hundreds of ways through our people but he chose to wash the money through Reid."

The homeless man nodded, then added, "As you know, I have only been in this country a few months, but it is already apparent Mr. Park is caught up in the Hollywood glitz; too many free tickets and too many red-carpet front-row seats."

With a wry smile the neatly dressed North Korean operative shook his head. "I wouldn't want Mr. Park to hear you talking like that. He doesn't take criticism well."

Both knew Park had a well-deserved reputation for disposing of those who committed mistakes, expeditiously and with considerable violence. If necessary, they all were willing to show H. Daniel Reid how North Korea's Office 39 handled people who created problems. "We need to resolve the matter quickly but not be foolish in our efforts."

"Could you overhear their conversation?" asked the man.

"He was hiring the big American to kill the girl."

"Jenny?" asked the boss.

"I think so. He didn't say a name but as Mr. Park suspected it makes sense it would be her. The American was charging fifty thousand dollars and Reid quibbled over the price," said the homeless man, taking another sip of coffee.

"He is cheap for a rich American lawyer."

The homeless man spit out the coffee as they both laughed out loud, knowing Park often complained about Reid never picking up a check when they went to dinner.

The homeless man continued, "Reid said the girl was pregnant. Do you think she is?"

The man shrugged.

"Reid believes he is the father. Why else would he want her killed?" said the homeless man.

"From what I've seen of her in the clubs, he might want to wait until the baby is born to determine paternity. I'm not sure Reid is the only man she's been with."

"I heard you danced with her a time or two; any chance it's yours?" asked the homeless man with a grin.

"I never went there."

"Don't tell me your kindness toward her was out of guilt," said the homeless man.

"I did what I was ordered to do. Park wanted her husband killed in a manner no one suspected was murder. The others were collateral damage."

"I think collateral damage includes Jenny and her current lifestyle," said the homeless man.

The other man raised an eyebrow. "It may play a part."

"Do we talk to her?"

"I'm not making that decision. We don't speak to her unless ordered to do so. She would immediately run to her father and we don't need the headache."

The homeless man nodded. "We have a headache now. Maybe we should let this cowboy handle the matter. The lawyer and his hired gunman are meeting again tomorrow afternoon at three."

"Where?"

"Here at the pier."

"Good, I will tell Mr. Park. If he orders it, you and I may have to put in more blood work and eliminate this attorney and his contract killer."

CHAPTER TWELVE

Mohammed entered the Koreatown restaurant through the alley entrance and spotted Kareem, who had his back turned, busy stocking the bar. Though several people were seated at tables in the dining area, the bar was empty as the lunchtime crowd was still a half hour away. Mohammed stayed near the back in the darkened hallway, waiting to be acknowledged.

Candy was at the hostess stand and saw the Lebanese man she knew Kareem so admired. She gave him a huge smile and bowed slightly before walking over to Kareem and saying quietly, "Mohammed is here."

Kareem turned and nodded for Mohammed to come to the bar.

"I'm just about done. He's upstairs," said Kareem.

"Do you want me to take him up?" asked Candy.

"No, I'll do it. Just give me a minute."

Mohammed appeared uncomfortable in the bar but took a seat waiting for the prison convert.

"Can I get you a drink?" said Candy.

Kareem snapped his head at the offer.

Mohammed feigned surprise. “I’m shocked you would offer me alcohol.”

“I mean Coke or club soda. I know he not drink,” said Candy awkwardly, knowing the importance of the man to Kareem.

Mohammed patted her hand as if offering forgiveness, and Candy rewarded him with a smile. With that Kareem escorted Mohammed upstairs to meet with Henry Yeong.

CHAPTER THIRTEEN

In Los Angeles's Korean community, it is known as "Sa E Gu," or "four two nine," the first day of the L.A. riots.

On April 29, 1992, after seven days of deliberations, a jury sitting in suburban Simi Valley acquitted five white police officers of assault in the videotaped beating of Rodney King, an African-American. King was on parole for armed robbery when he fled a routine California Highway Patrol traffic stop in March 1991. In the lengthy police pursuit to effect his arrest, vehicles reached speeds in excess of 110 miles per hour. King's subsequent apprehension at the intersection of Foothill Boulevard and Osborne Street in the San Fernando Valley was caught on tape by George Holliday, who lived in a nearby apartment complex. With his camcorder, Holliday recorded King being hit with batons and kicked by the arresting officers.

Within hours, video clips of the beating headlined every news broadcast and the ensuing trial of the five Los Angeles policemen captured international attention.

Immediately following the April acquittals, the Los Angeles riots erupted, lasting six days and nights. Murder and arson accompanied massive looting. Fifty-three people died and thousands were injured. More than four thousand National Guard troops and active-duty U.S. Army soldiers and Marines were called in to quell the anarchy, arson, and murder.

One of the hardest-hit communities was Koreatown, along the Wilshire Boulevard corridor, where hundreds of locally owned businesses were damaged or destroyed. When the police and fire departments withdrew from the violent street confrontations with rioters, Korean-Americans living in the community armed themselves and rallied to protect the Korean-owned businesses. Television news crews captured gun battles between the businessmen and looters, with some in the media labeling it a race war.

Following the riots, Koreatown fell into disrepair as many residents fled the area for safer suburban communities. But by 2005, a stagnant overseas economy brought new Korean investors to the United States and there was a rebirth in the Mid-Wilshire community, now an urban success story.

For Jake Kruse, however, Koreatown was just one more criminal community playground.

It was late in the afternoon as the undercover agent threaded his way through traffic and pulled down a side street just off Wilshire Boulevard. "Where is this place?"

Before Tommy Hwan answered, Jake slammed on his brakes and pounded the horn. A female driver pulled out from an alley without looking and almost clipped the front of the undercover vehicle.

"You know what's worse than eating down here?" barked Jake.

"What?" said Tommy, tattoos peeking out from below both sleeves of his counterfeit Polo shirt.

"Driving down here."

"Don't push your luck, whitey."

Jake wanted to add evidentiary value to the conversation. "When you set up the meeting this morning, you didn't tell me

Reid was so short. I towered over him during the negotiations. The boots allowed me to up the ante for the hit, but I could have gone barefoot."

"Did it work?"

"He's paying fifty thousand dollars and the only thing he remembers about me is I'm a lot taller than he is and I wear Tony Lama ostrich-skin boots."

"So when you get popped and are standing in a lineup with all your white-trash mayonnaise-sucking buddies, as long as your boots are off he won't recognize you." Tommy was grinning ear to ear as he spewed his idea of jailhouse humor.

"You're real funny, my short little Asian friend, but tell me more about Reid," said Jake.

"He is Mr. Park's attorney."

"When do I meet Park?"

"I'm not sure you ever will. You have no need to meet him. At least not yet," said Tommy without hesitation.

"What's the deal with you dog-munchers? You brag about some round-eye helping you smuggle in all kinds of counterfeit crap from the Empire of Evil but you won't introduce me to your friends and family. I'm not sure my delicate ego can take your slights," said Jake, concentrating on the road ahead but giving Tommy a quick glance.

"You'll be meeting one of my business associates in a few minutes. Assuming you behave yourself, I might take you home to mother."

"Tell me more about Reid, the attorney."

"He's a player. Reid and Mr. Park are big in Las Vegas. That's where I go to launder money for both of them. I've brought Reid a few paying clients over the years and take a little street tax for my referrals," said Tommy in a matter-of-fact manner.

"You're a capper?" asked Jake.

"You might say that. I introduced him to some Korean high-flyers and for that he was very generous."

In mock protest Jake said, "But Tommy, I believe referral fees from attorneys are illegal and unethical. Shouldn't we report him to the bar association?"

Tommy gave a halfhearted laugh. "Yeah, it's illegal. He trusts me and like I said, he's been good to me. Before I made a run to Vegas last Friday, he pulled me aside in his office and asked me for some very specific help."

"You don't think he's trying to set us up, do you?" said Jake, trying to sound cautious in taking on such an assignment.

"No. He deals with Hollywood filth and hip-hop drug scum. The only murderers he defends are actors who kill their wives. I told him you were a professional and could get it done right."

"Okay. I'll give it a shot and feel him out a little more tomorrow. I'll probably take the job, but we need to be sure he doesn't get cold feet and decide to switch sides."

"If that happens I can get some people from overseas who will eliminate the government's key witness, and you'll have the perfect alibi since your Caucasian ass will be sitting in county on a contract killing beef."

"You are so reassuring." Jake paused for a prolonged moment, then changed the subject. "So when do I get to meet this girlfriend of yours?"

Jake hoped to engage as many of Tommy's associates not only to identify the full scope of the criminal conspiracy but to enhance his credibility by throwing out Tommy's friends as being the undercover agent's friends.

"She'll be at the restaurant. She's working today."

"How serious is this?"

"I really, really like her."

"Really?" said Jake mockingly.

"Yes, really."

"You gonna make an honest woman of her and pop the question?"

Tommy gulped. "I'm not sure I'm that serious."

"You need to hurry and legalize it. Otherwise you can't get conjugal visits in prison."

Tommy again gave a halfhearted laugh, but even after two months of their joint criminal ventures he had trouble reading the man in the driver's seat.

In a slightly playful tone, Jake continued, hoping to get a further rise out of Tommy. "Is her name really Candy? That sounds like a screen name for some interstate escort service. I bet she spells it with a *k* and an *i*. What is it, Kandi Wantsum? I can see the Internet ads now."

Tommy wasn't eager to engage his co-conspirator in roguish banter. "It's Candy with a *c* and a *y*. I keep trying to figure out if I don't like you because you're white or I just don't like you. You are closing fast on the edge of a very steep cliff. One misstep and you might be tomorrow's headlines, assuming they find the body. I'm not even sure why I put up with you."

Jake flashed an engaging smile and, for the benefit of the device recording the conversation and any jury who might ultimately hear it, said, "Because I am only charging you and your boss two kilos of crystal meth for the container of counterfeit jeans I helped you smuggle across the border last week. I also seem to recall promising you a third on my most recent murder-for-hire contract, which you brought to me. You should be a little more grateful and forgiving."

"Once I no longer need your services I won't need to be forgiving or grateful."

"Come on, Tommy, don't tell me you're going to de-friend me on Facebook. We're BFFs."

Jake slowed as he came to a four-way stop, waiting for Tommy to give directions. Tommy pointed left and Jake turned north.

Tommy wasn't married to any particular gang or criminal enterprise. He was more a freelance broker and floated between the various factions of Asian organized-crime families throughout Los Angeles. His value to the FBI's investigation was immense, and he was an unwitting accomplice in what the Bureau hoped to be a successful run at a major crime problem plaguing the City of Angels.

Jake charged plenty for his services, if for no other reason than to thin out the herd. Trey Bennett, the FBI case agent, was interested only in targeting those Asian organized-crime figures deemed to be in senior management. In the Korean community only a few names surfaced. Tommy knew each of these players without a scorecard, and according to intelligence collected by the FBI, he had done business with all of them over the past several years.

Today was to be Jake's introduction to a perennial all-star, Yeong Chun Doo, or his Americanized name, Henry Yeong. Tommy had brokered a recent shipment of counterfeit Dolce & Gabbana jeans for Yeong and now this major player asked to meet the "round-eye" who was capable of easing logistical headaches. If everything worked out, Yeong would be solidifying his prospects for a long-term stay as the guest of the U.S. government in a federal prison.

CHAPTER FOURTEEN

It had taken more than two months for Jake to move from a "street hood" to a "delivery specialist" in the organized-crime hierarchy. Of the numerous crimes he and Tommy Hwan conspired to commit, Jake always fulfilled his end of the bargain, so his credibility was solid.

The smart move for the low-hanging fruit was to never introduce someone higher up on the tree. Had Jake been a real criminal and the situation reversed, he wouldn't have made the introduction, chancing Yeong would cut him out of any further deals. When Henry Yeong extended the invitation through Tommy, Jake understood the young criminal entrepreneur's reluctance to introduce Henry to his round-eye co-conspirator with the valuable connections at the border. Jake took the high road, promising Tommy a piece of everything regardless of whether Yeong decided to pull an end run. Tommy, happy to remain in the payment cycle, was pleased with Jake's proposal, knowing he couldn't very well go against the orders of someone like a Henry Yeong.

"There it is," said Tommy, pointing to the restaurant.

Jake drove past slowly, sizing up the business. The chipped and faded exterior paint was less than inviting. Then he spotted a *C* in the window, meaning the health inspectors deemed this eating establishment just a little better than dining in a toxic waste dump.

"Can't you ever take me to a place with a Zagat rating?" said Jake with genuine disgust.

"We're not here to eat," said Tommy.

"Don't worry, I won't be. Health inspectors must come to Koreatown to make their quotas."

"I can take your racial insensitivity and ethnic slurs, but I suggest you clean up your act once we get inside. Mr. Yeong doesn't like American humor."

"You don't think I got a shot on Korean Comedy Central?"

When Tommy pointed to a parking spot across the street from the restaurant, Jake shook his head. "Does this place have a back entrance?"

"Yeah," said Tommy, "through the alley."

"We'll use that. I'm betting they don't get much non-Asian business. No sense bringing undue attention to ourselves."

Jake pulled around the corner and parked. When they hopped out of the Range Rover and headed down the alley they were greeted by the smells of backstreet L.A.: rotten produce and putrefied water.

A rat darted out from behind a dumpster.

"Is this the year of the rat?" asked Jake.

"Does it matter?"

"I don't like rats," said Jake, knowing the irony in that statement.

"Actually rat is good. It's the symbol of luck. The rat is clever, quick-witted, and successful."

"Sort of like me, huh?" said Jake.

"There you go, whitey, flattering yourself again."

Jake and Tommy crossed the alley and Tommy pointed to a

wooden screen door just past a large green dumpster. Even with the lid closed the smell of garbage was pronounced. As Tommy grabbed a broken handle on the frame and opened the back door to the restaurant, Jake noted the torn netting, which allowed the flies to enter at will. Both stepped into the kitchen and were greeted by the contrasting aromas from the alley: sesame oil, garlic, ginger, peppers, and *gochujang*, all used in traditional Korean cooking. Two employees were busy with the dinner rush and paid little attention to the recent visitors.

The place wasn't exactly appetizing but the undercover agent loved playing the bold and brazen role. As Jake walked past the servers' counter, one of the cooks threw a plate of *yaki-mandu*, Korean egg rolls, under the heat lamp. Jake grabbed one, popped it in his mouth, and kept walking. The cook shouted something, which Jake assumed to be Korean expletives referencing the undercover agent's mother in some capacity.

Tommy turned in time to see Jake munching on the Korean appetizer and smiling ear to ear.

The restaurant was larger than Jake expected. From the street he assumed there were not much more than a few tables, but there was a fully stocked bar running the width of the building and several dozen worn tables scattered throughout the darkened open area. Ragged Asian décor accented the walls.

Only about a third of the tables were occupied but it was early, and based upon what Tommy said, he guessed things didn't pick up until later in the evening. All the patrons were older and appeared non-menacing, so Jake figured the diners weren't part of some Asian hit squad ready to take him down.

Jake was drawn to a tall African-American man standing at the far end of the bar and the attractive Asian woman seated on a bar stool across from him. The slender female had long black hair, a perfect complexion, and appeared to be in her early twenties. She shot out from her seat when Tommy entered the dining room, offering a seductive smile as she raced toward Jake's criminal associate. Tommy responded with a quick embrace as the two met at the middle of the bar.

"How you doing, baby," said Tommy.

"I fine, especially now you here."

Jake was following and Tommy turned to introduce the two. "Candy, this is Jake."

She did a slight bow. "Mr. Jake, it nice to finally meet you. Tommy tell me much about you."

Her smile seemed genuine and Jake countered, "Tommy has told me a lot about you. He said you were beautiful, but I thought that was just blind love. You really are very beautiful."

"Thank you, Mr. Jake," she said. Her quick blush and tilt of her head were convincing.

"Please just call me Jake."

She continued her smile and nodded. "Thank you, Jake."

Tommy was pleased Jake found his girlfriend so attractive but needed to get on with business. He turned to Jake. "Sit at the bar. I'll go upstairs and see if Mr. Yeong is ready."

As Tommy headed toward the stairs Candy said to him, "I need talk to you."

"Can we talk later? Mr. Yeong is waiting."

"It only take minute. It important. Please, Tommy," begged Candy.

Tommy stopped, hoping any further delay wouldn't upset Yeong.

"Did you hear about Sonny?"

"No."

"He dead."

"What?" said Tommy with genuine surprise.

"Two nights ago someone kill him. Shoot him."

"No way. Where?"

"He at home. It in paper this morning," said Candy.

"Look, we'll talk later. I've got to see Mr. Yeong. He's waiting."

Tommy walked toward the stairs, shaking his head, confused by the news he had just received.

As the two were talking, Jake straddled a bar stool covered with aging red vinyl and tried to listen in. The African-American at the far end of the bar turned out to be the bartender and strolled down to Jake with minimal enthusiasm. "What can I get you?"

"Give me a Hite."

"We don't carry it."

"But it's Korean," said Jake, studying the bartender.

"Yeah, and so is Taedonggang, Cass, and OB."

"Then give me one of those."

"We don't carry them, either."

Jake shook his head. "What do you have on tap?"

"Bud, Bud Light, Select, and Michelob."

"Make it a Light. . . . Real ethnic bar you got here. You carry all the authentic Korean brands, huh?"

The bartender, wearing what the undercover agent assumed to be a counterfeit Polo shirt and knockoff Dolce & Gabbana jeans, caught the sarcasm dripping from Jake's mouth as he drew a Bud Light from the tap.

"You own this place?" asked Jake.

"Nope," said the bartender abruptly, obviously not seeking to engage in conversation or get tipped.

"Why do you work down here?"

"I'm a bartender. I needed a job. They had an opening. Besides, ricers drink as much beer as peckerwoods."

Jake caught the references. Peckerwoods, a term typically reserved for whites in prison, was not necessarily one used in sensitivity training.

"When'd you get out?" asked Jake as he took a drink.

"A couple of years ago."

"Still gotta tail?"

"What are you, five-o?" asked the bartender.

"I did a little time back east," said Jake as he extended his hand. "The name's Jake."

"Yeah, I heard Tommy introduce you to Candy."

Jake waited, cocking his head as if to say, "And . . ."

The bartender said, "Nice to meet you," without introducing himself or shaking Jake's hand. He then walked to the far end of the bar and continued his conversation with Candy, which apparently Jake and Tommy had interrupted.

The undercover agent had taken only a few sips of his beer when Tommy returned through the hallway and joined their quiet discussion.

Jake could barely make out what Tommy, Candy, and the bartender were saying but they appeared to be discussing the murder of Sonny. No one seemed to be offering an easy explanation, though Jake overheard Candy say she was always uncomfortable around the victim because he asked too many questions and seemed to be in everyone's business, a trait not appreciated in Koreatown. Tommy excused himself and looked to Jake. Using his index finger in a circling motion, he signaled to the undercover agent, who left a couple of bucks on the bar and headed for the back.

"It's time. He's ready," said Tommy.

Tommy kissed Candy on the cheek as he and Jake headed down the dimly lit hallway to the stairs.

CHAPTER FIFTEEN

Once they were away from the others, Jake said, "Sorry to hear about your friend Sonny."

Tommy shrugged. "No great loss but I'd like to know why he was hit."

"Is anyone offering any explanations?"

"Not yet. At least no one has heard anything."

Jake tried to act disinterested but sought answers for the investigation. "Did you guys do much business together?"

Tommy didn't seem to mind the inquiry and answered without hesitation. "No. He was kind of a fixture in Koreatown. He did a little of this and a little of that."

"On the up-and-up?" asked Jake.

"Yes and no. As I understand it he got hurt in the riots back in '92."

Jake interrupted. "You mean injured?"

"No, not physically but he got slammed financially. He lost several businesses. Then a few years later he came back strong with overseas financing. He played both sides and moved a lot of paper."

"What do you mean?"

"He was into negotiable notes. Not all of which were legit."

"You mean counterfeit securities?"

"Something like that. I never quite understood what his game was. He was involved with several financial institutions both here and in Korea. He was a little too slick for me and never invited me to play. He ran with the big dogs."

"Like who?"

"You're meeting one today."

"Yeong?"

Tommy nodded. "It's Mr. Yeong to you."

"Just keep your ears open. I don't want anything coming back on us if this Sonny got smoked because of his walk on the wild side of Koreatown. We may be strolling down the same side of the street," said Jake.

"That wouldn't happen. I never had any business dealings with him unless you consider buying him a drink a business relationship."

"You aren't wasting any money on me. Why'd you buy him a drink?"

"He spent a lot of time here in the bar and I figured if I bought him a drink or two he might cut me in on some scam he had going, but nothing ever materialized."

"Maybe you were lucky you weren't involved. One of his deals may have gone south and he got laid out because of it."

Tommy nonchalanted the comment as the two climbed the stairs.

When they came to a door at the end of the corridor, Tommy knocked twice.

Four men were in the small office, a space hardly fitting for a Mr. Yeong, someone Jake's FBI colleagues believed to be a major player in the world of Asian organized crime. Three of the men, whom Jake didn't recognize, stood immediately when Tommy and he entered. Two of them flanked Yeong and the third took up a position to the right and slightly behind Jake. They stayed there, unmoving, throughout the meeting.

Though the men were small in stature, Jake saw the pronounced bulges on their hips. The semi-automatic weapons they carried under their stylish Kahala Hawaiian shirts evened out any size discrepancy. Yeong, the oldest of the four, at least fifty, remained seated, smoking a cigarette.

Jake concentrated on the faces, sizing up the opposition. He wanted to establish his dominance as much as Yeong and his associates did.

The office was cold and dank. The curtains were closed and a single low-wattage lightbulb hung from the ceiling, requiring several seconds for Jake's eyes to adjust to the darkness and the smoke.

Jake extended his hand but Yeong didn't take it. "Mr. Yeong, thank you for trusting me enough to allow me into your office. Tommy and I have done two containers for you without incident. I am glad to have built this bond where we can finally meet." Jake smiled and added, "You knew where I lived, but I never knew where you did business."

"I do business all over the world. I'm not limited to this office," said Yeong, whose thin smile quickly faded.

Jake's face projected confidence, not a hint of fear. "Sir, I've enjoyed my business relationship with Tommy. It's a pleasure to deal with honorable men, and I hope we can continue to do business for the long run."

Yeong said nothing but took a deep draw off the cigarette. His silence only added to the mystique of the setting. He pulled two packages from beneath the scarred wooden desk where he was sitting, each the size of a Tolstoy novel. Yeong slid the packages across the desk and gestured for Jake to take them.

Jake hefted one of the packages. He guessed around two pounds—about right for a kilo of crystal methamphetamine, the new drug of choice in Los Angeles. In the early eighties it was cocaine, a party favor for the rich and famous. By the end of that decade crack or rock cocaine, a simpler, less expensive alternative to freebasing, became popular in the inner city. The Crips and Bloods financed criminal empires with the cheap high and the South Central economy flourished as criminal entrepreneurs learned the basics of the free enterprise system.

The twenty-first century saw the rise of crystal meth—"crank," "speed," or "ice," as it was known on the street. The terminology changed almost monthly and even an experienced undercover agent had trouble keeping up with the street slang, but regardless of what the dealers and dopers called it, the highly addictive man-made stimulant became a multibillion-dollar industry in the underground economy.

The concoction that started out as a moneymaker for outlaw biker gangs became an epidemic criminal opportunity for anyone with an elementary knowledge of chemistry. It was as popular in the farmlands as it was in the inner city or corporate boardrooms. The stuff was so ubiquitous in Southern California that it was an accepted form of currency. By mid-2014, a kilo of high-quality crystal meth was worth more than thirty thousand dollars. Jake was only too happy to receive his payment in the controlled substance, ensuring lengthy prison sentences for all involved in the transaction.

As he examined the tightly wrapped package in clear plastic, Jake said, "It's tough to tell in this light but from what I can see it looks good. The color is better than the last batch of meth I bought, but that was from Mexicans. It had a yellow tinge that frightened my customers."

Yeong, always the businessman seeking to promote his product, nodded and said, "This is made in a government laboratory near Pyongyang. The state security forces protect the factory. The North Korean People's Army ensures safe delivery *and* it is the finest in the world."

Jake examined it more closely, smelling the outside of the package and holding it closer to the light. He paused for effect, hoping to gain more admissions on the tiny recording device he was wearing. "It does feel a little light. Did you weigh it?"

Tommy's eyes widened and he snapped: "Jake, I can assure—"

"You are questioning my integrity?" asked a clearly aggravated Yeong, interrupting Tommy.

Yeong's three associates said nothing but readied for a combative response.

Jake held up an apologetic hand and answered in a calming voice. "Not at all, sir. I'm questioning whoever packaged this. Tommy assures me you are a most trustworthy business partner."

Yeong's irritation was still evident. "I can assure you my people are accurate and there are no extra thumbs on the scales."

"If you say so," said Jake, with less respect than a man of Yeong's position presumably deserved.

"No one has ever questioned my packaging. I have satisfied many who return often for my product. If you wish to challenge me, then I suggest you return to the Mexicans and their off-color product. I'm sure you can find someone else willing to supply your needs, but they cannot give you the quality I am offering."

Jake turned on the mea culpa and the sincerity in his response was evident. "I'm sure you're right. Excuse me for even appearing to question you. That is not what I meant."

What he meant, he obtained: an extended conversation with a supplier who displayed significant knowledge of an illegal enterprise.

Yeong, momentarily placated by Jake's response, said, "You know, you don't have to take meth for payment. If you are fearful about reselling the contents of these packages, I can arrange to pay you in cash, or counterfeit clothing, maybe even jeans? There's a big markup with Dolce & Gabbana. I can even pay you in cigarettes." Yeong held up his cigarette, implying it may have been manufactured in North Korea but packaged as an American brand.

Though it wouldn't minimize the criminal culpability, Jake wasn't happy. Yeong's choice of words almost made it sound as if Jake had forced him into the illegal barter of drugs for the shipping container.

"Mr. Yeong, you know smoking's bad for your health, even the counterfeit brand you're holding. There's a warning label on every package," said Jake in a casual tone with mock concern.

Yeong was still uncertain how to read the American and replied, "You accepted cash for the previous container."

Jake held up one of the kilos and said, "This is fine, Mr. Yeong. All those who buy your product know you have the best ice made by man. Your reputation throughout Southern California puts you number one with a bullet on any Top Forty chart. I have customers who pay top dollar for this. The risk to me is worth the profit."

Yeong didn't speak for a moment. Then, as though he had made up his mind, the Korean gangster said in a quiet voice, "There is always great risk, which is why I am most cautious in my dealings. Only on Tommy's guarantees have I invited you today. I know there are many agencies of the government here who investigate drugs. Those who are caught face devastating consequences. Be extremely wise in your choices, as I am. Limit your dealings to only those you can trust."

Jake shook his head slowly, knowing the man across from him wasn't nearly as wise or as careful as he thought he was. "Mr. Yeong, I appreciate your concern but I'm very careful. As you have seen I have a well-established business which caters to very specific needs."

Yeong smiled. "I am well aware of your business and that is why I want you as part of my family."

Jake feigned confusion. "You want me to be an Oriental?"

Yeong corrected him immediately. "We do not like that term."

"I'm sorry, Mr. Yeong, I forgot. Tommy told me. I didn't mean to be insensitive."

Tommy looked at Jake, trying to determine if in fact he forgot. Yeong was an important figure in Koreatown and Jake's continued showing of disrespect might upset the delicate conspiracy the younger criminal capitalist was hoping to create.

Yeong finished the first cigarette and crushed it into a green ceramic ashtray shaped like a dragon. He took deliberate efforts to remove a gold Cartier cigarette case, identical to the one Daniel Reid possessed, from inside his jacket. Yeong grabbed a second cigarette and placed it to his lips, eyeing the bodyguard on the right. Without being asked, the henchman offered a light and Yeong took several long puffs, looking away as if contemplating his next statement.

Jake questioned if he'd crossed the line but then Yeong spoke. "I would like to negotiate for the exclusive use of your contacts at the border. Your connections at the U.S.-Mexican ports of entry are important to our enterprise. We have many different kinds of things we want to 'import' into the United States. We have learned it is much safer to bring containers into this country from Mexico than it is to import them directly from overseas into a U.S. port like San Diego, Long Beach, Oakland, or even Seattle.

"Our partners in Asia are counting on my organization to seize this opportunity because they want to make a significant increase in the quantity and types of imports. That is why I am inviting you to become part of my business family."

Jake nodded slowly and hoped he appeared to be considering the offer. He knew from previous conversations with Tommy and from intelligence reports he had reviewed preparing for the assignment that Yeong was in competition with Park Soon Yong for King of the Hill in the Korean organized-crime community. "That's an interesting proposition but I'm a pragmatic man. It would have to be financially beneficial for me to limit my dealings to just your organization."

"Don't let a reckless desire for success destroy your life. Confucius says, 'If you try to do too much, you will not achieve anything.' "

"I thought Confucius was Chinese."

"He was but he was still a very wise man. If you bet wrong in this business the consequences are far too great."

"Well, in the words of one of my favorite philosophers . . ." Jake began to sing, "I'll take your bet and you're gonna regret 'cause I'm the best that's ever been."

Tommy shook his head. "Jake!"

"I don't understand," said Yeong, confused by Jake's off-key addition to the conversation.

"Charlie Daniels, 'The Devil Went Down to Georgia,' " said Jake with a huge smile.

Yeong blew smoke into the air. "Confucius also said, 'A superior man is modest in his speech but exceeds in his actions.' "

Jake nodded as if in agreement, but then said, "Modesty doesn't become me. But my actions prove my success."

"We can do very well if you will be smart. Continue to bring my containers through the border and I will see you are rewarded quite well. Take my cash but leave the ice," said Yeong, taking a long draw on the cigarette. He then reached into a drawer and Jake readied for the unknown, his weight shifting to the balls of his feet, prepared to attack. When Yeong's hand surfaced he was holding six bundles of hundred-dollar bills, totaling sixty thousand dollars, and threw them on the table.

Jake shook his head and decided to reset the conspiracy for the purpose of the recording device he was wearing. "Mr. Yeong, I agreed to bring these containers across the border for sixty thousand dollars cash per container. These two keys of meth cost you what, forty thousand dollars at the most, maybe even as little as thirty? I can have my people break down these packages into eight-balls and resell it all for two hundred K—maybe as much as a quarter of a million. You save money. I make money."

Yeong nodded but then said, "What you say is correct, but breaking down the packages takes time—and reselling brings additional risks. In six weeks we have done two containers. That is a hundred twenty thousand in cash. Is that not enough to satisfy your needs?"

Jake could not have scripted the conversation any better. "I have expenses, Mr. Yeong. It's not all profits. You're a businessman, you know that. With this payment in the yaba I can make a whole lot more than a hundred and twenty. Let's continue to work together. Our common goal is lining both our pockets with American currency."

Yeong nodded, grabbing the bundles of hundreds from the table and sliding them back into the top drawer of the desk.

Tommy interceded. "We need to leave now."

"But I'd like to continue to talk long-term business plans with Mr. Yeong. We're just getting started. I think this relationship might evolve into substantial profits for all of us," said Jake.

"It's not wise while we're all together with what you're holding in those two packages," said Tommy, just a hint of irritation in his voice. "We can meet again tomorrow or the next day to discuss long-term plans."

With that Yeong clapped his hands twice. "Very wise, Tommy. You are learning." With the back of his hand Yeong gestured for everyone to leave.

Jake threw the two kilos into a nondescript brown paper bag Yeong provided.

"We'll talk more next time. I'd like to explore a long-term business proposition. We might be able to make it work if you make it worth my while," said Jake as he was leaving.

"We will talk again soon," said Yeong.

Tommy hustled Jake out of the office and back down the stairs.

CHAPTER SIXTEEN

As they began the long walk down a now-dark alley toward the Range Rover, Tommy fumed, "You made Mr. Yeong angry."

"What do you mean?" asked Jake, knowing exactly what he meant.

"You know Mr. Yeong doesn't like being called Oriental."

Jake smiled but said nothing.

"Why do you do that?" asked Tommy.

"Because I can get away with it," said Jake with a smirk, celebrating the fact he had just added one more nail to the coffin of several gangster entrepreneurs.

Tommy shook his head. "If you want to keep taking your fee in Mr. Yeong's yaba, I suggest you show the man a lot more respect."

"Oh, come on. Don't give me that respect crap. This is all about the money. I've got what he needs. If he can't handle my insensitivities, I'll just move on to someone else. A lot of people will pay for my services. If this is going to work, he doesn't have to like me. All he has to do is trust me—and pay me."

"Why should he trust you? I don't know that I do," said Tommy.

"Well, apparently he doesn't trust you. He wouldn't even front you two kilos of ice to pay for the container we smuggled into the United States. I'd watch my back around him. From now on, you ought to insist on half payment up front."

Jake knew he had three solid counts against Yeong: two containers of counterfeit goods smuggled across the U.S. border and now the crystal methamphetamine. He needed to move quickly to Park, whom he had not met but who had brokered the Rolex watch deal through Tommy. The investigation might be short-lived because of the lawyer's solicitation to commit murder. The undercover agent wanted to get Tommy off Yeong and on to Park. This was an opportunity to plant seeds of doubt and fear, maybe even a little paranoia.

Jake continued. "I'd drop this guy like used dental floss. From everything you've said Park is more honorable."

"You don't question the integrity of a man like Mr. Yeong."

Jake wasn't about to back down. "When I get back to my place I'm weighing this. If it's light your next container's gonna be light."

Tommy raised his voice slightly. "You never challenge a man like Mr. Yeong in his office in front of others."

"You call that a challenge? I never even put a gun to his head."

"You must always leave a man with his dignity. To do otherwise is to make an enemy."

"That must be more Confucius because I can't think of a country song with that line in it," said Jake.

Tommy looked over his shoulder.

"They aren't coming," said Jake.

"You think you know our ways but you're wrong."

"I'm still trying to catch up on all these Asian customs."

"You better hope you live long enough to learn them."

★ ★ ★

Jake needed to drop Tommy at his car, which was parked in a strip mall two miles from the restaurant. The undercover agent knew Tommy was agitated by the performance in Yeong's office, so he decided to lighten up the conversation as they were driving.

"Candy's beautiful," said Jake.

After a prolonged moment Tommy said, "You really think so?"

"Absolutely. Better keep a close eye on that one. Somebody with money will grab her in a heartbeat."

"That's why I'm working so hard to please her."

"Whatever generates our revenue stream pleases me, my friend," said Jake.

With the tension eased, Jake decided to press the investigation.

"What's the deal with a black bartender in a Korean bar serving only domestic beer?" asked Jake, trying to sound as if he were only making conversation and not all that interested.

Tommy seemed forgiving in his response. "His name's Kareem. He did time with Candy's brother at Folsom. They were in the same unit for a year or so and Kareem got to know the family. After Kareem got off parole and needed a job, Candy convinced Yeong's manager to hire him to tend bar."

"The bartender's name is Kareem?" said Jake, glancing over at Tommy.

"Yeah."

"Is he Muslim?"

"I'm not sure. He doesn't worship at my mosque," replied the Korean sarcastically.

"Funny, Tommy. Is Candy's brother still in?"

"Yeah, and he's not getting out anytime soon." Tommy paused briefly before asking, "Why are you so interested in all this? Are you writing a book?"

"No, just seemed odd, a black guy with a Muslim name working in a Korean bar."

"Submit it to Ripley's," came Tommy's quick response.

CHAPTER SEVENTEEN

Jake dropped Tommy at his car and headed south on Vermont Avenue toward the freeway, hoping to get out of Koreatown quickly. He raced in and out of traffic, constantly checking his mirrors, looking for a tail. He doubted Tommy and the crew would try to follow him, but he was carrying more than four pounds of a controlled substance under the front seat. Like every good dope dealer he wanted to get it to the next stage in the distribution process without interference. For Jake, it meant Trey Bennett, his case agent.

Using the speed-dial function on his phone, he punched in the code for Trey.

"I'm out of there," said Jake over the speaker.

"How'd it go?"

"It went. I'm heading over to the Santa Monica Freeway and will eventually get up to the Westside. Meet me in the parking lot across the street from this morning's tryst, Cupcake," said Jake, smacking his lips, making kissing sounds.

"You're sick."

"You're cute."

When Jake pulled off the 405 Freeway at Sunset Boulevard, he called Trey. "Everything look good?"

"Yeah, the parking lot's clean."

"I'll be there in two. Is junior with you?"

"Yeah."

"With drugs in the car, I don't want to stop at some minimart. Have him run across the street and grab me a Dr Pepper at the liquor store."

"Got it. He'll be waiting with drink in hand when you get here."

As soon as Jake pulled onto the side street leading to the Brentwood public parking lot he spotted Trey Bennett's Ford Fusion. Jake checked his mirrors one last time before pulling into the lot. Trey and Brian Carter were waiting outside the car.

"At least you took off the ties," said Jake as he exited his car, handing the paper bag to Trey, who was wearing clear latex gloves.

Brian handed Jake the soda and Jake fished out change from his pocket to repay the newest member of the team.

"Thanks. I was getting thirsty but always hate using a drive-thru or stopping at 7-Eleven. Need to get straight home to papa when you're holding product."

Trey was thrilled when he looked in the paper bag and saw the latest compensation in the undercover operation. "Two keys is a big score. Congratulations."

Jake briefed both agents as to how it went down in Yeong's office and then looked at Brian. "With Tommy's prior drug conviction, it's a double-up. He's looking at a twenty-year minimum mandatory sentence just for making the introduction. Yeong's looking at a dime."

Trey handed the bag back to Jake, who grabbed an ink pen from inside his Range Rover and began initialing and dating both packages of meth and the paper bag.

As Brian was observing the ritual, Jake said, "Chain of custody . . . Allows me to tell the twelve upstanding citizens who decided not to avoid jury duty that these are the kilos of ice I just obtained from Yeong and Tommy."

Brian nodded.

"Any idea who his butt boys were in the restaurant?" asked Trey.

Jake shook his head. "Not yet. He didn't introduce any of them or call them by name. I'm not even sure they spoke English. I just know when Yeong raised his voice they jumped and got ready to pull on me." Jake took a long draw of his Dr Pepper, then added, "I almost feel sorry for Tommy. He's such a dupe. I can't believe he took me to Yeong. Tommy's looking at the big two-o and he never even touched the product."

"Mandatory ten and twenty years," said Trey with a broad grin. "I love those federal sentencing guidelines. Makes all the paperwork worthwhile."

Jake feigned offense. "Paperwork? How about the possibility I could have caught bubonic plague just walking through the restaurant? That place is a *C* for crying out loud. Is that what you mean by 'worthwhile'?" Then, failing to get a rise out of Trey, Jake paused, took another sip, and added, "By the way, Yeong wants an exclusive on my border-crossing contacts. It's all on the microchip. You will note Yeong is willing to pay me a lot more for my services than the Bureau."

Trey refused to bite at Jake's provocative banter in the presence of a new agent. "That's a huge step. How do you want to handle it?"

Jake shrugged. "I downplayed it and told him I'd have to think about it. If I were really a crook it makes sense. I'd want to limit my exposure. But Reid and this contract killing may cut everything short. We may not have much of a window in which to operate and I really want to move on to Park. When you get to the office, download the audio, weigh the stuff in this paper bag, do a field test on the contents, and let me know the results. Yeong claims it's the highest-quality meth Asia produces, so I assume it will test positive. But let me know, especially the weight. I'll call Tommy tonight and tell him how pleased I am with the product, and assuming the weight is good, I'll say I want to meet with Yeong right away to discuss this new business relationship. It will at least get us one more recorded meeting and maybe give you a chance to identify his spear-carriers."

CHAPTER EIGHTEEN

It was a little past nine when Jake made it home. The wood-frame structure was old and lonely, tucked away in the Malibu hills five miles from the ocean. Two bedrooms and a bath gave him just enough room to house what few belongings he had. He didn't mind the solitude; in fact, he preferred it.

He grabbed a beer from the refrigerator, turned on the TV, and quickly scrolled through the cable news shows in an effort to catch up on what was happening in the rest of the world. On every broadcast, the hot news was all about how a new nuclear nonproliferation agreement with Iran would guarantee "peace for our time."

Jake noted FOX News Channel was the only place where reporters and commentators questioned the wisdom of the UN-sponsored international agreement. Both Megyn Kelly and Sean Hannity pointed out that the nuclear weapons deal with the ayatollahs in Tehran was remarkably similar to the 1938 Munich appeasement deal with Adolf Hitler.

As he prepared for a few hours of sleep, Jake picked up Katie's Bible from the table beside the bed. It was still opened to a verse in Job: "Man's days are determined. You have decreed the number of his months and have set limits he cannot exceed."

Katie always said Jake lived like he believed those words; taking risks as if God ordained his bravery, knowing no matter what he did, his final day was part of God's plan. But there were times when he wondered whether he was taking reckless chances or actually living under the watchful eye of God.

There was no doubt in Jake's mind the verse brought Katie comfort, knowing her life and Jake's were in God's hands. A set of his best friend's dog tags served as a bookmark for the opened page; a thin layer of dust on both . . .

Jake stared at the words he'd read so many times and said to himself, *I believe in You, Lord, but why do You let terrible things happen to those who love You and those I love?*

While brushing his teeth, Jake's undercover cell phone rang. He activated the internal recording device and answered.

"Yeah."

"Jake?" said the voice.

"Maybe. Who's this?"

"It's Daniel Reid. We met earlier today." He said it as if Jake must have so many contract killings lined up he wouldn't remember the morning meeting at the pier.

While rinsing his toothbrush, Jake said, "So, did you change your mind?" *Always give the target a chance to back out. They seldom do, but it precludes a successful entrapment argument at trial.*

"No. I just need to meet you earlier," said Reid.

"Do you have the money?"

"Yes, of course. Can we meet at noon instead of three?"

"Sure. Is there a problem?"

"No. I just found out I have a court appearance downtown at one thirty and there's no way I can make it to Santa Monica by three."

"I'll see you at noon, same place as this morning. Bring the money and all the four-one-one."

"I'll be there with everything you need."

"Perfect," said Jake with a double meaning . . . a counterfeit contract killing and an all-but-certain criminal conviction for solicitation to commit murder.

CHAPTER NINETEEN

The music was loud, almost deafening. It was enough to make an audiologist cringe, but then again loud enough to make him rich when these same young people sought hearing devices in a few years.

In the 1990s the rave parties were reserved for abandoned warehouses with word-of-mouth advertising, makeshift lighting, and boom boxes. The police fought hard to shut them down for a variety of reasons, mainly the guaranteed drug usage. Overdoses were as common as heartburn after eating at a skid-row restaurant advertising "Mom's Home Cooking." Now the parties were mainstreamed, with professional promoters using social media to draw more than ninety thousand fans to venues such as the Los Angeles Memorial Coliseum.

Sophisticated sound systems, laser light shows, and fog machines were the norm, with some clubs featuring top-name entertainers. The day of the week didn't matter. Weekends or weekdays saw crowds lining the streets to get in. The drugs were still common: ecstasy, crystal meth, K-water. All that and more, easy to obtain with just a nod, a smile, and the exchange of a few "Jacksons." Oddly enough, the petit dealers at these events preferred twenties to hundred-dollar bills. Even street thugs, pimps, and hookers know "Benjamins" are the most common counterfeits.

Jenny, H. Daniel Reid's pregnant paramour, loved the party scene. She was a regular at big-name clubs in and around downtown Los Angeles. Tonight she was at her favorite nightspot, planning to waste just a little more of her life. The atmosphere and the drugs were intoxicating, a welcome relief from the self-loathing she felt—and the tears she occasionally shed.

As Jenny waded into the mob, she spied Candy and waved frantically, trying to get her friend's attention. Through the noisy crowd and the flashing lights Candy caught a glimpse of Jenny's manufactured commotion. She and Tommy danced toward her, elbowing their way through the drug-induced throng.

CHAPTER TWENTY

DAY 4

THURSDAY, MAY 1

The noon sun and blue sky were testimony to another beautiful cloudless Southern California day. Jake made his way down the crowded Santa Monica Pier, continuing his mission to purge the judicial system of one more gutter-dwelling lawyer. In the morning the concrete and steel finger pointing into the Pacific was occupied by fishermen; by noon it was sightseers, lunchtime diners, and panhandlers hitting up the tourists. The sound of the 1922 carousel provided an amusement park atmosphere as vendors hawked their goods while street performers entertained the more than four million people who visited each year.

Though Jake was convinced Reid really wanted to have his pregnant girlfriend killed, he wanted to make sure it was just that and not a law enforcement setup, a blue-on-blue situation. He sized up the crowd on the pier and no one jumped out as a plainclothes cop. As he neared the meeting spot, he spied the attorney nervously waiting for the hit man. Jake was on time and glad Reid wouldn't keep him waiting.

He gave another cursory look over the crowd. It seemed safe

and he approached the target. Reid extended his hand and Jake grabbed it, pulling the lawyer toward him, subtly running his hands up and down the attorney's back. As Jake released the hug, he smiled, turned toward the water, and leaned on the rail, watching the ocean waves break on the shore.

"You still don't trust me?" asked Reid, almost sounding hurt, joining the fictitious hit man on the rail. Both were looking north up the Malibu coast.

"Why should I? You called me on the recommendation of someone neither of us trusts and asked me to kill your pregnant girlfriend. Not exactly the request of an honorable man worthy of respect or confidence," said Jake, reinforcing for the audio recorder why this undercover meeting was necessary. He inched closer to Reid, ensuring his hidden digital audio/video recording device picked up the conversation without a lot of ambient noise.

"I'd hate to go through life being that distrusting."

"That makes us even."

"How so?" asked Reid.

"I'd hate to go through life being a bottom-feeder who lacked the stones to pull the trigger when a problem arose."

Reid wanted to verbally attack and rip this undereducated Neanderthal, but fear and necessity were strong motivators to couch his criticism in less caustic terms. "I don't think that kind of personal attack is necessary. This is strictly a business relationship. I also don't change the oil on my Aston Martin or butcher my own beef. I don't like to get my hands greasy or bloody. I can afford to outsource those services. You provide a service I need and I'm willing to pay. Quite handsomely, I might add."

"Capitalism at work."

Reid attempted to restore his wounded ego. "Someday you might need the services of 'a bottom-feeder,' as you call me. When that time comes you will want the best." He paused as if delivering a closing argument to a jury hanging on his every word, and added, "I am the best."

"Let's get back to capitalism." Jake looked around the pier, more for show than security. "Did you bring the money?"

Jake angled his body just a few inches from Reid, who was now practically speaking into the microphone.

Reid pulled an envelope from inside his suit coat pocket and handed it to Jake. The business envelope had the return address of the law office in the upper left-hand corner. *Harvard might be prestigious but they obviously graduate some dumb ones. Thanks for the additional piece of circumstantial evidence.* Without looking at the contents, Jake stuffed the white envelope up under his shirt and into his waistband.

"There's twenty-five thousand in there. You get the second half when I know the job is done."

"That was the arrangement. You better not be short. If it is and I think you're playing me I walk away and keep the deposit."

"Why would I short you on this end? I want her dead," Reid said emphatically.

Perfect. The attorney just kept digging the hole deeper, burying himself with his bravado.

"When do you want this done?"

"I'll be in Hawaii all next week for a legal conference. That's my alibi. Several hundred lawyers will provide all the eyewitnesses I need. In fact, I'm the keynote speaker at the Wednesday luncheon. Can you do it then?"

"If I'm building an alibi, lawyers wouldn't be at the top of my list for 'must have' witnesses."

Reid wanted to respond but looked away, a show of weakness. The undercover pit bull decided to continue the attack. "How come you guys never have conferences in South Central L.A.? I know a perfect little motel on Figueroa and I bet I can get you a deal. Give back a little to the community."

"You're kidding, aren't you? Why would I hang out with a bunch of gangbangers when I've got Polynesian beauties catering to my every whim and all tax deductible? It's bad enough those hip-hop cretins soil my office when they seek my counsel. I sure don't want to socialize among them. Besides, your perfect little hideaway on Figueroa isn't next to a golf course. Apparently you don't know very much about continuing legal education."

Jake shook his head. "A touching display of altruism."

"So can you do it on Wednesday?"

"I don't see why not. You got all the info I need in the envelope, right? Her name, address, a picture, vehicles, employment?"

"Yeah, it's all in there."

"You said she's Korean?" asked Jake.

"No, *I* said Asian. *You* said Korean," shot Reid. "Why *did* you say Korean?"

Jake knew he'd slipped up the instant he said it. Undercover agents are killed for the little mistakes, not the big ones. *Focus.*

"So what is she?" he quickly countered.

"She's Korean."

"Then what's the problem? Tommy's Korean and Tommy referred me. Maybe they all look alike to you but I happen to know there's a difference."

Reid stumbled on Jake's swift response. "There . . . there isn't a problem. I just never said Korean."

"North or South?" fired Jake.

"How should I know North or South?"

"She's your pregnant girlfriend. I'd think you would have asked at some point while you were bedding her."

"She was a good time and now she's expendable. She could have gone away quietly but she wanted to flex her scrawny little muscles and make demands."

Jake dodged a bullet as Reid pulled out his Cartier cigarette case and removed a cigarette. He tapped it on the holder and placed it in his mouth. Still wanting to maintain his power position, Jake flicked the cigarette from the attorney's mouth. "Don't you read the warning label? Those things will kill you."

The cigarette fell to the ocean as Reid nervously slipped the case back into his jacket.

"How'd you meet her?" asked Jake.

"I do some work with her father."

"Legal?"

"You mean am I his attorney or is the work I do legal?"

Jake turned up the intensity. "I just want to know what I'm getting into. Is this Kim Jong Un's half sister? Will I have to be looking over my shoulder the rest of my life for some fresh-off-the-boat, North Korean commie assassin?"

"Not if you are as good as you say. Look, her father is connected. Is that what you're asking?"

"Connected to what?"

"Just connected, that's all. He's a criminal and has his stubby little yellow fingers into a lot. He's a facilitator. If you need something, he can facilitate."

"Does he have a crew?"

There was a slight anger in Reid's response. He wanted the job done and to get on with his life. He wasn't expecting the third degree from some knuckle-dragger hit man in cowboy boots. "Yeah, he's got guys who do what needs to be done. This is not some cakewalk. You'll have to earn your fifty thousand."

"I suspected I would."

"That's why I want this done professionally. If she were working out of some Oriental massage parlor I've got rappers who would trade services with me."

Jake nodded. "I'm gonna do it right. I need to be safe and you need to be satisfied."

"That's why I wanted the best. I think you have all you need in the envelope. You'll have no problem finding her. Her father launders money through some off-the-Strip casinos in Vegas. She'll be there on Wednesday doing a run. Maybe you can make it look like a robbery or carjacking. I made the reservations for her at the Bellagio."

"She's going out in style."

"Just make sure she goes out."

CHAPTER TWENTY-ONE

Following morning prayers Mohammed and Kareem retreated across the street to the near-empty diner, where the cell leader quietly held court at a table in the back. Mohammed sipped his tea as his student sat listening.

Kareem was grateful anyone at the mosque was willing to share a moment. The fellowship he once found in prison turned to awkward stares or to being completely ignored by those with whom he now worshipped. The new follower of the Prophet had heard enough platitudes about the five pillars of Islam. He'd been drawn to the movement by exhortations from a prison-visiting imam to wage violent jihad against the enemies of Islam. For Kareem, the United States of America was such an enemy. He also believed the heretics, apostates, and infidels populating the country deserved to be punished—and he was an implement of retribution for their wrongdoing.

The ex-con's favorite verses from the Koran included the commands "When you meet the unbelievers in the battlefield, strike off their heads and, when you have laid them low, bind your captives firmly," and "Prophet, make war on the unbelievers and the hypocrites and deal rigorously with them. Hell shall be their home; an evil fate." He recited them often, a gangster theology that resonated with the life he knew on the street before his conversion—and his new purpose in life as "an instrument of Allah's wrath."

Mohammed rewarded Kareem's successful assassination of Cho Hee Sun with more insights into his personal experience as a faithful warrior in Allah's army. "I was fifteen when the Jews invaded Southern Lebanon, occupying our nation, attacking those brothers we invited to live within our borders."

"You mean the PLO?"

"Yes," said Mohammed, nodding, putting down his cup of tea. "The Little Satan's Army crossed into our land, violating our sovereignty and assaulting our guests. An attack on our brothers was an attack on us. We had a duty to drive out the Zionists."

Mohammed grabbed a Koran, raised his arm as if brandishing a weapon, and smiled. "This later gave birth to the Hizb Allah-al-Thawra al-Islamiya fi Lubnan, or Hezbollah, the Party of God. My brothers were trained by the Islamic Revolutionary Guard Corps and were inspired by the Ayatollah Khomeini, who encouraged us to attack the apostates, knowing Allah would protect us. The Supreme Leader understood whoever wielded the sword would conquer the earth."

"Were you part of the fighting?"

Mohammed nodded. "I fought alongside my brothers and later received the same training. It was much more than the hand-to-hand combat techniques we have seen in the al-Qaeda videos they give to Al Jazeera and CNN. We were a tightly disciplined group and superbly trained with advanced skills to defeat any army. We learned how to use bombings and assassinations effectively.

"Until they built their wall, the Zionist occupiers were unable to cope with our tactics and as the war progressed our small numbers grew, encouraged by our friends in Iran. From our ranks arose great leaders."

Mohammed paused as if gathering his thoughts. "Imad Mugniyeh was such a leader, a pillar in our organization. He led the destruction of American and Jewish interests for three decades. In 1979, when the Ayatollah came to power in Iran, those who hated the Shah for turning his back on Allah seized the American Embassy in Tehran. They held fifty-two hostages for more than a year as an impotent United States looked on. It cost their President Carter his job and proved our advance can never be stopped when Allah wills. Imad was inspired and trained by those same valiant warriors and set up his organization in Lebanon. He was responsible for the bombing in 1983 of the American Embassy in Beirut, and then a few months later he destroyed the crusaders' Marine barracks. Once again we proved the weakness of the Great Satan, who ran when confronted by power. Even their new president withdrew his troops rather than face the wrath of Allah's soldiers."

"You mean Reagan?"

Mohammed flicked his wrist as if backhanding a pesky insect. "The name does not matter. America cannot stop what Allah has ordained. Imad was responsible for the killing of the American CIA station chief in Beirut and the hijacking of their TWA Flight 847. The Americans knew they could not stop him. They even put out a reward of five million dollars, hoping to coax a traitor within our midst. They had no way of finding him though he operated under their noses. He was called Abu Dokhan, 'the father of smoke,' because of his ability to evaporate in thin air when pursued. They suspected him of masterminding the bombing of the Jews' embassy in Argentina, a Zionist community center in Buenos Aires, and the Khobar Towers in Riyadh. He was a great warrior in the cause of Allah. It took the enemies of Islam until 2008 to find him. Then he was martyred in Damascus by a Zionist car bomb."

Kareem said nothing as he sipped his tea but the eyes spoke volumes, his zeal evident.

Mohammed continued, looking beyond Kareem, as if prophesying the future. "As the Americans like to say, he put us on the map. Now merely the name Hezbollah strikes fear in weak infidel nations. We have more than twenty thousand warriors. They are on every continent, with more missiles than most governments. Even leaders of the United States call us the 'A Team' and refer to al-Qaeda as the 'B Team.'

"Our purpose is to plant the banner of jihad here in America and avenge Imad Mugniyeh's murder." His voice rose slightly as he clenched his fist. "We must bring this nation to its knees in submission to the one true God. I want the Zionists and Crusaders to know they can cowardly kill a man of greatness like Imad Mugniyeh with a car bomb, or Osama bin Laden with their foolhardy SEAL teams, or Anwar al-Awlaki with their drones, but it will never stop our cause. We are stronger than one man. Allah is our God. He is the Righteous God of vengeance. He will be their judge and they will learn too late they are on the wrong side of this battle."

Kareem nodded in agreement, his eyes wide with enthusiasm.

Mohammed paused for a long moment, then, looking directly at Kareem, said, "You will be a great soldier for Allah. I want you to join me tomorrow to speak with Rostam."

CHAPTER TWENTY-TWO

As Jake drove from the pier to the café in Brentwood, he spent a few extra minutes "dry cleaning" to lose anyone who might be tailing him. The verbal slipup with Reid heightened his "situational awareness"—and he cautiously employed all but the most drastic of the countersurveillance techniques he had learned at Quantico and since.

By the time he arrived at the café he was certain he hadn't been followed. From the car he called Trey Bennett.

"Yeah," said Trey, noting the caller ID.

"You got the 'newbie' with you?" asked Jake.

"He's my little shadow. Where I go, he goes."

"Well, isn't that sweet. J. Edgar would be so proud of you," Jake parried. Then, serious, he added, "Look, I'm already here. I don't want to be paranoid but meet me inside. I'll grab a booth in the back."

"Okay."

Jake entered through the side entrance of the café and was soon joined by Trey and Brian Carter.

The waitress approached before the agents settled and all three ordered iced tea. She left menus but Jake was anxious to get back over the hill and wanted only a drink.

"How'd it go?" asked Trey after the waitress left.

Jake handed him the memory chip from his recording device in a chain-of-custody envelope. He then pulled out the package Reid passed to him on the pier and handed it to Trey. "We'll need to preserve all this and check it for prints. And since it's a 'lick-seal' closure, you probably ought to see if it has his DNA on the seal. But meanwhile, I have to see the contents. It has all the information I need on the girl."

"You want me to open it here?"

When Jake nodded, Trey, who was sitting next to the wall, surreptitiously pulled a pair of clear latex gloves from his tan leather attaché case.

With his hand under the table, Jake activated the spring-loaded switchblade he kept in his rear pocket, the sound drowned out by the chatter and clatter in the restaurant. "Here, you can use my letter opener," he said, slipping the open knife across the table.

"Aren't those illegal?" asked Brian.

"Remember, Brian, we're here to enforce the law, not follow it," said Jake.

Without changing expression, Trey said, "Brian, I'm your training agent. I order you not to listen to a word this man says. He has been permanently banned by OPR from advising agents on any matters pertaining to rules, regulations, or FBI protocols."

If the letters F-B-I were uttered to instill fear in the criminal populace, O-P-R brought a similar trepidation to FBI agents. The instructors at the Academy pounded into new agents during the twenty-week program the role of the Office of Professional Responsibility. It was the Bureau's answer to a police department's internal affairs division, and Trey's mentioning OPR put the probationary agent on alert. He hoped his training agent was joking but wasn't certain.

"Did you count the money?" asked Trey, looking at a stack of hundreds wrapped by a rubber band.

"No, but it's all there. He won't take a chance on shorting me unless he just can't count. He went to Harvard, so his math skills are probably above average."

"These are all old bills," said Trey.

"So?"

"Seems odd with the new hundreds out last year there wouldn't be a few of them in the mix."

"It all counts toward a conviction, so who cares," said Jake.

"As soon as we're done here I'll get it processed and get you the information on the girl," said Trey as he pulled the photo from the envelope.

"She looks young," said Brian.

"Apparently she doesn't look pregnant, at least not yet. Reid wants the problem disposed of before her father figures out his daughter is in the motherly way," replied Jake.

He then explained the details of the meeting with Reid, the rookie taking notes. Brian would prepare the FD-302 report of the meeting, minimizing the paperwork for Jake. When Jake got to the Vegas part of the story, Trey balked.

"You didn't agree to Las Vegas, did you?"

"Sure, why not?" said Jake with a playful grin.

"Jake, come on, you know why."

Brian put down his pen. "What's wrong with Vegas? Sounds like it's a necessary trip for this operation."

They both looked at Brian and simultaneously said, "Because Los Angeles won't get credit."

Jake's grin was ear to ear.

"Why did you agree to go to Las Vegas?" asked Trey, almost pleading.

"Listen to the recording. It makes sense. There is no good reason why a contract killer wouldn't want to do this in Las Vegas. You gotta listen to the way Reid set up the hit."

"Jake, we just got an all-agents email to restrict travel due to budget cuts." Again Trey was pleading, because he knew he had to sell his superiors on any trip outside the Los Angeles office's area of responsibility.

"Who's your AUSA?" asked Jake, referring to the assistant United States attorney who would be prosecuting the case. "He can still indict it here and make the travel element just another overt act in the commission of all these crimes."

"Adriana Corbet."

"You're golden. She's the best prosecutor in the section. She'll work with us. Heck, if we agree to take her to Vegas, she'd convince the bean counters this is a necessary element of the offense."

Trey shut his eyes and shook his head. "I should have just closed the case."

Jake laughed. "We may not have to go to Vegas."

Trey looked up, a glimmer of hope in his eyes.

"We're going to have to approach the girl," said Jake.

"Why?" asked the newly minted special agent.

Jake took another sip of his iced tea, then said, "It makes for a stronger case if we get the second payment after Reid thinks the girl is dead. Otherwise he can always say he changed his mind and was trying to locate the hit man to cancel the order."

"And a jury will buy that?" asked Brian.

"You'd be surprised what a jury buys. Ever hear of O.J.? How about Casey Anthony? You'd be even more surprised by what a judge will buy from a Johnnie Cochran. We must have all the elements covered and we want them on tape," said Jake.

"So what do you do?"

"We get the girl to cooperate. I have a friend who's a Hollywood makeup artist. We squeeze a little fake blood on our victim, take pictures of the gore, color of course, and get one of our National Academy pals in the LVPD to plant a story and the images in the Las Vegas 'blogosphere' so we don't get accused of misleading the press. Then I present everything to our Perry Mason make-believe and he hands me another bag full of cash."

"Do you think the girl will cooperate?" asked Brian.

"When we play her the tapes, she'll be more than willing." Jake took the last sip of his iced tea, the ice falling to his lips as he tipped the glass upward.

"What about her father?" asked Brian.

"I think we need to keep him out of the equation. He might just want to inflict a little Pyongyang justice on our distinguished member of the bar."

Trey's cell phone rang and when he looked at the caller ID he said, "I have to get this." Trey excused himself and went outside to take the call.

Jake turned to Brian. "So where are you living?"

"We're renting a place in the West San Fernando Valley just off the Ventura Freeway," said Brian.

"Good," said Jake. "I spend a lot of time that direction. Let's meet later this afternoon and trade Marine Corps war stories."

Without showing a trace of emotion Brian said, "With all due respect, sir, Trey told me not to be alone with you until I'm off probation. He said you could ruin a bright future faster than a senatorial sex scandal."

Jake's face dropped and there was a brief uncomfortable silence as he searched for a comeback. Then he spied the hint of a smile on the probationary agent.

"You're pretty good. I almost bought it. You may have a future in the UC program."

Trey returned to the table and saw the two grinning. "What's up?"

"Nothing," said Jake. "Junior here might make a pretty good undercover agent. He's got the gift of deceit."

Trey shook his head. "I'm not ready to handle two practiced liars."

CHAPTER TWENTY-THREE

As three o'clock neared, the two Korean operatives staked out the pier seeking to locate the attorney and the cowboy. The warm May sunshine made for a pleasant assignment. With school out, parents and their children and teenagers on bikes, Roller-blades, and skateboards dominated the crowd.

The homeless man trudged up and down the pier, occasionally begging for change, just to appear authentic. The other man, garbed in casual attire, covered all the attractions: the carousel and old-fashioned soda fountain, the arcade and food court, even the Heal the Bay aquarium and science center. Both predators struck out in finding their prey.

Park had given the order and wanted the lawyer disposed of but wanted nothing coming back to him or his daughter. The men seeking Reid were professional killers and valuable members of Park's entourage. They could easily strike at any time, duplicating a Hollywood-like Mafia contract killing with a suppressed, subsonic .22 round to the head, a mysterious residential explosion and fire, or even the communists' preferred assassination technique: a sudden stop after a long fall from a great height.

The assassins could have waited outside Reid's office and attacked him as he walked to his car in the parking garage, but that manner of death might be too easily caught on a surveillance camera. Park wanted to make sure the killing didn't come back to him or his organization. The men were hoping to find Reid at the pier and follow him to where they could make the homicide appear to be a common street crime or perhaps a carjacking, not the work of a disgruntled client.

H. Daniel Reid didn't know it, but he was a dead man walking. The two men dispatched to eliminate him were unaware of all the particulars, but they didn't need to know. Mr. Park had simply ordered the lawyer killed. If someone else got in the way—like the guy in the cowboy boots, with whom Reid met the day before—so be it.

The homeless man and his companion had no idea who the guy with the ostrich boots really was. They didn't know his strengths or his record. And they didn't care. They would take out the cowboy, too, if he got in the way. Mr. Park's mission in the United States was far too important to allow interference from these bourgeois interlopers.

After searching the pier for nearly an hour, the two returned to a concrete table near the beachfront coffee stand.

Speaking in Korean, the homeless man said, "I don't think we missed them."

"We didn't. I don't think they came."

"But why? Do you think we were detected yesterday?" asked the homeless man.

"I don't see how."

The homeless man reached into the pocket of his ragged, urine-stained trousers, pulled out an iPhone 5, and said, "I will call his office."

In seconds the smartphone found the number and dialed the

law offices of H. Daniel Reid. After speaking with the receptionist in perfect English, he ended the call and said to his colleague in Korean, "Reid is in court all afternoon."

The older man smiled. The deed would be completed another day.

CHAPTER TWENTY-FOUR

Jake was driving in bumper-to-bumper traffic on the 101 Freeway when his cell phone rang. He spied the caller ID and turned down the volume on Charlie Daniels blasting from the speakers.

"Hey, what's up?"

"You were right," said Trey Bennett.

"About what?"

"The front office hit the roof when they learned the killing was to take place in Vegas. They accused you of setting up the entire episode for a weeklong boondoggle in Sin City. I was ordered to produce copies of the recordings to verify you did this on purpose. OPR even came up in the conversation. I'm not sure your marriage to management is going to last."

"We're like fire and kerosene."

A sense of perverse pride washed across Jake's face; he knew he was viewed as a bureaucratic liability by those cloistered in the corner offices of the federal building; so quick to exploit his successes but so unwilling to chance failure. Any good undercover agent ruffled a few feathers in the front office, and Jake more often than not upset the entire henhouse. He loved these little episodes because they guaranteed he would never be assigned to a management position in the FBI. He also knew the recordings would exonerate him of any wrongdoing.

"Tell the turd sniffers at OPR if I wanted a boondoggle, I would have set it up in Maui."

Trey laughed. "That's what I told them . . . and then I spoke with Adriana Corbet at the U.S. Attorney's Office. She says we have both jurisdiction and venue. She doesn't see a problem and said she and her husband would gladly accompany us on the trip to Vegas to make sure all the legal issues are resolved."

"I bet she did." You could hear the smile in Jake's voice. "A couple of years ago she worked a human trafficking case for us involving L.A., Vegas, and San Francisco. On the trips to Vegas we had to pry her away from the tables with a crowbar. What was even more amazing, she won big every night."

"As she pointed out, we'll arrest Reid when he's in L.A., not Vegas, so it won't even become an issue."

"I love it when the feather merchants get their collective panties in a bunch. I'm so glad to stir the pot."

CHAPTER TWENTY-FIVE

Jake squeezed the Range Rover into a parking spot on Ventura Boulevard and spied Brian Carter waiting in front of Three Amigos, Jake's favorite Mexican fast-food spot in the Valley.

"Nice ride," said Brian. "I meant to ask when we met yesterday. Is that your personal car?"

"Hardly. You probably thought everyone in the FBI drove a Malibu or Ford Fusion."

Brian nodded.

Jake smiled. "This is why you get into the undercover program, the few, the proud, the ugly: better cars, no ties, and an adrenaline rush hard to beat. We're blessed on the West Coast with some truly stupid criminals with exotic tastes. When they take a fall we build up our war chests. While you were still at Quantico, this Rover belonged to a Mexican meth dealer with strong cartel ties who's now doing twenty at the supermax in Florence, Colorado."

The two agents entered the tiny restaurant and Jake grabbed a table in the back before ordering his standard fare, the Steak

Burrito Supreme. Carter followed the experienced agent's recommendation and soon both were chowing down.

Brian spent the next few minutes discussing his eight years on active duty, including three deployments to Afghanistan, where amenities such as running water and electricity were luxuries. IEDs and gunfights were the norm. In his last tour he was part of a village stabilization project assisting the ALP, the Afghan Local Police. That too consisted of almost daily patrols preparing the Afghan people to stand on their own as the United States transitioned to a support role. Though he was doing what he trained to do, he soon realized the toll his frequent deployments were taking on his new wife.

"Unless you've been through it, no one understands the impact a combat deployment has on a marriage," said Brian. "We were lucky. We didn't have children. I don't know how those moms did it, repeatedly playing the single-parent role for months, sometimes up to a year or more at a time."

Before taking another bite, Jake said, "You're right. I think it's much harder on the family. We're out runnin' and gunnin' doing what we signed up to do while those who love us wait at home, fearful every time the phone rings, praying a Marine in 'Dress Blues' and a chaplain never ring the doorbell."

"Yeah, but is it any better when you're undercover?"

"Undercover work can be extremely dangerous. When you're downrange in a war zone you expect contact, maybe every day. Undercover work is much more subtle. You're among them without becoming one of them. I've certainly experienced those pucker-factor moments undercover, but not every day like on a combat tour.

"In UC work you don't worry about getting hit when you're on patrol or having your troops killed as much as you worry about being discovered. It's a different kind of concern. It's not sidestepping IEDs. Typically you're on your own, no backup in sight and no friendlies in harm's way. It's better to be quick with the tongue than the trigger, though every once in a while, accurate shooting is a big plus."

Jake smiled, then quieted as a customer passed their table, headed to the restroom in the back.

Between bites, Jake asked, "Did most of the guys you served with get out?"

"Maybe a third of the company-grade officers stayed in. With three and sometimes four deployments it was tough on the families. I loved the Corps and would have stayed had I been single."

"If the Marines had wanted you to have a wife they would have issued you one," cracked Jake, repeating the legendary "Old Corps" maxim.

"I hear that."

"Those who got out, where'd they go?"

"Mainly the private sector," said Brian.

"You mean security work?"

"No, business, sales. A few went into law enforcement. I have one buddy who went into the DEA and another guy, my best friend in the Marines, he and I were at the Basic School together and as second lieutenants were part of a special operations group that did some work in South America. Gabe got out after three deployments in four years and joined the Agency. He was an intel officer and spoke Korean. Gabe Chong, so naturally everyone called him—"

Jake interrupted, "Cheech."

"Yep. You know how the Marine Corps operates. Gabe is a Korean speaker, so they sent him to South America. At least the Agency is using his skill set. I saw him a month ago as he passed through L.A. heading for points west."

"The Marines are a lot like the Bu. Different bureaucrats, all singing from the same sheet music," added Jake.

"Well, Gabe will be a great spook. Sharp guy, went to Berkeley."

"A Marine at Berkeley? I bet he was popular on campus."

"And how about you? When did you serve?"

"I went through the PLC program, two summers, then was commissioned when I graduated from college. Spent four years on active duty and got out in 2003. I was a rifle company commander with RCT-3 in the initial invasion of Iraq. A lot of my guys got hurt and killed on the way to Baghdad and later on in Anbar Province . . . too many. I was wounded in Fallujah by a suicidal bastard using an RPG as a sniper rifle.

"While I was recovering in the hospital and writing too many letters home to the loved ones of the Marines I lost, I decided I couldn't do that forever. Colonel Newman, our regimental CO, visited me in the hospital and tried to talk me into staying in the Corps. But I needed to move on and told him I wanted to join the FBI. He understood and encouraged me to keep at the rehab so I could pass the Bureau's physical qualification test. He also wrote a gold-plated fitness report that went in with my application."

"You talking about Major General Peter Newman?"

"Yeah, you know him?"

"Gabe and I were with him in Venezuela as part of that special operations group I mentioned. The unit was formed under the Threat Mitigation Commission, which Congress later shut down. We spent the Marine Corps Birthday, 10 November 2007, at the Simón Bolívar International Airport. It hit the fan that night. We lost one of the finest Marines I ever knew . . . Sergeant Major Amos Skillings . . . He received a posthumous Medal of Honor. Afterward, it was General Newman who encouraged Gabe to apply to the Agency because of his Korean-language skills and spec-ops background. Peter Newman knew how to lead. Gabe and I would have followed that man barefoot into hell itself."

"I remember hearing some scuttlebutt about what happened in Venezuela—but not much. It was all very hush-hush, wasn't it? Russian agents, Iranian nukes."

"Yeah," replied Carter, looking clearly uncomfortable. "You have the general outline, Jake, but I really can't say more—I want to be able to pass my next polygraph. You know what I mean?"

Jake nodded and said, "Sure, but from what little I know about that unit and that operation, it really was hell." Then quieter, he added, "I'm not sure Gabe is that much safer in his new job. I lost my best friend a few months ago on an OGA mission in Afghanistan. He was my best man when Katie and I got married. He'd found the girl of his dreams. They'd been married less than six months when he was killed. Joe was a MARSOC operator and loved the world of special ops. I'm not sure a day goes by I don't think about him. When I got the word he'd been killed it was the second-toughest day of my life. Joe had something to come back to. I don't, at least not anymore."

"Trey said you've had a tough year. I guess he was right," replied Brian.

Neither said anything for a long moment. Jake choked back his emotions as he changed the subject. "It'll be a different kind of combat for you now. It's more mental than physical. You might spend an entire career and never fire your weapon in the heat of battle, yet each day you will be challenged to outthink some of the most sophisticated criminals in our society. I love that type of warfare. And if you get into the undercover program, you will find an indescribable rush. Going face-to-face with somebody playing for the other side and never blinking, that's what it's all about. Unlike the Marine Corps, you won't have fire teams, squads, or platoons to maneuver. It is usually just you, all alone. I can't get enough."

Brian nodded without saying a word.

CHAPTER TWENTY-SIX

The front porch of the tiny cabin brought a measure of comfort but failed to erase the loneliness. An easy life is rarely meaningful and a meaningful life rarely easy. Jake's life had been meaningful in ways he never anticipated. Slouching in his favorite chair, he drained the second beer with a final gulp, wishing he could reverse some of the "meaning" and find more of the "ease" . . . it *had* been a rough year.

The smoke from his Macanudo Hyde Park lingered as he stared at the bright stars in the clear Topanga Canyon sky. Katie hated the cigars, failing to appreciate the mild almond and fresh herb scents. She described the cigar's fine aroma as "burning horse dung."

A smile crossed his face as memories of his wife flooded his mind. She loved him through all his scars, visible and hidden. The heartache that seared his soul for so many months abated somewhat when he focused on the great times they shared.

His cell phone rang, interrupting the moment. Noting the caller ID, he answered on the second ring.

"This better be important."

"We need to meet first thing in the morning," said Trey Bennett.

"What's up?"

"Can't talk about it over the phone."

Jake shook his head. "Don't tell me you're getting a case of the for-reals."

"Maybe I am but we need to meet first thing."

"Where?"

"The JTTF."

"Who called the meeting?"

"The front office."

"Is this because of Vegas?"

"This has nothing to do with your wasteful trek to Glitter Gulch. The meeting's in the SCIF at eight."

Jake screwed up his face trying to determine why the meeting had to be conducted in the top-secret portion of the building GSA leased for the Bureau and several other three-letter U.S. government agencies. "You want to give me a clue as to what this is all about?"

"No can do, big guy, but I think for once the brass wants to see you and you aren't in trouble."

"And some people don't believe in miracles," said Jake.

It was difficult to imagine why a lawyer's solicitation to commit murder necessitated a top-secret summit. Mandatory morning meetings with an administrator usually resulted in a restless night's sleep. Jake joked he committed a felony a day but with sufficient warning he could provide an alibi and defense for even his most egregious conduct. So far he was golden on this assignment. Maybe he could sleep soundly tonight.

CHAPTER TWENTY-SEVEN

DAY 5

FRIDAY, MAY 2

Jake got in a five-mile run before heading to the Joint Terrorism Task Force "off-site" in the West San Fernando Valley. The traffic was bearable but any trip down the Ventura Freeway at this hour was cause for a sedative when the drive was complete.

Thanks to the traffic, he arrived a few minutes late. The JTTF, a single-story nondescript building, was hidden in one of the many industrial parks in the Valley. He made his way to the Sensitive Compartmented Information Facility, or SCIF. It was a large, secure conference room, specially designated for the discussion of classified information. The doors and walls were built to prevent acoustical intrusion, and precautions were taken for the limited number of visitors allowed access. To prevent eavesdropping or tracking, all electronic devices were left outside the room. No cell phones, laptops, iPads, electronic notebooks.

Meetings in the SCIF were usually limited to members of the FBI's "secret squirrel division," as the agents referred to those who worked counterintelligence matters. Most agents never darkened the door of the SCIF and Jake had no idea why a squad working cases involving Asian organized crime and now a lawyer who wanted to eliminate his pregnant girlfriend needed access to the secure facility.

Trey Bennett was removing his cell phone and placing it in a gymnasium-style wall locker as Jake approached.

"You sure know how to ruin a morning. What's going on? Is our lawyer part of a terrorist sleeper cell?"

"I pinky-finger swore not to tell," said Trey with a weak, crooked grin. "We can talk about it when we get inside."

Jake gave him a look as if to say, "You've got to be kidding me!" Instead he whispered sotto voce, "So where is Tonto, your faithful Indian companion, this morning?"

He gave Jake a hard look and replied, "Carter's not cleared for this," and knocked on the door.

Jake, suffering somewhat from being over-caffeinated, refused to get serious. "Shouldn't we knock three times, wait for a response, then recite the appropriate counter catchphrase?"

"You mean like 'I've got the yoyo.' And those on the other side of the door say, 'I've got the string.' "

Jake flashed a huge smile. "Exactly. You know how much I love this cloak-and-dagger stuff."

Before Trey could shout out the secret password of the day, the door opened and the two entered.

Jake surveyed those in attendance. Some faces were familiar, others new. The "heavies"—those seated at the large conference table—were wearing suits and ties. The attire alone spelled government bureaucrats, so he headed toward a back-bench seat along the far wall.

Olivia Knox, the Assistant Director in Charge (ADIC) of the Los Angeles Field Office, was seated at the head of the table, surrounded by her subordinates and supplicants.

Trey was right. This was big. Olivia Knox didn't casually call meetings with street agents. Though she left most operational issues for her command structure to handle, she and Jake had been known to butt heads during her two-year reign in L.A.

Most FBI field offices were led by a Special Agent in Charge (SAC). Three offices—New York, Washington, D.C., and Los Angeles—were so large that an ADIC was the designated head, with multiple SACs one step below on the management flowchart.

Olivia Knox was respected throughout the Bureau and her name was prominently mentioned anytime there was an opening in the highest levels at Headquarters. Her opinion mattered to most but for Jake she was still just another bureaucrat.

"You going to Vegas with us?" whispered Jake as he passed her.

She glanced at the undercover agent's boots, jeans, and open collar, glared into his grin for an instant, grimaced slightly, and said to the rest of the room, "Let's get started. I have an important meeting I need to chair downtown."

Jake's competitive streak carried over from the ball fields of his youth to the FBI. Whether the opponent was a crazed serial killer or a bureaucrat, his ego required he keep the upper hand. The character trait kept him alive on the street but was far less appreciated by those in management. He gestured as if to say, "By all means."

Knox began. "For those of you who don't know him, this is Robert Bauer, the SAC for the Secret Service here in Los Angeles. I've also asked Rachel Chang, our supervisor of the Asian Organized Crime squad, to be here. I'm debating transferring this matter to the JTTF but may allow her to continue handling it. Rachel's new to the division, fresh from Headquarters, but she worked in the Asian Unit back there, so she's familiar with the issues in this investigation."

Jake had yet to meet Rachel, but the undercover operation targeting Tommy Hwan and his extended criminal family was being worked by her squad. The original supervisor handling the matter was transferred back to Washington soon after the UC portion of the investigation began. Trey had been running it unencumbered until Rachel arrived. For two weeks, she had been unable to find or make the time to meet with Jake, which was fine with him.

Trey mentioned her to Jake in passing and though her stay in L.A. had only begun, Trey said she seemed okay.

For Jake the jury was still out on L.A.'s latest find from HQ. As far as he was concerned, street agents had to prove they didn't have what it took to be in the FBI. Administrators had to prove they belonged . . . for Jake, Rachel Chang had yet to prove her worth.

Stuart Upchurch, the Special Agent in Charge of the Organized Crime Division, sat next to Charles Hafner, his Assistant Special Agent in Charge (ASAC). Upchurch, who was retiring at the end of the month, was respected by the street agents because he had a hands-off approach to managing cases. Hafner, on the other hand, was a piece of work. He was the proverbial empty suit who couldn't find his backside with a GPS device. Hafner had a rabbi at Headquarters and the bullpen scuttlebutt had him stepping into Upchurch's slot if a more meaningful position didn't open up back east. He had spent an extended assignment on the Headquarters inspection staff and parlayed that into an ASAC position in L.A.

Assistant Special Agents in Charge were a different breed, especially in an office as large as L.A. In the smaller offices an ASAC served just below the division's top gun, so the responsibilities were more visible and pronounced. In the larger offices they represented one more layer of bureaucracy and most were blue-flamers hoping to land an administrative position elsewhere after checking off another box. Hafner came from the Headquarters mold: good-looking, stiff collar, silk tie, perfect white teeth, risk-averse, and worse than useless.

"We want to keep this in our division and work it off Rachel's desk," said Hafner.

Knox nodded as if the ASAC's input was all she needed to finalize her decision. Knox didn't introduce a man with salt-and-pepper hair, in his late forties, who sat in the opposite far corner, a cup of coffee in hand, balancing his chair on two legs and resting against the wall.

Knox then introduced Jake as the UC who met with the attorney, Reid, yesterday. Jake wasn't thrilled his undercover role was now exposed to outside agencies, but he also couldn't mask the confusion on his face. He remained silent but was having trouble coming to grips with why a murder-for-hire case was plaguing the JTTF and Secret Service.

There was a knock on the door and the gate guard glanced down at the flat-screen display on his desk, rose, and opened the portal. In walked a young, wiry Asian male, late twenties and athletic. He looked like a Korean Bruce Lee.

Jake was stunned! The new entry was one of Henry Yeong's henchmen from the meeting in the restaurant. The two locked eyes before a slight smile appeared on the face of the newest visitor to the SCIF. He sat next to the mysterious man in the back of the room. Jake suppressed his alarm and the urge to interrupt the proceedings but focused his attention on the late arrival.

Olivia Knox reviewed the facts of the case to date and Jake had no quarrel with her presentation. Since outsiders were present she offered borderline praise for Jake's undercover work, then she came to the meat of the issue. "Yesterday, Daniel Reid handed Jake a twenty-five-thousand-dollar deposit for the hit, all in hundreds, every bill a Supernote."

There was an audible gasp from several of the administrative minions.

Knox gave a primer to those in the meeting. "It's no secret North Korea's a criminal empire. Since the imposition of economic sanctions, drugs and counterfeit goods have played an integral part in the country's survival. They are one of the world's largest producers of opium, meth, and knockoff pharmaceuticals. We've seized tens of millions of dollars' worth of counterfeit cigarettes and clothing manufactured in Pyongyang and its outlying towns and villages. Nothing occurs there without being approved by the government. All of its criminal activities are tightly controlled by Kim Jong Un's regime loyalists just as it was under his father. We would be here all day if we had to rehash the incidents of North Korean diplomats linked to drugs, black-market arms shipments, human trafficking, and counterfeiting."

Knox paused to catch her breath, but it made her next statement appear more dramatic. "One of the greatest threats to our economy and our national security is the Supernote. It's been around for years but it took two multiagency undercover cases, headed up by the FBI, 'Smoking Dragon' on the West Coast and 'Royal Charm' on the East Coast, before any administration acknowledged North Korean government officials were printing the bills. Back in 2006, President Bush warned North Korea we were aware of their activities and reminded the leaders in Pyongyang that counterfeiting another nation's currency is an act of war. Though the details are not relevant to this meeting, you should know it was because of these discreetly delivered warnings that North Korea returned to the nuclear weapons talks a few months later.

"The quality of the counterfeit one-hundred-dollar bill is so good, imperfections are almost undetectable. The bills are printed on a special intaglio press with optically variable ink. Even the paper has the long, parallel fibers used by our Bureau of Engraving and Printing. . . ."

Jake was impressed. Knox appeared to know a great deal about the Supernote.

She continued, "Those joint investigations slowed the flow of counterfeit bills into the U.S., but as the payment to Jake indicates, we didn't stop it. North Korea's the reason we modified the hundred-dollar bill last year. Certainly it's our government's hope the new bill will deter counterfeiting, but I wouldn't be surprised if Pyongyang is busy engraving new plates so they can start counterfeiting our most recent hundreds. The first samples of North Korea's work showed up in 1989. This is the third time we've redesigned the bill since then and in our two previous attempts North Korea kept up with our enhanced security. It's just a matter of time before they are producing their latest version of the Supernote."

"But even if the new-design bill is as tough to copy as Treasury hopes, the old U.S. currency is still in circulation—and so are the virtually indistinguishable North Korean Supernotes," interjected Bauer, the Secret Service SAC.

Knox nodded. "As we saw yesterday, they are flowing through the global economy and will pass muster at any bank. When the new bills were issued last year there was an estimated nine hundred billion dollars—that's billion with a *b*—of the old currency still in circulation. The old bills will gradually be phased out when they are too worn, but that will take years. From all our intelligence, Kim Jong Un is flooding the Asian and European markets with the old Supernotes trying to beat the phaseout."

Robert Bauer added, "They are literally laundering the most recently produced Supernotes and aging the paper. The bills look as if they've been in circulation so as not to attract close scrutiny."

Trey looked at Jake and nodded an affirmation.

Olivia Knox smiled, something few in the room had ever seen her do, and said, "It's one thing for our Treasury to crank out more bills as part of an economic stimulus plan, but when a foreign government is manufacturing our money, it's important that we stop it. Now it's an imperative."

Knox paused for effect and every eye turned toward her as she continued, "Everyone here knows North Korea has used Supernotes to finance terrorism and R&D on ICBMs and WMDs—nuclear, chemical, and biological. They've been getting away with it for years. We now have credible information from reliable sources that the regime in Pyongyang may have closed a barter deal involving Supernotes with another hostile power that poses a real and present danger—an existential threat, if you will—to the U.S. homeland.

"I am not at liberty to say more about this right now, but I can tell you that what started out as an organized-crime investigation may have grave national security implications—and I can tell you the potential damage goes well beyond weakening our dollar and strengthening an adversary's global influence.

"I called this meeting because yesterday's payoff to Jake appears to validate a new classified National Intelligence Assessment that the DPRK—the so-called Democratic People's Republic of Korea, which we endearingly refer to as North Korea—is now engaged in a full-court press to accelerate conversion of Supernotes into goods and services of tangible value.

"The contents of the bag Reid passed to Jake represent one of the largest bulk uses of the Supernote we've seen in the United States since the arrests in August 2005. No matter how you slice it, the Supernotes are a serious assault on our monetary system and our national security."

"So what made you decide to even check the quality of the currency Reid passed off yesterday?" asked Jake, leaning forward, fully engaged in the conversation, his attention diverted from Bruce Lee's stunt double.

Bauer, the Secret Service SAC, took the question. "Park has been known to our office for a long time as a mover and shaker in the world of Korean organized crime. We've never been able to prove his involvement in the Supernote, but he's been on our radar and we were aware of your operation." Then, nodding toward Rachel Chang, he continued, "Yesterday, when Rachel told us of the payoff in U.S. hundreds, we asked to take a look. We knew Reid was Park's attorney and suspected any currency he passed could have originated with Park and might be Supernotes. We guessed right."

"You're not saying you think Park's financing his own daughter's execution?" asked Jake.

"Not at all. We suspect Park and Reid have no intention of declaring their illegal gains to the IRS, so a lot of Park's legal expenses are settled through cash payouts. In all likelihood, Park paid Reid for other services rendered and Reid used those same bills to pay you."

Knox jumped back in, "With Russia and Ukraine, there are many national security issues, but Headquarters wants to expedite *this* investigation. We need to pursue the Supernote as far and as fast as we can."

Then turning to Jake—and every head in the room turned with hers—she said, "Jake, how quickly can you come up with more on the Supernotes?"

The undercover agent paused a moment, then said, "Off the top of my head, I really don't know. The twenty-five thousand was a down payment on a murder that is to take place next week. Then the lid comes off. We can't hide a contract killing. We'll need to go overt and make an arrest."

"Then we have a week," she replied without hesitation.

"Give or take a nuclear apocalypse," said Jake.

"I'm open for suggestions as to how we proceed," said Knox.

No one said a word. Jake turned toward the odd couple on the other side of the room to see if they were going to contribute. Since they didn't appear to be on the cusp of responding, Jake took the lead. "How about this? I remain in my cover and I approach Park and tell him of Reid's plans."

"How will you get to Park?" asked Olivia Knox.

"I'll convince Tommy Hwan to introduce me. He's the guy who brought Reid to me, so now it makes sense for me to warn his boss and give Park a chance to buy out the contract."

"Then what?" said Hafner, questioning the investigative strategy.

"Saving his daughter may not be enough to have Park bring me into his inner circle but it should give me some cred with him. Then we'll see where that leads us."

"I don't know. The chances for success seem remote and time is of the essence," said Hafner.

Jake threw up his hands, looked toward Bruce Lee and his silent partner, and said in all sincerity, "I'm open to a better idea."

If the action-film look-alike or his partner were about to speak, Hafner's next query cut them off at the pass. In a derisive tone the aspiring bureaucrat interjected, "What do *you* suggest we do with Reid? Park will have him killed if you tell him about the contract."

"Do we care what happens to this scum-dwelling lawyer?" asked Jake.

"Yes, Jake, we do care," said Knox without hesitation.

"Especially with a room full of witnesses," whispered Trey Bennett.

"I'll come up with a reason why I need Reid alive. I'll convince Park to hide his daughter until we can spring a double reverse on the attorney."

Knox, Upchurch, Hafner, and Bauer traded thoughts on Jake's strategy before the ADIC proffered her reluctant approval.

As the meeting broke up and everyone began filing out of the SCIF, Jake approached the two strangers Knox conveniently forgot to introduce. He extended his hand. "Hi, I'm Jake. Thanks for your contribution to the discussion this morning. I suppose Henry Yeong could have introduced us the other day and saved the awkwardness of meeting this way."

The younger of the two men smiled as the older man remained stoic.

The Bruce Lee of the two-man cabal said, "I'm Gabe."

Jake put it together quickly. "Cheech."

When the older man's head snapped, Jake's suspicions were confirmed. "Semper Fi."

Gabe smiled as the older man muttered, "How do you know? What's going on here?" The spook squinted across the room toward Olivia Knox as though he was about to protest. She was deep in quiet conversation with Bauer and Hafner and didn't notice the accusatory stare.

Jake gave no quarter. "I'm a trained investigator. What's the Agency's involvement in all this?"

The older man said nothing.

"I hate all this need-to-know horse pucky. You got a name? I don't like talking to ghosts; too many conspiratorial thoughts for my weak mind and overactive imagination."

The older man said, "You can call me Wilson."

"Is that a first name or last name?"

"Wilson will do."

"You guys and your off-the-books, black-budget operations. Do you just sit around in SCIFs and make up this crap? Look, Wilson, I'd really like to play your silly little games but my ass may be hanging out on this one. I would like to think I've got most of the facts before I run off into some Pyongyang parallel universe."

Neither man said anything, so Jake pressed on. "Look, we're supposed to be on the same team. We all know, information is power. So I'd like some information. At least if I end up being fed to mad dogs in a North Korean dungeon like Kim Jong Un's uncle, I'll know it was for a good cause." Still no response.

Olivia Knox, now aware of the growing confrontation, moved toward the three men. Hafner trailed her like a poorly trained retriever.

As she approached, Jake said, "You know, I'm not thrilled my UC role has been outed to the Secret Service and now the CIA. I'm also not interested in being cannon fodder for the next election cycle. Why not fill me in?"

Before Olivia could respond, Gabe stepped forward and took the initiative in defusing the controversy. "Jake, the Agency's been looking into the Supernote for a long time. The bills have been showing up here for years. We assumed since Henry Yeong was a major player in Korean organized crime, both here and in Asia, he was likely involved in distribution of the counterfeit currency. Yeong's tentacles reach well beyond Los Angeles and I have verified he is involved in converting the counterfeit currency overseas. I just can't connect Yeong with bulk distribution of Supernotes here in the United States.

"With yesterday's payoff, it would appear as though Park may have an exclusive deal with the North Koreans for distribution of Supernotes in this country. Since Yeong and Park are ostensibly competitors for illegal goods coming into the country, I don't see any way I can get to Park."

"The last time I scanned the rules and regs, the CIA wasn't allowed to operate within the United States," said Jake.

"Actually we can with the right approvals. I first met Yeong in Hong Kong, where I was hired to be part of his security team after two of his goons just happened to get popped for roughing up a prostitute. In the past month I've traveled with Yeong to China, Japan, Macao, Singapore, Kish Island, South Korea, and now here to the U.S. Like you, and all of us working undercover, I have to live my legend. As part of Yeong's PSD, I couldn't very well avoid this leg of his world tour. Since he isn't a U.S. citizen the approval process was relatively simple," said Gabe, nodding at Wilson, who simply grimaced and said nothing.

Knox interrupted. "Jake, the Director of National Intelligence and the Attorney General have signed off on the paperwork. The appropriate authorities are well aware of the Agency's involvement in this. Yesterday, given the new urgency to find out about what's happening with the Supernotes, Headquarters authorized me to call this meeting so all of us from every agency involved in this operation understand our respective roles."

"So are you still in charge of this investigation?" Jake countered. "Or has the Attorney General made a power play to take over?"

Olivia glared at her recalcitrant UC agent and said, "I'm still in charge . . . at least for the time being."

"And what's the game plan—to out me and allow the spooks to continue to march?" Then with sarcasm Jake turned toward Gabe's partner and asked, "Is your name *really* Wilson?"

Ignoring Jake's question, Gabe continued. "Being part of Yeong's security team doesn't mean much. Some days he lets me drive. Other days I sit around the office and fetch coffee. I've yet to break into Yeong's inner circle and am not sure I ever will.

At this point you may have a better chance of penetrating both Yeong's and Park's operations."

"How'd you get in? Is there another friendly inside Yeong's organizational structure?"

Wilson finally spoke up. "Look, we're getting way beyond 'need-to-know' here. Gabe was hired for Yeong's personal security detail in Hong Kong because friends of ours arranged to have a couple of Yeong's goons arrested. Yeong is an officer of the DPRK Ministry of State Security. He is a graduate of the Kumsong Political Military University in Pyongyang. From what we know, Park has a similar background. Gabe was hired by the Ministry of State Security to fill one of the unexpected vacancies in Yeong's travel team."

For a moment Jake said nothing, then turned to Gabe and said, "DPRK Ministry of State Security. So you're a NOC," the CIA term for an operative working under non-official cover. Most American intelligence officers work from U.S. diplomatic missions under official cover—with titles like "trade counsel" or "economic advisor"—complete with black passports and diplomatic immunity. NOCs have no such protection. As they say in the business, "You get caught spying with diplomatic immunity you get deported. NOCs who get caught spying get decapitated."

Gabe smiled. "Yeah, I'm a NOC."

"And your backstopping is secure?"

Wilson huffed, "This has gone far enough! Our backstops for Gabe are just fine. Your concern is noted. Need I remind you, we're in the business of creating legends."

"Thanks for that," said Jake dryly. Turning back to Gabe, he continued, "We don't need to know each other's backstory, but it's good for us both to know there is another 'friendly' downrange if someone starts throwing live ordnance."

"Right," Gabe replied with a smile. "There is something else that may be helpful," he added. "Are you familiar with Office 39?"

"No," answered Jake.

"Office 39 is a secret agency within the North Korean government—separate from the Ministry of State Security. It answers directly to Kim Jong Un and provides money for the Great Successor to run his mafia-like criminal enterprise. Office 39 is responsible for the production and distribution of the Supernotes, the manufacture and distribution of counterfeit cigarettes, clothing, and pharmaceuticals, as well as the distribution of heroin and crystal meth. Revenues from these activities fund terrorism and WMD research and development.

"In the DPRK, grass is a vegetable. It's a country totally dependent on international aid to feed its people. Yet the government pours hundreds of millions of dollars into terror and weapons of mass destruction, which eventually become revenue generators themselves. But the 'seed capital' has to come from somewhere—"

"That 'somewhere' is the illegal contraband you've seen so far in this UC assignment," interjected Knox.

"Sounds like a well-oiled criminal conspiracy," said Jake.

Gabe nodded. "It is, and Yeong gets his share of the grease. As ADIC Knox just said, crime is an integral part of North Korea's economy. By some estimates Office 39 brings in more than a billion dollars a year."

"I guess that makes Yeong a worthy target," said Jake.

"And Park," said Gabe.

"Let me see what I can do," said Jake, starting toward the door. "Nice to know you'll have my six when I'm out there."

Gabe slowly nodded, then to Wilson he said, "I think we owe him the rest."

"The rest of what?" said Jake, stopping abruptly, anger seeping through the words.

Wilson nodded.

Gabe said, "I've had trouble penetrating beyond the gunsel role in Yeong's organization. The only other inside person we had on this side of the Pacific was killed earlier this week in his home in Beverly Hills."

"That sounds like Cho Hee Sun, known as 'Sonny' out here," said Jake.

"How do you know?" shot Wilson in a tone that sounded to Jake as if he was being accused of Sonny's untimely demise.

"I know I'm only an FBI agent and not some CIA superspy, but the Bureau has a new requirement. We now have to be able to read before the FBI will hire us. And guess what, Wilson, it was in the *L.A. Times*, and Sonny's enemies and friends have been discussing his unfortunate end all over town since it happened."

Gabe intervened. "We were told the murder looks like a contract job. Nothing was taken. He was shot through the door. Apparently, no one even broke into his house—before or after he was killed. Does that square with what you know?"

"Yep. So far that's what I've heard. But what was Sonny's role in all this?" asked Jake.

"His brother in Hong Kong used family connections in Pyongyang to get me hired on with Henry Yeong's security detail."

"Sonny's brother in Hong Kong works for *us*?" asked Jake.

At this, Olivia Knox motioned for Robert Bauer, the Secret Service SAC, to join them. As Bauer approached she said, "Bob, tell Jake about his recently deceased friend, Sonny."

Bauer shrugged and said, "Cho Hee Sun worked for us. He was a U.S. Secret Service informant. We actually recruited the brother in Hong Kong first. Thanks to information the brother provided from Hong Kong and North Korea, we jammed Sonny up on counterfeit securities he was pushing here in the States."

Jake threw up his hands in frustration and turned to Olivia Knox. "When were you going to clue me in on all this? Had Reid not paid me off in Supernotes, I can only assume I'd still be out in the cold, running around with informants getting whacked, spies inside the organization, and me and my ass hanging out like some donkey waiting for anyone to pin on the tail. This is like a singalong with no words. You guys are truly amazing."

No one spoke.

Jake looked at Trey. "Did you know about any of this?"

Trey shook his head and the undercover agent believed him.

Jake took a long breath, shook his head, looked at Gabe, and said calmly, "So you're one degree from removal."

"It looks that way."

"One last question—Marine-to-Marine. You mentioned that you accompanied Yeong to Kish Island. What was he doing there?"

"I don't know exactly," answered Gabe. "It was a big hush-hush, three-day powwow with about fifty big shots from Pyongyang and twice as many Iranians. Not all of them were towel-heads. Some were IRGC."

"Was Park there?" Jake asked.

"If he was, I didn't see him. We've identified about half of those I could get images of using the AV recording device I was wearing. Seems like at Kish on both sides a lot of them were nuclear scientists, missile engineers, and—"

"That's enough!" Wilson interrupted. "This conversation is superfluous to the purpose of this meeting and I insist we wrap it up. Now!"

Olivia Knox nodded, looked at her watch, and said, "That's right. Recess is over, boys. Time to get back to work."

As the gaggle moved toward the door, Jake edged up to Gabe and whispered, "Watch yourself. Somebody is playing for keeps and the stakes in this card game are pretty high."

Gabe nodded. He didn't know it, but he'd been dealt a bad hand.

CHAPTER TWENTY-EIGHT

Tommy Hwan and two members of Park's crew were almost done loading boxes of counterfeit Rolex watches into the back of an old Ford Expedition. The SUV was packed and if Tommy was successful at entering the merchandise into the stream of commerce, as he had so many times in the past, a lot of people paying a discounted price for a Submariner or Oyster Perpetual Date Sea Dweller would be dumping good money into the coffers of Office 39 in the DPRK.

Most of Tommy's imports would be sold on the street or online. The majority of consumers would know the watch was a knock-off because of the price and would actually prefer the cheaper counterfeit, hoping to fool their friends. Others would pay close to full price only to learn the return policy from the online vendor didn't fulfill the Better Business Bureau truth-in-selling requirements.

Tommy's entire initiative was focused on criminal behavior. Had he applied his intellect and sales skills to legitimate commerce he might be a candidate for the Fortune 500 "Entrepreneurs to Watch" issue. But Tommy liked to party and most of his profits quickly evaporated once the music started.

Jake walked into the warehouse through the alley entrance.

"Tommy, I need to see you before you pull out," hollered Jake above the noise of Rain, Korea's answer to Justin Timberlake. The rock star's music was blasting through a stolen sound system.

The Korean "fixer" pointed toward his office and Jake made his way there as the crew finished loading the SUV.

As Jake entered the office he grabbed a Hite from the refrigerator, plopped himself in a worn leather chair, and began drinking the Korean beer. As he was staring out the window contemplating his approach, Tommy walked in.

"You wanted to see me?" said the criminal entrepreneur, grabbing a beer for himself before sitting down at his oversized desk.

Tommy flashed a counterfeit Rolex at Jake. "You want one?"

Jake smiled and slid his sleeve halfway up his arm, displaying a Rolex Oyster for Tommy to see.

"Is that real?" asked Tommy as he popped the tab on the Hite.

"Is that one?" said Jake, referring to the watch Tommy was holding.

"Nope."

"This one is," said Jake, then matter-of-factly continued, "Took it off a dead guy. He should have sold it and paid off the debt he owed my client. Said he didn't want to part with a family heirloom. He lost his life and the watch."

"Dead men don't pay very well."

"I was hired to send a message and I sent one."

Jake had gotten the watch from the undercover inventory, but he spun the tale to reinforce his credibility as a hired gun—and because he liked screwing with Tommy's head.

The Korean street thug, apparently unimpressed with Jake's watch-acquisition story, said, "I let those guys go on. They're taking the watches to some camel jockey who hopes to sucker his

Dearborn rug merchant brother-in-law. What did you need to talk about?"

There was a sense of urgency in his voice when Jake said, "I need to meet Mr. Park."

"I'm not sure I can make that happen. Why would he sit down with any white guy, especially you?"

"We've been at this for two months and you're still ticking like a cheap Timex. I need to see him and I need you to make it happen."

"Why?"

Jake took a long sip. "The 'why' isn't important. 'What' is important. If I don't meet him and people get killed, I'll make sure the word on the street lays it all on your skinny little backside."

"And that threat is supposed to make me want to help you?"

Jake offered an evil grin. "It's your memorial service if you don't make the introduction. Look, it's important I meet with him. Make it happen and I'll give you a twenty-five percent discount on your next container."

Tommy shook his head slowly and deliberately. "That's not much incentive. Park isn't the type of guy you mess with. If I make an introduction and any of this goes sideways I might just end up as man-sushi."

Jake laughed. "Sushi's Japanese."

"We all look alike to you anyway, and I'm not interested in being displayed on the Food Network as an Asian three-course meal."

Jake leaned forward to convey sincerity and lowered his voice just a bit for effect. "Think of the money you'll pocket."

"But why?"

Jake leaned back in his chair. "Look, all I'll tell you is somebody wants to shaft Park."

Tommy raised his eyebrows and threw open his hands. "So let him. Don't tell me you've grown a conscience."

"No, but I recognize if you do big favors for important people, the returns have an exponential effect."

"For a white boy who makes his living with a gun, you've got a pretty big vocabulary."

Jake smiled. "I read a lot."

"I just don't know. It seems pretty dangerous."

"You'll save money. My fees eat into your profits."

Tommy paused, maybe more for effect as well. He looked out the window and while taking a long gaze into the parking lot said, "I'll see what I can do."

"You won't regret it."

Tommy turned to Jake and now it was his turn to lean forward in his chair. "If you screw this up I won't have time to regret it. Just keep me out of it once I get it arranged."

"You've got a deal."

"And I want a fifty percent discount."

"A third," countered Jake.

Tommy nodded.

Jake threw his hand across the table and the two shook.

"I'll set it up for tomorrow," said Tommy.

CHAPTER TWENTY-NINE

Following the Maghrib, or sunset prayers, Mohammed, Rostam, and Kareem retreated to the small office in the back of the strip mall mosque. The tiny place of worship certainly wouldn't warrant inclusion in a book on the great cathedrals of North America, but it served the needs of a radical Islamist sleeper cell operating in metro Los Angeles. A single lamp, providing muted light, shrouded the room as if the demons of terrorism hovered overhead.

Rostam, Mohammed's most trusted associate, had an air of superiority and, though several inches shorter than Kareem, still managed to look down his nose at the black American convert. The Hezbollah fighter's beard was thick, his hair shoe-polish black, and he often questioned why Mohammed included the convicted felon in the terrorists' mission. Mohammed and Rostam had discussed many times the threat jihadist wannabes posed to their objective. Rostam believed the homegrown terrorists had adversely impacted the cause by alerting law enforcement authorities to the Islamist hidden agenda.

Mohammed countered that, in fact, "Jihad Jims and Janes" springing up in America's heartland helped the cause by instilling fear in a nation of sheep and distracted law enforcement authorities from the lethal work of Allah's *real* warriors. "Let them waste their dollars erecting new security walls that will be breached by our brothers."

Now, in the presence of their latest recruit, Rostam was silent about his concerns. The three men exchanged small talk about a new Islamic center being built in the Midwest before taking their seats at a scarred table that rocked whenever someone leaned on one side or the other. It annoyed Kareem, who was constantly shoving folded napkins under one leg or the other in an effort to stabilize the battered piece of furniture.

As Kareem engaged in his ritual repair, Mohammed engaged in a ritual of his own that had nothing to do with religion. He turned on the small transistor radio positioned on a nearby shelf. "All News KNX 1070" had become a constant part of every discussion in this room—not from any desire to keep up with current events, but because the IRGC had schooled Mohammed that such background noise made it more difficult for listening devices to pick up conversations.

Mohammed offered Kareem and Rostam tea and both accepted as Mohammed, acting as teacher, led the discussion about the new Islamic center. "The mega-mosques serve a purpose. There is great propaganda value in having moderate imams proclaim that jihad is simply a personal struggle against the sin and weakness in one's soul. The peace-loving leaders in these places do us no harm. They will never rise at Friday prayers to condemn the actions of men like Nidal Hasan or the martyrs who blow themselves to pieces while killing infidels."

"But these places serve as magnets for our cowardly brothers and sisters, those who think we can have sharia without bloodshed," countered Rostam.

"This is true," responded Mohammed. "But as long as one in a thousand attending prayers in these places comes to know that we will never succeed with weakness, never conquer through Da'wa, lip-service jihad, then we will raise sufficient numbers to conquer through the sword."

Rostam smiled. "Perhaps you are correct. Even their Justice Department supports the building of our mosques. You are a good teacher."

Mohammed took a sip of tea before continuing. "Americans are mindless. They refuse to drill for their own oil, seeking to protect the environment. They do not care that their petrodollars have long funded our cause."

"So when they are conquered, they will have clear skies," said Rostam, grinning.

"Inshallah," said Mohammed. *If Allah wills.*

All three laughed.

"Their days are numbered. Whoever has the sword will have the earth. Very soon the battle flag of jihad will be flying over the White House, their Stars and Stripes a mere footnote in the history books," added Rostam.

Mohammed's voice rose slightly as he leaned forward in the chair looking past the two men. "We do not have to be satisfied with mosque building. We were not sent here to 'convince' through their political system. We are here to remind the infidels that September 11, 2001, is the model, not the exception. We are here to strike fear in the hearts and minds of the infidels and rejoice when they are slain. The Prophet has told us, 'The writ of Islam will be obeyed in every country and must be pressed by force.' It is our mission to make it so when the time is right."

Rostam nodded. "All that you say is true. But to wage war we need money. Much of our funding from the Islamic charities has been cut off. We can no longer count on financial support from our friends who have been so generous in the past. The sanctions against Tehran have hurt us the most."

"You are correct, Rostam," Mohammed said with a smile. "That is why the Prophet instructed us in the holy book and the Hadith to destroy our enemies and always be alert to making new allies; new friends. And now our spiritual leaders have done so."

The cell leader had the full attention of his protégés. Rostam spoke first: "Who are our new friends?"

Mohammed waited a moment and then said, "The people of North Korea."

Kareem still said nothing, but Rostam was stunned. "How do you know this? How will the North Koreans help us with our jihad here in California?"

Mohammed cut him off. "I know this because I have received a communication from our sponsors in Beirut. They have told me that a great agreement has been forged between the Islamic Republic of Iran and the Democratic People's Republic of Korea. Included in this covenant is an arrangement for providing us with funds to carry out our mission."

"How will they do this?" asked Rostam.

"Through North Korean enterprises operating in this country," replied the teacher.

"You mean their black market in knockoff cigarettes, jeans, and watches?" Rostam was clearly uncomfortable with the idea. He leaned forward and asked quietly, "Mohammed, please tell me, how did you receive this message."

The imam cum cell leader reached into a pocket, pulled out two cheap throwaway cell phones, slid one to each of his co-conspirators, and said, "From now on we are going to use phones like these. They can be bought at Walmart for twenty-five dollars. Use only cash to buy them. Make or receive no more than five calls of less than a minute each and then smash the phone, throw it away, and get a new one. Make sure I have your new number each time you get a new phone. From now on, this is how we will communicate when we cannot meet face-to-face."

"But why must we communicate this way?" asked Rostam.

"Because," answered Mohammed, "thanks to the defector Snowden we now know how the NSA collects information. This will make it much harder for them to intercept our communications in what they call 'real time.' "

Rostam nodded and said, "How will they get the money to us?"

"I don't know the details yet. All they have told me is that it's through North Korean enterprises in this country," said Mohammed.

"And you believe them?" said Rostam. "They've told us before that money was coming and it never got here."

Finally Kareem spoke up. "I don't know about agreements with Iran, but we all know Korean businesses generate lots of cash."

Rostam's tone and expression revealed his skepticism. "How do you know what they make? Because they pay you so well at their infidel bar, shaming the word of Allah, that you are able to share your meager tips with us?"

Before Kareem could react to the insult, Mohammed intervened. "Kareem is working there at my direction. We need him there to protect our interests."

Unconvinced, Rostam stared at Kareem and asked, "And just how much money does your employer Henry Yeong make on his counterfeit goods that he would have something to spare for us?"

Kareem thought for a moment, doing the math in his head, and said, "I don't know all his overhead or exactly how many partners he has to pay off, but in addition to the cigarettes, phony-label clothing, watches, handbags, athletic shoes, and luggage, he's also moving knockoff Viagra, OxyContin, meth, and ecstasy. My guess is he grosses somewhere in the neighborhood of five million a month." Kareem paused to let the figure sink in, knowing his importance was about to increase in the eyes of Rostam and the teacher. "And if what I've learned is true we should be able to pick up a quick three million in the next few days."

Rostam choked on the tea he was sipping as he and Mohammed fixed their gaze on the recent convert.

CHAPTER THIRTY

CIA "NOC" Gabe Chong, or "Cheech" as he was known to his Marine Corps friends, stood transferring his weight from one leg to the other, occasionally leaning up against the wall. He remained focused on the activities of the others, shifting his eyes back and forth, watching all in attendance. Six young, athletic Asian males surrounded the two older men sitting at a table in the center of the room.

The occasion: an extraordinary meeting between the two most powerful Asian crime bosses in Los Angeles, Henry Yeong and Park Soon Yong. The venue: Henry Yeong's restaurant. By agreement, each "don" was accompanied by three security men. They were paired off in a circle around the table.

Gabe's sport coat was open. His weapon, a Daewoo DP51 given to him by the supervisor of Yeong's PSD, rested comfortably in a shoulder holster and was easily accessible. He wanted to give the appearance of being relaxed, so he engaged his partner from Park's detail in quiet conversation while they waited for the two principals to begin the meeting.

The hastily called dinner meeting at Yeong's restaurant had been convened by Henry Yeong—to deal with the instructions he had received from Pyongyang and the matter of Cho Hee Sun's execution. Yeong suspected Park of being behind the murder and thought it was likely perpetrated by Park's security personnel. Park, on the other hand, knew he had not called for the execution and suspected either an outside organization or an unrelated reason for Cho's death. Park ordered his men to watch Yeong's people and be on the lookout for potential intruders from the outside. There were no other patrons in the restaurant, as a sign in English and Korean greeted would-be customers with an awkward "Sorry, Closed for Private Party, Come Please Again."

Gabe watched as Candy repeatedly refilled the empty cups of the two men seated at the table, offering all her coveted smile.

It had been three days since the body of Yeong's criminal associate, Cho Hee Sun—"Sonny" to the Americans—was discovered at his Beverly Hills residence, a single gunshot to the head. Cho's brother, originally an informant for the U.S. Secret Service—and now a CIA asset—had convinced the North Korean Ministry of State Security to hire Gabe for Yeong's PSD when two members of the crime boss's security detail were arrested in Hong Kong.

Gabe had been on the job for more than a month, but other than lots of frequent-flyer miles, he had little to show for all the travel. He was providing security for an organized-crime boss but the information he was gathering was unlikely to ever be used in an American courtroom. He had collected hours of audio and video on a tiny recording device—and dutifully passed more than thirty micro-memory chips to Wilson, his "coordinator." But Gabe also knew that unless he was brought into Yeong's inner circle, he wasn't likely to accomplish his mission: "Find out everything you can about what's going on between Pyongyang and Tehran."

Gabe's bosses in Washington were excited about Yeong's visit to Kish Island and the images of the North Korean and Iranian participants he brought back. But there was precious little audio and Gabe had not been allowed inside the meetings Yeong attended.

Sonny Cho's murder threw a wrench in the works. Some at CIA headquarters in Langley who knew about the connection between Cho's brother and Gabe's job on Yeong's PSD urged that Gabe be pulled off the assignment. Others said the mission was too important a national security matter to pull him out at the first sign of trouble. Wilson left it up to Gabe.

Gabe had learned in the Marine Corps to run *to*—not *from*—the sound of gunfire. His hope was not only in situational awareness developed in combat and instilled in the training he received at the CIA's "Farm" in Virginia but the intelligence-gathering devices available to the federal government. So far Cho's murder remained a mystery . . . to the Korean criminal community, the Beverly Hills police, and Gabe's government handlers.

Though Gabe had tried to distance himself from Cho, all the members of Yeong's security team had shared beers at the bar with Cho. Some of them, Gabe included, had even dined with Sonny at the same table where Park and Yeong were now sitting. It was not unusual for the "off-duty" members of the security team to gather at the end of a long day of doing Henry Yeong's bidding to down a few cold ones and complain about management . . . criminal syndicate management. Since Candy was the perfect hostess and gorgeous, the men enjoyed spending time with her, sharing stories even if embellished, and hoping to be rewarded with her smile. Gabe concluded that nearly every member of Yeong's cadre should be equally suspect and that would ameliorate the risk of being discovered.

To his credit, Wilson pointed out the risks. "Look," he told his young charge, "there were less than two degrees of separation between you and Cho. Both of you were tasked with investigating the Supernote: you by the CIA and Cho by the Secret Service. The reports and audio files you've sent in show he was a big talker and he claimed to have dated both Park's daughter, Jenny, and that bar princess, Candy. The profile on Cho says he fancied himself to be a 'ladies' man,' though how a guy with his looks and personality could have been is beyond me."

"Yeah," said Gabe with a smile, "and his breath was rancid."

Wilson continued, "Your aud/vid recordings make it clear you were practicing good tradecraft by trying to avoid Cho, but there are several where you caught him spinning yarns and bullshitting Candy and others about the work he supposedly did for Yeong. More than once he can be seen and heard asking others about the Supernote. When I saw what you had gotten, I called Bauer at Secret Service and suggested they pull Cho in and whip him into shape. Sounds weird, but Bauer was acting as case officer for Cho and was afraid his boy might skip the country if he leaned too hard on him.

"Of course, Langley didn't want that to happen because of the link between you and Cho's brother. If Cho had split, we would have had to pull you out. Unfortunately, we don't know for sure how much Sonny told others about your connection with his brother and your getting hired on with Yeong's PSD.

"I called Langley and asked them to ping NSA for anything they can suck out of their 'music collection' from Cho's phone calls and computer files, but the hackers at Fort Meade say it will take two to three weeks to search for it."

Gabe nodded and said, "It figures. Another case of too much data."

"To the extent that there is any good news in all this, NSA is now hitting every phone number and URL we know of for both Park and Yeong and all their known associates for any live hits that mention your name."

"In real time or delay?"

Wilson reflected a moment, then said, "The FISA order says real time because your life is at risk. But you and I know that means hours at best—not minutes—and it's usually seconds that really matter. You want to stay in or we can pull you. It's your call."

The young CIA Clandestine Service officer reflected on what Wilson said. Gabe had observed Cho's sleuthing tactics to be less than perfect and twice warned the Korean gangster to work the silence. Finally, he considered that everyone knew Sonny Cho truly enjoyed hearing himself talk and that anyone who cared would conclude Cho's big mouth had somehow gotten him killed. After reflecting for a few moments on what Wilson had told him and what he already knew, Gabe said, "I'll stay in."

Though they weren't participants in the discussion at the table, Gabe and Li from Park's security detail could easily hear all that was being said by the two crime bosses. Gabe hoped his miniature recording device was capturing the audio and video of this unprecedented meeting. What the tiny lens couldn't catch were the security personnel of both participants posted outside at the front and back doors.

Every U.S. agency involved in this operation knew that unlike the Italian Mafia, there is no "commission" overseeing Korean organized crime in Los Angeles. Yeong and Park called the shots in Southern California. But only Gabe and a handful of others knew both men had been sent to Los Angeles by the North Korean regime, relying on Pyongyang's criminal empire to furnish the contraband being distributed in L.A. and throughout the United States.

Depending upon their respective overseas contacts, they could get a long list of contraband products from a variety of sources in North Korea, China, Russia, Indonesia, Mexico, Latin America, and Southwest Asia. Both the Park and Yeong organizations had networks of "shoppers" scouring a global underground marketplace for everything from sophisticated phony pharmaceuticals to the counterfeit Rolex watches Tommy Hwan was distributing.

The two crime bosses had vied for the lucrative privilege of distributing Supernotes in the Americas. By listening carefully to the conversation, Gabe discerned Office 39 in Pyongyang made the decision: Park would have exclusive rights for distribution in the United States and Mexico. Yeong was now the sole distributor in the Middle East, Africa, and Asia—but not China or South Korea. Others, apparently unknown to Park, Yeong, or U.S. authorities, were given distribution rights in Europe and Latin America.

"We have had our differences," said Park.

"We have," replied Yeong.

"But I had no reason to kill Cho. He served you, not me. He never betrayed me nor have we engaged in any type of business venture."

"He dated your daughter," said Yeong.

"Briefly, after her husband's death, but Jenny had no interest in him. He offered little to her and she moved on to others."

"So I have heard," said Yeong, a little too quickly.

"Do you want to explain that comment?" asked Park, a hint of anger in his voice.

"I didn't say that to offend you. I only know Jenny has dated others."

Park seemed somewhat satisfied with the answer and continued. "I don't wish to speak ill of the dead. Cho had some success in business but was a weak man who constantly demanded reassurance of his manhood. He was much too needy for my daughter, demanding to have his ego constantly stroked."

Yeong thought briefly, then nodded. "Maybe you are right."

"He also talked too much." Park flapped his fingers as if imitating lips moving.

Yeong nodded and took a long sip of his tea. "By that do you mean you suspect he was speaking to the police?"

"What do you think? He knew few of my secrets and could discuss my work only in generalities. He could, however, tell them of your activities in more detail," said Park.

"But do you suspect him of being an informant?"

"I spent little time with the man but I must say a man who likes to talk often seeks a listening ear. If the police or FBI offered that listening ear he might have spoken at length."

Yeong put the teacup down and looked out toward the street, his mind questioning whether his business associate would have revealed secrets to the authorities. It never occurred to him Cho could be an informant. Fear washed over him as he reflected on all the crimes he committed or discussed in Cho's presence that would be of interest to the authorities.

"Did he have enemies?" asked Park, changing the direction of the inquiry.

Henry Yeong turned toward Park and shrugged, throwing open his hands. "We all have enemies but I know of none who would wish him dead. There may have been men who would like to see him fail in business but that doesn't call for his murder."

"Possibly he cheated someone in the past who was now seeking retribution." Then Park smiled, knowing Cho was heavily engaged in several of Yeong's criminal enterprises. "He spent time in prison. Could the Americans have recruited him while he was locked up?"

Yeong understood the smile, tugged at his collar, and replied, "Perhaps."

"Was he working on any special projects for you?"

Now Yeong smiled. "Those 'special projects' as you call them do not concern you."

"Then I think we have nothing further to discuss. I can assure you I had nothing to do with his death. I'm sorry for your loss," said Park.

Yeong waved the back of his hand, as if saying Cho's death was not that important. "My concern is not his death but our survival. We have both received orders from those who dispatched us here many years ago from our home country. The message I received said we are to cooperate in the distribution of certain currency."

Park simply nodded.

"The courier also said we will be informed in the next few days about other matters in which we are to cooperate."

Park nodded again and said, "Yes, that is so. But I suspect you already know something of these other matters since you went to the meeting at Kish Island."

"How do you know I went to Kish?" asked Yeong.

"I have my sources."

"Well," Yeong continued, "I do not know all that was decided in Pyongyang after the meeting at Kish, so we should await the new instructions. But until then, I wanted to make sure you and I are not at odds or that somehow you blamed me for an indiscretion and took it out on my associate. I did not want to see a war between friends because of a misunderstanding."

"We are fine."

"Good. Los Angeles is a large city. There is much we can accomplish without stepping on each other's toes. I would hope if we have concerns we can bring them to each other over a cup of tea rather than an assassin's bullet," said Yeong.

Park held up his cup and smiled. "I would prefer doing this over a glass of *soju*."

Gabe watched as the two men rose and bowed. What he had just witnessed was a treasure trove of intelligence that went far beyond Cho's unresolved murder. The young clandestine officer did his best to conceal his excitement but knew he couldn't just run out of the restaurant and report to Wilson.

What he didn't see or hear was the call Candy made on her cell phone from the kitchen, nor did he know . . . Kareem answered on the second ring.

CHAPTER THIRTY-ONE

As Park's people cleared the room, there was a collective inaudible sigh of relief the meeting had ended without incident. Gabe tracked them out the door and watched as Park and his security team entered a dark GMC Yukon parked on the street.

The CIA operative walked back into the restaurant, where Yeong was talking quietly with the other two members of his three-man security detail. Concern still covered Yeong's face.

"Were you satisfied with his answers?" asked Gabe in Korean as he approached Yeong.

"I'm not certain. Did Cho ever strike you as the type of man who would cooperate with the police?"

"No. I thought of him as a loyal soldier," said Gabe.

"I do not understand why Park would have suggested otherwise," said Yeong, shaking his head.

Gabe knew the real answer. Few living in Beverly Hills were willing to trade a luxurious lifestyle for a crowded cell and prison cuisine. The thought of being sent back to a minimum-security lockup was enough to turn Cho into an informant and spill all he knew about his closest associates.

"You knew him best and you're a wise judge of character. Did you ever see a flaw in this man's core?" asked Gabe, knowing the irony since an undercover government operative was asking the question.

"I never saw any such flaw, but I wonder if Park did and had Cho killed to prevent a problem in the future?"

"Wouldn't he have told us tonight if that were so?" asked Gabe.

"No, I don't think he would and he certainly hasn't reassured me of his innocence in this matter," said Yeong.

"So why Cho was murdered is still a mystery?"

"Yes, it is."

Gabe saw an opportunity to get out of the restaurant and deliver the information he collected. "Do you want me to see what more I can find out from Li, the guy on Park's security detail I was standing next to during the meeting? He and I did the advance before everyone else arrived. I got to know him. His family and mine are from the same Pyongyang neighborhood."

Henry Yeong thought for a long moment before answering. "I don't think that's wise. We'll leave it for the police. I've asked on the street and haven't found any satisfactory answers, but further inquiry might lead the police back to me."

"Then we'll abide by your decision."

Candy approached as Yeong and Gabe completed their exchange. "If nothing else I go home unless you want me lock up."

"No, Candy, we are fine. I will have Gabe close up. Thank you for being here tonight. You can go now."

She bowed and before departing rewarded the CIA operative with one of her sought-after smiles.

Turning to Gabe, Yeong said, "You seem anxious to leave. Were you planning to accompany her?"

"No, sir," said Gabe, perhaps too quickly, for he really was hoping to get off duty and report to Wilson.

"You don't mind closing up, do you?"

"Of course not," said Gabe, reconciled to a delay in delivering the explosive information he had just obtained. *At least this will give me a chance to "bag" Yeong's lair for more intelligence after they leave.*

"Make sure you turn off the lights in my office upstairs," said Yeong.

"Yes, of course," Gabe replied with new respect for the North Korean agent's powers of perception. To reassure Yeong he had nothing else to do tonight, Gabe hastily added, "I haven't had anything to eat since breakfast. Would it be okay if I made something before locking up?"

"Certainly, just clean up your mess," said Yeong in English.

In Korean Gabe responded, "Now you sound like my mother," bringing a laugh from everyone.

CHAPTER THIRTY-TWO

When Henry Yeong and his two bodyguards left the restaurant by the alley entrance, Gabe was immediately conflicted. The information he already had in his head and hopefully recorded on the hidden device was of vital importance, but there might be even more here in Yeong's criminal compound. He hesitated not because he lacked a search warrant; he simply wanted to ensure he could safely and quickly maneuver inside the building. Constitutional niceties were someone else's concern. He was a spy, not a cop, and he didn't have the time to determine if he was pushing the needle of a moral compass a few degrees off true north. He was, after all, gathering intelligence, seeking information about activities that posed a risk to U.S. security, not preparing a case for prosecution.

Gabe's fear was getting caught and having to explain to Yeong or one of his thugs why he was snooping around the premises. To provide added security he locked the back door before heading to the dining room.

Gabe placated his desire to get to Wilson by telling himself Yeong's order to close up the place alone was a degree of confidence in Gabe's loyalty not previously acknowledged. If Henry Yeong suspected Gabe of working for the government or involvement in Cho's death, the Korean crime boss would never have allowed him unfettered access to the business. Gabe knew nothing more about Sonny's death than the others and was increasingly confident he had not been tainted by whatever suspicions the Koreans had about Cho.

In that, Gabe was dead wrong.

During many visits to the restaurant, the undercover CIA officer had repeatedly looked for security devices, cameras, or other such surveillance. He'd found none. And since he previously accompanied others on the closing procedures Gabe was familiar with the duties, even to the point of knowing how to set the alarm near the back door. He double-bolted the front door, lowered the shades, and turned out the lights in the dining area.

Before heading to the kitchen he did a hasty perusal of the hostess stand, opening the drawers and giving a quick read of a tattered reservation book. Nothing stood out as being of value or even mildly informative. Most of the notations were written in Korean, and since he was fluent it didn't create a problem once he was able to decipher the sloppy handwriting. The restaurant enjoyed minimal success and served more as a cover for Yeong's criminal activities. He could survive an IRS audit, but his lifestyle wasn't based solely on the income from those in the neighborhood seeking a Korean food fix.

This was Gabe's first time alone in the restaurant and he assumed any information of value was in Yeong's office upstairs, even though the man spent little time there. Figuring the crime boss would conceal evidence of his criminal activities where he felt most comfortable, Gabe wanted to concentrate his efforts in the upstairs room where Yeong had delivered the two kilograms of methamphetamines to Jake two days earlier.

Though the small office didn't appear to be a place where a ton of secrets were likely to be stored, Gabe didn't want to miss the chance to surreptitiously explore. He hoped the walls might have hidden compartments holding the intelligence nuggets he was hoping to gather. After a search of Yeong's desk he would begin examining the office walls, floor, and ceiling.

As he headed up the stairs to do a hasty search of Yeong's office, there was a loud banging at the back door. Gabe jumped as his stomach took a quick somersault. He assumed it was one of the homeless who frequented the alley asking for handouts as the evening crowd waned. He hoped the nighttime solicitor would move on.

There was a brief pause in the heavy knocking before it started again. This time it was accompanied by someone calling his name, "Gabe."

He didn't recognize the male voice and Gabe moved closer to the door.

"Gabe!" More banging.

"Yeah, what do you want?" said Gabe in a commanding voice, irritated his search had been interrupted before it even began.

"Gabe, open up. I need your help."

When Gabe relented and opened the door, Kareem was standing there with a heavy-duty lug nut wrench in his right hand.

Gabe nodded from behind the closed screen door. "Yeah."

"Sorry to bother you, man. I just saw Yeong leave and he said to ask you for help. My battery is dead and I need a jump."

"Why are you here?"

"I was partying down the street and parked in the alley. I guess I left my lights on," said the bartender with enough sincerity to be believed.

"Yeah, I can help you," said Gabe with some reluctance. "Do you have jumper cables?"

"Yeah, I got a pair."

"What's with the wrench?"

"Hey, it's dangerous out here. I don't have a gat but thought if some homeless dude wanted my wallet this provided the answer." Kareem waved the wrench like a weapon.

"Where are you parked?"

"On the other side of the alley."

Gabe opened the screen door and stepped out into the alley. As they crossed toward the car, Kareem imperceptibly fell behind a step and before Gabe realized it the wrench came crashing down across the top of his head. He collapsed immediately, blood streaming from a large gash.

Kareem wasn't interested in sparing Gabe further injury, quickly dragging him behind the Honda Pilot and then opening the hatch. Before throwing Gabe's limp body into the back, Kareem wrapped the CIA operative's hands and feet with duct tape, taped his mouth, and covered the rear cargo area with blankets to soak up the blood still flowing from the head wound.

Grabbing the hose used to wash out the trash bins, Kareem flooded the immediate area and watched the fresh blood in the alley flow down the drain. He laid the hose on the ground, allowing the water to continue running, and raced to the rear door of the restaurant, where he turned off the lights, set the alarm, and locked the door.

With the alley clean, at least of Gabe's blood, Kareem shut off the hose, got into the Honda, and drove less than a mile to his next destination.

CHAPTER THIRTY-THREE

"Gabe," said Candy softly into his ear. "Please, Gabe, wake up," as she gently stroked his face and continued her pleas.

Gabe began to stir. Through blurred vision, he focused on a comforting Candy standing in front of him.

"Gabe, I so glad you awake. I worry about you. I care for you."

"What's going on?" mumbled Gabe as he slowly realized he was restrained to a metal chair bolted to the greasy concrete floor of a run-down garage. He had no way of knowing he was less than eight blocks from the restaurant where he'd been bludgeoned unconscious.

"You must whisper. I no want Kareem to know I here."

"Where are we? What's going on?" asked Gabe as he struggled to loosen the duct tape securing his arms.

"Kareem think you bad. I no want to see you hurt. Please tell him everything."

"What are you talking about?"

"Please, Gabe, you must tell Kareem the truth. Only then will he let you live. Kareem bad person. I no want to see you hurt. We could be friends."

"Where am I?"

"Kareem is in the other room. He would hurt me if he know I try to help you. Gabe, please tell him."

"Tell him what?"

"Tell him who you work for. I no want to see you hurt." Her eyes were begging and she rewarded him with a tender smile. "I know I can help you if you tell truth. Kareem listen to me. He know I like you. He would not hurt my friend but you must tell truth."

"Help me get these off," said Gabe, continuing to fight at the restraints.

"I cannot. He hurt me if he catch me helping you. You must tell him who you work for, then he let us both go."

"I work for Yeong. You know that," said Gabe, confused by the inquiry.

"He think you work for Cho and he know Cho work for police," whispered Candy, looking over Gabe's shoulder trying to determine if her presence at the auto repair facility in the aging industrial complex had been detected.

"What?"

"Cho tell me one night he work for police."

"He did what? Why would he tell you that?"

"He think it make him important in my eyes. He always trying to impress me by who he know. He say he can help my brother in prison because he work for police."

Gabe fought against the duct tape wrapped around his arms and legs but was unable to free himself. "Get a knife and cut me loose."

"I afraid Kareem catch me. Only way for you to go free is to tell Kareem who you work for. He only want truth. Once you tell him he let you go."

"I work for Yeong. Tell Kareem that's the truth."

"Cho tell me you work with him and you both could help me if I told about Supernotes."

Gabe hesitated with a response. He'd been betrayed by the Secret Service informant and his fate seemed settled unless he could escape.

"I see you talk much in corner. If you tell Kareem truth he forgive you. He very forgiving man. His religion require he forgive if you tell truth. Please tell him, then Kareem let you go and we could be friends. I always like you. You good person, not like Cho."

"Help me get out of here and I'll tell you everything."

"Please tell truth. I want us to be happy. I want us to be together but it not happen if Kareem mad. He would chase us down until you tell truth. Tell him and we can go away unhurt," begged the young female with a beautiful smile.

"Get me a knife and we can both get out of here. I'll protect you. I promise."

The silence hung between them. Then the long moment was broken by Mohammed's shout. "Enough! It's not working."

Mohammed and Kareem entered from the shadows as Candy stepped back, failing in her attempt to deceive the undercover operative.

From his back pocket, Mohammed grabbed a thick black glove, the fingers lined with lead. He slipped it on to his right hand and backhanded Gabe, the loud crack of lead on bone being drowned out by Gabe's wail.

Kareem, no stranger to blood and pain, looked around the garage as if questioning whether others heard the cry, but calmed remembering the industrial complex was empty at this hour.

"Who do you work for?" asked Mohammed.

Gabe looked at him with pained incredulity, then toward Kareem. "You know who I work for."

This time a backhand from the left side. "Who do you work for?"

"I work for Mr. Yeong."

"Liar," said Mohammed, repeating the backhand.

"I work for Mr. Yeong."

"Who did Cho work for?" bellowed Mohammed.

Gabe was now struggling to simply survive the attack. "He worked *with* Mr. Yeong," he mumbled through the blood gushing from a broken nose and smashed lips.

Mohammed threw a powerful right hand to the base of the rib cage. "Who else?"

It took Gabe a few moments to catch his breath. "I didn't know he worked for anybody else until she just told me. I sure as hell didn't know he worked for the cops. I would have killed him if I knew he was ratting us out," said Gabe.

"Why is your English so good?" said Mohammed.

Through the bruising, the blood, and the pain, Gabe offered a limp smile. "Good teachers."

Mohammed slapped him hard and repeated the question.

"I grew up here. I went to school in Northern California," said Gabe, spitting blood as he turned his head from left to right.

"But you came here with Yeong when he returned from a trip to Hong Kong and North Korea," said Kareem.

"Yeah, so what? My father was from North Korea. He came here just before I was born, working for a unified Korean trade delegation. I still have family in North Korea. Even though I'm a U.S. citizen I got a Korean visa through them." Gabe wasn't sure they would buy the legend the CIA created, but if they stopped beating him long enough to do an Internet search of immigration regulations and a government records check, it would back up his story.

Kareem, Candy, and Mohammed looked at each other, not sure whether to accept the explanation of the tortured man.

"Why did you return to North Korea?" asked Mohammed.

"After my father died I was allowed to return. I visited our family and found work there."

"What kind of work?" asked Kareem.

"I worked for the government."

"The North Korean government?" asked Mohammed.

"Yeah, what other government operates in North Korea?" said Gabe with an attitude that cost him another sharp backhand across the face.

"How do you know Cho?" barked Mohammed.

Gabe returned to his cover story. "I know Cho's brother. He lives outside of Pyongyang but he does a lot of business in Hong Kong. He was in Hong Kong when some of Mr. Yeong's security men were arrested by the Hong Kong police. He called me up in Pyongyang and asked if I wanted the job. I flew to Hong Kong and joined Mr. Yeong's security team."

"I didn't think anyone could leave North Korea?" asked Kareem in an almost civil tone.

"Sure you can, as long as the right people in the government approve."

"Why would the North Korean government allow you to leave?" asked Mohammed with genuine curiosity, standing in front of Gabe, poised to strike again.

"Why do you think?"

Mohammed backhanded Gabe. An evil smile crossed Candy's face.

"Okay, okay. The North Korean government wanted me here. They wanted me to watch Yeong, to protect him. They sent me."

Kareem looked at Mohammed. "What do you think?"

"I'm not buying it," said the cell leader.

Gabe protested. "It's the truth. You didn't have to beat me to learn this. You only had to ask. Check it out."

Candy cocked her head. "He's lying."

Mohammed threw a backhanded slap, snapping Gabe's head to the left, then grabbed him by the hair and whipped Gabe's head back. "Cho never told you he was working for the police?"

Blood from his battered nose and mouth was filling his throat faster than he could swallow it, but Gabe managed to gurgle, "Never. I would have killed him. I was sent here by the North Korean government."

"Maybe he didn't know. Maybe Cho made up the story," said Kareem.

"He know. He working with Cho," said Candy.

"You're crazy," said Gabe defiantly, earning him another backhanded strike to his face, which was now swelling and bleeding profusely.

"Maybe he's telling the truth," said Kareem, questioning whether they might have misread Gabe's role.

"He's lying," said Mohammed.

"How can you be sure?" asked Kareem.

"It no matter. We can't take chances," said Candy, excited by the blood.

"Doesn't matter?" said Gabe, spitting blood. "You are beating me for no reason."

Mohammed had psychopathic skills and prepared to exercise them again. He grabbed the little finger on Gabe's right hand and twisted it back, wrenching it out of the socket, ripping muscle and tendons.

Gabe screamed, gasping for relief before shouting, "I'm telling the truth."

The jihadist repeated the performance with the ring finger.

Again more screams and denials.

Mohammed grabbed the lug nut wrench and stood next to Gabe, waiting for answers. When no response was forthcoming the terrorist wiggled the wrench as if waiting for a waist-high fastball. With a powerful two-handed swing he crushed the undercover operative's right kneecap, the bones splintering.

Gabe cried out, fighting the pain surging through his body.

Candy, wired by the carnage, said, "Make him talk."

"You'll tell us the truth," whispered Mohammed. The Iranian-trained jihadi picked up a single-edge razor blade from the workbench. He then sliced away at Gabe's pants, exposing his left thigh.

"What do you want?" screamed Gabe as Mohammed held the razor in front of the captive's face.

Gabe knew in that instant he was straddling death at the hands of a jihadist—just as Navy diver Robert Stethem had been in Beirut, aboard TWA 847. Even in his agony, Gabe remembered the hidden micro-recorder was documenting this terrible ordeal and he resolved in that instant to get the maximum information from the man who was killing him. "What do you want from me?" he managed to say through a mouthful of blood, broken teeth, and a fractured jaw.

"I want the truth about what you know of the nuclear weapons arrangement between Iran and North Korea," said Mohammed, his face pressed near to Gabe's ear.

"Nothing. I don't know what you are talking about," gurgled Gabe.

"Then die, infidel," said Mohammed as he used the razor to slice deep into Gabe's exposed thigh. There was a gush of blood as the femoral artery was severed.

"Tell me what you know and you live," breathed Mohammed in Gabe's left ear, waving a tourniquet and bandages in the CIA operative's face.

Though Gabe's resolve remained strong, his body was rapidly failing as the hemorrhage from the gash in his thigh compounded the effects of the wounds he had already endured. He sucked in a breath and said a quiet prayer, the bruises, cuts, and broken bones bearing testimony to the savagery.

In his last moment he looked up into the muzzle of Candy's .45-caliber M1911A1 just as she pulled the trigger. His lifeless body slumped in the chair, only the duct tape preventing him from collapsing to the floor.

The three conspirators who had watched the young American die never bothered to question the success or failure of their mission. Two potential obstacles—real or imagined—Cho and Gabe, had been removed from their calculus.

There was little left to do. Kareem picked up the spent shell casing and, after a quick cleanup of the garage, Candy headed home. In their haste to prepare for Isha, the last of the daily prayers, the two jihadists dumped Gabe's body in a nearby alley in hopes it would look like another random street crime, a common occurrence in Los Angeles.

When the beat cop found the body, he assumed it was that of a foreign tourist, murdered for a wallet. The pockets were empty. There was no ID, passport, or driver's license.

The subsequent electronic report from the L.A. County medical examiner's office included a dental imprint and morgue photos of the "unidentified male victim" and close-up images of an "Eagle, Globe, and Anchor" tattoo above the words "Semper Fi" on the right bicep of the deceased. Only later would the CIA's Office of Personnel Management realize Gabe had answered "no" on question 143 of the hiring application: "Do you have any identifying marks, scars, or tattoos?"

There was also a notation about the victim's personal effects and clothing being held for next of kin:

"One pair, New Balance athletic shoes, size 10 C [blood spattered]; one pair, white cotton sport socks w/o label [blood spattered]; one Jockey label boxer underwear, size 28; one North Face label, size 28 x 33, dark green trousers [damaged and blood spattered]; one Kirkland label, size large, dark blue polo shirt [bloodstained]; one Casio label wristwatch w/ dark green, nylon wristband [bloodstained]; one hand-stitched leather belt w/o label, w/ faux-brass buckle, size 28–32."

CHAPTER THIRTY-FOUR

DAY 6

SATURDAY, MAY 3

Jake had been looking forward to this meeting all morning. He hopped out of the car and handed the keys to the parking valet. He was immediately struck by the warm breeze blowing in from the ocean. He loved the Malibu heat. Two hours earlier, when he met with Henry Yeong and Tommy to discuss an exclusive use of his services, there was a chill in the air. Now as it was nearing noon, the famous California sunshine had turned it into a beautiful day.

Jake pocketed the claim check, questioning whether anyone ever read the fine print, and headed into Gladstone's, a beachfront restaurant favorite.

Two couples were ahead of him as he made his way to the hostess stand. He waited patiently to give his name but as he scanned the outdoor patio he spotted her. He jumped out of line and strode toward the wooden plank table near the back of the patio. She stood and the two embraced. At eight months pregnant it wasn't quite as easy to get his arms around her.

"I'm glad you were able to make it. I can never count on your schedule—too many criminal variables," she said.

Using a very poor French accent, Jake said, "Quiet, don't blow my cover. The Bureau thinks I'm meeting some hooker named Natasha working for a Mob-run escort service."

"Jake!"

"No, my name is Pierre and I am businessman from Paris garment district. You are Natasha. I told madam running operation I like big Russian women."

"You are impossible," she said, hitting him playfully as they both took a seat.

As the two began to peruse the menu, Jake said, "I know you have this craving for seafood but wouldn't you be satisfied with Long John Silver's? I think I have a coupon in the car."

"You don't think I'm Gladstone's worthy?"

"Oh, you are worth the French Riviera. It's just that I can afford fast-food fish and chips, not the market price for the Iced Seafood Tower."

"You don't even know what the market price is. Maybe you can afford it."

"Trust me. I've eaten here before. I can't afford their market price anything."

A bleached-blond college-age server, who was probably wasting his daddy's savings on a higher education at UCLA or Pepperdine, came to the table dressed in a blue logo T-shirt, white trousers, and the Gladstone's blue apron. "Can I get you something to drink?"

"We'll both take iced tea," said Jake.

"I better not have caffeine," she said. "Do you have any decaf tea?"

The server shook his head.

"Then just bring her water with lemon," said Jake.

"You got it, dude."

When the server left, Jake, shaking his head in disgust and

employing his weak French accent, asked, "So, Natasha, dude, how are you feeling?"

She smiled. "I'm great. A little tired. I slept until almost nine this morning. I had to hustle to make the doctor's appointment, but she said everything looks fine and I'm right on schedule, maybe even a little ahead."

"You think junior might punch out early?"

Offering a smile, she said, "I'm ready if he is. He's got to be a lot like his dad."

There was an awkward silence, neither quite knowing what to say, as they both looked out toward the ocean pretending to breathe in the salt air.

"How's your week been going?" she asked.

"You know, same ole, same ole. Set up a contract killing, scored some meth from members of an ethnic minority group, and wasted a breakfast meeting this morning on two mopes who will be eating prison food soon. Just risking it all to keep the world safe from democracy," said Jake with a mischievous grin.

"*For* democracy, not *from* democracy," she said, shaking her head.

"Whatever. Have you decided what you want?"

"I'll take a cup of clam chowder . . ."

"I can afford soup, good choice . . ."

"And the Niçoise blue crab salad."

Jake gave her a look.

"Pierre, I'm eating for two."

Just then the surfer dude brought the iced tea and water with lemon. Jake ordered . . . the crab salad and soup for her, just the soup for him. He didn't have a coupon!

CHAPTER THIRTY-FIVE

The sun was beginning to set but the day's warmth refused to wane as the shadows lengthened. As promised, Tommy arranged for a "meet and greet" with Park Soon Yong.

Jake followed Tommy's black Lexus LS F Sport through the tree-lined streets of San Marino, an exclusive community near Pasadena, part of "greater" Los Angeles. Occupying an area less than four square miles, some thirteen thousand people called the city home. Over half those residents were of Asian descent. Even in a residential market downturn, the typical San Marino home carried a $2-million-plus price tag. Large lots and massive structures were the norm; upscale and expansive, just the type government employees like Jake could never afford.

Yet he was savoring the moment. Here was a lawman, listening to a CD of Peyton Tochterman singing "God and Country"—a song about Red Roundtree, America's oldest bank robber—while trailing a Korean mobster driving a luxury car built in a country that once enslaved his own ancestors, on the way to a mansion occupied by an agent of a government committed to bringing down all these trappings of "bourgeois capitalism."

It just doesn't get any more surreal than this! Jake said to himself. But then it did.

As the two cars approached the destination address, a dark 2013 BMW 640i Gran Coupe was leaving the residence. Through the lightly tinted windows, Jake thought the driver appeared to be Middle Eastern, perhaps Mexican or Latin American—but certainly not Asian. Jake did a quick head turn as the car passed, catching the license plate. Grabbing a pen from the glove compartment, he scribbled the numbers on a piece of scrap paper.

Jake followed Tommy to the driveway, where they were greeted by ten-foot beige stucco walls, a large black steel gate, and enough surveillance cameras to give Fort Knox a sense of inadequacy. At the entrance a security device was mounted on an arm extending over the yellow brick paving stones. Tommy punched some numbers into the keypad and Jake, his window down, could hear the device calling a phone. Like a drive-thru call box at a fast-food restaurant, a voice came over the speaker.

"Good afternoon," answered a female voice.

"It's Tommy Hwan. My friend in the car behind me and I are here to see Mr. Park. He's expecting us."

Within seconds the giant gate opened and the cars slowly entered. Jake wasn't sure what to expect and wondered if he was about to be ambushed by a North Korean hit squad.

The long, winding driveway bisected a well-kept botanical garden and perfectly manicured lawn. The U-shaped home had a five-car garage on the north end of the drive. The garage was connected to the house by an enclosed walkway. Pyongyang's answer to Al Capone lived in opulence.

"Sin pays," said Jake as he exited his car.

"I'd downplay your cute little witticisms if I were you. Show some respect. Mr. Park is an important man and not one who will take pleasure in your Western comedy."

"Witticisms? Now who's using big words? I'll try to contain my comic alter ego."

He watched Tommy punch the doorbell and a melodious tune could be heard through the large oak door. Patience was not one of Jake's virtues and the wait seemed longer than normal. He was hoping the crime boss wasn't racking a round in the chamber of a high-powered automatic. He wanted to pound on the door, but knowing the importance of the man on the other side, he stepped away from the portal and "bladed" himself, trying to become a thinner target should bullets start flying.

Tommy gave Jake a questioning look as if to say, "Should I ring the bell again?" But before he could open his mouth a twenty-something female opened the massive door. Though she wasn't stunning, her almond eyes were accentuated by shoulder-length black hair and a perfect porcelain complexion.

"Hi, Tommy," said the female with a beautiful smile.

Tommy gave her an extended hug and she returned the embrace, looking over his shoulder, and with that same smile eyed Jake. Then Tommy introduced the undercover agent to Jenny, H. Daniel Reid's former love interest and the target of Jake's fictional assassination attempt. *There's no accounting for bad taste. Why would a girl living in such luxury be attracted to some aging barrister just because he belches big bucks?*

Jake and Tommy stood in the entryway and watched Jenny as she casually walked down a long hallway to an open door.

"Father, Tommy and his guest have arrived."

Jake heard a voice say, "Show them in."

Jenny returned and ushered the men toward the hallway. An older female and young girl walked out from the kitchen as the men passed. Tommy stopped and in Korean greeted the woman. She smiled and bowed. Tommy turned to Jake. "This is Soo Min, Mr. Park's wife. And this is Gracie, their granddaughter."

"I'm Jake. How do you do?"

Soo Min smiled and bowed without speaking. Gracie bowed and held up four fingers. "I'm four. How old are you?"

Jake smiled. "A little older than that."

Jenny continued to lead the men down the hallway to the study.

Jake was hardly surprised when he entered Park's office. Everything this man did was beyond excess. The marble floor and oak-paneled walls shouted wealth. His large antique desk was situated to overlook the Olympic-size swimming pool in the backyard, the water cascading down a man-made falls.

The criminal kingpin was sitting in a high-back brown leather chair and Jake quickly spotted two Asian males posted in opposite corners at the far end of the room, quietly standing guard. He saw the bulges beneath their matching dark green Tommy Bahama shirts and assumed the two were well armed. There was a strange familiarity with the smaller of the two men; his manner, his eyes. Jake couldn't quite place it but it was unsettling. He needed to focus but the nagging question persisted.

Tommy strode to Park and bowed. "Mr. Park, thank you for seeing us. Allow me to introduce my friend, Jake. He is the one who has been assisting us in our business."

Park nodded toward the security guards, then said to Jake, "You will understand if my men perform a cursory search."

Jake smiled, lifted his shirt, and turned around slowly, displaying the Glock 19 resting in the small of his back. "With your permission I'll remove it. I have no intention of using it but understand your reluctance to discuss business with an armed man." Using two fingers, Jake carefully withdrew the semi-automatic and laid it on a nearby dark walnut antique Korean medicine chest.

Anger and embarrassment flashed across Tommy's face; he had been unaware Jake was armed. "Sir, I can assure you I had no idea this man brought a weapon into your home."

Park waved him off. "He is a careful man. It is okay. Should he have chosen to use the weapon he would not have left alive." Smiling, Park spoke in Korean to the larger of the guards. The man stepped forward, picked up the firearm, deftly dropped the magazine into his palm, set it on the chest, cleared the 9mm round out of the chamber, and placed the empty weapon beside it. As the big man returned to his post along the wall, he slid the round into his pocket.

Jake was unapologetic. "I didn't mean to dishonor you by bringing a weapon into your residence. I have enemies who might strike at any time . . . so when we leave, I would like to have the bullet your man removed from my pistol. I may need it."

"No offense is taken. I understand. And of course you may have your bullet . . . when you leave."

The preemptive strike of revealing the weapon prevented a pat-down, which might have uncovered the recording device. He might not have been armed during the conversation, but it was being preserved for posterity.

"Tommy has told me a great deal about you," said Park.

Jake smiled. "He has told me little about you but I am aware of your importance in the community."

Before the conversation expanded into the area Jake wanted to explore, Gracie, the little girl, now dressed as a ballerina, came dancing into the office performing a make-believe ballet for her grandfather.

As she completed her performance, she curtsied. Her grandfather applauded wildly. "Gracie, that was beautiful. You are a most excellent dancer."

Soo Min and Tommy applauded as well and Jake reluctantly joined in with what could only be described as mild enthusiasm.

Gracie floated over to Jake, a Caucasian giant to this diminutive four-year-old. "I'm going to be a ballerina. Will you dance with me?"

Before agreeing, Jake looked toward Park for permission. He wasn't quite sure what was proper protocol and typically didn't care. He was portraying a crook, not a diplomat, but asking permission seemed like the right thing to do. Gracie saw him seeking approval. She turned toward her grandfather and with the eyes of youthful innocence asked, "Papa, can he dance with me?"

Park smiled, pleased the visitor had sought permission. He nodded in agreement toward Jake.

Gracie let out a faint squeal and grabbed Jake's hand. For the next several minutes the two danced around the floor, the now-uninhibited undercover agent and the crime lord's granddaughter. The tough-guy persona was buried for the length of an imaginary song.

Tommy seemed to enjoy the scene almost as much as Mr. Park, only Tommy's reactions lacked the sincerity of the crime boss. Tommy loved seeing the round-eye making a fool of himself.

As the youthful ballerina extended the dance beyond an imaginary song or two, it became apparent the performance was as much an excuse to avoid bedtime as to entertain her grandfather. After a few too many sashays around the spacious office, Soo Min looked to her husband. "It is time for bed."

Park then gave the order to Gracie. "It is time for you to go to your bedroom. Jake and Tommy and I have business to discuss."

Gracie agreed without an argument. She bowed to Jake and when he kneeled down, the young ballerina gave him a huge four-year-old hug. She then ran over to her grandfather and gave him a hug and a kiss.

Soo Min and Gracie walked down the hallway, hand in hand, the younger swaying to another imaginary song. Gracie kept turning around, waving to Jake with her free hand.

"My granddaughter likes the tall American."

Jake smiled, a genuine smile. "I think your granddaughter is pretty special."

Park instructed one of his security guards to close the door, but before he could, Jenny brought in a tray with three cups and a steaming pot. "Father, may I offer you and your guests some tea?"

"Yes, of course. Though I suspect my guests might want something stronger than tea," said Park.

Jenny provided an impish grin. "Do I need to remind you what the doctor said?"

"Tea is fine, Mr. Park," said Jake as Jenny poured the tea and offered cups to her father, Jake, and Tommy, but not the two security men.

"I understand you were able to assist with a container of valuable watches that arrived the other day," said Park.

Jake nodded.

"That is good," said Park. "And I understand we have another container arriving soon."

"Yes," said Tommy.

"And you are helping us get that container past the customs officials in San Diego." It was a statement, maybe even an order, rather than a question.

Jake smiled. "That's what I do."

With his daughter still in the room, Park continued the conversation, inquiring more into Jake's background. The undercover agent provided the basic legend he invented detailing his investments. He downplayed his criminal history, as most crooks would in any initial meeting. Jake had been at this long enough to know how much to reveal, often like a first date, just enough to keep the suitor interested.

"Father, would you like me to stay?" asked Jenny.

"No, we are fine, thank you, unless you would like to stay?"

Jenny shook her head as she made her way to the door, closing it on the way out.

Park waited until she left the room before he rose and slowly ambled to the wet bar. With a conspiratorial smile he offered both visitors a drink. Though the men declined, he poured himself half a glass of *cheongju*, the clear rice wine that served as Korea's answer to Japanese sake. He held up the glass and said, "My daughter does not have to know about this."

"Sir, we don't wish to take up a lot of your time. I need to discuss something very important," said Jake.

Taking a sip of his drink, Park said, "We are here to do business; please speak. Tell me why you've asked to meet me."

Without breaking eye contact with Park, Jake said, "It might be better if we talk alone."

"I don't think that is necessary, unless you don't trust the man who introduced us," said Park.

Jake looked at Tommy. "I trust him as much as I trust any man who deals in smuggled goods."

Mr. Park let out a hearty laugh and pointed to the two henchmen serving as security guards. "Maybe everyone should leave and allow me to speak with the visitor in the privacy of my office. Please take his weapon with you." Looking at Jake he said, "You may retrieve your toys on the way out."

Jake shrugged as if to say, "No big deal."

"Sir, if you don't mind I'd like to stay," insisted Tommy.

Park looked at Jake, then back to Tommy. "It's your associate who asked you to leave. Maybe you should have worked out the logistics before you came."

"I'd like to stay," said Tommy, defiantly looking at Jake.

"Tommy, I don't think that's a good idea. Let me talk with Mr. Park alone. After the discussion, if he wants me to share our conversation I certainly will, but this matter is personal."

"But I don't want to leave," said Tommy, attempting to regain a position of strength after being slighted by Jake.

"Tommy, your friend has a point. I will listen in private to what he has to say, then I will decide how much to share."

As Tommy headed to the door, he turned briefly and corrected Park. "He's a business associate, not a friend."

Tommy still didn't trust Jake and carrying the concealed weapon into Park's home only fueled his anxiety. The young Korean criminal entrepreneur had spent more than a year cultivating a relationship with Park and he feared Jake was about to undo all that—perhaps intending to cut him out of the action.

As the two security guards escorted Tommy to the hallway, he glared at Jake. When the trio reached the doorway, the larger of the two guards said, "Mr. Park, we will be standing outside the door in case you need us."

Park nodded without saying a word. As the door closed, Park gestured toward the bottle of Chung Ha, Korea's most popular brand of *cheongju*, but Jake again declined the drink.

CHAPTER THIRTY-SIX

"Mr. Park, this is a somewhat delicate situation and I hope you understand I come with the best intentions."

"Go on."

"I believe you know an attorney named H. Daniel Reid."

"But of course, he handles many of my legal affairs. I can assure you it is all on the up-and-up," said Park, taking a casual sip of the *cheongju*.

Jake flashed a wry smile. "Mr. Park, I am aware of your reputation and I have spoken with Reid. I know it's not all on the up-and-up, but I'm not here to discuss your criminal enterprise."

Park took another sip of his drink. "Then what is so important we need to meet in private?"

"Reid contacted me the other day. He hired me to kill someone."

"And you are capable of doing such a thing?" asked Park, as if contract killings were on par with real estate transactions.

"Yes, but that's not important—"

"Then what is important?" asked Park, interrupting Jake.

"He hired me to kill your daughter," said Jake.

Park's reaction was more sedate than Jake expected. The crime boss slowly turned toward the wet bar and poured another drink. He took a sip, then just as slowly turned to face the FBI agent. He eyed Jake as if trying to determine how much to reveal to the visitor. "Did he give a reason for wanting my daughter dead?"

"Yes, sir, he did," said Jake, acting cautiously but eager to get to the meat of the undercover meeting.

"Is she carrying his child?"

"You suspected?"

"Yes, I suspected. Now, why did you come to me?"

"Sir, he offered me fifty thousand dollars to kill Jenny. He wants it done next week while she is in Las Vegas handling business for you. He'll be at a legal convention in Hawaii. I have no issue with killing anyone but I don't kill children, born or unborn. Also, once he identified Jenny and I realized she was your daughter, I knew this was a task requiring the utmost discretion. I know what an important man you are in this community. I thought you might like to buy the contract and who knows, maybe in the future we could do business if you would ever need me for such services."

Park opened the top drawer of his desk and pulled out a Cartier tricolor gold cigarette case identical to the one Reid and Yeong carried. He opened the container and offered a cigarette to Jake, who shook his head. "These are the Indigo, a most popular brand in Korea."

"No, thank you. That's a beautiful case, though. Reid and Yeong have similar ones."

"I gave them as gifts but apparently one recipient has betrayed me." Park paused briefly, as if debating whether to enlighten him. "My daughter has had many problems, not all of her own making. Her husband died a year ago and she has lived with us ever since."

"I'm sorry to hear that," said Jake.

"To compensate for her pain she has spent far too much time

masking her grief in nightclubs and other such unwholesome places. Her mother and I recognize she must grieve in her own way, so we have been tolerant of her actions."

"It's not easy being a widow and a mother," said Jake, who understood loss.

"Oh, she is not a mother, at least not yet. Gracie is not hers. As you may have determined in the short time you have been here, Jenny has little to do with Gracie, who was my other daughter's child. Lily and her husband were killed tragically the same time Jenny's husband died. We have provided for my daughter and for Gracie, as you can see. Perhaps we have overcompensated."

"Your love is apparent, Mr. Park."

"My daughter has assisted me in some of my business dealings but seeks too much reward for far too little effort. She views me as her personal ATM machine."

"I'm sure once the grief dies she will appreciate all you and your wife have done," offered Jake.

"One might hope. She has become quite fond of the nightlife in the Korean community. Apparently she partied once too often with my attorney."

Park then removed a cigarette, tapped it on the case, and placed it in his mouth. He looked at Jake, waiting for him to make the next move. The undercover agent was confused until he realized Park expected him to light the cigarette. Reaching deep into both pockets, Jake withdrew empty hands.

Park nodded toward an object on the desk, but rather than prolonging the moment, Park picked up the gold Tiffany antique lighter shaped like an owl. He popped open the head and lit the cigarette.

Jake watched with an apologetic grin.

Park took a long drag before removing the cigarette from his mouth and slowly blew out the smoke. "You would sell Reid out for fifty thousand dollars?"

"I will kill him for fifty thousand dollars."

Park nodded, placing the cigarette back in his mouth. After a quick puff Park asked, "If you are so quick to break faith with my attorney, how do I know you won't play me? Maybe even going back to Reid in an attempt to renegotiate the contract on my daughter."

Jake smiled and walked toward the wet bar. "Maybe I'll take that drink now."

Without saying a word, Park walked to the bar and poured him a drink, refilling his own glass as well.

Jake took a small sip, then said, "Mr. Park, I'm a pragmatic man. Reid, on the other hand, is a street-hustling shill whose law degree legitimizes his three-card monte act. Since he doesn't have the fortitude to pull the trigger or do the honorable thing, he seeks out mechanics who can fix his problem. My contempt for his kind is long-standing. He needs to go down on principle alone. I view it as pulling one more weed from the garden of life. You, however, command great respect and lead an enterprise only a fool would challenge. Reid's a fool who chose to fight a losing battle. I don't need many friends but I certainly don't side with losers."

Park smiled and lifted his glass to Jake. "You have chosen wisely."

"Are you buying out the contract?"

"You will do wise not to harm my daughter and soon I will reward you with suitable compensation. As to H. Daniel Reid, I will see to it the problem is resolved. You need not trouble yourself. I was aware of your meeting with my attorney and I will handle it."

"Aware?"

"My men observed you meeting."

Jake smiled. "The homeless man."

Park nodded.

"I presume both the Green Hornet and Kato were on the pier," said Jake.

Park smiled. "Yes, but don't assume they are cartoon characters. They provide many services and do so quite well."

"Such as standing in the hallway guarding my Glock and keeping an eye on Tommy."

Park smiled as he handed Jake a business card with his cell phone number. "I think we may need to speak again soon."

Jake offered a sincere smile. "Sir, it is an honor to meet you. I look forward to a long and prosperous business relationship."

Park simply nodded.

CHAPTER THIRTY-SEVEN

A third security guard was entering Park's home as Jake retrieved his firearm, the now-empty magazine, and a handful of bullets. By the time he got out the front door, Tommy was already entering his car.

Jake headed toward the Lexus and stood by the driver's-side door as the two men stared at each other across an uncomfortable silence. Tommy finally rolled down his window and snapped, "I don't want to talk here."

"Okay."

"Follow me in your car." It was an order, not a request.

The four men and one woman in the Honda Pilot watched Tommy and then Jake leave the crime lord's residence. As they were parked in the shadows and down the street from the house, their presence went undetected by either man. Tommy was blinded by his anger, and Jake was forced to concentrate on following the black Lexus as Tommy sped out the driveway.

After the cars turned at the stop sign at the far end of the block, Kareem Abdul, the assassin-bartender, eased forward, parking the Pilot just beyond the range of the security cameras. The three Arab men from the mosque who accompanied Kareem on the mission were in the backseat. The windows were down and all five welcomed the cool night breeze. Tensions were high and the diluted smell of nervous perspiration lingered.

Candy offered each a piece of Korean confection but the men refused. She casually unwrapped the piece, tossed the cellophane wrapping out the window, and popped the candy in her mouth, enjoying the flavor combination of ginseng extract, honey, sugar, and peppermint.

"How much longer?" whispered one of the Arab men from the back as he and the others shared a look.

Earlier in the week Candy had reported to Kareem that Park's two most trusted security men never spent the night at the residence. However, each evening one of Park's many underlings stayed at the house as a precaution should anyone breach the grounds' costly security system. The guard was housed in a small room just inside the front door and to the left. His quick elimination tonight would remove the only real impediment to success.

"His security detail is probably ready to call it a night and will leave soon. Give everyone a chance to settle down. Let Park relax after his company leaves. We don't need anybody still on high alert," said Kareem, sipping his second cup of coffee.

This morning at the mosque, following sunrise prayers, the men had reviewed their respective assignments, studying the detailed floor plan of the house Candy provided. Inside the warehouse where Gabe Chong had been murdered, Kareem measured off a mini-replica of the home, with tape and string serving as the makeshift residence.

The team practiced moving commando-style from room to

room, clearing each as if in combat. Though not perfect, they developed a level of discipline and sophistication they believed would be adequate for tonight's mission.

Mohammed valued Kareem's expertise and was grateful he brought this opportunity to the attention of the cell. The entry was to be through the front gate, breaching it as Kareem had done before on home invasions prior to his stint in prison. Tonight all were armed and prepared to resolve any resistance with controlled violence. The only three who needed to survive the assault were Park, his daughter, and the granddaughter, all of value to the cell. The death of any of the three diminished the chance the terrorists would prosper.

The three Arab men in the backseat were anxious. This was the first mission for the Hezbollah terrorists since they had been smuggled across the Mexican border into the United States.

If they were successful tonight, the proceeds from this operation would be sufficient to bring more of the fighters from their special unit on the long trip from Beirut to Caracas and up through Mexico. The trio were seasoned warriors. But all their missions in the Middle East had been direct action against opposition leaders or attacks against American military personnel in Iraq, Afghanistan, South Sudan, or Turkey. All of them had served with Hezbollah squads in Syria, propping up the Assad regime in Damascus.

They were experts at rigging improvised explosive devices and assassination shots resulting in death to infidels and apostates.

Tonight's mission was more complicated. The three men believed in themselves and each other but not in Kareem. They knew from Rostam that the black prison convert was a newcomer to the jihad. They were prepared to die as martyrs for the cause, but they weren't certain about the man at the wheel. They were good soldiers and accepted this assignment because Mohammed had ordered their participation. And like good soldiers they kept their doubts to themselves and hoped the worst wouldn't happen.

It was a false hope.

CHAPTER THIRTY-EIGHT

Jake wasn't too sure what to expect when Tommy stuck his arm out his car window and waved them to the curb just three blocks from Park's residence. The only thing he knew for sure was that the young Korean criminal was furious at him for being forced to stand in the hallway with the two security men while Jake and Park conversed in private.

Both cars pulled to a halt midway between two lampposts. As Jake hastily inserted loose rounds into his magazine and reloaded his Glock in the front seat of the Range Rover, Tommy jumped out of his car and headed toward the undercover vehicle.

Jake could see the agitation in Tommy's face and quickly activated the hidden recording device. By the time the enraged Korean criminal opened the Rover's passenger-side door and sat down, Jake had both hands on the steering wheel but was ready to react if necessary.

"Why didn't you want to talk back there?" asked Jake, trying to defuse what he now believed to be a potentially volatile situation.

"Why did you carry a gun into Park's residence?" demanded Tommy, his anger flaring.

"Whoa, partner. Let's turn it down a notch or two," said Jake, a take-command expression on his face.

Tommy repeated the question a bit more sedately but the hostility simmered.

Jake was turned in his seat facing Tommy, watching his eyes, prepared to strike should the street thug decide to attack; never underestimate the enemy. Jake responded with subdued sarcasm. "I always carry a gun. We live in a dangerous world."

"I've had enough of your crap. Are you a cop?"

"You've gotta be kidding me," said Jake, shaking his head.

Tommy inched closer, seeking to get in Jake's face, not the wisest move in this situation, his dark eyes raging. "No, I'm serious. Are you a cop?"

"No, Tommy. How many deals have we done?"

"That's not important."

Jake took the offensive. "What do you mean it's not important? We've done close to a half-dozen deals. I've brought your containers across the border. I've been to your warehouse where you store all kinds of swag. Has it ever been raided? Has anyone been arrested? Have you even been stopped by anybody in law enforcement? Cops? Deputies? Chippies? Feds? Would a cop allow you to get away with all that?"

"Tell me again you're not a cop. If I ask, you have to tell me; otherwise it's entrapment. I know the law."

In at least half of his undercover assignments, the target asked the same question. Thanks to Hollywood the bad guys believed a law enforcement official if asked had to answer honestly. Jake wasn't about to take the time to educate this criminal entrepreneur. From experience Jake knew Tommy would be able to discuss the finer points of the law with his attorney after the indictment.

"Tommy, read my lips. I'll speak very slowly. I . . . am . . . not . . . a . . . cop."

Tommy still wasn't convinced, his eyes boring through the undercover agent.

Jake threw up his hands as if in mock surrender. "Okay, you got me. I'm a supersecret undercover agent assigned to thwart international criminal conspiracies. I'm MI6, CIA, FBI, as well as LAPD and somewhere at home I think I have a sheriff's badge. I'm really the Lone Ranger and I'm here looking for Tonto, my faithful Indian companion. . . ."

Jake could tell his over-the-top rant had worked to calm his accomplice. He continued in a quieter tone, intending to sound conspiratorial. "Do you want to know why I needed to meet with Park? Would that make you feel better? But since you're so big on the law, as I understand it, if I tell you, you're part of the conspiracy. In on the score, in on the beef; that's the way the game is played. So tell me, do you want in?"

Tommy thought hard. He stared out the passenger window, the night growing darker by the minute as Jake's aggressive offense played with the Korean street thug's mind.

"Yeah, I want in," said Tommy with some reluctance.

There was a pregnant pause before Jake answered, "Reid hired me to kill Park's daughter, Jenny."

"What?"

"You heard me. Reid's willing to pay fifty thousand dollars for me to kill Jenny, and if I take the contract you get a third."

"Why?" asked Tommy, now almost pleading for an answer.

"The why isn't important."

Tommy sat there trying to gather his thoughts.

"So do you want your third of the fifty grand?" asked Jake.

Tommy sat in disbelief, his head pounding, his hands beginning to shake. He began to massage his temples, believing that might relieve the stress. There was prolonged silence before he spoke again. "Did you tell Park I brought Reid to you? Please, Jake, tell me you didn't tell Mr. Park I had anything to do with this."

"Tommy, are you in or out?"

"Jake," said Tommy, again almost pleading.

"Your name never came up. I gave Park a chance to buy out the contract. There is no way I'm going against a man as powerful as Park. I may be crazy but I'm not stupid. I want to be on his side when this comes down. Besides, he knew about it."

Tommy jumped on Jake's last statement, incredulous at the thought as his head snapped to the left, focusing on Jake's eyes. "What do you mean he knew about it?"

"Those gunslingers he had in his office, the two boneheads he sent to babysit you in the hallway . . . they were at the pier when I met with Reid."

"Are you sure?"

"Tommy, I was there and so were they. The best thing we did was come here tonight. Park knew all about it, or at least he would have figured out the details eventually. We're golden. We're on the A-team, the varsity, and if all goes well, we're in the starting lineup."

Tommy breathed an audible sigh, slowly blowing out the tensions that choked him seconds before. He smiled as he turned to Jake. "Do I still get a third?"

Jake gave his passenger a playful swat to the back of his head.

"Are you happy now?" asked Jake.

"Yeah," said Tommy, still with the smile on his face. "But if I find out you're a cop I'll kill you."

Looking Tommy in the eye, Jake said, "Good! That makes us even."

"How so?" asked Tommy.

"If I find out you're a cop I'll kill you."

Tommy offered a nervous smile as he exited Jake's car. "I'm going back to Mr. Park right now and clear this up. I need to get out front on this. I'll talk to you tomorrow."

"Whatever."

CHAPTER THIRTY-NINE

The black GMC Yukon pulled from the driveway and headed north. In what would prove to be a fatal security lapse, the Green Hornet and Kato failed to look south and see the five sitting in the Honda Pilot.

"Get ready to move," whispered Kareem.

Just as he started the engine and prepared to drive forward, Candy spotted Tommy pulling up to the security gate. "Wait!"

"Why would he return?" asked one of the terrorists in the backseat.

"Quiet," whispered Candy—unaware that a woman giving orders to a radical Islamist would be an unforgivable offense.

They watched Tommy punch the call button on the security arm extending out over the driveway.

"Yes," came a male voice in heavily accented English loud enough for those in the Honda Pilot to hear.

"Mr. Park, I'm sorry to bother you again. I know it's getting late. I just spoke with Jake. May I come back in and explain about Reid?"

"You'll need to wait a minute. I have to deactivate the alarm system."

Hearing the exchange over the speaker at the gate, Kareem said, "Get ready!"

"For what?" asked one of the men from the backseat.

"Change of plans. As soon as Tommy pulls forward we move."

"This was not the plan," said the man in the backseat as he looked to the others.

"It is now! Take out the security cameras as we rehearsed. Everybody gear up! Now!" said Kareem, handing latex gloves to his four passengers.

He reached into the backseat and grabbed an aluminum baseball bat he kept behind the driver's seat. It served as a convenient legal weapon that wouldn't be questioned by the police if he was pulled over. He handed it to the shortest of the three men in the backseat. "Jam this between the brace and the gate after it swings open."

As Tommy's Lexus cleared the gate and headed down the driveway, the Honda Pilot pulled in a few seconds behind. Inside the SUV, everyone was wearing black cotton balaclavas, the preferred attire of terrorists and thugs. The masks had holes for only the mouth and eyes, covering the head and neck.

Two of the men jumped from the backseat of the vehicle. One fired paintball pellets at the overhead camera focused on the front gate. The balls splattered and within seconds an opaque film covered the lens, obscuring visibility. The other man jammed the metal baseball bat into the gate's hinges, preventing it from closing.

Kareem drove through the open portal, stopping long enough to pick up his two co-conspirators, then slowly made his way up the driveway after giving Tommy enough time to enter the residence.

From the driveway the occupants of the SUV saw lights come on in what Candy had told them was Park's first-floor office. Kareem turned to the others and said quietly, "We go now."

CHAPTER FORTY

As the team exited the Pilot, the men maneuvered with military precision toward the door. Using a heavy steel handheld battering ram, two men instantly destroyed the lock. As the door burst open, the third terrorist tossed a flash-bang grenade, designed to stun anyone within ten yards of the detonation. The bold flash of light essentially blinded an individual for five seconds while the loud blast deafened and incapacitated those in the room.

The grenade performed as advertised—momentarily disorienting everyone on the ground floor of Park's residence with a thunderous explosion.

Kareem was the first to enter and looked left, his AK-47 in a combat-ready position. The security guard stumbled through the open door of his office located exactly as Candy detailed. From just a few feet away, Kareem fired a burst of five rounds, all striking the intended target.

The raiding party moved quickly, clearing the living room. Two of the men and Candy moved down the long hallway to the bedroom seeking Jenny and the child. Kareem and the other terrorist headed toward Park's office. Pale smoke from the flash-bang and gunfire permeated the room and the smell of the pyrotechnic metal oxide mix hung in the air.

Park raced to the antique oak desk in his study and ducked down behind the heavy piece of furniture. Tommy followed, squatting next to Park.

"Do you have a gun?" asked Tommy.

"It's in the safe," said Park, pointing to a large oil painting on the far wall concealing a safe.

Before Tommy could mount a counterattack, the masked intruders kicked in the door to the study and Kareem rolled a second flash-bang into the room.

Tommy, not knowing the lethality of the device, threw himself on Park in an attempt to shield his boss. Though the flash-bang was far from deadly unless it detonated next to someone's head, Tommy's act of loyalty to his criminal mentor was the stuff of underworld legend.

The grenade's concussion filled the room with noise and smoke. Two invaders rushed forward, circling the desk, with Kareem shouting in English for the two men to surrender. As Tommy moved to his left off Park, there was a moment of hesitation as he tried to recall where he had previously heard the voice of the lead gunman.

Adrenaline is a survival aid. It prompted Tommy to jump up from the floor and grapple with the nearest attacker, wrestling him to the ground. With a stranglehold around the Middle Eastern intruder's neck, Tommy viciously bit the man's ear, a pathetic shriek evidencing the pain, both men now struggling to survive.

With his free hand, Tommy reached for the intruder's AK-47, which had fallen to the floor during the melee. Kareem, stunned the attack was unfolding in ways no one anticipated, saw Tommy grasp the weapon. As the two men wrestled for control of the dropped weapon, the bartending "wannabe" jihadist opened fire.

The burst of ten rounds from Kareem's AK-47 had a predictable effect. Both Tommy and Kareem's fellow jihadist were hit multiple times.

Tommy's arm was shredded from the blast, flesh hanging from shattered bone. But with his good arm the Korean street hustler attempted to lift the intruder's weapon and take aim at Kareem.

It was a futile effort. The "convert to the cause" unleashed another burst of fire at the young Korean criminal capitalist and finished him. Turning to the man Tommy had tried to shield, Kareem screamed at Park, cowering behind the desk, "Stay where you are! Arms, spread-eagle! Now!"

Park submitted to Kareem's commands and sprawled on the floor, hands held far from his body. With his weapon trained on Park, Kareem moved to his Lebanese companion and noted the man was no longer struggling for breath as he lay in a large pool of blood.

Keeping the muzzle of his AK pointed at Park, Kareem squatted next to his terrorist partner and felt for a carotid pulse—he found none.

In the immediate aftermath of the grenades and gunfire, Kareem heard the whimpers of a child as the other three assailants pushed Soo Min, Jenny, and Gracie into the room. Blood poured from a large gash above Soo Min's eye where she'd been pistol-whipped by one of the misogynistic Lebanese terrorists.

The attacker had Park's wife by the hair, maintaining control as she fought her captor and struggled to get free. Jenny, a hood over her head, was compliant, controlled by the flex-cuffs securing her hands behind her back. The third intruder held the little girl, who screamed when she saw the slaughter.

"What happened?" asked the terrorist, referring to his friend lying on the floor as he tried to subdue a frightened Gracie.

"Later," said Kareem.

One of the masked intruders picked up the weapon lying next to Tommy and slung it across his shoulder.

Soo Min struggled again, seeking to escape, and the jihadi pulled her toward him. She lost her balance but before she hit the floor, the attacker yanked hard on her jet-black hair, preventing her from collapsing. She screamed in pain and fear. The intruder swung the weapon, smashing it against the back of her head, opening another wound. Then he threw her to the floor.

Park, ignoring threats from Kareem, struggled to his feet to aid his wife but was greeted by the sharp slash across his face from the barrel of Kareem's AK-47, draining him of what little strength remained. He crumpled to the floor and Kareem shouted, "If you get up again I will kill you!"

"Let the women go!" shouted Park.

"We don't need the old one. You can have her but you'll see the other two again when you answer our demands," said Kareem as he threw a note at Park.

With that the attacker dragged Jenny and Gracie from the office, the young child's shrieks echoing down the hallway. Park may have been a criminal and the agent of an enemy regime, but he was also a grandfather.

As the attackers were preparing to depart, the North Korean crime boss made another attempt to aid his unconscious wife. Kareem, in an act of gratuitous cruelty, turned from the doorway and smashed the butt of his AK-47 into the old man's face. "Stay down!" he shouted as he fired off three rounds into the wall of the office. "We'll be in touch."

CHAPTER FORTY-ONE

Jake pulled from the curb and flipped a disc into the CD player. Elvis blasted from the speakers. Though he was exhausted, he was celebrating two back-to-back high-risk meetings. Every time he could walk away from one of these events without getting killed or discovered it was a victory. Tonight was a doubleheader win for the good guys. He had managed to sell himself to a criminal kingpin—and the subsequent "rededication ceremony" in the front seat of the Range Rover proved successful with the crime boss's gangbanging associate.

Though Jake had often been told by others he couldn't "carry a tune in a covered basket," he joined the King of Rock and Roll in a lively, off-key rendition of "Jailhouse Rock." He checked his mirrors, took several side streets, and circled two cul-de-sacs. He was clean but tired. An hour of undercover work is like an eight-hour day to mortals, and he had been balancing too many nonstop undercover days and nights without respite.

After crooning with the King he headed east on Huntington

Drive. He turned right on Rosemead Boulevard and then right again into the North Woods Inn/Kohl's parking lot, the prearranged meeting spot.

As he negotiated his way through the parking lot, looking for Trey Bennett, he hoped this would be a quick debrief and a chance to get home to his firm but very lonely mattress.

Jake spied them and groaned. Instead of just Trey, there were three others standing next to a tan, government-issue Ford Taurus parked beneath a "mushroom cap" sodium-vapor light a few rows back from the Kohl's main entrance. Jake shook his head when he realized Trey was accompanied not only by their immediate boss, Rachel Chang, but by ASAC Charles Hafner and Wilson, the Agency spook.

Trey and Rachel were in casual attire but Hafner and Wilson were in business suits. All four were drinking coffee from white Styrofoam cups as they chatted, awaiting Jake's arrival.

When Trey spotted Jake pulling into a parking space about fifty yards away where there were no lights, he hustled over to the Range Rover before Jake could exit the vehicle. "You okay? Everything go well?"

Jake nodded. "Could not have gone better. Why are you guys parked under a light and why all the suits? Nice cover, by the way, suits in a department-store parking lot after dark. Never would suspect they're feds."

Trey shrugged and grimaced as Jake stepped from the Rover and the two walked toward the others.

Before reaching the administrators Trey said, "As you can see, we have company tonight. . . . Please be on your best behavior for a change."

"Why?" Jake replied. "You worried about your next promotion?"

"Not really. You've already made sure that won't happen. But do me a favor, would you?" Bennett responded. "I just want to get some sleep tonight. And this case has suddenly generated all kinds of extra attention from Washington. Think of your responses to these nice people who are senior to both of us as courtroom testimony. Just answer their questions. Nothing extra. No embellishments. No insults. Okay?"

"Okay," Jake said, pulling a scrap of paper from his pants pocket and handing it to Trey. "I'll be a good boy as long as you run this plate ASAP. This car was leaving Park's driveway as we pulled up."

Trey looked at the number, nodded, and said, "Deal."

When the two men joined the other three, the first to speak was Hafner, the ambitious Assistant Special Agent in Charge. It was the first time Jake had known the bureaucrat to attend an after-hours undercover meeting.

Hafner was practically giddy with excitement, a goofy grin running ear to ear. "How'd it go? You get us what we need?"

In compliance with Trey's appeal, Jake was all business. "It went well. I'm confident Park bought my act. I had some issues with Tommy Hwan but in the end he's on board."

"What issues?" asked Rachel Chang.

"Tommy tried the 'are you a cop' crap and I needed to head him off. All is now good. He's convinced I'm the real deal," said Jake, noticing Hafner was fidgeting, wanting to move the inquiry along.

Interrupting, Hafner asked with the officiousness of a determined bureaucrat, "Did Park bring up the Supernote?"

Jake shook his head and said, "Never came up."

Hafner pressed. "Did you bring it up?"

"Nope, never was an opportunity to discuss it."

"Why not?"

Jake paused before responding. He could trade barbs in the locker room with the best of them. He could laugh at himself and enjoyed the playful banter with his fellow street agents, but administrators needed to walk softly when questioning his investigative strategy. "What do you mean, 'why not'? I'm asking you, 'why?' Why *would* I bring it up? Why would we even talk about it? I have no reason to inquire about counterfeit money. It makes no sense."

Hafner either wasn't listening or didn't comprehend Jake's logic. "But we need to pursue the Supernote. That's the whole purpose for your meeting Park. Why didn't you bring it up? We're getting a lot of pressure from Washington. Headquarters is being hammered by the State Department. We owe it to them to resolve this quickly. The highest levels in Washington want and deserve answers."

Jake looked at Trey and Rachel before dealing with the idiocy confronting him at this late hour. "In my undercover capacity I don't even know he deals in Supernotes."

"But Reid paid you with Supernotes," said Hafner.

"But I don't know that."

Hafner failed to grasp the distinction. "Of course you do. That's what the meeting in the SCIF was all about."

"Jake Kruse knows but Jake Goode doesn't," offered Jake in a somewhat detached voice, with just a hint of sarcasm.

Rachel Chang intervened. "Boss, he's right. In his undercover capacity he doesn't know the money was counterfeit. He would have no reason to bring it up since there isn't any way for him to identify the bills as being bogus."

Hafner gave a halfhearted "whatever" look before he said to Jake, "The point here is that you need to get on with finding out everything you can about the Supernotes."

Jake was just below erupting but maintained his composure. "And what scenarios do you have in mind? I welcome an opportunity to discuss our options."

"You're operational. You come up with the plan. I'm telling you to get it done and get it done quickly," Hafner said like a petulant child.

Jake looked at the others before facing Hafner. "If you think you can do it any better, pal, I'll make the introduction."

Jake did an about-face and walked toward his car, not waiting for a response.

Hafner started to chase after him but Rachel held out her hand, blocking his pursuit. "Boss, I think it's best to let it go. Trey and I will touch base with him tomorrow."

Through it all, Wilson never uttered a word.

CHAPTER FORTY-TWO

Jake was steaming when he got into the Rover. He also knew better than to let it show. He took a deep breath, started the vehicle, eased methodically out of the parking space, and headed toward the Rosemead Boulevard exit. While waiting for the light to change he was thinking about the confrontation that had just occurred—and how much it distracted from accomplishing the mission.

He was a hardened warrior—and wanted nothing more than the satisfaction of removing the cancers of society. He had proven himself on the battlefield in Iraq, and on more than a dozen undercover assignments since joining the Bureau. But he also knew "fighting the good fight" included too many skirmishes with administrators who didn't understand or refused to acknowledge the complexities of undercover work on the street.

Hafner was one more self-proclaimed beacon of brilliance from Headquarters who spent too much time jockeying for the throne at D.C.'s puzzle palace. He would never grasp an essential reality:

every undercover assignment is an unscripted one-act play with the actors fluent in the language of deceit. Jake needed to get home before he went Waco on this ASAC. He resolved to remove the administrator from his Christmas card list.

As the light turned and Jake pulled out onto Rosemead and headed toward home, his cell phone rang. He fished through his pocket for the phone and answered on the third ring. "Yeah, this is Jake."

It was Bill Holodnak, a former Marine on the Joint Terrorism Task Force. "Jake, I'm in the wire room working Park's phones."

"I was there less than an hour ago."

"Well, apparently since you departed, there was some kind of home invasion at Park's. He just got off the phone with someone, maybe one of his security people. From what our interpreter says, Park was saying his daughter Jenny and his granddaughter were kidnapped."

"What?" shouted Jake. "Are the police there? What happened?"

"I'm not sure but I think Tommy's dead."

"No! Was Park hurt?"

"I think he's hurt but is going to be okay. There was a lot of confusion but I've got our Korean translator listening to a playback of the call."

"Did you call the police?"

"I called 9-1-1 but the dispatcher said they were already notified. I know it wasn't Park. We would have picked it up on the wire. It must have been a neighbor or maybe the alarm company."

Jake pulled the Rover to a halt in the parking lot of a bank and said, "This may work to our advantage. Call Trey. He's with Rachel and Hafner. I just left them. Tell Trey what happened and that I'm heading back toward Park's home in San Marino."

"Roger," Holodnak replied. "Anything else?"

"Not right now. I'm going to call Park on a cell phone number you may not have on the wire warrant. I'll record it in case you can't listen in. I'm going to call as if I have an idea on how to handle Reid, his attorney. Maybe he'll tell me something about what just happened."

"That might work. I'll notify the others now. I called you first since your stake is personal," said Bill.

"Thanks," said Jake.

"I've got your six. Be careful."

"Thanks, Bill. I'll give Park a call."

Jake ended the call and reached into his pocket for the number Park gave him. He activated the internal recording device on his phone and punched in the number.

Park answered on the first ring.

"Hey, Mr. Park, it's Jake. As I was driving I got to thinking about how to handle Reid. What if we—"

Before Jake completed the sentence Park interrupted. "Where are you?"

"What's wrong? You sound upset."

"I need you back here immediately. I need some help, especially from someone outside the family."

"Sure. I stopped to get gas and a bite to eat. I can be back at your house in a few minutes."

"The police may be here when you arrive. Tell them I asked for you."

"What's wrong? Why the police?"

"Just get here," ordered Park.

Jake heard the weak sound of sirens in the background as he ended the call. Instead of heading for home, Jake turned west on Huntington and backtracked to Park's home in San Marino. This time he made the trip without "the King."

CHAPTER FORTY-THREE

When Jake arrived at Park's home, the San Marino police were on the scene. Red and blue flashes shot into the night sky like strobe lights at a seventies disco. The media were also on hand, reporters across the street attempting to get a few facts to piece together a story and helicopters circling, their bright lights attempting to get footage for the eleven o'clock news. Uniformed officers blocked the entrance at the gate. Jake couldn't very well flash his FBI credentials to gain access. He would have to bluff his way through the cordon—and still avoid being plastered on the front page of tomorrow's *Los Angeles Times*.

He drove down the block, parking around the corner from Park's home. Grabbing a baseball cap from the backseat, he pulled it down low on his head, put a new memory chip in his recording device, and locked his Glock in the glove compartment.

He slipped behind the shrubbery of a nearby home and made his way down the driveway, where he walked with purpose toward Park's drive, appearing to the media to be a nosy neighbor.

Approaching a uniformed officer at the gate, Jake said, "I'm a friend of Mr. Park's. He called and asked me to come over. He's not real comfortable around uniforms. Where he comes from, people wearing uniforms aren't exactly on the side of the citizen. I think I could help gain his cooperation."

The police officer nodded and said, "Let me call my sergeant." With that he walked a few feet away and spoke into the radio attached at his shoulder. The other officers remained vigilant just in case one of the perpetrators had remained at the scene, risking capture to further satisfy his bloodlust. An evidence technician inside a patrol van was discreetly videotaping the crowd so detectives could review it at a later stage of the investigation. When the officer guarding the gate returned seconds later he said to Jake, "I'll escort you to the house."

"That's okay, I know the way," said Jake, acting naïve about proper police procedures that prevent citizens from freely roaming around a crime scene.

"I'll escort you. Let's go," said the officer in a command voice.

After turning the corner of the driveway, beyond the site of the media or neighbors, the officer said, "As a precaution I need to pat you down."

"I understand."

The officer gave a cursory search, asked Jake to remove the wallet from his back pocket and then hold his undercover driver's license while the cop used the camera on his smartphone to photograph it. Then, using a field interrogation app on the phone, the officer asked, "Is this address on your license current? You're not a neighbor?"

Jake's undercover address—an apartment he rarely frequented—was downtown. "Yes, that's my address. I know Mr. Park from work."

When they arrived at the front door Jake saw the destruction. Having executed early-morning arrest warrants, Jake had burst through enough doors to recognize the work of trained professionals. The intruders had skillfully centered the ram just below the doorknob and shattered the wooden frame, defeating the lock and dead bolt.

A female detective came to the front door. "Is this the guy Park called?"

"Yes," said the uniformed officer. "I patted him down, he's clean. I sent the FI card to your phone."

The detective nodded and extended her hand. "I'm Kelly Rodriguez. I'll need you to sign the log-in sheet."

"Jake Goode," said Jake. "What happened? Do you have any idea who did this?"

The dark-haired detective shook her head. "I'm hoping you can help. Park doesn't seem too interested in cooperating. He's not much of a talker."

Jake maintained his serious façade. "He's from a police state. I don't think he had much success with uniformed authorities."

"Maybe you can convince him this isn't a police state."

"At least not yet," said Jake.

She gave him a look and he knew what she was thinking. *Oh great, just what I need at a triple homicide, some left-wing nut job with an agenda.*

Jake knew he wasn't making a friend but he wasn't interested in earning his Merit Badge this evening.

With a hint of resignation, Rodriguez said, "Maybe hearing it from you will make him realize it's in his best interest to work with us. The sooner we can get the information out on the air, the quicker we may be able to find who did this."

"I'll do my best," he said with feigned sincerity.

Jake stepped through the front door and immediately spied a dead body to the left, a sheet covering the corpse. In the living room a paramedic was treating Park, placing a bandage on the large gash above his eye. A second team had already taken Park's wife, Soo Min, to the hospital.

Jake headed to Park, who stood up, pushing aside the paramedic. "No more. I am fine."

"But sir . . ."

Park offered a slight bow as Jake approached. "Thank you for coming." Then, almost in a whisper, he said, "Walk over here."

"Sir, if you are refusing any further treatment I'll have to ask you to sign this form."

Park waved him off. "I will sign your paperwork later."

The paramedic began cleaning up the mess he caused treating the wound as Park and Jake walked to a quiet corner. The detectives watched intently.

Park said, "They have Jenny and Gracie. At least five men broke into my home. When Tommy tried to stop them he was killed. Jake, Tommy was very brave. He saved my life. Do not say anything to the police about Jenny and the girl. I will handle this matter."

Jake balked. "But it's a multiple murder. Your house is a bloodbath. The cops are swarming all over the place."

Park answered quietly but sternly. "I will handle the kidnapping in my own way. Let them investigate the murders. I will do the rest."

"Do you think Reid is behind this?"

"He would never be that stupid."

CHAPTER FORTY-FOUR

Good to his word, Bill Holodnak notified his FBI superiors about what he knew of the attack at Park's residence. Charles Hafner, still smarting from the confrontation with Jake, had just gotten to his car with Wilson when the call came in from Holodnak. He turned on the speaker so the CIA officer could hear the report from the wire room.

Immediately after receiving the report and pressing END CALL on the keypad, he turned to Wilson and said, "You want to go see Park?"

"How are you going to make that happen?" Wilson asked.

"I know the San Marino chief of police. He's a graduate of the FBI National Academy."

The ten-week school in Quantico, Virginia, for state and local police administrators was the product of J. Edgar Hoover's efforts to enhance law enforcement professionalism throughout the United States. The coveted school provided graduate-level studies in criminal justice and was a great resume booster for any law enforcement official. On a more practical level it encouraged cooperation between the FBI and local law enforcement with a common bond of training.

The FBI hierarchy in L.A. frequently socialized with National Academy graduates in the region. When time was of the essence, this networking bridged bureaucratic obstacles.

The CIA operative considered the offer for a moment and said, "I don't want our respective bosses in Washington to get their knickers in a knot over this, but if you can get us in without a lot of fanfare, we might be able to get to the bottom of what Park is doing with the Supernotes and make 'em all happy back in D.C."

Hafner immediately dialed the chief and explained that he and a colleague wanted to go to the crime scene at Park's residence on a "not to interfere basis" and see for themselves whether there were any connections to a matter of national security.

The local lawman immediately agreed and said that a Lieutenant Jon Osborne, one of his department's senior detectives, would meet Hafner at the entrance to the residence.

Hafner and Wilson arrived about ten minutes after Jake. Lieutenant Osborne was waiting at the gate as the duo exited Hafner's car. He left the blue lights hidden in the grille flashing for effect.

Hafner explained the situation, detailing the FBI's interest in Park but not mentioning the Supernotes, Jake's undercover role, or providing the true identity of Wilson. Since the detective received his marching orders directly from the chief, he was only too eager to support the FBI. Privately, the detective hoped his assistance might lead to an appointment to the career-enhancing National Academy.

The three men walked up the driveway to the front door and were immediately granted access. The game was on as soon as Osborne entered the house accompanied by the ASAC and the CIA official.

Jake immediately spied the new arrivals and was stunned Hafner and Wilson would intrude in the midst of his undercover operation.

Lieutenant Osborne, tall and thin, flashed his badge. "Mr. Park, I'm Lieutenant Osborne. I'm a detective with the San Marino Police Department. You want to tell us what happened here?"

Park was hardly impressed by the lieutenant but maintained his humble posture, walking slowly back to his chair and taking a seat. "I've spoken to your other detectives. I've already told them. Men broke in and tried to rob me."

Osborne was attempting to act efficient and commanding. "We know that. We need a description of the men who broke in."

Park replied meekly, "They were wearing masks."

"How many?"

With a slight tone of annoyance Park said, "I've already told your men, at least five."

"At least?" asked Osborne. "You don't know for sure?"

Park lifted his head slowly and looked the police lieutenant in the eye. "I was in my office. I only saw five. One is lying dead in my study."

An air of mistrust flooded the room, with Park playing the frightened immigrant to perfection. The lieutenant said, "Good thing the neighbors called the police. I'm not sure you would have reported this."

Park became more conciliatory. "Lieutenant, my friend has been killed, as has one of my security personnel. Both died protecting me from just this type of intrusion. If I could help I would. Please, the men wore masks and gloves. There is nothing more I can tell you."

The police detective was polite but firm. "Sir, would you accompany us to your office?"

Park nodded and slowly rose from his seat. He grabbed Jake's arm more for show than need but Jake could tell the events of the evening had taken a physical as well as emotional toll on the crime boss.

The lieutenant, Hafner, and Wilson followed behind Jake and Park, Hafner grunting as if upset it was taking the elderly Korean so long to make his way down the hallway to the study.

When they entered, Jake immediately spotted two more bodies

covered with sheets. The coroner's team was preparing to remove the deceased to the county morgue on North Mission Road. Routine autopsies would be performed but an armchair detective could identify the cause of death. Evidence, however, in the form of bullets and fragments would be preserved in the hopes at some point they could be matched to a weapon and the shooter.

The evidence technicians were photographing the crime scene and attempting to dig spent rounds out of the walls and ceiling. Cartridge casings were scattered throughout the floor and cardboard numbers were placed by each object, providing reference for the crime-scene photographs.

The lieutenant lifted the sheet of the intruder, lying in a large pool of dark blood where the twentysomething man had bled out from his wounds. He was dressed in black but Jake was surprised by his appearance. The dark curly hair and full beard were matted from the sweat and mask but the man was obviously Middle Eastern, not Asian as Jake expected.

"Do you know this man?" asked the lieutenant.

Park looked at Jake before answering. He put his head down as if in submission and said quietly, "He is one of the men who broke into my house."

"We know that," said the lieutenant, exasperated. "Did you ever see him prior to this evening?"

Park shook his head as he took a seat. "I have never seen this man before."

Everyone's attention turned to the two coroner assistants who removed the sheet and carefully placed Tommy in a black body bag. As they lifted the limp body onto the gurney, Charles Hafner, the FBI ASAC, chose that moment to insert himself into the investigation.

Hafner bellowed for all to hear, "Park, it's no secret who and what you are. Who was behind this? Rivals seeking to eliminate the competition?"

Park remained humble, his head lowered, though Jake noted a slight edge to the response. "I am a businessman."

Hafner took a step forward. "You and I both know that's a lie. It's either stupidity or guts to do this to a man like you. What did they want? They didn't just break in here for grins and giggles."

Park kept his head down in either genuine grief or an effort to hide his contempt and anger. "I do not know why they broke in here. They left without taking anything."

Hafner moved in closer to the seated crime boss. "Is that so? Mind if we look around. Have you checked the entire house? Maybe you should accompany us on a walk through the house and check out every room. Maybe something important is missing and you just didn't look close enough."

"They took nothing."

"You live alone? This is a pretty big house." Derision was evident in the question.

"I live with my wife, my daughter, and my granddaughter."

"We know your wife went to the hospital but I haven't seen your daughter or granddaughter. Where are they?" asked Hafner.

Park said nothing.

Hafner continued to plow ahead. "Where are they tonight? Were they home when this happened? It's late and it seems strange they aren't here. Come on, Park, tell us what really happened."

Jake's face reddened and his temper was about to crest. He was at his best in the midst of chaos. He calmed in a shootout. He almost welcomed commotion and disorder. But Hafner, the bureaucratic bumbler, was on the verge of wrecking the entire operation.

Though Jake worked at staying cool he decided an act of honor would enhance his credibility with Park; he sprang for the attack. "It's Mr. Park to you and he told you all he can. This man has just been through a home invasion. His friend and an employee were killed. His wife was attacked. With the property taxes he pays you'd think the police could protect him. I'd suggest you hit the streets and try to find who did this. Or is it just easier to harass the victim? You guys are amazing."

Hafner was staggered. He wasn't expecting his subordinate to intervene, but with the ASAC's lack of real investigative experience, maybe any move the undercover agent made would have come as a surprise. He held up his hand to object and said, "Listen, Jake . . ."

The idiot blew it!

Hafner was large on volume and weak on sense. No one had addressed the undercover agent by a first name. Park had his head down and didn't react to the gaffe.

Jake pounced on the mistake, interrupting the ASAC, hoping his theatrics would mask Hafner's blunder. "You think you can waltz in here and challenge this man's integrity. I'm assuming you got lucky and found that badge in the first Cracker Jack box you opened. Armed and ignorant is a horrible combination."

Hafner was overmatched but, swallowing his pride, he played the role. "Who are you? Has anyone checked this man's ID?"

Jake whipped out his wallet and shoved his driver's license into Hafner's face. The undercover agent was into his role and pushed back hard, real anger spilling over. "Here's my ID! Now how about your badge number? Is this where my tax dollars go, to pay your salary? I think it's time you and your people left. If you have any further questions, send someone else tomorrow. Mr. Park answered your questions the best he could. He has tried to cooperate. Maybe your next questions should be directed to his attorney. Is this the way you conduct a murder investigation? I happen to know Mr. Park is a close friend of the mayor. With a phone call or two I'm sure by this time next week all of you will be worrying about parking ticket quotas."

The lieutenant, unaware of Jake's undercover capacity, jumped between Hafner and the agent. As a patrolman he had deescalated enough domestic disturbance calls to understand the importance of a timely intervention. "Maybe he's right. We'll give Mr. Park a chance to rest. We'll be back tomorrow, sir."

With a weak smile, Park nodded as everyone began to slowly exit the room. "Thank you, Lieutenant."

CHAPTER FORTY-FIVE

While the technicians finished photographing the crime scene and uniformed officers collected the evidence-gathering equipment, the senior on-scene tech approached Park and Jake with a request. "Since you and your wife described the intruders as men wearing gloves," he said to Park, "there isn't much point in us dusting the place for fingerprints. But I notice this place has an extensive video surveillance–security system. It would be very helpful to our investigation if we could have access to the backup files either here or at the alarm company."

"I will look into it," Park said wearily. "But not tonight. It will have to wait until tomorrow."

"But sir," began the evidence technician, "that could be a terrible mistake. Many of these systems automatically delete files after a certain length of time and we don't want to lose—"

Jake, still concerned about Hafner's blunder, seized the opportunity to again play the role of Park's ally and interrupted. "Look, you heard the man. He's been through hell tonight. His wife has been taken to the hospital and he needs to deal with that. Tomorrow will have to do."

The crime-scene investigator shrugged and departed. When all the police were gone, Park ushered Jake back into his office, where his demeanor immediately changed from meek victim to warlord. He summoned his security chief, instructed the heavyset guard to contact the families of Tommy Hwan and the dead security man, then dismissed him with instructions. "Make sure they have all departed the house and grounds and we are not interrupted."

When Park and Jake were finally alone, the crime boss sat at his desk and opened the bottom drawer, withdrawing something concealed beneath a stack of papers. He handed Jake a half sheet of paper with cutout letters from a magazine. "Here's the ransom note they left. They're demanding three million dollars."

Jake debated whether he should be the CSI technician preserving the note for prints or the criminal cohort anxious to kill those responsible. "Cutout words on a ransom note seems a little too Hollywood. Why not just pound out a note on a computer? I'm not sure it's possible, but if you turned this over to the police they might be able to get fingerprints or maybe even DNA off the letter," said Jake.

Park shook his head, his anger surfacing. "No more police! I'll cooperate long enough to get information from them, but we give them nothing more."

"They may not be competent, but I'm not sure they'll give up easily," said Jake. "They will be back. Your neighbors here will demand it. I'm also guessing without your help this will never get solved."

"I don't need their help. I will resolve this in my own way." Park punctuated this by slamming his fist on the desk.

Jake let Park's anger simmer, then, pointing to the ransom note, he said, as if asking himself aloud, "I wonder why three million? Three million seems like an odd amount. Why not a million or five million?"

Park was confident in his response. "There is a reason for that amount. The demand provides a clue and a reason why I can trust you."

"I don't understand. Who do you think is behind this?" asked Jake, sensing he was close to information that was key to the investigation.

"I may tell you everything at the appropriate time. I need to do some checking. When I find those responsible they will pay with their lives."

Jake shook his head; his response was sincere. "But we need to get Jenny and Gracie back safely."

Park nodded, his dark eyes filled with rage. "Jenny and the child are my first priority. Once they are safely in my protection I will eliminate those who chose to challenge me."

"But who? Could it have been Reid? If he's too weak to pull the trigger, could he really orchestrate a kidnapping?"

"It is not Reid," said Park, putting his elbows on the desk, resting his face in his cupped hands as he gently probed with his fingertips the abrasion on his cheek where Kareem had struck him with the muzzle of the AK-47.

"Could it have been Yeong?" asked Jake.

Park looked up at the American and said definitively, "It is someone within our circle."

"But why would he challenge you? Tommy was more fearful of you than he was of Yeong. He always said you had the strength and controlled the community."

Park nodded.

Jake continued. "Kidnapping doesn't seem the smart move. Does Yeong have anything to do with Arabs? Tommy never mentioned anything about Middle Easterners being mixed up with the enterprise."

"Yeong is a businessman and, like me, is willing to deal with anyone who can be trusted. We both have gone outside the family in our various ventures."

"Did you know the intruder who was killed?" asked Jake.

Park slowly rose from the desk without responding and headed toward the wet bar. He held up the bottle of *insamju*, Korean vodka, offering Jake a drink. When Jake nodded, Park poured two drinks, handing one to Jake. "I don't know, but I think Tommy recognized one of the intruders just before he was killed."

"Is that the person who shot Tommy?"

Park nodded.

"What about the others?"

Park took a sip. "The one who shot Tommy seemed to be in charge. He's the one who threw the note at me and did all of the talking."

Jake debated how far to push the inquiry. He was almost conducting the interrogation Hafner wanted but didn't want to appear to be a cop.

"In what language? Did you recognize his voice?"

Park shook his head and said, "He spoke English, without an accent. But I did not recognize the voice."

Park took the Cartier cigarette case off the bar and removed a cigarette. Without waiting for Jake to assist, he lit it, drawing several puffs as the conversation paused.

"Do you know a guy named Sonny?" asked Jake.

"We call Cho Hee Sun 'Sonny.' Is that who you mean?" said Park as he slipped the cigarette case in his pocket.

"When I was with Tommy the other day, he and his girlfriend Candy were talking about a man named Sonny getting killed a couple of nights ago."

"That was Sonny. It was in the papers. He was killed at his home in Beverly Hills."

Jake took a brief sip of the Korean vodka made with ginseng root. "What part did he play in all this?"

"He worked with Yeong. I had little to do with him. He was a successful businessman who was involved in our business as well. He moved much of what Tommy brought in from Korea, but I'm

not sure Tommy knew very much, since Sonny was higher up on the distribution chain."

"Could his death and the kidnapping be connected?"

Park paused before answering and his response was as if the question triggered a thought. "I'm not sure."

"Why did you hesitate?" asked Jake.

"Like I said earlier, I will find out who did this and when I learn their identities I will tell you, assuming I need your help."

"Whatever you need, just ask."

Park nodded, crushed the half-smoked cigarette into an ashtray, and began making his way to the door. "Excuse me. I need something for the pain."

As Park headed toward the bathroom, Jake continued down the long hallway and began looking around the living room for clues. Even though the police had searched the crime scene, the tension between Park and the law enforcement officers had to have affected the thoroughness of the examination. And Jake's dance with Hafner certainly abbreviated the search for evidence that could be useful in a prosecution.

Jake bent down near an antique table and picked up a small sticky object the size of an almond.

Park looked puzzled as he entered the room.

"CSI: Hong Kong," said Jake, holding up the object and smiling uncomfortably. "Could this have come from one of the attackers?"

Park shrugged and said nothing.

Jake was serious about the clue and thought it might hold an answer. But he also feared his performance could arouse Park's suspicions about this overly intuitive criminal co-conspirator. Jake stood straight and walked toward the Asian crime boss, allowing a closer examination of the object in his hand. Putting the evidence to his nose, Jake said, "I think this is candy. It smells like peppermint."

He held the object out for Park. "It makes no difference," Park said.

"Maybe it will help the cops identify who did this."

Park shook his head slowly and with thoughtful deliberation said, "I am not interested in helping the police. First we get the return of Jenny and the child. Then we kill those who did this."

Park crossed the expansive living room and opened the sliding glass doors leading to a large patio. He stepped out and looked toward heaven as if seeking comfort.

Jake followed. Staying in character, he wasn't about to lecture Park on the merits of the U.S. criminal justice system. Anyone with Park's background would administer his own brand of street justice, never seeking satisfaction from the courts. Park, the hunter, had become the prey, for a few very violent moments.

Standing silently beside the crime lord on the darkened patio, Jake thought to himself, *Those behind this abduction may be able to run but they'll never hide from a man with Park's power. Whoever did this is already dead; they just don't know it yet.*

After the two men stood in silence for nearly a minute, Jake asked quietly, "Do you have the money? It may be key to getting Jenny and Gracie back safely."

Park pulled out his gold cigarette case and after opening it offered one to Jake, who shook his head. Park removed a cigarette and tapped it on the case before putting it in his mouth. After lighting and taking a long draw, he slowly blew the smoke into the still night.

"I will when the container arrives on Friday."

Jake was genuinely surprised. "You can make three million off one container?"

Park shook his head. "I can make three million off the next container. You must ensure that it arrives on time. Jenny and the child cannot afford any delays."

"I've cleared the container through Customs and paid off my guy at the port of entry. There shouldn't be a problem. I'll check with him tonight just to make sure."

Park took another slow draw on the cigarette and said, "Thank you," as he blew out the smoke.

"Will you be okay tonight?"

Park tamped out his cigarette. "I am fine, Jake. I must call some people. Just deliver my container."

CHAPTER FORTY-SIX

As soon as he reached the Range Rover and pulled away from the curb, Jake was on the phone to Rachel Chang. "We need to meet, ASAP!"

"I'm with the ASAC at the San Marino Police Department headquarters, mending fences," she replied.

"Good, I'm heading that direction," he said, making a turn at the next intersection that tested the advertised traction of the SUV's high-performance tires.

"Jake, cool down before you get here. Come around to the parking lot in the back. I'll have Lieutenant Osborne, your new best friend, clear in your vehicle."

"Not a good idea," the undercover agent replied. "I don't know how big Park's network is. He may well have spotters watching the station or someone on the inside. I can't take the chance one of his goons could put me or this vehicle up on YouTube as I pull in there."

"How about the pharmacy parking lot at the end of the block?" she replied.

It took him less than ten minutes to negotiate the traffic. By the time he pulled into the parking lot and spied Rachel on her cell phone, he had dialed back his visible anger. But when he saw Hafner sitting in the government Ford, he slammed the door anyway—just for emphasis.

The ASAC jumped out of the car as Jake approached.

"What the hell was that all about?"

"What?" said Hafner, not quite sure whether to adopt a more forceful demeanor.

"Don't give me that crap!" Jake yelled. "Nobody told me you and your buddy Wilson were going to show up at Park's. You almost blew my cover. No one knew about the kidnapping but Park, me, and the kidnappers. Then you start running your mouth about the daughter and granddaughter and calling me Jake when no one addressed me by name."

If the leadership skills he learned in the Marine Corps taught him anything, it was to praise in public and criticize in private. While on active duty he employed the principle daily when dealing with those he commanded. But when it came to FBI administrators, Jake's leadership traits had gone the way of the Oldsmobile. Maybe if he burned fewer bridges he'd find more support from the Bureau's command structure, but tonight his volatile nature was on full display.

Rachel quickly stepped in, attempting to head off a career-ending confrontation between Jake and Hafner.

"Jake, relax. It's okay. Park's not suspicious at all," said Rachel.

"How would you know?" snapped Jake.

"I just talked to Bill Holodnak in the wire room. Park and his security chief were on the phones as soon as you left calling some people we have yet to identify," said Rachel with a calming professional confidence. "Park has called up additional security personnel and they are on their way to the house."

"Good," said Jake, still hot.

Rachel inched away from Hafner, trying to direct Jake's attention on her rather than the ASAC. The ploy worked as Jake focused on her next statement. "Bill said Park was very appreciative of you being at the residence while the cops were there. He said, 'The round-eye is a strong ally,' so he's not suspicious at all. In fact your little two-step with the ASAC enhanced your credibility."

Hafner flashed a self-congratulatory grin as if it were all part of his investigatory scheme.

Jake settled down momentarily after hearing the reassurances from his supervisor. She had been a street agent and had done UC work on a nasty sex-trafficking ring and had what her peers and subordinates considered to be street smarts.

"What happened after the police left?" asked Rachel, still trying to divert attention from Hafner.

"He showed me the ransom note for three million dollars."

Hafner nodded and said a little too enthusiastically, "That's good."

Jake barked, "What's good?"

Rachel answered, "That he showed you the note."

Exhausted by the events of the day, Jake replied simply, "Yeah, well, why wouldn't he? He needs to trust someone. He doesn't suspect me of being behind the home invasion."

"Does he have the money?" asked Hafner.

"No."

Hafner nodded again. "Good."

Jake's suspicions grew. "Whattaya mean, 'good'? What's going on here?"

Rachel remained cool. "Nothing, Jake. We're trying to figure out what Park's next move is."

"His next move is to get his daughter and granddaughter back."

Hafner smirked. "And how does he do that without money?"

"He'll have to get it. He said he was going to make some calls this evening."

"Any idea where he'll get the money?" asked Hafner.

"Maybe he's taking up a collection. Calling in a few markers. I don't know, maybe a garage sale."

"That's it?" asked Hafner.

Jake glowered. "How about you? You got any ideas? You seem to be on top of things."

Rachel Chang was beginning to understand the admonition she'd received from Jake's last supervisor. "He's great undercover; maybe the best we've got, but keep him away from people." She'd laughed when she heard the warning but had come to realize the wisdom in it.

"Jake," said Rachel, "if Park doesn't have the money, he'll need to reach out to those who do. We may be able to identify the broader scope of the conspiracy. Maybe he'll seek the Supernotes for payment. The phones are lit up now. Let's see where we stand in the morning. It's been a long day for everyone. We could all use some rest."

Before they parted, Jake handed the evidence envelope with the microchip to Rachel and said, "I know I'm supposed to give this to Trey, but since he's not here, you should take it back to the office. There's a lot on it that may mesh with what Bill is picking up on the phones."

As he watched the transaction, Hafner couldn't resist one last bureaucratic dig: "We really don't want administrators testifying in court on chain-of-custody evidentiary issues."

Jake stared at the ASAC for a long moment, but he had the self-discipline to say nothing. Instead he shook his head, got into the Range Rover, and drove out of the parking lot, headed for home.

CHAPTER FORTY-SEVEN

DAY 7

SUNDAY, MAY 4

As the morning sun made its way over the tops of the mid-block high-rises, a metallic black 2013 GMC Yukon XL Denali turned right onto Wilshire Boulevard and two men jumped from the vehicle. They confronted a young Korean male, a minor player in Henry Yeong's criminal enterprise, walking westbound. For a Sunday, the street was crowded with pedestrians and cars, but no one seemed to notice the abduction. One of the two who sprang from the black SUV jammed a semi-automatic into the back of the young Korean.

"Mr. Park needs to speak to you."

The young man realized it would do no good to run, hoping he could talk his way out of a violent confrontation. He accompanied the two males a few feet to the back door of the vehicle. All three entered and the driver turned at the next corner. Driving only a few hundred feet, he turned again into an alley that paralleled Wilshire.

When the vehicle stopped, Park, who was in the front passenger seat, turned to confront the young man just snatched off the street in broad daylight. "Do you know why I need to speak with you?"

"No," said the young Korean.

Park nodded. All five men exited the vehicle with the two heavies holding the frightened man by each arm.

Park repeated the question. "Do you know why I need to talk with you?"

"No," said the young captive, fright pulsating through his body, raw, fear-induced beads of perspiration appearing on his forehead.

Park nodded and the biggest of his thugs slammed his fist into the man's stomach. As the victim doubled over, Park repeated the question a third time.

The second gangster grabbed the victim by the hair and straightened him. Gasping for breath the man said in Korean, "I have no idea what you want."

"I think you do," said Park. "Where are my daughter and granddaughter?"

"I don't know. I wasn't part of it and I swear I've heard nothing. Please believe me," replied the man meekly, struggling to breathe and to stand, his legs weakening as the two abductors propped him up for another assault.

The smaller of the two gangsters cracked the terrified man across the mouth with the barrel of the weapon and blood spattered on the front of Park's pristine shirt.

Park looked down at his shirt, waving his hand toward the stain, and said, "This blood I can clean, but yours can never be replaced when it drains into the alley. Tell me where my daughter and granddaughter are."

"You must believe me. I have no idea. I swear my boss was not behind the kidnapping. We do not know who took Jenny and the girl."

"You are lying," said Park in a gentle voice, shaking his head slowly. With that, the crime boss pulled from his waistband a North Korean Type 68, 7.62mm x 35 semi-automatic pistol equipped with a Maxim suppressor.

Park nodded to the smaller of his two accomplices, who proceeded to pull out his smartphone, press "video app" on the keypad, and point the tiny lens at the young man they had detained on the street just minutes before. The digital device, made in the Republic of Korea, recorded it all:

An off-camera voice asking in Korean: "Where are Jenny and Gracie?"

The terrified, already bloodied face of a young man, replying: "I do not know! Please, do not kill me. I have a wife and two children."

The off-camera voice saying: "Wrong answer."

The camera moves slightly to show the barrel of the automatic weapon and the three-inch-long suppressor. Then there is a soft *pop* as the pistol fires a single round.

A bloody hole appears just above the nose of the young man. His eyes roll back and his face disappears at the bottom of the screen. There is a hole—and a gruesome red stain—on the wall behind where the young man was executed.

The off-camera voice says, "Leave him. I want everyone in our community to know that as many as necessary will die until Jenny and Gracie are free. The person who provides information leading to their safe return will receive one million dollars."

At 6 a.m. Pacific Daylight Saving Time, the horrific "snuff video" was posted on YouTube. It immediately went viral—first on Korean-language websites and then globally. FBI Headquarters in Washington learned about it from the DoD/NSA Cyber Command at Fort Meade, Maryland. The Los Angeles Field Office received it from FBI HQ at 6:47. Though no one in Washington could identify the voice of the shooter, Jake Kruse would know exactly who it was.

CHAPTER FORTY-EIGHT

Sleep rarely comes easily to an undercover agent. For Jake Kruse it never did. Even supposedly routine assignments came with their own brand of tension, the need to be constantly "on guard" and a nagging "what if" uncertainty about being exposed—caught in the open—with no cavalry riding to the rescue.

Jake's key to survival and success was an innate ability to keep track of the "who am I?" question—and his skill at projecting that persona every waking minute, even while in church, which he would be missing this morning. He had to believe in himself *and* in the person he was portraying, and be so comfortable in his character that *every* response in *every* situation came naturally—and appear believable to the criminals he was deceiving.

Living two lives at once requires extraordinary self-confidence. It means never becoming complacent. The consummate undercover agent lives like a spy in enemy territory—and lives to tell the story. Jake Kruse knew he was very good at living by his wits. But he also went regularly to the range and practiced putting ten rounds into an eight-inch circle at twenty-five yards—just in case.

Despite a restless night's sleep, Jake hopped out of bed when the alarm went off at six thirty. He grabbed his workout clothes and hit the trails. Running cleared his head but it also brought immediate goal-oriented satisfaction, something undercover work seldom did.

With UC assignments, significant accomplishments could be weeks, months, maybe even years down the road. On two particular assignments Jake never knew the final results, nor would he ever. On both occasions he was tasked with compromising foreign dignitaries working in the United States. Though much of his undercover work was secret, at least until the indictments were unsealed, on both of these missions he was required to sign nondisclosure agreements preventing him from ever discussing the targets or the nature of the assignment. He was successful both times in "neutralizing" the subjects.

In one instance, he set up an embassy official in such a way that his government would have killed the diplomat had the foreign power learned of his dealings with an American undercover agent. Jake assumed the short, squat, swarthy individual was on the FBI's payroll singing dutifully about Middle Eastern affairs, grateful to be alive. In the other assignment, one of the three targets would never sing again, and Jake could only assume the two remaining subjects were used in a never-disclosed spy swap.

Jake pushed himself this morning, aiming for a six-minute-mile pace. But throughout the run, a question kept nagging: *Who is behind the Park kidnapping?*

He intentionally arrived early for the meeting at the Koffee Kombine on Ventura Boulevard. The place was open—a counterintuitive location for clandestine encounters. The patio was nearly empty—yet perfect. The church crowd would be joining them soon, but the participants in this morning's meeting had a clear view of others approaching. The ambient noise from the street traffic prevented surreptitious monitoring of their conversation.

When he could, Jake always chose locations like this for conferences with colleagues—and his criminal co-conspirators. He reconnoitered entries and exits in advance—and knew where to look and what to look for. It gave him a measure of certainty in situations that could quickly get out of control—far preferable to exchanging information in a "brush pass" at a supermarket vegetable stand. From experience he knew the more obvious he was, the less obvious he would appear.

He ordered coffee and was reading the *Times* sports section when Trey Bennett pulled up to the curb in his silver Ford Fusion. Jake watched over the top of the newspaper as Trey threw the FBI radio microphone over the rearview mirror and hopped out of the vehicle. The hanging mike was a common sign to meter maids and patrol cars to extend "professional courtesy" and not ticket an illegally parked government vehicle. Even on Sunday these meters needed feeding.

Trey walked into the patio but before he could sit, Jake looked up at his friend and said quietly, "Please don't ever do that again when you are coming to a meeting with me."

"Don't do what?"

"Don't hang your mike. Here's a quarter. I know all agents are cheap but you just signaled everyone—the good, the bad, and the ugly—that you're a cop. I'd like to maintain some semblance of secrecy. It might just keep me alive." Jake flipped him the quarter and Trey sheepishly retreated to the car, pulled his mike, and pumped the quarter into the meter.

When Trey returned he apologized.

"Don't be sorry, be cautious."

"Yeah, like meeting you in broad daylight on the busiest surface street in the Valley is cautious."

"Hey, if you want to do the paperwork to rent a motel room for every meet, that's fine with me. I thought you'd appreciate I'm only sticking you with coffee, but we can do the Ritz any time."

"A bit testy this morning, aren't we?" said Trey, trying to lighten the moment.

"Screw you and the horse you rode in on," said Jake without the hint of a smile.

The waitress approached and both men quieted. She topped off Jake's cup and filled Bennett's when he said he wasn't ordering breakfast.

Trey took a long sip of the coffee, then said, "That plate you grabbed from the car as you arrived at Park's house last night comes back to Sharaz Ali al-Sattar."

"Am I supposed to know him?" asked Jake.

"Only if you follow Iranian TV. He runs Iranian International Television, which has production facilities in Hollywood. From everything I could find in our files, the entire operation is funded by Tehran."

"No way."

"Yeah," said Bennett. "I haven't had time to listen or watch the playback of all you recorded with Park last night, but has he given you any clue that he is engaged with any Iranians or Mideasterners?"

Jake thought for a moment and said, "Not a word. But if Park's involved with the Iranian community here in L.A., that would be a stunner. It's way out of our lane, but it looks to me like the Iranians dropped off the charts last year after they closed that interim nuclear weapons deal in Geneva."

"You're right about that," said Trey. "Crime stats on Persian perps are way down from a year ago. Some ayatollah must have issued a fatwa to knock off the wife beatings LAPD would report and the clandestine caviar and illicit pistachio imports CBP used to catch."

Jake was still thinking about the car leaving Park's place as he and Tommy arrived. "What does Bill Holodnak say? Does he have any calls between Park and this Iranian we saw leaving his place last night?"

"Nothing."

"Park must be communicating by means we aren't monitoring," Jake said. "That has me concerned. I don't like going in blind *and* deaf. Can we get the judge who issued the wires warrant to broaden the fishing license?"

"I'll try," Trey said as he made a note in his iPhone.

"That could be important," Jake said. "There is no doubt in my mind the dead guy at Park's last night was Middle Eastern. He could have been Lebanese, Syrian, Iranian, Iraqi, whatever. But Park is convinced it has to be someone with connections to the Korean underworld. He has some ideas but wasn't interested in sharing them with me last night. Have you seen any forensics to ID the dead guy?"

"That's going to take days if we get it at all," Trey replied. Then, consulting the notes he had made on his phone, he continued, "Here's what the medical examiner's office told me this morning: There was no ID on the corpse. Initial assessment, large trapezius muscles, indicative of carrying a military backpack and/or wearing an armored vest. Dental work appears to be Middle Eastern or south European—gold, not amalgam. Stomach contents, were—"

"Stop!" said Jake, holding up his hand. "I'm not interested in what he had for breakfast. Just let me know if we figure out who the guy was."

"Got it." Trey continued, "Listen, it will come as no shock to you but you didn't make any new friends last night with the ASAC."

Jake leaned back in his seat. "Yeah, like I'm inviting him over for Monday Night Football. Do they study to be that stupid or is it genetic? The guy's an idiot."

Trey took another sip of his coffee, then said cautiously, knowing the messenger might get caught in the cross fire, "He wants to send you back to Quantico for an emergency psych assessment."

Jake laughed derisively. "You've got to be kidding me."

Trey shook his head. "I'm serious. He told Rachel to set it up ASAP."

Every six months undercover agents are subjected to a psychological assessment designed to determine if they are on the brink of a breakdown or total collapse. The stresses are real and the testing can sometimes identify symptoms of a "breakdown" before the agent and his handler appreciate its existence. Jake had sat through far too many semiannual evaluations and somehow managed to win almost every session on the couch. He'd win this one, too, but the timing couldn't be worse.

Jake lowered his voice to what those who knew him best described as his "Dirty Harry" level: "This is nuts. I'm in the middle of what may be an international criminal conspiracy, a triple homicide, and a double kidnapping and he wants to yank me?"

Trey looked around the patio, motioned for him to lean across the table, and said, "Jake, I know he's an idiot, but he's an ASAC idiot. You can't just jump in a guy's face like you did last night and expect to walk away, especially in front of witnesses. He has to take a stand; otherwise he looks weak."

Jake shook his head and mouthed the words as if shouting but whispered, "He *is* weak. I've seen too many like him since joining the Bureau. One more overeducated bureaucrat who hides behind the manual. Keep 'em off the streets and let the real agents do the work."

"You're preaching to the choir, but part of my job is to keep you on the street and away from Headquarters and shrinks, especially in a fast-moving case like this one. I'm on your side, Spider-Man, but you're making it tough."

Jake lowered his head. His contempt for administrators plagued him at the most inopportune times . . . usually in the middle of an investigation. He knew Trey was right. "You got my back?"

"You know I do. Just stay off the high ground for a day or two."

Jake smiled, nodded, and said, "Deal. As long as you promise not to hang your mike when we're meeting."

"Works for me," replied Trey. "Just don't answer your phone unless it's me or the bad guys."

"Thanks for the heads-up." Jake nodded to the waitress, who refilled their cups.

When she left the patio, Jake took a sip and asked, "What's really going on with the Park kidnapping? Are we behind it?"

"Jake, you can't really believe that?"

I watched Hafner and the spook last night. There's more to this than anyone is telling me. And now Hafner wants me back east for a psych eval, which will take me out of play for at least three days."

"You watch way too much TV. Don't go paranoid on me. Next thing you'll tell me is Hafner's an agent for the Trilateral Commission and he's really running the world from the basement of the World Bank."

"Is he?"

"No."

"Are you sure?"

Trey paused, a little too long, conspiratorial thoughts beginning to surface. "How the hell would I know? If I asked him and he told me the truth, he'd have to kill me. Then where would you be?"

Jake held his look for a pregnant moment before a smile surfaced. "There's a reason why it's a secret society."

"You aren't cleared for the secret handshake," said Trey, dismissing the conspiracy theory and somewhat relieved his agent wasn't going there, either.

Jake turned serious. "But I am cleared. It's my butt out there, not yours and certainly not Hafner's. I need to be cut in on what's really going on—in the depths where I can't see. It is, after all, my ass that's on the line."

"Jake, it's need-to-know. I'm up for my five-year security evaluation and they're putting everyone on the box."

"Take a Darvon the morning of the polygraph," said Jake.

"Does that work?" said Trey, surprised there might be a way to beat the polygraph exam.

"No, but you'll be more relaxed when they tell you you failed."

"Come on, Jake. Don't ask me. Just continue to march and keep me updated as you go."

Jake shook his head, almost in disbelief. "Well, I need to know and I need to know yesterday."

Trey said nothing.

"I can't believe you're siding with management," said Jake, a comment reminiscent of the grade-school barb "You throw like a girl."

Street senses prevailed. Trey looked around before responding. "The Agency says Park's a North Korean IO. They believe he has access to millions in Supernotes and will probably use them for the ransom."

Jake nodded. "I guess it makes sense the DPRK has intelligence officers operating in L.A. Their entire government is a criminal enterprise, so why wouldn't someone profiting from its contraband be connected back to Pyongyang? This gets more interesting by the minute."

As the waitress approached and refilled their coffee cups, both men quieted until she left.

Trey lowered his voice. "A ransom payoff in Supernotes doesn't cost anyone anything. It just floods our economy with more bad paper. But that's not all. It turns out NSA didn't know it in 'real time,' but they picked up overhears about the kidnapping . . . before it went down—"

"Before it went down!" interrupted Jake.

Trey shook his head slowly. "*Kidnapping* is a predicated word. They couldn't trace the calls because they were prepaid disposable phones."

"So we let Jenny and the little girl get kidnapped."

"This is way above my pay grade and yours. But it looks to me as though the folks in Washington and Hafner thought this might force Park to use the Supernotes for the ransom."

"I don't believe this," said Jake, shaking his head. "Three people were killed and we could have prevented it!"

"It's not that simple. Nobody thought anyone would get killed. They didn't know the 'who,' the 'where,' or the 'when' of the kidnapping until after it all went down. That's because of the incredible volume of information NSA collects. It's like trying to get a spoonful of water while standing under Niagara Falls.

"Everything I just told you apparently became evident in the past twenty-four hours. If we warned Park about the kidnapping, he would know we were on to him. This whole North Korean issue is important."

"More important than a life?"

Trey didn't hesitate with an answer. "Yeah, Jake. Even innocent people get caught in the cross fire, but maybe preventing North Korea from playing a key role in a nuclear holocaust is more important than some Asian gangbangers getting clipped."

Jake calmed. He didn't want to get into a moral-equivalency argument with Trey since he knew firsthand what it was like to put other people's lives on the line. He had to do that in combat as a Marine—and nobody has pleasant memories of those times.

"So whose phones did we pick up on Park's wiretap?"

"That's the other thing. It wasn't on our warrant for Park. It was a call from Lebanon to a 'throwaway' cell phone in L.A."

"What?"

"It was a short call, but NSA is certain the conversation was about the Park kidnapping."

Jake rubbed his eyes, trying to sort out all he was hearing. "How are we playing the kidnapping?"

"Again, we're in a box. Park never reported it and if we go to him he'll know either we've got the house wired or we have someone on the inside. From where I stand that someone looks like the gringo sitting across from me."

"But we have to do something. Trey, we can't let this little girl and the daughter get killed. They really are the innocents in all this."

"I know. We talked about it last night after you left. Rachel thinks you should try to convince Park to call us but is leaving the final decision up to you. For some reason she trusts your judgment," said Trey with a slight smile.

"I was just getting ready to say how much I really think she is a great supervisor with tremendous instincts."

"Don't let your ego get in the way of the investigation," said Trey, still smiling.

Jake shook his head after taking a sip of coffee. "I don't think trying to convince Park to call the Bureau is the right move. If we bet wrong, I'm out. I think the better road is to stay close, within his wingspan, and be available for him."

"You might be right."

"I hope I am."

"I hope *we* are," said Trey, who took a final sip of his coffee. "I don't want any of this to come back to bite you or me."

"We're okay. Thanks for cutting me in. We're going to get this done, but I may decide the front office doesn't need to know the how or the where."

"Jake, one other thing: don't go toe-to-toe with Hafner. He's got suck at Headquarters; tread lightly or you might find yourself in Adak, working security clearances for government contractors."

CHAPTER FORTY-NINE

After pulling onto the freeway following the meeting with Trey, Jake punched Park's number into his cell phone. The Korean crime kingpin answered on the first ring. "Mr. Park, it's Jake. Have you heard anything?"

"No, Jake. My people have been looking since last night but have found nothing."

"Have you spoken with Henry Yeong?"

"I called him and he denies any involvement."

"Do you believe him?"

"I'm not sure. We are still inquiring with his soldiers. It has to be someone with knowledge of my enterprise. We are questioning many within our special part of the Korean community."

He caught the full meaning of Park's words. Most members of the large "Korean community" in Los Angeles were hardworking, law-abiding, legal immigrants who had nothing to do with the criminal underworld inhabited by the likes of Park and Yeong. Many were devout Christians and their heroes were people who made Hyundais, Kias, and LG phones, appliances, and flat-screen TVs. They didn't admire or respect Korean criminals—but they knew enough to stay out of their way.

Jake paused. "I met Yeong through Tommy. Do you think it would make sense for me to approach him?"

"No. That won't be necessary," Park replied. "We will handle it. You have a much more valuable mission."

Jake paused for a second. "Yes. I understand—the container. I spoke to my friend on the border. The delivery is set for around three tomorrow. The container is being processed through Customs today and will be released tomorrow late in the morning. Do you still want it delivered to Tommy's warehouse?"

"Yes, Jake. Tommy ran the warehouse but I paid the bills. I have access."

"I will meet you then at the warehouse tomorrow unless you need me sooner."

"No, but thank you, Jake. I will see you tomorrow at three."

"Everything will be set for your delivery, sir. Please let me know if there's anything I can do before then."

"I will, Jake, and thank you again. Your friendship at this time is much appreciated."

Jake ended the call and when he turned up the volume on the CD player Charlie Daniels came blasting through the speakers. Since he was targeting an Asian crime syndicate, "Still in Saigon" seemed appropriate.

Jake could barely hear the ringtone above Charlie singing, "My younger brother calls me a killer and my daddy calls me a vet."

He fumbled to turn down the music and grab the phone. By the fourth ring Jake had the phone in hand and noted the caller ID was blocked. He flipped on the internal recording device before answering.

"Yeah," he said in a less than welcoming greeting.

"Jake?"

"Maybe, who's this?" Still borderline nasty.

"Jake, it's Charles Hafner, the ASAC." Jake almost choked. *Oh, that Charles Hafner, the ASAC guy. Glad I didn't confuse you with the other Charles Hafner.* Since he assumed he was in for a lecture on late-night decorum, he debated leaving the recording device on for OPR evidentiary purposes. Or maybe he would post the conversation on the FBI's intranet to demonstrate the officiousness of L.A.'s latest contribution to the managerial hierarchy. He took the high road and decided against it.

"Hang on just a second. Let me shut this off. I wasn't sure who was calling and I'm recording this."

"Yes, please turn it off."

Please. Jake sensed maybe he had the upper hand as he deactivated the recording device.

"Okay, it's off. What's up?" asked Jake casually, with no hint of respect.

"Sorry to bother you on a Sunday."

"It's okay. I'm working."

"We may have a problem. Have you heard from Gabe Chong?"

"No, not at all. I don't even have his contact information. We met during the powwow at the SCIF and our only connection on the street was the meeting at Yeong's restaurant. It made no sense for us to exchange numbers, just in case one of us lost our phone or was compromised."

"I understand."

"Why are you asking?" said Jake, wondering whether this discussion should be taking place on a cell phone, but he thought better of bringing up the issue since Hafner initiated the call.

"Gabe is supposed to report twice a day—at nine and nine. He's missed the last three check-ins. Wilson and his people have been unable to contact him."

"Has he done this before?"

"Never."

"That doesn't sound good," said Jake, appreciating the urgency in Hafner's voice.

"Especially in light of the Secret Service losing their local source," said Hafner.

"It might be related but we should be careful how much we say on the phone," cautioned Jake.

"You're right," the ASAC conceded. "Should we meet somewhere to discuss this?"

"Have you told Trey or Rachel?"

"Not yet. I wanted to reach out to you directly in case you had any idea on Gabe's whereabouts. The Agency wants us to put out a BOLO on him as though he's a person of interest in an unrelated criminal case."

"With his picture and bio data?" Jake asked. "That's pretty high risk all around, isn't it?"

"Yes, it is," Hafner replied. "But this is coming from Washington. There is a lot of pressure to get answers to their questions."

"I don't get it," Jake said bluntly.

"Get what?"

"I don't understand why we're pushing this case at warp speed."

Hafner paused a moment before responding, then said, "It's very complicated. There are a lot of fingers in this pie. And as you said, it's not stuff we should talk about on the phone. . . ."

"I got that," the undercover agent said curtly. "But under the circumstances—with people getting killed and kidnapped, I think it's best if I minimize contact with people on our side. Can you fill in Trey and Rachel on what you know? I have a regularly scheduled meet with Trey later today and he can pass the details on to me then."

"That makes sense."

"Give me a few hours to do some checking before you put out the BOLO on Gabe. I need to be careful, but I think it's possible his disappearance may be somehow connected to Sonny's murder and the incident at Park's residence."

"Please be careful. I'm tempted to pull you out but the mission is too important. Since we have our marching orders from back east, I'd hate to do anything without clearing it first with Headquarters," said Hafner cautiously, recognizing the career-crushing impact a dead undercover agent could have on a blue-flame administrator.

"Yeah, I'd hate to get whacked. There's always so much paperwork after the funeral," said Jake, knowing the mere thought would cause Hafner to pop Pepcid the rest of the day.

CHAPTER FIFTY

The Sunday lunch crowd at the restaurant was still an hour or so away. Candy sat at the far end of the bar eating a kimchee beef burrito, Seoul's answer to Southern California fusion. Her iced tea, sweetened with three packets of Splenda, did little to soften her mood. Kareem was behind the bar arranging glasses, trying to coax a smile, but Candy was in no mood to dispense favors.

"There no reason to kill Tommy," whispered Candy in anger.

"He fought back," protested Kareem quietly.

"You and Jabari broke into Park's home while Tommy there. What did you expect him to do? Tommy worship Park and constantly seek his favor. Of course he protect him. If Tommy had fault, it was loyalty. I see that in all he do."

"If he had a fault it was committing a felony a day," said Kareem under his breath so as not to incur further wrath from Candy. "We lost Jabari, too."

After taking another bite of the burrito, Candy sneered, "Your friend knew he taking risk when he take assignment. Besides, doesn't this qualify him for virgins?"

"I wish you understood," said Kareem.

"Understood what? You commit crime hoping to make profit. Isn't that why most people commit crimes?"

"I did it for the cause."

"Yeah, I hear you talk about mission, faith, and cause but maybe I have cause, too."

"I wish my cause was your cause."

"I have my own jihad," she said with a fake smile.

Kareem shook his head and with resignation in his voice said, "Your brother was never interested in the faith. I tried to convince him of its value but he never wanted to listen. Maybe if he adopted our ways he wouldn't still be sitting in prison."

"My brother and I have lot in common. We never want anyone or anything to interfere with good times."

"Was Tommy that important to you?"

"He was convenient but murder just brings more police."

"You don't think kidnapping interests them?" asked Kareem, knowing the cops take the crime very seriously and often call in the FBI.

"As I understand, Park never report kidnapping."

Kareem nodded, continuing his chores behind the bar. "I'm sorry Tommy was killed."

Candy dismissed the apology with several more bites. Finishing lunch, she took the last sip of her iced tea. Grabbing the dishes to return them to the kitchen, she said, "I be back later. I check on things and continue clean up your mess from last night. Have one of girls seat customers."

Kareem continued his work behind the bar preparing for the lunch crowd. Shortly after Candy left, he happened to look to the hallway to see Mohammed standing in the shadows and quickly made his way to the terrorist leader.

Hidden in the darkened passageway, Mohammed whispered, "It did not go well last night."

"The kidnapping was successful but we lost a faithful soldier," said Kareem, fearful Mohammed was upset.

Mohammed remained calm, his face expressionless. "He died for the jihad. He is being rewarded in the next life. It was a good plan. I should have given you more men, anticipating others might be in the house."

Kareem was afraid to lie to his mentor. "I changed the plan at the last minute."

"How?"

Kareem screwed up his courage, bracing for criticism. "We saw the security people leave just as we suspected they would, but then Tommy, Candy's friend, came back unexpectedly. When the gate opened I saw it as an opportunity to breach the alarm system without any effort. I didn't think Tommy would be a problem."

"You were wrong."

"Yes, I was."

Mohammed maintained his stoicism. "It is my fault. I should have been there with you. Rostam said as much when I made the decision to proceed."

"Rostam did not want us to do this, did he?" said Kareem, looking his mentor in the eye.

"No," Mohammed admitted. "He believes the promises of our brothers in Beirut—that this new arrangement will assure us of funds for jihad. But Rostam is not responsible for paying our debts; I am. The expenses of bringing fighters here from the Bekaa Valley, Syria, Chechnya, and Iraq have been great. Our brothers in Beirut may indeed come through in the future. But this operation is something we can control. We will be more careful in the future. Is everything still a go for the rest of the plan?"

Kareem nodded.

Before exiting down the hallway and heading back to the mosque, Mohammed said, "As Allah wills, we shall succeed."

He knew it was high risk, but if he was to learn anything about Gabe, Jenny, and Gracie, he would have to cover some familiar ground. Jake parked the Range Rover across the street from Henry Yeong's restaurant and jaywalked through traffic to the front door.

Business was less than brisk. There were just six patrons in the dining room and only two people at the far end of the bar. As he climbed onto a stool the burley bartender sauntered over, less than enthusiastic to see the return of his only peckerwood customer.

"Yeah," said Kareem, wiping off the area in front of Jake.

"Give me a Light."

The ex-con drew a Bud Light from the tap.

"Is Candy around?"

"Nope, she left a half hour ago. I doubt if she returns today. Her boyfriend got capped last night."

Jake focused on the bartender, who wouldn't return the look. "Tommy was my friend, too."

"So you mourn him by drinking a beer before noon?" said Kareem as he reached for a basket of peanuts and slid it in front of his customer.

"I mourn in my own way. Maybe when you catch a cold, I'll hoist one to you as well. Heard anything about what happened?"

Kareem shrugged and opened his hands, feigning innocence. "Should I?"

"According to the news, it was a home invasion. I thought maybe you would have heard something."

The bartender shook his head. "*Nada*. I just pour. In case you haven't noticed, business isn't all that great today and this is Mid-Wilshire, not San Marino."

"Yeah, but you listen and this is Koreatown. And as you

probably know, Tommy and I delivered goods for your boss and Mr. Park. Whoever did this killed my friend and snatched Mr. Park's daughter and granddaughter—and all of them just happen to be Korean."

"Is that so?"

"If you come up with anything I'll make it worth your while."

Kareem offered a wicked smile. "My loyalties don't run too deep. If I hear anything I'll let you know and drop a dime."

Jake laughed. "You must have been away a long time; it's a quarter now."

He didn't finish the beer but threw a five on the bar. As Jake headed to the front door, he grabbed a couple of pieces of candy from the bowl on the hostess stand.

CHAPTER FIFTY-ONE

"In the movies they always get really cool vans, decked out with the latest spyware," said Jake.

"Well, this ain't the movies and you aren't James Bond," said Trey as both men stared out the heavily tinted windows in the back of a beat-up van. The vehicle was parked in the darkened alley about seventy-five feet from the rear entrance to Henry Yeong's restaurant; the only light came from the opened door of the restaurant.

Activity had been minimal and time seemed to drag. So far the traffic consisted of a produce truck making a late-night run at an all-night market farther down the alley and a couple of homeless people pushing shopping carts. All were quickly dismissed when it was apparent they played no role in Yeong's business.

Jake looked at his cell phone and realized it had been less than two hours. "Somehow Hollywood has never quite captured the sheer boredom of a surveillance."

"That's because on TV they have to get it done within a

one-hour episode and the case agent isn't locked in a van with an ADD undercover nut job."

Jake unscrewed the top on his third Coke Zero as both men talked without looking at each other, focusing on the alley.

"That stuff runs right through me," said Trey, referring to the diet soft drink. "I'd be going like a racehorse if I drank as much of that stuff as you do."

"That's why I save the bottles and caps, so I have something to pee in, and why I never sit on a surveillance with a female."

Just then Trey passed gas and a broad smile covered his face.

"You idiot!"

"That's why I never sit on a surveillance with a female," said Trey, proud of his accomplishment in confined quarters.

Jake opened a sliding window on the side of the van next to the building, but his efforts did little to air out the vehicle.

"You had Italian for lunch. I smell the garlic."

Trey grinned like a five-year-old learning to appreciate bodily functions, then whispered, "This isn't one of your brighter moves."

"You mean sitting in a surveillance van with some flatulent-friendly immature adolescent?"

"No, sitting in this alley waiting to accost a godfather wannabe. Can you live with this if it all goes south?"

"I can live with it as long as I'm only an unindicted co-conspirator," said Jake with a smirk.

"Boldness and stupidity never seem like a good combination," said Trey just above a whisper.

In an equally low voice Jake said, "If you've got a better plan I'd like to hear it. I'm convinced Yeong and his thugs know what happened to Jenny and Gracie. And since Gabe works for Yeong, somebody in this establishment must know where he is."

"Jake, just worry about getting Park's container in. Let him and his goons find the daughter and the little girl. If the San Marino cops and the LAPD are telling us the truth, Park's men are covering every inch of Koreatown. And if our missing clandestine

service officer has gone to ground in the neighborhood, they will likely find out what's going on with him as well. You don't need to be involved. Let Park's heavies handle Henry Yeong."

"Everyone is telling me to ignore Yeong. According to Hafner and Rachel, Park's the big fish, the North Korean IO. If something bad has happened to Gabe and Yeong's crew didn't do it, isn't it likely Park's people did?"

Trey nodded. "That's certainly possible since he was hired on as part of Yeong's security travel team. It's also possible Yeong is behind the kidnapping and Gabe is now guarding the girls wherever they are being held and can't communicate."

"Well, if we find Jenny and Gracie in the hands of Yeong's goons, we not only save the girls but think of the credibility I gain with Park and his syndicate."

"You've already got credibility."

"I need to find Jenny and Gracie. You're the case agent. This is all so detached for you. It's just another investigation. But for me it's personal. These two, especially the little girl, shouldn't become pawns in some surreal and sanguinary parlor game because Park wears a black hat."

"Pretty big words for an undercover agent, Jake. But Jenny's already a pawn. That's how we got here in the first place. Reid wanted her killed and she became our pawn."

"I just can't sit back and do nothing. I can't throw my badge around but I can continue to help even in my undercover capacity."

"Let Park handle Yeong," Trey repeated, slowly shaking his head.

"If you want out, then go."

"Like I'm going to sneak out of the back of a van at ten o'clock on a Sunday night in the middle of a Koreatown alley and hail a cab to the federal building. I'm in. Just be careful."

As Trey finished his sentence, a young Asian male dressed in black exited the back entrance to the restaurant. Looking up and

down the narrow passage and seemingly satisfied, he turned back to the opened door, nodded, and a second male in jeans and a Hawaiian shirt walked out.

"Were those two guys with Yeong when he paid you off with the two kilos of meth the other night?"

Jake threw up his hands. "In this light they all really do look alike."

"You're a huge help."

Jake grabbed a pair of binoculars and focused on the men. "Hey, *Don Ho and Johnny Cash,* turn around," whispered Jake since both men had their backs to the van. Almost as if he heard, the shorter of the two men, the one in the Hawaiian shirt, Jake's Don Ho, turned. "Yeah, that's one of them."

"Now what?" asked Trey.

"Get ready to move."

Both FBI agents pulled out size XXL L'eggs knee-high stockings and pulled them down over their heads as Don Ho opened the screen door and Henry Yeong cautiously exited, evidently seeking some fresh air, as if any could be found at night in an L.A. alley.

The three chatted briefly before Yeong reached into his jacket and pulled out the Cartier gold case. Without offering either bodyguard one, the crime boss removed a cigarette, tapped it lightly on the case, and slipped it back into his jacket. Johnny Cash, the bodyguard dressed in black, whipped out a lighter and lit Yeong's cigarette. Yeong took several long draws, blowing smoke rings into the air.

Jake and Trey could hear a phone ring and watched Don Ho reach into his back pocket for a cell phone. He answered and quickly gave the phone to Yeong, who turned away from the van and began talking while still smoking the cigarette.

Though neither agent inside the van could hear what was being said, Jake could tell Yeong was dominating the conversation. Whoever was on the other end of the call was doing a lot of listening.

Only Don Ho seemed interested in the call.

The other member of the security detail was more focused on four women standing at the far end of the alley. Dressed like they were auditioning for an Asian porn flick, the girls had his full attention.

The Korean Johnny Cash reached toward his right shoulder, where he had a pack of Marlboro Reds tucked into the rolled-up short sleeve of his shirt. He grabbed the pack and slowly removed a cigarette, placing it in his mouth. He finessed the pack with his left hand, rolling up the sleeve to hold the pack in place. Reaching into his front pants pocket he pulled out the lighter again and, after two unsuccessful attempts, managed to light the cigarette.

Yeong was still engaged in the telephone call and asking Don Ho for input. After several minutes, the crime boss handed the phone to the shorter bodyguard, who continued the conversation. Yeong tamped out his cigarette on the brick wall and walked back into the restaurant, apparently satisfied with the call and the alley fresh air.

Jake and Trey quietly exited the van and padded toward the two Korean bodyguards. Trey had his Glock 23 drawn, hanging near his right side. As the two approached, Jake nodded toward the man in black.

Trey focused on the henchman and said quietly, "Hey, man in black, Johnny Cash."

The Asian male turned just as Trey grabbed him, flipped him back around, and threw him up against the brick wall, smashing the cigarette, which fell to the ground. With his left hand Trey grabbed the long black hair and yanked the man's head back, restricting his breathing. The Glock now pointed at the man's head, Trey asked, "Do I have your full attention?"

The man nodded and grunted the best he could.

Leaning into the man Trey did a cursory pat-down and discovered a Daewoo DP51 automatic lodged in the small of his back. Trey carefully removed it and slipped it in the front of his pants. "I hope you have a permit," said Trey, knowing the answer.

At the moment his partner grabbed Johnny Cash, Jake rushed the second bodyguard and shoved him against the wall, forcing him to drop the cell phone. Jake braced the man with his left forearm planted solidly in the back of the Korean's neck. The street thug struggled briefly but relaxed when the FBI agent whispered, "I'm not here to kill you. I want answers."

"You have a strange way of asking questions," said Don Ho, his face still planted in the wall but trying to identify the attackers.

Continuing to whisper, Jake said, "Tommy got killed last night. You know anything about that?"

The bodyguard struggled to shake his head but didn't say a word.

"We can do this the easy way or the hard way. I prefer easy but I'm always willing to go the extra mile. I assume you would rather wake up tomorrow breathing air instead of sucking dirt, so let me repeat the question. Did you have anything to do with Tommy's killing?"

"Why would we kill Tommy?" mumbled the man, his face still pressed against the wall.

"You tell me," whispered Jake.

Trey maintained a vise grip on the other bodyguard as Jake continued the questioning. "A woman and little girl got kidnapped. You and your friends know anything about that?"

Don Ho struggled to turn his face, trying to get a look at his assailants, forcing Jake to lean in even harder, increasing the pressure.

"I don't know who was behind the kidnapping or the murder," mumbled the man.

"Why should I believe you?"

"Because it is the truth." He tried to shout the answer, but with his face planted in the wall it was difficult.

Trey stabbed his gun closer and pressed it against the ear of the man in black. "You want me to kill Johnny Cash? It might encourage your friend to open up and help us."

Jake knew Trey was bluffing but liked the way he was getting into the role.

"Not yet but the night is young."

Trey tugged a little harder on the bodyguard's hair, pulling the neck back ever so slightly, enough to be painful but not enough to cut off the air supply and crush the trachea. He whispered, "You speak English? Maybe you want to answer some questions."

The man maintained his silence as Trey shifted his weight, leaning into him, using body weight to secure the man's detention.

Jake whispered, "So you don't know anything?"

"We had nothing to do with it. I swear."

"Tell me one more time."

"I swear. We had nothing to do with the kidnapping and if we knew anything we'd tell Park."

Confident he couldn't be recognized, Jake tacked to a different subject: "You know Gabe Chong." It was a statement, not a question.

Don Ho mumbled, "Yes. He works security for Mr. Yeong."

"When and where was the last time you saw him?"

"Two days ago, here at the restaurant."

"Where is he right now?"

"I don't know."

With that Jake flipped the man around, kneed him in the groin, and, as he folded, threw him to the filthy pavement, facedown. After he placed his foot on the back of the henchman's neck, securing him to the ground, he turned his attention to Trey's captive.

When Johnny Cash struggled to eyeball his attackers, Jake threw two quick left elbows, which snapped the henchman's head, disorienting him and weakening his resolve. Blood poured from his nose.

Ordered to the ground, he quickly complied, proning himself out in a puddle of scum. Trey bent over and twisted the man's face away from the two FBI agents, then reached into the thug's left back pocket and removed his wallet.

Searching the contents, Trey said, "I've got a driver's license but it's fake. There's no hologram and the lamination is sloppy. Can't find a green card but he does have a Blockbuster video rental card and plenty of cash. This guy isn't legal."

Jake said, "Take the DL and video card; at least we've got a name and we'll ruin his date night if he can't rent a movie."

Jake reached down, picked up the cell phone, and tossed it to Trey. "Check to see his recent calls and take a look at his directory."

Trey scrolled through the phone, calling out names, almost all Asian.

"Who were they just talking with?" asked Jake.

Trey punched up that feature and reported the results. "No name but a 310 area code, five minutes, thirty-five seconds."

Jake pressed harder, the man's face buried in the ground. "Who were you just talking to?"

The man said nothing.

Jake dug his heel hard into the man's neck and repeated the question.

"Mohammed," he croaked.

"This isn't a knock-knock joke. Mohammed who?"

"I just know him as Mohammed."

"What was the call about?"

"He's looking to buy some stuff."

"What stuff?" said Jake, grinding his foot deeper into the man's neck.

"Counterfeit stuff—watches, clothes, cigarettes. He's a regular. He sometimes makes small purchases of meth. I swear that's all I know. It's the truth," said the man, struggling to speak and breathe.

Jake said to Trey, "Keep the phone." Then, whispering in his best Clint Eastwood imitation to the two men on the ground, he said, "You two, keep your eyes on the street. If you lift your head or turn toward us, I promise you will both have closed-casket funerals because I will blow your faces into Beverly Hills."

With that Jake and Trey rushed to the van. Jake jumped into the driver's seat. The engine kicked over on the first attempt and he goosed the accelerator, squealing out of the alley toward Wilshire Boulevard as the two FBI agents removed the stockings from their heads. The four women who had been at the end of the alley when the altercation began were nowhere to be seen.

"That went well. You're kind of fun to play with when you aren't cranky," said Trey with a broad grin. "Where'd that elbow come from? Is that legal?"

"Marquis of Queensberry rules only count in the ring. You always cheat on the street," Jake said, laughing.

"What do you expect me to do with this cell phone? Given the way we obtained it, the U.S. Attorney is never going to allow us to use anything we get from it as evidence at trial."

"Let's worry about the rules of evidence after we rescue two kidnap victims. Ask the tech guys to dump the SIM card for previous calls and check the names in his directory against our files. We need to find out who this Mohammed is. At least one of the attackers at Park's house was Middle Eastern and we had the Iranian broadcaster's plates. Maybe they're somehow involved in this," said Jake.

Trey thought for a moment and said, "If Korean mobsters are working with Iranian-connected Middle Eastern bangers, this case will be one for the record books."

As Jake ran a yellow light on Wilshire, he glanced toward Trey and said, "Stranger things have happened. Remember we had that mafia gang two years ago that teamed up with the Mexican drug cartel to deliver khat from Uganda to the Somali expat community?"

"Yeah," Trey replied. "That was the stuff that was tainted with some kind of chemical, killing seven of the buyers—and the ACLU sued the Bureau and the DEA for not stopping the shipment before the stuff hit the streets."

"Well, I don't think that's going to happen here," said Jake. "By the way, did you notice neither of the two guys we took down tonight seemed to know how to defend himself? I thought they all knew karate."

Trey laughed. "I think that's Japanese."

"Whatever."

CHAPTER FIFTY-TWO

DAY 8

MONDAY, MAY 5

Jake arranged with his ICE contacts for a two-man FBI undercover truck-driving team to pick up Park's container at the Otay Mesa border crossing at ten in the morning. Unlike his nighttime antics with the two border thieves a week ago, this pickup was uneventful.

Jake's UC budget for this operation included rented space at an offload transit facility in the Valley. The shipment would arrive there at about two. Instead of shadowing the delivery, Jake was en route to a "cloth-napkined" Studio City restaurant.

He parked on the street to avoid the valet, saving himself the paperwork hassle of trying to get reimbursed for a tip. Though it really wasn't necessary, he entered the restaurant through the rear door and made a quick stop at the restroom before heading for his noon appointment.

While washing his hands, Jake questioned why Olivia Knox, the Assistant Director in Charge of the FBI's L.A. office, had arranged for this hastily called meeting. He assumed it had to do with his nocturnal confrontation with ASAC Hafner and/or the psych eval Trey had mentioned. That had to be why she had set the meeting for a very public venue, where he was less likely to go postal.

"Welcome to the Bistro Garden," said the hostess as he approached.

"Thanks," said Jake. "I'm supposed to meet someone and I'm not sure if she's here yet."

"Are you Jake?" asked the hostess.

He nodded guardedly.

"She's already seated. Please follow me."

With that Jake accompanied the hostess to a table in the back corner. Olivia rose as he approached, offering her hand and a smile.

"Thanks for coming," said his boss. She was wearing a chic, well-tailored, navy blue Elie Tahari pantsuit. Though he thought, *She's trying to look younger than she is,* he had to admit she was a picture-perfect representative of the FBI management team.

The contrast with his attire, a clean but faded Polo shirt, jeans, and cowboy boots, was stark. He said, "Please pardon me for being underdressed for this occasion, but when the ADIC says 'meet me for lunch, come as you are,' I figure it was a good thing you called after I was dressed."

"I'm glad you were wearing pants," she said with just the hint of a smile. "I appreciate you being here on such short notice—and am very aware how engaged you are right now with this investigation. I didn't want to put you in jeopardy by having you come to the office."

"Thanks. Under the circumstances it's probably best I steer clear of the federal building."

"I think it's safe here. I didn't see any Korean crime lords, suspected terrorists, or defense attorneys."

Jake offered a cautious smile.

"I understand you and Hafner went at it the other night."

Here it comes, a counseling session or at least her way of saying they are ordering an emergency psych evaluation. He could feel the bile churning in his stomach but had the self-discipline to remain silent.

"We are all under a lot of pressure with this investigation and maybe I've been pushing Charles too hard." She paused, taking a sip of water, then said, "I have some bad news and I wanted you to hear it from me."

Jake stared, waiting for her delivery.

"The LAPD found Gabe Chong's body early this morning. He was tortured and murdered."

Jake was stunned, his mind racing to find the right words, but nothing came. After a prolonged moment he said, "Have you told Brian Carter?"

Knox was confused. "No, why would we?"

"They were best friends in the Marine Corps."

"Oh no," she said with genuine sympathy, sorrow gripping her face.

The server approached. "May I get you something from the bar?"

Knox shook her head and ordered iced tea. Jake ordered a Coke. When he left, Knox continued: "I'm not sure under the circumstances we can tell him. This is extremely sensitive and if it gets out he was with the Agency there will be ramifications, both in D.C. and overseas."

"Where'd they find him?"

"An LAPD patrol unit found him in an alley off Wilshire Boulevard in Koreatown after a call on their tip line. At first they thought he was passed out drunk, but when they turned the body over they saw the carnage. He'd been beaten, his legs broken, his femoral artery slit, and he was shot in the head."

Jake swallowed hard. "How long had he been dead?"

"The coroner hasn't pinpointed an exact time but at least forty-eight hours, based upon rigor. He said it would have been an excruciating death. I don't understand how anyone could inflict such torture on another human being."

Jake sat there without saying a word, trying to comprehend all he was hearing. Almost in a whisper he said, "I think every human is capable of evil, given the right circumstances."

"We need to pull you out immediately."

Jake was silent for a moment, then said calmly, "That would be a mistake. I'm deep into Park and he may be responsible for what happened to Gabe. It's possible Gabe was a reprisal killing in the turf war between Park and Yeong. At least give me a chance to discover why Gabe was murdered and turn his death into a victory."

"Jake, we have our orders from back east."

"I thought my orders were to find out everything possible about the North Koreans flooding the globe with Supernotes," said Jake with a little too much force.

"It was, but the mission's changed. Gabe's death changes a lot. We can't risk the same thing happening to you."

His voice rose slightly. "But I can risk it. I know how far I can push. You have to trust me on this one."

She shook her head. "The safest course of action right now is for us to terminate the operation. Headquarters agrees. That's why they've ordered you to come in. They're getting their marching orders from State. I'm sorry I even invited Gabe to the meeting in the SCIF. I wish he hadn't been read in on our project. He probably gave you up."

"He didn't," said Jake without hesitating.

"How do you know?"

"He's a Marine. *Semper Fidelis*, always faithful."

"You're putting a lot of trust in a man you just met the other day."

"It's a brotherhood thing. Besides, if he had given me up I'd be dead by now."

The server returned with the drinks and asked if they were ready to order. Knox said they needed a couple of minutes. As soon as he left, Jake continued. "I am meeting Park this afternoon when I deliver a container to his warehouse. Let me meet with him and see where we stand with the kidnapping and Tommy's murder. The whole thing will be recorded and I'll be armed. I would think our Headquarters and the Agency would want to know if Park is behind Gabe's murder. I don't know if I can find out, but at least we have a chance."

"I don't know," Knox said, shaking her head as she maintained eye contact.

"Look, Park has already told me he needs this container to pay the ransom for his daughter and granddaughter. If we pull out now, if we go overt, or refuse to deliver the container, both Jenny and Gracie die. I don't think you want to explain that to OPR or State or the press."

"Jake, Hafner's already gone over my head calling for your removal as the undercover agent in this investigation. He called Headquarters early yesterday morning—"

Jake interrupted. "That must have been before he learned Gabe was missing. He called me yesterday, asking for help, all polite and proper. What a piece of work! Where do you find these guys?"

"Jake, that's not important. What is important is if anything happens to you or to the kidnap victims while you are involved in your undercover capacity, we will be subjected to all kinds of second-guessing," she said as she took a sip of iced tea. "If we tell Park we know of the kidnapping, we remove ourselves from any legal liability."

"What about moral responsibility?"

"Jake, I just don't think we can allow you to continue. We have our orders."

Jake shook his head slowly. Without being confrontational, closer to a plea, he said, "Come on, Olivia. Don't go Bureau on me. Trust me. You have in the past and I've always come through for you."

She laughed. "Do you have any idea how many sleepless nights you've given me?"

"Call me. I don't sleep, either," said Jake with a slight grin.

She smiled, pausing before speaking. "As you've probably figured out, this is a highly unusual and sensitive case. The Director has been briefed daily and is keeping the Attorney General and the President updated. Up until today, it seemed like everyone in Washington wanted to know what the North Koreans are up to. Now it seems as though there are some in the administration and Congress who want this operation shut down."

Jake shook his head and said, "Sounds to me like this is becoming another bad case of political indigestion—just like Fast and Furious, the IRS Enemies List, and Benghazi."

"Well," Knox continued, "there are certainly people in Washington who want to shut this case down."

"Why?"

"I'm not sure. We've kept Headquarters updated. The 'drones' at Hoover and DOJ have immediate access to our entire case file. They know everything once we input the information. Something has changed. It's more than Gabe's death but it's something State's not sharing."

Jake said nothing.

Knox leaned forward almost as if the two were about to engage in a romantic conversation. In a voice just loud enough for Jake to hear she said, "Look, the regime in Pyongyang is dangerous and unstable. Lately they have been very bold.

"The NKPA has shelled South Korea, tested nuclear weapons, and test-fired ICBMs capable of delivering a nuclear warhead. Kim Jong Un even declared the 1953 armistice nullified. Blackmail is their favored avenue of political negotiations. We know North Korea has enough weaponized fissile material for at least six atomic bombs. They've admitted to possessing thirty-seven kilograms of plutonium."

"Sounds like a worthy target," said Jake, not giving any ground.

"They are, but the FBI doesn't make foreign policy. That's the purview of the White House and the State Department. We take our orders from DOJ and right now those orders are for me to pull you out. It's above my pay grade and it doesn't matter whether I agree or not. They don't always clue me in on everything that goes on in the Washington decision-making process. I can only pray those issuing a final verdict have our nation's best interests at heart."

When the server returned to take their order, Knox said, "I'm sorry. We just got to gabbing. It's been years since we've seen each other and we have so much catching up to do. Give us just a sec."

She said it without stumbling, like a skilled liar. Jake was impressed.

Picking up the menu, Knox said, "Maybe we better look at the menu and we can finish this discussion after we order."

As Jake was opening the menu, Knox said, "I love their cold poached salmon."

Jake looked at the price and quickly said, "I'll probably just get the club sandwich."

Knox moved a stray hair behind her left ear and said, "This is coming out of my budget, not yours."

"In that case, I'll take the sliced filet mignon sandwich and fries," said Jake with a smile.

Knox laughed and signaled the server, who took their order.

"Okay, where were we?" she said. But before Jake could assist, she continued, "Oh yeah, I remember. Look, here's the bottom line. Without the proceeds from their criminal activities, North Korea can't afford to do any of the nuclear and missile research they conduct."

Jake gave her a look.

Knox continued, "It takes tens of billions of dollars. It's not just the Supernotes. They counterfeit everything—from clothing to cigarettes to pharmaceuticals. It's a multifaceted conspiracy and if our information is correct there may be more than a billion in Supernotes already in circulation. We have no way of telling how

CHAPTER FIFTY-THREE

As he started the Range Rover, Jake heard his backup cell phone, the one Katie used to carry, chirp in the door pocket. He pulled it out—saw the caller ID was blocked—and answered with a curt "Hello."

A voice he recognized said, "It's Grizzly Six. If you're not alone, just answer 'yes' or 'no.' "

Jake smiled. No one who ever served with Peter Newman would ever forget his radio call sign.

"I'm alone. Good to hear your voice, sir."

"And yours, Jake," said the retired Marine major general. "I'm calling because I just left a meeting where your name came up several times."

With a hint of levity, Jake said, "I hope you weren't meeting with bill collectors or IRS agents."

"No," Newman replied. "Unfortunately, it was much worse than that. Do you have a few minutes?"

Now serious, Jake said, "Yes, sir. I have time—but we're on an open line. And I'm in bad-guy territory."

much counterfeit money is floating around the international markets."

"And this doesn't make our case important?"

"Of course it does, but State wants us to put this operation on hold and the AG agrees. Regardless of where you've been or where you're going, we need to shut this down."

"So Gabe died for nothing and two victims of a kidnapping don't come home because somebody in D.C. wants us out of the game? We're going to let two innocents die and nobody cares."

"I care, Jake," said Olivia with a sincerity Jake believed.

"Then I have to meet with Park this afternoon. I'll get the container to him; otherwise he can't pay the ransom."

She paused for an extended moment, her eyes gazing in the distance. Jake maintained his focus on her, refraining from offering any more comments. When she turned back toward him she said, "Jake, you can meet with Park. I don't want to see the little girl or the daughter killed. Turn over the container, but I think then we have to pull you out."

"So you'll give me until the end of the day?"

"If that's how long it takes to get the container processed and unloaded, you have until the end of the day."

"Okay. Midnight. That's all I need."

As the server approached with their plates, Jake stood up. "I hate to ask this but an emergency just came up at work. Could you box this up for me?"

Jake smiled at Knox as he followed the server to the swinging doors into the kitchen. Before leaving the restaurant via the same back door he had used to enter, Jake waved to Olivia, mouthed the words "Thank you" while holding up the Styrofoam container, and blew her a kiss—hoping it would drive her a little bit nuts.

"I know where you are; I'm looking at the GPS locater on your phone. But this is important and time is not an ally today. How long before you can call me back from a secure phone or a hard line so we can have a ten-minute conversation without committing too many security violations?"

Jake pulled over to the curb to give the call his full attention. He looked around, saw the Marine recruiting substation in the strip mall less than a hundred yards from where he was parked, and said, "I'll call you back, collect, in five from a hard line."

"Good," said the general. "But use the 800 number I gave you. It's direct."

"Roger that, sir."

It took less than three minutes for Jake to flash his Marine Corps League membership card, his FBI credentials, and the promise of an FBI baseball hat for him to be seated in Gunnery Sergeant Barry Simon's office. He dialed the 800 number. The general answered on the first ring.

Newman got straight to the point. "Since we talked a few weeks ago, CSG has been contracted to do vulnerability evaluations for a bunch of three-letter organizations back here. I just left a damage assessment meeting—where you and another of my Marines were prominently featured. You with me, so far?"

Jake knew his former commander had retired as a major general when the Senate wouldn't approve his third star—and that he had taken over as the CEO of a company called Centurion Solutions Group. But other than hearing about CSG being awarded some classified contracts with CIA, NSA, DIA, and the FBI, Jake didn't really know much about the company's business. In response to the general's "you with me?" query, Jake responded, "Yes, sir."

Newman continued: "You know about Gabe?"

"Yes, sir."

"Have the people you're working for told you the op you are on is being shut down?"

"I was told just a few minutes ago the plug gets pulled at midnight tonight."

"Were you told *why* it was being shut down?"

"I was told it's because of what happened to Gabe and for my safety. But I think there's more to it than that."

"There's a lot more to it," interrupted the general. "DOJ and State are probably telling your boss out there it's about safety. But the real reason the operation is being shut down is because the White House does not want it to become known the DPRK is working with the IRGC to build nuclear weapons and ICBMs."

Jake was stunned. "Are we talking about the same case? I'm working a counterfeit goods violation and a kidnapping. My targets are Korean gangsters moving containers of illicit merchandise into the United States."

"Yeah, I know," Newman continued. "But what nobody bothered to tell you is Pyongyang and Tehran have found a way to skirt compliance with this new nuclear arms agreement by having the North Koreans build nuclear warheads and ICBMs for the ayatollahs."

"How does that connect with the California Korean Mafia moving containers of knockoff jeans, watches, and cigarettes into the States?"

"Here's the short form," Newman said after a brief pause. "The Senate has to ratify the so-called International Agreement on Iranian Nuclear Research and Development in the next thirty days. If it becomes known North Korea is doing uranium and plutonium enrichment and ICBM R&D for Tehran to avoid detection by the International Atomic Energy Agency, the Senate will vote down the treaty."

"But how do containers full of counterfeit goods and drugs play into the North Koreans building nuclear weapons for Iran?"

"The North Koreans oversold their own nuclear fuel enrichment and ICBM R&D capability—and Tehran bought Pyongyang's BS. Now agents for the DPRK are scurrying all over the globe, buying up advanced centrifuge components, nuke warhead electromechanical technology, and high-tech industrial robotic machinery for building ICBMs."

"But that stuff has to cost a whole lot more than they can raise with a few dozen containers of phony Rolex watches and the other stuff I'm seeing."

"You're right," Newman replied. "That's why there's a flood of Supernotes here in the United States and all over Europe. The North Koreans are paying for all the illicit technology with counterfeit hundred-dollar bills."

Jake pondered the information for a moment, then said quietly, "All the more reason why the right thing to do is keep this case going, not kill it."

"This isn't about right or wrong, Jake. It's about institutional arrogance. The nuclear arms deal with Iran is the only diplomatic claim to fame this White House has left. If this treaty goes down the tubes, so does the president's legacy as a great statesman."

"So justice doesn't matter. Gabe's torture-murder doesn't matter. And Iran cheating on a nuclear arms treaty doesn't matter. All that matters is the ego of—"

"Stop, Jake. You're preaching to the choir," Newman interrupted. "Here's something else that matters to me: not losing another of my Marines—meaning you."

"Yes, sir."

"At the meeting I just left, the Agency rep described how Gabe was brutally tortured before he was killed. Langley is convinced he was compromised by someone inside the operation."

"That's possible," said Jake. "It could have been Cho Hee Sun, the guy they called Sonny. He was killed out here last week. But it could have also been Sonny's brother in Hong Kong. There are a lot of different agencies playing in this sandbox—and way too many people with a 'need-to-know' who don't know anything."

"Well, here's a little of what I know from the NSA rep on this damage assessment team: This fellow Park Soon Yong that you have contacted is the big gun for the DPRK. Park is in charge of disbursing counterfeit currency in the United States and buying the high-tech toys the North Koreans need to make good on their deal with the Iranians. He's apparently waiting for a large shipment of cash—real or counterfeit, nobody seems to know—so he can purchase the items on Pyongyang's shopping list and ship them back to North Korea. And finally, the Agency seems to think Park is somehow involved in Gabe's murder. I hope you have someone to cover *your* six—because Gabe didn't."

"Many thanks for the intel, General. It's good to know since I will apparently be off this case at midnight. You just gave me more straight scoop than I've gotten from the Bureau since this op began—"

"Oh yeah, since you mentioned the Bureau: do you have a fellow by the name of Hafner in the FBI office out there?"

"Yes, sir, he's the ASAC. Why?"

"Well, he was on the secure video link for part of this damage assessment meeting. Hafner said you were being pulled off the case and sent back here for a psych eval. I took the opportunity to tell him that it would be a waste of money. Anybody who leaves the Corps to join the Bureau has to be certifiable."

"Thanks, General," said Jake with a smile. "I'll continue to use you as a reference in my ongoing search for meaningful work. Please give my fond regards to Mrs. Newman."

The sign-off was classic Newman: "Keep your head down, Jake. Call if you need a QRF. You mean a lot to me. *Semper Fi*, Marine."

CHAPTER FIFTY-FOUR

Jake finished backing the trailer up to the loading dock while waiting for Park to arrive. He shut down the diesel engine, pondering what he had learned from Peter Newman and wondering about the contents of the forty-foot container. If the general was right, the steel box held currency—real or counterfeit—to be used for buying centrifuges and other nuclear weapons components for the North Korean government. But if Jake understood Park correctly, the crime boss intended to use some or all of what was in the container to pay a three-million-dollar ransom.

It was a few minutes after three and Jake was surprised there was no one here to open the warehouse. Time seemed to be of the essence and he assumed Park and his minions would be on-scene when he arrived. Wondering if there had been a problem, Jake had begun to punch in Park's number when he spotted the GMC Yukon turning the corner.

Park was driving, accompanied by the Green Hornet and Kato—the two-man security team Park considered to be most reliable. A rental box truck followed Park with three Asian men cramped in the front seat. Both vehicles turned into the alley entrance of the warehouse and Jake knew that in a matter of minutes the loading-dock door would be opened.

As the door slowly rose he spotted the six men through his sideview mirrors. They scrambled around, moving cargo inside the warehouse, making room for the contents of the container. He jumped down from the cab, approached Park, and asked, "Any word, sir?"

"Nothing yet, Jake. Please, let's hurry."

Jake pulled the one-page bill of lading from his back pocket and handed it to Park. In his other hand Jake gripped a long pair of bolt cutters. He and Park walked to the back of the shipping container and Jake grabbed the thin metal seal attached to the lock.

Jake examined the serial numbers on the seal and read them off to Park, who compared the numbers to those listed on the bill of lading.

Park said, "Not that I doubted you but the numbers match. Open it."

Jake wanted to reinforce his integrity. "Mr. Park, I want to assure you no one has tampered with this container since it left Korea. As you can see, the seal is intact."

Park nodded but was anxious to get the container unloaded. "Yes, I see that. Just get it open."

Using the bolt cutters, Jake easily clipped the seal and opened the cumbersome steel doors to a container packed from floor to ceiling with . . . rolls of fabric!

Jake was shocked. How would yards of cotton and polyester fund the three-million-dollar ransom to save Jenny and Gracie? This couldn't be the large shipment of cash Newman had told him about just a few hours ago.

After one of the workers backed the box truck within a few feet of the container, Park ordered the unloading to begin. The men quieted and began the arduous task of unloading the multicolored rolls of fabric, encased in clear plastic, each numbered on the outside in four-inch figures. Park's two bodyguards stood at the ready. Though weapons weren't visible Jake assumed the men were well armed.

Jake and Park stood off to the side as Park carefully watched each roll come off the truck. Two men would awkwardly grab a roll and toss it into the box truck, where the third man restacked it. To Jake each roll was identical: six feet wide, a foot in diameter, fifty feet long when unrolled. Park was anxious, mumbling with each roll that was removed. Jake noted the frustration but said nothing.

It was a warm afternoon and sweat was pouring off the men as they moved the rolls of fabric from the container to the truck.

"You guys want something to drink?" asked Jake, knowing Tommy kept a refrigerator full of beer and soda in his office.

The men didn't respond and Jake wasn't sure if they understood English. Park didn't seem anxious to translate and before Jake could ask a second time, Park pointed to a roll of fabric and hollered, "That one."

The two workers holding the roll looked at Park. Park repeated his declaration in Korean. The men stepped toward Park and placed the roll in front of him. Satisfied after examining the number, he ordered the men to deliver the fabric roll to the office.

Jake was as confused as the workers.

Once inside the office, the men placed the roll on the table next to the desk. Park ordered the workers to return and continue unloading the container. He instructed the Green Hornet and Kato to remain in the hallway.

Jake pulled out two Cokes from the refrigerator. "Do you want me to give them anything to drink?"

Park offered a dismissive backhanded wave as he closed the door. Jake popped the top to his drink and took a long sip as Park ripped at the thick clear plastic encasing the roll of fabric. Unable to tear it and seeing Park's frustration, Jake whipped out the switchblade from his rear pocket, the blade springing open. The crime boss smiled as Jake easily cut the wrapping.

"Why rolls of fabric?" asked Jake, still trying to come to grips with the criminality of this latest act.

"Imported fabric is a customs violation if it's out of quota. It carries a civil not a criminal penalty. I wanted to minimize the risk of getting this shipment through the Mexican ports and into the United States." Park paused, then said, "I still do not know who kidnapped my daughter and granddaughter. Someone from our community, maybe even someone from the inside. I can trust no one, not even my own people."

Jake started to speak. "Mr. Park, I would never—"

Park interrupted. "Jake, I trusted Tommy. He died trying to save me. Now I must trust you. You knew nothing about the contents of this container, only that I was bringing it in, just as you had done for me before." Park, still focused on the rolls, said, "Now, help me unroll the fabric."

"Mr. Park, I don't understand."

"Unroll the fabric." It was an order, not a request.

As Jake and Park unrolled about twenty feet of the six-foot-wide fabric, allowing it to fall to the floor, they came upon stacks of hundred-dollar bills wrapped neatly, several rows deep.

Jake was genuinely astonished. "What the . . ."

Park held up a bundle. "These are Supernotes. Counterfeits made in North Korea."

Jake grabbed a bundle and held it up to the light. It even had what appeared to be a genuine Federal Reserve wrapper. Removing a single bill, he examined it closely. "I've heard about these. They look perfect."

Park nodded. "They almost are. This is how I will get back my Jenny and Gracie."

Jake looked confused. "You're going to pay the ransom in counterfeit bills?"

"Yes."

"Isn't that dangerous?"

"Why? They won't be able to tell the difference and neither can the banks. Whoever took my family will not be any wiser as to the legitimacy of the currency."

Jake cautioned, "But if they get caught with the bills, it could come back on you."

"As long as my daughter and granddaughter are safely returned, it doesn't matter. I will get my money back."

Jake considered asking *how*. Instead he said, "Is there enough here to pay the ransom?"

Park nodded. "There are three hundred packets of ten thousand dollars each. That's three million, just like the ransom demand."

Jake understood. "That's why you think someone within your organization is in on the kidnapping. The kidnappers knew about this shipment and the exact amount."

Park said, "It seems a little too convenient the ransom is for the amount I just received."

"Who knew about the Supernotes?"

"Tommy knew the money was coming in but didn't know it was Supernotes. I told him I was bringing in the money to buy certain hard-to-get items for shipment back to Korea. He and my superiors in North Korea are the only ones who knew of this shipment and the amount."

"Your superiors. Who are they?" Jake asked.

Park pondered the question for a moment and said, "They are the people who sent me this container and its contents. They are expecting me to purchase certain items with this money. I will tell you more when the time is right."

"Why did Tommy know about the amount of money in this shipment?"

"I had to trust him because I needed to make sure this container arrived. I was unwilling to chance having it shipped through the Port of Long Beach. I knew I could get it safely into Mexico but had to be guaranteed it would clear the border in San Diego. You successfully brought in my previous container and I knew from Tommy you brought in a container for him and two containers for Yeong. You proved your value and reliability."

Jake took a sip of the Coke. "So I guess I was hanging out if this didn't make it across the border."

"You passed. That is all that matters."

Jake said, "So other than those overseas, no one but Tommy and you knew the contents of this container."

"You are correct, Jake, but no one overseas would be behind this."

"Why would you say that?"

"I am the purchasing agent for some very difficult-to-obtain items needed in North Korea to fulfill their obligations to others."

"And you're going to buy these items with Supernotes?"

"Yes."

"So what are you supposed to buy with this cash?" queried Jake casually.

Park looked long and hard at him before responding. The North Korean intelligence officer's life had become decidedly more complicated in the last seventy-two hours. He needed a replacement for Tommy and decided on the spot the "round-eye" could be trusted.

"I not only import goods. I'm also in the export business and I need your services for both," said Park.

"What do you export?" asked Jake.

"The three million was sent here to buy advanced magnetic-suspension centrifuges and special electronic switches and equipment."

"I don't know much about electronics, but if the money's right I'm in."

Park smiled. He understood avarice and said, "I have been told that the parts are for manufacturing what the American military calls permissive action links—PALs. I need a Caucasian to buy this equipment here and elsewhere to deflect suspicion."

"What's a PAL?" asked Jake, hoping all this was being picked up on his miniature recording device.

"Every nuclear weapon has a PAL—it is how nuclear weapons are armed. Each weapon has a different PAL code. The correct code must be entered or it will not detonate."

"And you can buy centrifuges and PAL devices here?"

"No, but a round-eye with three million can buy a test shipment of the necessary parts. If the equipment is satisfactory to our scientists in Pyongyang and their client, we will be sent much more money for other acquisitions."

"So who is the client, and does he have the money to make this worthwhile given the risks we're going to take?" asked Jake.

"I am not supposed to know, but it is Iran. The Iranians have shut down their fissile material enrichment operations to comply with the new international agreement on Iranian nuclear arms. That's why Pyongyang and Tehran have signed a compact to do all that work in North Korea."

Jake shook his head and said, "The ayatollahs just contracted it out?"

"You could say that," Park commented. "But now I must have your help, Jake—and you will be very well compensated."

Jake paused before responding, staggered by Park's open discussion of nuclear weapons caught on his undercover recording device. "But how can you use this cash for buying nuke weapons stuff if you've already passed it on as ransom to the kidnappers?"

"You are very astute, Jake. That is why I trust you. You are correct. We must deliver this cash to the kidnappers, recover Jenny and Gracie, and then retrieve the money—and we must do this quickly before my superiors in Pyongyang realize what I have done."

The undercover agent paused for a moment, then said, "Someone with the kidnappers must have known you were receiving this money—and the amount. That's why the ransom was set at three million for Jenny and Gracie. If you and Tommy are the only ones here who knew the timing and the amount, then it must be someone from overseas. Do you have enemies inside your government?"

In almost a whisper Park said, "I am dealing with honorable men overseas. The family is sacred. They would never target the family."

Jake shook his head. "We still don't know who's behind this kidnapping."

Park pointed to two burlap bags. "As I said, there are supposed to be three hundred packets of bills, ten thousand dollars per packet. Each of us will count a hundred fifty packets and put them in a bag. Place both bags in my car and we will return to my home to see if there is any news."

CHAPTER FIFTY-FIVE

By the time Jake and Park finished counting and bagging the packets, the three loaders, the rental truck, and the rolls of fabric were gone. Jake followed Park and his two bodyguards as they left the warehouse and drove east to San Marino. He checked his mirrors, carefully searching for surveillance, either friend or foe. He spotted nothing out of the ordinary but knew his fellow FBI agents were professionals who could elude detection. He couldn't risk their interference either. Not now; too much was at stake.

Jake knew he was trapped between two—perhaps three—rival gangs and the possibility Park had enemies in his own organization who wanted to bring him down. He also knew from his previous undercover experience the high-wire act without a net is always more entertaining to the patrons than the participant. Jake just hoped to avoid the high winds and a plummet to the asphalt below. He waited until both cars pulled onto the freeway before punching the speed-dial feature on the phone.

Trey picked up on the third ring after spotting the caller ID. "Jake, let me put you on speaker. I've got Brian here with me."

There was a click. "You there?" asked Trey.

There was an awkward pause as Jake wrestled with revealing Gabe's death. He caught himself in a role he'd accused so many of playing. He was comforted by the fact he needed to make the notification in person, not over the speaker from his cell phone.

"Yeah, I'm on my way back to Park's house. Any word?" asked Jake.

"On what?"

"On anything," said Jake, frustrated he had to spell out his interest in the investigation.

"I'm not hearing anything from Hafner or the Agency."

"Figures. Did you come up with anything on the bartender?"

"Yeah," said Trey, rummaging through the papers on his desk. "Turns out your drinking buddy's slave name is Jerome Johnson. He legally changed it to Kareem Abdul five years ago after he converted to Islam while at Folsom. He's a two-striker. Both convictions are for armed robbery."

"Is he still on paper?"

"Nope, got off parole last November," said Trey.

"That explains why he can tend bar at Yeong's place," said Jake.

"I thought alcohol was prohibited for traditional Muslims. Wasn't that the whole issue with the Somali cabdrivers in Minneapolis refusing to transport passengers carrying booze?" asked Trey.

"It is. It's called *haram*, forbidden in Islam. We were schooled on the culture before we deployed," said Brian.

"Those 9/11 hijackers didn't have problems with partying before the attacks," said Trey.

Brian continued. "That's the great thing about martyrdom. It cleanses you of all your past sins. You are absolved of everything and once you pull the pin of the suicide vest you are whisked straight to Paradise, where your seventy-two virgins await."

"So you think he's ready to martyr himself?" asked Trey.

"No, but a terrorist cell can be very forgiving if he's putting in work. Financial success can trump martyrdom," said Brian.

"What about Candy?" asked Jake.

"Squeaky clean. She has a brother upstate in Folsom but she has no convictions, no arrests," said Brian. "Does that make her approachable?"

"That's a tough call. If she knows anything she might be willing to talk, assuming she thought as much about Tommy as he did of her. Let's hold off for now," said Jake. "Have you been able to pull up the crime reports on Kareem's two convictions?"

"Both home invasions; confessed to the first one, convicted of the second. The report mentions a drug problem and he needed a quick cash infusion. Did he strike you as using?"

"No, he's clean. If anything he might be on juice, steroids. He's a rock. I certainly didn't notice any needle marks and his eyes were clear."

"What's going on at your end?" asked Trey.

"I'm following Park back to his place. See if the kidnappers have called."

"We'd hear if they did."

"Is there any activity on Park's phones?" asked Jake.

"A few condolences."

"What about Hafner and the Agency? Are they giving you anything? Is NSA picking up any overhears?"

"Hafner's keeping us both in the dark. I think they believe my loyalty sides with you rather than management."

"Great, I can use a partner in Adak when I'm doing background checks for security clearances. Listen, I can't really talk about it now but we have until the end of the day to wrap this up. I need both of you guys on the ready."

"What are you talking about?" asked Trey.

"They're shutting this down at midnight. That means we have a little more than six hours. Just be ready. I'll explain it all later. I'll call you after I leave Park's place."

"Be safe," said Trey, ending the call.

CHAPTER FIFTY-SIX

When Jake and Park, accompanied by the crime boss's security team, entered the living room, Park's wife was waiting, dried tears caked on her face. Soo Min, her face badly bruised, was still bandaged from the wounds she received two nights earlier and was sitting nervously on the couch.

Park spotted the large bouquet of fresh-cut flowers sitting on the coffee table and offered an inquisitive glance.

"The flowers arrived about an hour ago. The card is addressed to you. I was afraid to open it," said his wife, handing the card to Park.

Park tore open the envelope and removed the card. He read the card once, closed it, and opened it again, rereading the message. "It is from the kidnappers. I must make a call."

"May I see it?" asked Jake.

Park nodded, handing the card to Jake, who grabbed it, not worrying about its evidentiary value, and read the contents. The note was in English, which the FBI agent thought strange if the kidnappers were Korean: *We know you have the money. Call us immediately.*

Jake noted the phone number—undoubtedly a throwaway cell phone.

As Park picked up the phone, preparing to call the number on the card, Jake shouted, "Wait!"

Both guards jumped, startled by the outburst and prepared to protect their boss.

"What?" asked Park, seemingly confused as he looked at Jake.

He shook his head purposefully. "You better not use your home phone."

"Why?"

Jake handed Park his cell phone, activating the discreet consensual recording button. "The police know who you are and that you were robbed the other day. They may have tapped your phones hoping you'll identify who killed Tommy."

Park nodded. "You are wise. I do not want them to know about the kidnapping."

"Exactly," said Jake with a look of confident reassurance. "Call the number using my phone."

Park smiled and said, "Thank you," in a moment of genuine gratitude.

"Ask for proof," said Jake.

"Proof of what?"

"Proof of life. Ask to speak to Jenny. Be strong. Refuse to give into their demands unless they can prove Jenny and Gracie are alive," said Jake with conviction and authority.

"You sound as if you have handled such a situation before." It was a statement, not an accusation.

Jake shrugged and offered a comforting smile, hoping he hadn't overplayed his hand. "Some people think I watch too much television. In Hollywood they always ask for proof of life."

Park walked toward the French doors leading to the garden and punched in the phone number listed in the message. Both guards followed him onto the patio as he made the call.

Jake sat on the couch next to Soo Min, comforting the older

woman, knowing he could play back the call when he departed the residence. "It's going to be okay. We'll get Jenny and Gracie back."

Park's wife said nothing, realizing her husband's chosen profession continued to destroy the only life she knew and the family she loved.

Jake could make out pieces of the conversation as both he and Soo Min focused on Park. The crime boss talked for several minutes, all in English, which again surprised Jake—reinforcing his conclusion the kidnappers were not a rival Korean gang. After a brief minute of cajoling, Jake heard Park say, "Are you okay?" There was a pause. "And Gracie?" Then Park responded, "It's going to be okay. I will bring you both home."

When the kidnappers came back to the phone Park said, "I will get you your money but if you harm either of them you will never live to spend the ransom." Park paused, listening to their response, then said, "Laugh if you want but I have not succeeded in this country on kindness alone."

With that the call ended. Park returned slowly from the patio, his guards following closely, and handed the phone to Jake.

Park thought for an extended moment before he asked, "Will you make the drop this evening?"

"Absolutely."

CHAPTER FIFTY-SEVEN

Jake had the window down, allowing the breeze to cool his face. His mind was spinning, as he planned how to navigate his next move. He knew Park and the kidnappers were both adversaries. And his own FBI would become an obstacle in another five hours. If he disclosed his plan, especially his intention to safely recover Jenny and Gracie, Hafner and the Bureau hierarchy would balk.

Logistically it was a nightmare. Legally it was questionable. No matter how you sliced it the chances of any rescue were slim. But attempting to convince Park to seek law enforcement assistance was futile and a SWAT entry made no sense; the deaths of Jenny and Gracie would be almost guaranteed.

Jake put his cell phone on speaker and played back the call Park placed to the kidnappers. Otis Redding was singing in the background and the voice was a distinct Middle Eastern accent; a strange combination. "The girls will not be hurt if you comply. Bring three million dollars to the Shanghai Hotel, room 212, at eight p.m. Do not be stupid. And whoever you send with the money, make sure he comes alone; otherwise your daughter and granddaughter die."

When Park demanded to speak to Jenny, she managed to say only a couple of words before the phone was yanked from her mouth. She begged for help, tears in her voice.

Jake replayed the recording, seeking more answers before calling Trey.

"Check indices and tell me everything we've got on the Shanghai Hotel," said Jake.

"The what?"

Jake repeated himself, then added, "If it's the same place I'm thinking, it's a whorehouse."

"Were you a patron or was this part of an official investigation?" asked Trey, not expecting an answer as he accessed the computer on his desk to search FBI records. "Got it. Yeah, it's on Olympic near Hoover in the Mid-Wilshire District."

"That's the one."

"You frequent the place?"

"No, but I did a dope deal there three years ago. It's a three-story building with girls running in and out all day. It's perfect for what I want to do."

"Do I want to know?"

"You are part of the plan . . . idiots!"

"Are you calling me an idiot?"

"No, them. I love it when their IQs are double digits below mine. Now we just have to play all the interests."

CHAPTER FIFTY-EIGHT

Jake pulled into the parking lot of a strip mall just north of the 10 Freeway, a few miles from Park's residence. He cruised slowly toward the lone empty parking space in front of the liquor store. Noting the five men congregating in front, he tapped his back as he exited the car, ensuring his Glock was securely nestled in the waistband. His biggest fear wasn't death; it was embarrassment.

He didn't want to get caught in the middle of an armed robbery, not having his weapon, and somehow the police and media learning an unarmed FBI agent failed to thwart a felony in progress. His destination was not the liquor store but the nondescript phone store next to it. Jake weaved his way past the men sharing a forty-ouncer hidden in a not-so-discreet brown paper bag. He smiled confidently, not wanting to be confrontational, but remembered the words of Marine General James Mattis preparing us for combat in Iraq: "Be polite, be professional, but have a plan to kill everyone you meet."

Jake was the only customer in the phone store, and the long-haired, pimply-faced teenager sitting behind the counter looked up from his iPad to greet a potential commissioned sale. "Can I help you?"

"I sure hope so," said Jake, acting confused by the many phones offered on the wall display.

"You've come to the right place. We've got all your cellular phone needs. You're actually in luck. The owner is running a special on the iPhone 5 and with a three-year service contract you get an automatic free upgrade each year on your contract anniversary."

Jake smiled. The kid was good and pushing hard for a sale, but the undercover agent was going to be a huge disappointment. "Look, I'm in a hurry and just want the cheapest prepaid phone you have in your inventory. It's for my grandmother so she can put it in her car in case of an emergency."

The clerk gave Jake a "cheapskate" look. "A lot of customers initially want the prepaid, minimal-use phone but quickly learn it's not the ideal plan. Let me show you some free phones that I can give you merely by adding your grandmother to our new family and friends plan. For less than a visit to Starbucks I can make your grandmother always available."

"Nice try but you don't get it. I don't want her always available. I want her to know this is limited use and only in the event of an emergency," said Jake, admiring the kid's persistence.

Without much of a fight, the young salesman selected a no-frills cell phone, which served the purpose but meant pennies in the young man's pocket.

Jake thought he'd ease the pain for the salesperson as he rang up the sale and was genuine in his next statement. "I'm in a hurry but I may be back. That three-year contract on a 5 sounds enticing. I'm looking to upgrade."

The clerk gave Jake an entrepreneurial grin. "I'll give you my card. I hope when you come back in you'll ask for me."

"You can count on it," said Jake as the teenager handed him the bag with the prepaid cell phone and a business card with his name and phone number on it.

Before Jake went to his car he stopped at the liquor store.

"You got aspirin?" Jake asked the clerk behind the counter. The man was short and dark, possibly Indian or Pakistani.

The clerk responded but Jake had no clue what he said. Jake repeated the question and the clerk pointed to shelves at the back of the store, where Jake found an assortment of high-priced over-the-counter drugs. He was looking for the largest bottle of aspirin and shook each bottle to make sure it met his needs. When he was satisfied, he found a roll of overpriced Scotch tape on another dust-covered shelf and stopped by the cooler to grab a Pepsi before heading to the cash register.

Once inside the car he popped three aspirin, washed them down with a swig from the Pepsi, wrapped the cotton from the aspirin bottle around the mouthpiece of the prepaid cell phone, then taped it in place with a couple of inches of tape from the roll he had just purchased.

CHAPTER FIFTY-NINE

Jake called Park as he approached the residence. When the gate opened he drove up the long driveway. Park was standing in front when Jake arrived, the Green Hornet and Kato by his side. As Jake hopped out of the car he said, "I don't have much time. I need to get back to the other side of town and I don't trust the traffic."

"I understand," said Park.

Jake handed him the cell phone and Park gave an inquisitive look.

"Just follow the directions on the card," said Jake, handing Park a three-by-five file card. "At the time specified on the card I need you to call this number and read exactly what I've written. Do you understand?"

Park nodded but asked, "Why the cotton?"

"I want your voice muffled."

"You mean in case the police have voice-recognition software?"

Jake hesitated with a response. That wasn't his reasoning but it sounded good. "Yes, exactly. You are a wise man, Mr. Park. Make sure you call exactly at seven forty-five tonight and read the message as I've written it."

Park smiled, sincerely appreciative of all Jake was doing to recover his daughter and granddaughter. In a final logistical act for tonight's drama, the North Korean intelligence agent handed him the two large burlap bags containing the three million in Supernotes. Jake recognized the grand gesture of trust it represented. Even if the counterfeit money cost Park nothing, the contents embodied the lives of Jenny and Gracie. Their safe return rested upon the shoulders of a man Park had met less than forty-eight hours earlier.

As Jake prepared to leave, Park grabbed him and gave him an uncharacteristic hug. "Thank you, Jake. You first approached me because you had been hired to kill my daughter. Now you are willing to risk your life to free my family. You are the only non-Korean I have ever allowed inside my organization. You know the most important thing tonight is to free Jenny and Gracie—after that we will worry about how to get the money back."

Jake nodded and said, "Yes, sir, I understand."

"Are you sure you do not want some of my men to follow you at a distance in case you need help?"

"The kidnappers said to come alone," the FBI agent replied. "If they spot your men, they will kill your daughter and granddaughter."

Park pondered that for a moment, nodded, and said, "You are right." Grasping Jake's hand, the North Korean intelligence officer whispered, "I will never forget you."

As Jake pulled away from the residence, he spotted the candies he had taken from Yeong's restaurant sitting in the cup holder. He unwrapped a piece and popped it in his mouth. As he let the confection rest on his tongue, the familiar smells of peppermint flooded the car. The memory took him back to the night of the kidnapping and the piece of candy he found on the floor following the melee. "Yeong's gotta be involved somehow," said Jake out loud.

CHAPTER SIXTY

Jake turned into the alley where Trey and Brian were waiting in a Bureau car. He pulled alongside as Trey rolled down his window, shaking his head. "This is never going to work."

Jake offered a confident smile and said, "Of course it will."

"I'm not sure I can go along with this," said Trey, hesitation in his voice. "There are too many moving parts."

Jake's extortionate smile continued. "Trey, do you remember yesterday morning when you told me about those top-secret matters?"

Trey looked puzzled. "Yeah."

In a tone half serious Jake said, "Well, if you don't go along I may have to tell Hafner about our conversation. Then we'll both be doing background checks in Adak."

Precisely at 7:45, Park picked up the prepaid cell phone and punched in the number Jake had written on the card. When

Yeong answered, Park slowly read the words: "The round-eye will be at the Shanghai Hotel, room 212 at eight p.m. tonight. You can get even then but you must hurry. Don't be late or you will miss him."

When asked, Park repeated the name of the hotel and the room number.

Jake, Trey, and Brian walked down the alley, their vehicles parked on a side street just off Olympic. All were wearing worn, paint-splashed coveralls Jake picked up at a used clothing store. Jake and Brian were also carrying oversized, mismatched plastic toolboxes. As they approached the rear entrance of the Shanghai Hotel, Trey said, "What's with you and the alleys? Why don't you ever use the front door?"

Jake snapped, "Knock it off."

"Whoa. Don't tell me you're having second thoughts."

"No, but this is serious. We need to focus."

"This isn't serious. This is crazy. You are diving into the shallow end, my friend. If you want to call this thing off I'm behind you all the way. We phone up the cavalry now. I drop a dime on SWAT or just make a call to LAPD. Tell them we have a kidnapping in progress."

Jake was focused as he opened the rear door. "This will work."

"Yeah, just keep thinking that," muttered Trey.

Jake paused before entering, then said, "Trey, we're in the business of worst-case scenarios."

"Oh, that's comforting." The sarcasm was evident.

The hallway smelled of stale sweat and the hotel had no shot of being mentioned in the AAA guidebook. Jake had been here before and knew his immediate destination.

"I did a couple of dope deals here several years ago," said Jake to Brian, excited but apprehensive as to what was about to happen.

"I always thought of you as a Hyatt Regency type of guy," said Trey.

Jake seemed to relax just a bit and smiled, saying, "I like to expand my acting horizons. Hate to be typecast as strictly a high-roller. I can work Beverly Hills or urban back alleys."

The floor creaked with every few steps as they tried to lighten the footfalls.

In a near whisper Trey said, "I bet this place hasn't seen any repairs since the Johnson administration."

"Lyndon or Andrew?"

Jake found the door he was looking for and the three descended concrete steps into a dark, damp basement housing the power, electrical, and fire sprinkler systems, and an ancient HVAC air handler. The noise was a few decibels below deafening as every piece of equipment was badly in need of repairs.

Jake removed the coveralls and was now dressed as a semi-casual drug dealer, his shirttail out, hiding his Glock 19 on his right hip and a mini-Glock stuffed in the small of his back. He had three magazines, fully loaded, in his left hip pocket.

"This is never gonna work," said Trey.

"Yeah, I heard you."

"What?" Trey spoke just above the noise of the basement power system.

"Yeah, I heard you. It will work. It has to."

Jake pulled out two black plastic cases from the toolbox he'd carried into the basement. He popped open the first one and removed a tiny transmitter. Holding it up to the light, he wanted to make sure he was installing it "sunny side up." He then dropped his pants, getting a "you've got to be kidding me" look from Trey.

Jake blew his case agent a kiss and mouthed the words over the basement noise, "Don't ask. Don't tell."

Allowing the transmitter to dangle at his ankle, he ran the microphone wire up his leg, near his crotch, placing the mike just above the belt line. As he rolled some tape around the wire on his leg, Trey smiled and said into Jake's ear, "Sweetie, that's gonna hurt when you pull it off. Shoulda shaved your legs before you decided to run with the big dogs."

"Try this," said Jake, handing the earpiece to Trey.

Jake walked to the far end of the basement and said, "Testing one, two, three."

Trey shook his head. "It's all static. I can't hear a thing."

Jake mouthed an expletive as he sat down, crossing his legs to get better access to the transmitter. He made some adjustments and again said, "Testing."

Trey ripped at the earpiece. "That about blew out my eardrum."

"Sorry, let me lower the volume. Too bad Hafner's spook friend couldn't lend us some of his equipment," said Jake as he made the adjustment.

"Maybe if you would have cut them in they would have," said Trey.

"Yeah right. How's that?"

"Better," said Trey.

"Good."

Jake opened the second black plastic container and removed a small transmitter device, disguised to look like a butane lighter, and placed it inside his front shirt pocket. "Back up," said Jake as he pulled up his pants and buckled his belt.

Grabbing the top shelf from the large toolbox, Jake tossed it aside.

When Trey looked in the oversized box he spotted bundles of currency, U.S. one-hundred-dollar bills. Trey picked up a bundle and began to examine it. "Is this what I think it is?"

"Need-to-know," said Jake, taking off his shirt and double-stuffing ten bundles of the hundreds—one hundred thousand dollars—inside his waistband.

Both Trey and Brian gave him looks of confusion.

"Can I trust you to keep an eye on the rest of my retirement stash?" said Jake as he grabbed the bundle from Trey and threw it back into the toolbox.

"This stuff looks perfect," said Trey.

"It almost is," said Jake, buttoning his shirt, concealing the money and the two weapons he was now carrying.

It was ten minutes to eight. He called Park and learned the North Korean kingpin had to repeat the name of the hotel and the room number. Turning to Trey and Brian, Jake said, "It's not Henry Yeong. He didn't know anything about the hotel or the room number when Park called him. I'm not sure who or how many will be up there. The timing is important, so when you hear a commotion, set off everything. It should be straight-up at eight."

Jake's confident demeanor washed away most of their misgivings. Trey, out of friendship, and Brian, because of that Marine Corps *Semper Fi* thing, were ready to go with Jake into battle.

CHAPTER SIXTY-ONE

As Jake climbed the stairs from the basement to the second floor, he remembered Katie's Bible verse from the book of Job. Maybe today was the limit he could not exceed.

As he was walking down the hallway toward room 212, two Asian women, practitioners of the world's oldest profession and painted for the evening, greeted him.

The shorter of the two said in heavily accented English, "You must be looking for friend."

"I'm looking for *my* friend."

She smiled. "Then you come with us."

The other woman seductively touched Jake's arm and, wrapping hers in his, said, "You want to party all night with us instead?"

"Business first, ladies. Then maybe we can celebrate."

The three walked to the far end of the hallway and, just outside the door to room 212, Jake stepped on a loose board, which moaned a loud, painful wail as he put weight on it.

"What's with all the squeaky boards in this place? Is the maintenance staff on sabbatical?"

Both women looked at Jake, confused by his complaint. The shorter woman knocked on the door and waited for a response. When the door opened Jake was greeted by a Middle Eastern man in his thirties with a thick, dark beard.

"He come alone," said Jake's escort.

The undercover agent entered as the ladies retreated down the hallway, seeking additional income for the evening. Jake's eyes swept the room. In the hotel's heyday it would have been a "parlor"—now it was just a drab, run-down "suite," with a sagging foldout couch flanked by two mismatched end tables. In front of the couch, a scratched and scarred coffee table, two battered wooden chairs, an incongruously placed wingback easy chair, and a vintage Queen Anne–style side table complete with a crystal lamp, circa 1940—all reminiscent of a much earlier era.

Kareem Abdul, the bartender, occupied the tattered wingback, a large-caliber semi-auto pistol and an open bag of salted sunflower seeds within easy reach on the side table. His tired, bloodshot eyes revealed sleep had not been a recent luxury.

The two others—both apparently of Mideast extraction—were standing and both had oversized semi-autos tucked inside the front of their waistbands. The one who had opened the door for Jake looked like a Doberman ready to pounce. The other, whom Jake guessed to be in his mid-forties, stood by the couch, his posture indicative of indifference instead of aggression.

The sounds of traffic from a busy Olympic Boulevard flooded through an open window and Jake noted the door to an adjoining room was slightly ajar. He took in the disheveled appearance of the three men, empty takeout food wrappers from Aladdin's Mediterranean Delights, the hot plate with a cheap teapot, five plastic teacups, the stench of stale sweat, and concluded: *This is amateur hour.*

"You are a huge disappointment," said Jake, directing his comment to the bartender.

Kareem surveyed the undercover agent. "You came alone. At

least you listened, but unless you're keistering three million in foldin' money, we got no business."

"I guess you weren't rehabilitated with that latest prison stint," said Jake.

"Shut up!" screamed Kareem, trying to establish his dominance, his eyes intense.

Jake sized up the situation, positioning himself to keep an open shot to the hallway door or the adjoining room. All three opponents were close enough that should Jake need to shoot he could easily drop them without much maneuvering. He hoped it wouldn't come to that but he didn't want the men spreading out, making a rapid assault more difficult.

"Aren't you going to introduce me to your friends? You know my name but I really feel at a disadvantage. Maybe we should print up name tags. We need a little guy-time before the fun begins," said Jake, trying to keep everyone distracted with his self-assured banter.

Kareem shook his head.

"So what do I call them, Dopey and Bashful? You didn't pick these guys up off Craigslist. Obviously they're two more pimps of war. Come on, Kareem, we're among friends. Surely their mamas call them something."

Kareem bit. "Mohammed and Rostam."

"Okay, now we're getting somewhere. So, who's who?"

There was a moment of silence before the older of the two said quietly, "I am Mohammed."

"Hi, guys. Nice to meet you. I'm guessing you're hoping to get rich this evening." Jake remained calm; his demeanor in the face of horror was unsettling to the three terrorists. . . . *If you have no fear, they have no power.*

Frustrated, Kareem looked to Mohammed, the cell leader, before returning to Jake and barking, "I need to see some green."

"I brought earnest money for the first round of negotiations," said Jake, noting Kareem sought Mohammed's approval.

The ex-con bartender spit a mouthful of sunflower husks on the floor and said, "I don't need no earnest money and there's no negotiating. I want to see three million."

Jake noticed the one called Rostam, his lips curled in disgust, was looking at the well-chewed detritus on the worn carpet. *These are not happy campers.*

In the hotel basement, Trey could barely hear what was happening in room 212. Between the static from the transmitter and the noise from the pipes, the conversation was garbled and barely audible.

He slammed his fist on the workbench as he tried to focus on the situation on the second floor, knowing Jake's life hung in the balance. Cupping his hands over his ears in an effort to block out the extraneous noises, he debated moving from the basement but wasn't sure of the layout of the hotel and whether two white guys would bring more attention to the pending eruption.

There was no panic in Jake's eyes as he looked directly at Mohammed rather than Kareem. "I've got your money," he said. "I want to see Jenny and the girl."

"You're not seein' nothin' till I see the money," said Kareem, trying to get Jake's attention.

"I brought the money, a little here and a lot outside. I want to see Jenny and Gracie," said the ever-defiant undercover agent, showing absolutely no fear.

Kareem laughed but didn't smile. "That ain't right, Batman, unless Robin is hangin' on the other side of the door. You came alone and I know you ain't dumb enough to leave a pile of cash in the hallway. I need to see a three and six zeroes *now*!"

"You'll see all the money when I see the girls, but here's a little taste," said Jake with calculated assurance.

He reached inside his shirt and Kareem's two partners immediately drew their weapons from their waistbands, pointing them at Jake.

"Whoa, fellows! Mohammed, Rostam, let's not get trigger-happy. I'm just reaching for some bundles of Kareem's Monopoly money, or is it Mohammed's play dough? I can't tell who's calling the shots but I'm guessing it's not you, Rostam. Kareem says you're just Mohammed's chai boy."

The bartender jumped out of the chair and shouted to Mohammed, "Teacher, I never said any such thing to this infidel."

"Well," said Jake, looking at Mohammed, "I guess that means you're the boss man."

Jake grabbed three bundles of the Supernote hundreds and threw them on the couch. Three pairs of eyes followed the bundles as they bounced on the stained cushions.

Jake continued to focus on Mohammed. "Now it's your turn to play nice. Let's get this over with. Bring in Jenny and the little girl."

Mohammed nodded toward Kareem.

"Bring them in!" hollered Kareem.

With that, Candy walked in from the adjoining room, a .45-caliber, M1911A1 auto pointed at Jenny, who was a step in front, her mouth gagged and her hands behind her back. With Candy's free hand she was holding Gracie's hand, tears running down angelic cheeks.

Jake looked at Jenny. "Are you guys okay?"

Jenny put her head down, refusing to look at Jake, and nodded slowly.

"Gracie, why don't you come stand over here with me?" said Jake.

"No," said Kareem.

"For an ex-con bartender you have no sense of fair play. You've still got Jenny and it's four to one. You have to like those odds. I want to make sure the little girl's okay," said Jake.

Kareem thought for a long moment, then looked to Mohammed, as did Candy. When Mohammed nodded, Candy released her grip. The tiny ballerina, confused and frightened, slowly made her way to Jake, who crouched down and cradled her in his arms, her head on his shoulder as she sobbed softly. "It's going to be okay, Gracie. You'll be going home to your grandfather soon." Turning to Candy, he said with a calm, deliberate delivery, "Tommy loved you and you had him killed. That's pretty cold."

Candy said nothing, focusing her attention on Mohammed rather than Jake.

Looking at Candy and Kareem, Jake said, "I'm confused by Mohammed and Rostam. Is this some eclectic UN kidnapping conspiracy? You must really believe in diversity and equal opportunity. This is a regular rainbow coalition. And Kareem, I'm not paying attention to you anymore. I thought you were my go-to guy, but since Mohammed is in charge, I'm directing all my comments to the boss."

Looking at Mohammed, Jake said, "What are we talking here? Al-Qaeda? Hamas? Maybe Hezbollah? I'm guessing you're Iranian."

"Wrong," said Mohammed.

"He speaks again," said Jake with a manufactured smile.

Kareem jumped back into the game. "I need to see the rest of the green and I need to see it now!"

Candy barked, "We know you have money!"

"Park wouldn't have sent you here without three million," added Kareem.

"Mohammed, you can play anytime," said Jake. "Like the rest of these guys I'm looking to you for direction."

Candy's frustration was growing as the tension thickened. "I know Park has much money. Tommy tell me. He always talk too much. He always try to impress. He tell me Park bringing in three million and you would deliver."

Kareem added an evil smile. "See, Tommy got his piece off my girl here. Now I want my piece. If I don't see the cash very soon, Gracie's next nap will be permanent."

CHAPTER SIXTY-TWO

In the hotel lobby Henry Yeong and three of his thugs entered the first floor and approached the window, where a thin, shaggy-haired white man in his early twenties had his feet propped up on the desk watching MTV. With little enthusiasm, he stood up and walked to the window.

"Yeah, can I help you?"

"Who's in room 212?" asked Yeong.

"We don't exactly check ID. Most people pay cash and I don't ask too many questions," said the night clerk with too much attitude.

One of Yeong's thugs reached through the window and grabbed the skinny employee by the shirt, pulling him across the counter. His feet were kicking, his eyes filled with fear.

"I'll repeat my question since my associate has your attention. Who is in room 212?"

He stammered, "Some black dude and a couple of camel jockeys."

"Did you see a white guy?"

The clerk answered tearfully and stuttered, "Yeah, he . . . he . . . he just walked up the stairs."

Kareem looked at Candy and, referring to Jenny, said, "Hurt her."

Before taking any action, Candy eyed Mohammed, who nodded. She raised the weapon above her head, preparing to strike Park's daughter, but Jake intervened. "Okay. Okay. I've got the money."

He pulled up his shirt and like a piñata bursting forth with Benjamins, the remaining seven bundles of newly minted counterfeit hundreds fell to the floor. Candy squealed with childish delight as the terrorists' behavior revealed their excitement.

Rostam slipped his weapon in his waistband and was joined by Kareem, who lurched to help gather up the bundles, tossing them on the couch as the two men collected their plunder.

Mohammed remained still but dropped his weapon by his side. Though it was more money than any of the room's occupants had seen in a lifetime, Mohammed was fairly certain the ten packets of bills on the couch amounted to far less than the $3 million ransom demand. He ordered, "Rostam, count one of the bundles."

Rostam tore off the brown paper Treasury wrapper and began counting the bills on the coffee table.

As Rostam counted out the contents of a single packet, Kareem stacked the other nine bundles in a neat row on the table, saying, "This will further our cause. We can bring America to its knees. Allah's word will reign supreme. Allah be praised."

The eyes of the others were focused on the man counting the money, but when Rostam said, "This packet is ten thousand dollars," it took only an instant for Mohammed to do the math.

He turned, pointed his weapon at Jake's head, and said, "This is only one hundred thousand. Where is the rest of it?"

"It's nearby. You'll get the rest once Jenny and Gracie are safe. I need you to let them both go. Jenny can have the keys to my car. I'll stay here. Once they call and tell me they are with Park, I'll take you to the rest."

"That wasn't the deal," bellowed Kareem, looking to Mohammed for reassurance.

"It is now," said Jake calmly, as Gracie, scared by Kareem's angry shriek, began to sob again. Jake held her close, her heart pounding with fear and uncertainty.

Suddenly Candy began to cackle mirthlessly. Everyone in the room but little Gracie turned toward the maniacal outburst and saw the reason for Candy's mocking laughter: both Candy and Jenny were pointing large-caliber semi-automatic pistols at the men in the room.

Neither Mohammed nor Rostam said a word. Kareem, on the other hand, moaned, "Ohh noo . . . Candy, noo . . ."

CHAPTER SIXTY-THREE

Candy's sights were set on Mohammed, who quickly dropped his weapon when she ordered. Jenny swept the room with her .45, poised to kill anyone seeking to interrupt the women's plan of action.

Jake, still crouched on the floor, his arms around Gracie, quietly addressed Jenny: "You've got to be kidding me. I risked my life for you and now you're part of it."

"What can I say?" said Jenny, shrugging, a growing smirk on her face.

"Is the pregnancy a lie, too?" asked Jake.

"How'd you know about that?"

"Reid told me."

Jenny looked toward Candy and the two laughed, both cunning and composed. "Yeah, that was a lie. Reid tried to buy it off cheap but I was negotiating for a little bigger payday."

Kareem's face bore defeat as he realized he'd been played, betrayed by those he trusted, even loved. He looked toward

Mohammed and saw the look of a cornered animal seeking a way to escape.

Jenny sneered, her weapon now pointed at Jake. "My father made me a widow. He had my husband killed because he thought Michael was stealing from him. He made Gracie an orphan when her parents got in the way of the hit on my Michael. Daddy Dearest lied to me about how they died and tried to buy my love and affection, but I knew he was responsible.

"Now it's payback time. Candy and I have been planning this ever since he ran his mouth about the three million coming in. He thought I never paid attention. I heard him scheming with Tommy. Thanks, by the way, for helping him get the container across the border."

Candy laughed. "Tommy say you reliable."

Jenny, poised and assertive, continued: "I guess he was right. Too bad he's not around anymore to help us spend it."

"But this money is going for a greater cause. This is for Allah," pleaded Kareem.

Jenny shook her head. "Sorry about that, Ali Baba, but this is not Al-lah's. This is all-ours."

Candy laughed at Jenny's effort at humor.

Jenny's focus was now on Kareem, her muzzle pointing at his chest, center mass. "I figured a street-smart guy like you might realize what was happening when we got you to eliminate Sonny and Gabe. They could have ruined this for us. That's why Candy accompanied you on your little nighttime romp to take out Sonny. Besides, I think she made it worth your while. You celebrated that night, right?"

From the hallway Jake heard the squeak of the boards and suspected the next phase of what now appeared to be his ill-conceived plan was about to be implemented.

Jake's whole strategy was based on a false assumption: that the kidnapping was at Yeong's behest. He planned to have Yeong and his bodyguards show up at the hotel after Jenny and Gracie were gone. Then, with the help of Trey and Brian, he would take down two Korean crime rings and shut down a North Korean–Iranian conspiracy to circumvent the new UN treaty on nuclear arms. And he had hours of audio-video recordings and $3 million in Supernotes to make the case.

From outside the door he heard the unmistakable sound of a weapon being racked. Crouched down and holding Gracie closer, the thought occurred to him: *Katie would know the verse in the Bible about pride going before a fall.*

As the doorknob began to turn, Jake's eyes darted around the room, seeking cover or concealment from what was now inevitable, unstoppable carnage, and he said to himself, *Oh dear God, help me and this child to survive this!*

In that same instant, Jenny looked at Candy, who smiled and nodded. When Jenny returned the nod both women opened fire; the crack of gunfire in the small room deafened everyone.

Jake grabbed his Glock 19 from his right hip and dove on top of Gracie, pressing their bodies tightly to the floor, protecting her from the barrage of bullets, refusing to join in the erupting chaos.

Mohammed reached for his weapon, seeking cover behind the couch, his combat experience prevailing. Staying on his feet meant certain death. Prone on the floor, he reached up without exposing himself, firing blindly over the arm of the couch in the direction of the women, his shots ringing out in a semi-measured pace of two- and three-round bursts.

Kareem, still coping with Candy's betrayal, was slow to grab his weapon. Jenny's first three rounds hit him in the chest. The bartender's prison-tuned physique was no match for the hollow-point ammunition ripping through his internal organs. He bellowed just once as he fell to the floor in the kind of agony he had so often inflicted on others. He briefly struggled to breathe, coughed up bright red arterial blood, and convulsed as his eyes went lifeless.

Candy got off several rounds before Rostam, frozen by the

madness, finally reacted. As the Hezbollah terrorist attempted to drop to one knee and return fire, he was hit in the head, never engaging in the gun battle, never firing his weapon. For all his bravado in the back room of the mosque, he lacked the skills to survive on the street. His reward would have to be elsewhere. He would not find it on the second floor of a battered Los Angeles brothel.

As the room erupted in gunfire, Henry Yeong and his men burst in, firing indiscriminately, spraying shots throughout the confined quarters, rounds striking in every direction—including the walls, floor, and ceiling.

Candy and Jenny were both hit but refused to go down. They continued firing, shooting into the void, exchanging shots with Yeong's men.

Yeong hesitated too long when he realized it was Candy shooting at him. His mind failed to register the peril. Before he could grasp the full extent of the situation he was hit multiple times, Candy having little concern with his authority or their perceived friendship.

Jake didn't join the battle. Instead, using his body to shield Gracie from the errant rounds flying around the room, Jake shuffled the child along the floor toward the adjoining room. The shooters, more concerned with firing at each other, ignored Jake and the little girl. Though it seemed like a lifetime, and for some it was, it really took just a few seconds for Jake to low-crawl out of the carnage, dragging Gracie through the doorway to relative safety in the adjoining room.

Mohammed continued firing, hoping a round would find its mark. When he emptied his first magazine, he quickly slammed in a second, releasing the slide and chambering a new round, to continue the battle.

Trey heard the first gunshots through the transmitter taped to Jake's leg, two floors above. He glanced at his watch—noted that it was two minutes before eight—and pulled the fire alarm, activating the sprinkler system throughout the hotel and automatically alerting the fire and police departments. Then Trey and Brian raced upstairs into the madness.

As they ran to the sound of the gunfire, high-pressure water from the sprinkler system sprayed in their faces, nearly blinding them. They could hear shots mixed with screams and moans, some trailing off into mere whimpers. Lives were being wasted and the two agents could only hope Jake and the kidnap victims weren't part of the bloodbath.

Jake pushed Gracie beneath the bed in their new refuge and crawled toward the open doorway, his Glock at a suppressed firing position. He did a quick peek around the door frame and saw Kareem was down, as were Rostam, Yeong, and two of Yeong's men. The weakening cries of Jenny and Candy flooded the room; both were on the floor, their weapons as empty as their lives.

Mohammed got off a shot just after Jake retreated behind the door. The door frame splintered, the round mere inches from finding its mark. Jake waited a prolonged three count, then took a second look and fired one shot just as Mohammed rose from behind the arm of the couch. The economy of a well-placed round was evident. Jake's aim was perfect. The terrorist cell leader's head pitched backward. He collapsed, his skull split open by the slug, his brains leaking onto the worn carpet. By the time he hit the floor he had already joined the others in the dead pool.

One of Yeong's men retreated down the hallway. He was immediately met by Trey and Brian coming up the stairs.

A ragged chorus of "Freeze, FBI!" rang out but the gunman continued, raising his weapon to engage the two agents.

Brian, no stranger to urban combat, dropped to one knee and fired a three-round burst; each one on target. Yeong's henchman was dead before he hit the floor, without getting off a shot at the approaching agents.

"Trey, Brian, they're all down in here!" shouted Jake, knowing it's not over until the enemy is neutralized.

"The hallway's clear!" hollered Trey.

The entire violent confrontation had taken less than two minutes.

Trey and Brian ran into the room, weapons at the ready. Seeing only bodies, Trey shouted, "Jake, we're in! Jake!"

"Roger, coming in," Jake responded from the adjoining room. "Sorry, I couldn't hear you; my ears are still ringing."

The three agents immediately began collecting weapons before administering any aid. Jenny, the only one of the assailants left alive, quickly drew her last breath and joined Candy, Kareem, Mohammed, Rostam, Yeong, and his three associates.

With Trey and Brian securing the room, Jake ran back to Gracie, who was sobbing, scared, and confused. He grabbed her in his arms and held her tight, trying to comfort another innocent victim of evil.

CHAPTER SIXTY-FOUR

Five LAPD units, three fire trucks, and two ambulances were at the hotel less than seven minutes after Trey pulled the alarm. A fireman shut off the sprinkler system while Trey and Brian provided an outline of what transpired in the room to an incredulous LAPD detective. Jake remained in the adjoining bedroom with Gracie, confident that there soon would be plenty of FBI agents of much higher pay grade on-scene to fill in the details.

As soon as Gracie dozed off, Jake called Park. "Your granddaughter's safe but your daughter's dead. She betrayed the family."

"How did Jenny die?"

"Yeong and a bunch of his goons showed up. All hell broke loose. I'll explain the rest when I get to your house. I got out the fire escape with Gracie and will come to you as soon as I can get to my car."

"What about the money?"

"Some of the bills were destroyed when the sprinkler system went off, but most of it is still hidden in the basement of the hotel.

We can come back later and retrieve it after the cops and firemen leave."

Park replied with a simple "Thank you, Jake."

As the crime-scene technicians began their gruesome work, Jake tapped Brian on the shoulder and motioned for him to come into the room where the child was sleeping. In a voice just above a whisper he explained what had happened to Gabe. Jake could see the mist forming in the new agent's eyes. Swallowing hard to suppress the emotions building in him, Jake grabbed the new agent, gave him a hug, and whispered, "Semper Fi."

Twenty-five minutes after the explosive firefight, ASAC Hafner, the CIA spook Wilson, and Supervisor Rachel Chang arrived on the scene wearing FBI raid jackets. Hafner elbowed his way past the police and demanded to speak to Jake in the adjoining room.

Jake was sitting on the bed; the little girl, beside him, was asleep. Brian Carter was in a chair next to the window reflecting on what he had just experienced and on the loss of a friend.

Hafner was visibly angry. But before he could raise his voice, Jake put a finger to his lips and pointed to the sleeping child.

Instead of shouting, Hafner hissed, "You were supposed to have pulled out of this assignment. Headquarters ordered it. I want to know when you knew about the Supernotes. Why wasn't I called? I'm your ASAC. I should have been notified immediately about this operation. I saw no ops order and I certainly didn't approve of any of this." Hafner waved his arm toward the slaughter in the next room and the hallway.

Though neither man knew it at the time, it would take days of "trajectory analysis" and countless hours of forensic work in the FBI lab to eventually determine which weapons fired which rounds. Based on a 3-D analysis of the mayhem, it was determined that several of the deceased had been struck by multiple weapons. Only one, Mohammed, had been hit just once. Jake, hoping to mitigate some of the ASAC's wrath, said, "If it makes any difference, I only fired one round."

Hafner simply glared, so Jake continued in a whisper. "It all came up suddenly. It was a very fast-moving operation. I didn't have time to put it on paper. I thought I had until the end of the day."

"That's no excuse. I should have been notified. I'm the ASAC. It's my career on the line. I'm going to ask you again and maybe I should speak slowly so you'll understand. . . . Why were you still in this operation and when did you know they were Supernotes?"

Jake feigned innocence with an accurate but calibrated version of the truth. "I didn't know for sure they were Supernotes. I suspected they were but I didn't have any samples to run past Secret Service. Park just gave me the three million for the ransom."

Hafner wasn't buying it. "So you had three million in samples!"

"But that was for the ransom. All the meetings and calls are recorded. If you listen to the recordings you should get a pretty good idea of how it all went down. I thought the Bureau's priority would be the safety of this child," Jake said, pointing to the little girl asleep in the bed. He actually sounded sincere.

Hafner waved some waterlogged counterfeit bills in the air. "These are ruined. We can't go back to Headquarters with soaked bills."

"They'd still be counterfeit, wouldn't they?" said Jake, deciding to prolong the ASAC's suffering by waiting to tell him $2.9 million in dry Supernotes was stashed in the two oversized plastic toolboxes sitting at Brian Carter's feet.

Hafner blasted through his agenda. "I've scheduled you for an emergency psych eval at Headquarters and I plan on asking for a polygraph as well."

Jake pointed to Gracie again and motioned for Hafner to lower his voice. Then, in a whisper he asked, "Psych eval? What for?"

Hafner rolled his eyes. "I don't like the way you respond to supervision. I think you have issues."

Jake laughed out loud, causing Gracie to stir. "Oh, I've got issues, huge issues!" he whispered. "But you don't think I can fake sanity? I'll pass. I always do. And forget the poly."

Hafner had no intention of backing down. "Why?"

Jake smiled and said, "If I don't pass the polygraph, there goes my credibility. The U.S. Attorney won't allow me to testify. If I don't testify, we won't get a conviction. And if we don't get a conviction, you don't get a promotion. You need an unblemished lamb for this sacrifice."

Jake spotted Olivia Knox standing in the doorway and decided to play his trump card.

"Besides, if I fail, it might screw up the centrifuge and nuclear weapons deal."

"What centrifuge and nuke weapons deal?" clamored Hafner.

Jake's smile morphed into a serious expression. "Probably won't be able to work it now, after you get the results of the psych eval and the polygraph."

Knox decided to end Hafner's torture. "Tell him the rest of the story, Jake."

He complied. "The Supernotes were sent to Park to buy centrifuges and other high-tech components for the nuclear weapons work Pyongyang is now doing for the Iranians. The ayatollahs in Tehran have contracted with the DPRK to do the fissile material enrichment and R&D that's banned by that new UN treaty."

Wilson, the CIA ghost, finally spoke. "That fits with chatter we've been picking up overseas."

"Am I cleared to know that?" Jake asked, still whispering.

A pregnant pause hung over the room as all parties looked toward Olivia Knox.

"Charles, I gave Jake until midnight tonight to wrap up the operation. Earlier today, we met and talked about what needed to be done. I personally approved his plan."

"But why wasn't I told about this?" said the ASAC, in a whispered whine.

Olivia continued. "Because when I called to tell you, Charles, you were on the phone with the State Department."

"But I *had* to talk to State," Hafner protested. "The Attorney General himself told me to make sure we didn't do anything that would screw up the permanent nuclear weapons deal with Iran. What did you *expect* me to do?"

Knox held up her hand. "I expect the same thing from all my agents. I expect them to do what's right."

Hafner, chagrined in front of his subordinates, muttered, "I guess I should cancel my trip to D.C."

"I think that's wise," said Knox.

Cradling Gracie in his arms, Jake walked past the police and fire lines and a growing crowd in front of the hotel. He proceeded virtually unnoticed to the undercover Range Rover. As he placed the somnolent child on the backseat and locked the seat belt around her, he said to himself, *Katie used to tell me, "All things work together for good to those who love God and are called according to His purpose."*

As Jake pulled out onto Olympic Boulevard his cell phone slipped down between the seat and the console.

He never saw the text message from Trey Bennett.

CHAPTER SIXTY-FIVE

As Jake arrived at Park's San Marino residence, the gate was open. He was greeted in the driveway by Park and his wife, Soo Min. Gracie awoke when Jake shut off the engine and he feared what the tiny ballerina remembered following the shooting. Her eyes had been closed and he assumed she was asleep in the hotel room but couldn't know if she had heard any of the conversation once Trey and Brian secured the crime scene. He could only hope any story a four-year-old could tell would be dismissed as fantasy by those who heard it.

Grateful grandparents smothered Gracie in kisses. When Soo Min took her into the house, Jake detailed the contrived events at the hotel as Park listened intently.

When he had completed his after-action report, Park said, "Is there anything else you'd like to tell me?"

With genuine confusion, Jake asked, "Like what?"

"Like the fact you're an FBI agent and your wife is pregnant?"

Jake froze; the chill of discovery and death enveloped him. He glimpsed the Green Hornet and Kato out of the corner of his eye. Both were standing in the well-lit driveway, their large-caliber, silenced semi-automatics in their hands. "I don't understand," said Jake, turning slowly to face Park.

"Tommy and some of his associates followed you to Gladstone's restaurant and saw you meeting your wife. He shared it with me the night he was killed. He thought it was strange you never said you were married. I assume she is due any day now."

Jake paused, then answered calmly, "I'm not married. The woman I met for lunch is the widow of my best friend. He was killed six months ago on an assignment in Afghanistan."

"No more lies, Jake! After we take care of you, we'll take care of your family. I must tie up all the loose ends. You didn't think I'd send you to the hotel unaccompanied? My confidence in you did not exceed three million dollars—even if the bills were counterfeit. I had to retrieve the money for the equipment I had been told to acquire. And I really wanted to trust you, Jake. Apparently my faith was misplaced once again. You betrayed me as did the others. My people knew once they saw the FBI raid jackets at the hotel. It all began to make sense," said Park.

There was a long pause. Jake said nothing, wondering if today was the expiration date God had set.

Before Jake could act, Park offered an abrupt hand signal to his minions. A shot shattered the momentary silence.

It wasn't the muted sound of a subsonic round the undercover agent expected as he flung himself to the ground and grabbed the Glock concealed in the small of his back. Rolling into a prone position, Jake spied the Green Hornet already inert on the driveway and Trey Bennett, now firing at Kato as he moved.

Wheeling toward Trey, Kato leveled his weapon and prepared to fire. But before the North Korean could get Trey in his sights, Jake cranked off four rounds—two "double taps"—and dropped the thug.

Jake pivoted, spied Park attempting to escape around the side of the residence, and gave chase across the well-manicured lawn. He quickly closed on the aging North Korean intelligence officer and yelled at the top of his lungs, "Stop, or I'll shoot!"

Surprisingly, Park stopped in his tracks, tossed his weapon on the ground, and threw his hands into the air. He had decided he wanted to live.

The gesture didn't stop Jake. His momentum carried him into Park, knocking the older man to the ground. The FBI agent, breathing hard, placed his right knee on the North Korean's neck, painfully establishing alpha-dog superiority, and pointed his Glock at the crime boss's head.

"I brought back your granddaughter and you were going to kill me?" He cracked the barrel of the weapon across the back of Park's head. "I ought to spread your brains across the grass."

"Jake, don't do it," said Trey, racing up behind them.

"No, Trey, I'm going to close this case tonight with one nine-millimeter slug in the back of this commie bastard's head."

"Jake, we need him."

Park moaned, "Please let me live."

"Come on, Trey. This piece of garbage doesn't deserve to live."

"Please, don't kill me. I can help you!" the Korean managed to croak.

"What can you do for us?" Jake asked, easing some of his weight off Park's neck.

"I can help your country. I can tell you about the Iranians and the centrifuges and how they are making nuclear weapons."

"Jake, he's right. He can help," said Trey.

Jake eased up on the trigger of his Glock and asked in a whisper, "Do you believe in God?"

"What?" said Park.

Jake cracked the crime boss across the back of the head one more time before he repeated the question.

Park wasn't sure how to answer, so he told the truth. "No."

"Too bad. The God you don't believe in just saved your life. He determined your days but I guess tonight your number wasn't up."

Trey tossed his handcuffs to Jake, who double-locked the cuffs on Park while telling the Korean crime boss, "As usual, you and your Stalinist buddies have it wrong. The pregnant woman I had lunch with isn't my wife. Katie died a year ago. The woman I met for lunch was her closest friend. Someone she loved, the wife of my best friend. Do you know the meaning of those words, *love* or *friend*, you miserable example of humanity?"

Park, clearly confounded by all that was happening and still fearful for his life, replied, "Yes." Then, as Trey and Jake helped him to his feet, he said, "These are hurting my wrists."

Jake looked at them in the dark and said, "They're a little tight but they'll stretch after you wear 'em awhile." He then ratcheted each cuff close to the skin, bringing on additional pain with the slightest movement. "I hope they fit okay. Sizing is always so difficult for me to estimate, but I'd recommend you not wiggle too much. These things leave scars."

As they walked Park back to the front of the house, Jake asked Trey, "How'd you know to come here?"

"After you left with the little girl, I watched you out the window of the hotel room. Hafner was strutting around on the phone, taking credit for the Supernote success once Brian showed him the contents of the toolboxes. I saw Park's two goons come out of the little deli across the street. When they followed you toward your car, I figured you would need some help and sent you a text message."

"I never saw it."

"Well, I came anyway."

"Thanks for having my back," said Jake.

"I'll always have your six. Isn't that what you Marines call it?" Then, as they heard the sounds of sirens wailing in the distance, Trey added with a smile, "Maybe we should get everything prepped for Hafner's press conference."

"We didn't leave many witnesses," said Jake.

"Doesn't matter, there's not much left to prosecute. I think he's on our side now," said Trey, referring to Park.

"I guess that means Hafner gets that psych eval he was pushing," said Jake with a grimace.

"I bet he does but my money's on you. Somehow you'll pass."

Jake's cell phone chirped. He fished it out of his back pocket. The text message read, "IT'S TIME!!!!"

"Trey, it's Natasha, Joe's wife! I have to get to the hospital. Their baby's coming."

"Go! I'll clean up here."

As he ran toward his car in the moonlight, he was grateful to be alive but still not sure why God allowed people like Park to exist. Jake had survived another series of near-death encounters and concluded he must have more to do before completing the days his Creator allotted. The birth of his best friend's son was yet another reason to live.

"Thanks, God," he whispered as he headed to the hospital.

EPILOGUE

No one was ever prosecuted for the espionage, murders, and other crimes committed during the course of what the CIA and FBI called "Operation Counterfeit Lies."

The Department of Justice and the Director of National Intelligence declared all the activities and events that took place during the undercover operation to be part of a Foreign Intelligence Activity. The DNI classified all files, debriefs, and audiovisual surveillance recordings as Top Secret.

The undercover recording devices and associated memory chips worn by Gabe Chong and Jake Kruse during the operation were placed in an FBI evidence container and transferred to the Office of the Director of National Intelligence. They subsequently disappeared.

All U.S. government participants in Operation Counterfeit Lies were compelled to sign nondisclosure agreements pledging to never reveal what they knew of the operation or the DPRK-Iran nuclear weapons deal.

Park Soon Yong agreed to become an undercover asset of the CIA and the FBI. To maintain his cover, the $2.9 million in Supernotes was replaced with real currency and he continues to operate a global import-export business from Los Angeles. His case officer is named Wilson.

Olivia Knox was promoted and assigned to head the National Counterterrorism Center under the Director of National Intelligence.

Charles Hafner has been named Special Agent in Charge of the FBI office in Anchorage, Alaska.

H. Daniel Reid and three of his former clients were arrested in Hawaii and charged with "possession with the intent to distribute cocaine."

Trey Bennett and Brian Carter are still assigned to the Los Angeles Field Office of the FBI.

The DPRK continues to refine fissile material and build nuclear warheads for Iran's Islamic Revolutionary Guard Corps.

Gabe Chong, "Cheech" to his Marine Corps buddies, will never be publicly recognized for his valor. Retired Marine Major General Peter Newman and FBI Special Agent James "Jake" Kruse were the only "outsiders" invited to the closed ceremony when Gabe's sacrifice was honored by an anonymous star on the wall at CIA Headquarters in Langley, Virginia. The tiny device hidden in Gabe's clothing recorded what happened to him. A portion of the classified citation for his National Intelligence Medal cites Gabe for "extraordinary bravery and devotion to duty. Despite brutal and prolonged torture that led to his death, National Clandestine Service officer Chong never revealed the identity of another U.S. Agent who likely would have been killed."

Jake Kruse remains undercover and knows he is the other "U.S. Agent" mentioned in the classified citation. He also knows that had it not been for Gabe's courage, his best friend's son would never call him "Uncle Jake."

FREEDOM ALLIANCE

HEROES SCHOLARSHIPS—For the Children of America's Fallen Heroes

The Freedom Alliance Scholarship Fund honors American military personnel who have been killed or permanently disabled in service to our nation by providing educational scholarships for their dependent children.

Since 1990, Freedom Alliance has awarded millions of dollars in college scholarships to the sons and daughters of U.S. Soldiers, Sailors, Airmen, Guardsmen, and Marines. These grants further education and remind all that their parents' sacrifice will never be forgotten by a grateful nation.

SUPPORT OUR TROOPS—Serving those who serve in America's Armed Forces

The Freedom Alliance Support Our Troops program provides direct financial and other assistance to active-duty military personnel and their families. Priority is given to those recuperating from wounds and injuries and to their dependents.

Through relationships with military and veterans' hospitals and rehabilitation facilities, Freedom Alliance provides emergency grants to families enduring financial hardship while members of our Armed Forces recover from wounds, injuries, or sickness suffered in the line of duty.

The Freedom Alliance "Gifts from Home" project ships thousands of care packages to service members deployed overseas throughout the year. Here on the home front, we provide gifts and sponsor activities for the spouses and children of deployed personnel.

Our Healing Heroes program offers "Hero Holiday" vacations for injured military members and their families and "Hero Hunts," fishing retreats, and outdoor activities to aid in rehabilitation.

Freedom Alliance, founded in 1990 by Lt. Col. Oliver North, USMC (Ret.), and Lt. Gen. Edward Bronars, USMC (Ret.), is a nonprofit 501(c)(3) charitable and educational organization dedicated to advancing America's heritage of freedom by honoring and encouraging military service, defending the sovereignty of the United States, and promoting a strong national defense.

For more information, or to donate, contact:

FREEDOM ALLIANCE
22570 Markey Court, Suite 240
Dulles, Virginia 20166-6919
Phone: 800-475-6620
www.freedomalliance.org
www.facebook.com/FreedomAlliance

"LEST WE FORGET"